•

Designed to Deceive

John Hallam Lott

•

WebVivant Press

www.webvivantpress.com

•

Global Edition

ISBN: 978-1-908708-03-8

Published by WebVivant Press

www.webvivantpress.com

*

CHAPTER ONE

Dover 1077

Noise and smells were everywhere! The shrieks of servant girls being groped were drowned by the banging of mugs, skillets, dishes and platters on trestles. Shouts to make way for venison pies, so big it took four men to carry them to the top tables. Barking, snarling and yelping of dogs as they fought over scraps or were kicked from the benches. Hundreds of people conversing at the top of their voices, infants bawling and mothers singing to them, all added to the din that signified supper in the Great Hall.

And the smell! Meats, fish, stale wine, small ale, sweat, flatulence, fog-sodden wool, candle fat and wood smoke which, thanks to inadequate roof ventilation, hung over the assembly like a toxic cloud.

Jean LeBrun did what he had been doing ever since he arrived here. He ignored everything going on around him and concentrated on getting more food on his stale crust than his neighbours. That is until he felt the hand on his shoulder; only another worse for wear diner fighting his way through the crowd to get outside for a piss, or so he thought. Then the fingers on the hand tightened. Jean looked up into the expressionless face of a man in his twenties. Dressed in the fashion adopted by most of the Squires and younger Knights of the Court, his aristocratic features were pale, under a tonsured head of black hair. His only adornment was a golden cross, hanging from his belt. He lowered his head to Jean's ear.

'Master LeBrun, come with me.'

Jean, his mouth full of food, frowned. The grip tightened.

'Now, Master LeBrun, the Earl of Kent does not like to be kept waiting.'

Jean rose to his feet, the hand was transferred from his shoulder to his elbow and he was propelled through the crowded Great Hall. Was he, he wondered, at last going to be told the reason for his summons to this unfriendly, fog-ridden island where he had spent the past two miserable months of his young life.

Jean was the eldest son of the Seneschal on one of Lord Odo's Normandy Estates. Aged seventeen, not especially handsome but possessed of an unruly mop of hair and more natural charm than he was aware. At home, the village girls loved him and he them. In fact, he wondered if his exile to these shores was not the result of a careless liaison which had come to the attention of his father. He had been given no reason for his banishment other than being told it was at the command of Lord Odo. His father, a conscientious Steward, considered that to be sufficient explanation and he was dispatched to the nearest port with money to buy a passage to Dover. For this journey he was granted the services of a surly servant and an equally intractable mule. Jean soon understood that the only role of the servant was to ensure the safe return of the mule.

Easy going and friendly, Jean had a good mind but did not take kindly to authority, which made life at home difficult for both father and son. He was quick at his lessons and enjoyed them but his favourite occupations were drawing on any available surface and bedding as many of the local girls as he could. Combining these activities brought him the best of both worlds since most of the girls were happy to pose for him in the nude. Jean was an extremely talented artist who took his gift for granted. He also took care to hide his erotic studies but was it possible that his cache had been discovered? Was that the reason for him being marooned here in England? If so, what could it possibly have to do with Lord Odo?

In spite of the confusion and bustle, there were some seated on the dais at the top of the hall who thought it their business to register anything unusual going on below them. One of these interested spectators was William, King of England and Duke of Normandy, whose eyes were everywhere, even when talking to those seated next to him. He was not in a good mood. He disliked visiting this island realm and spent as little time here as he could. In the last eleven years England had, with the exception of the occasional rebellion, been subjugated, whereas his lands on the other side of the Manche were under constant threat from his fellow Normans and Bretons. There were more than enough of those to keep him occupied, not least the one sitting on the other side of Mathilde, his wife, Odo, Bishop of Bayeux, William's half brother and Mathilde's uncle.

William threw him a covert look and Odo, sensing that he was being appraised, raised his cup in salutation. William nodded, turned back and took a reflective sip of wine. Brother Odo; the ungodliest Bishop in Christendom. Ambitious, lecherous, greedy and, even by William's standards, uncompromisingly cruel but they were related and he had, thus far, proved a capable defender of this region. William's problem was that he was not sure whose interests Odo was defending. His fingers drummed the arm of his chair and Mathilde, who read his moods better than anybody, dropped her hand over his to still it. To her right, Odo had risen to his feet, ready to leave the table. With a deference bordering on the insolent, he bowed to William who indicated his permission. Mathilde felt her husband's hand tense as he did so.

Jean was pushed into a small windowless room containing a rough trestle and two stools. He shivered and shrugged his shoulders closer into his woollen cloak. He was not invited to sit nor did his escort take a stool and for a few moments nothing was said. Jean stood in the middle of the chamber while his companion leaned against the wall, under a flambeau which provided the only illumination. Jean turned to him.

'Why am I here, what's going on?'

The young man didn't even look at him.

'You will find out, soon enough.'

'But ... who is this Earl of Kent and, come to that, who are you? You know my name, what's yours?'

This time Jean received a dismissive look but no reply. He turned away, shivered again and pulled his cloak even closer.

'Cold?' A powerful voice came from the doorway.

Jean wheeled round and found himself confronted by a nobleman. Impressively proportioned and richly attired, he regarded Jean with a mixture of distaste and impatience.

'I asked if you were cold.'

The tone matched the bearing and the dress and Jean felt a frisson of panic. He opened his mouth to reply but nothing came out. The newcomer shrugged his extravagantly furred mantle up onto his shoulders and sighed.

'You are Jean LeBrun, son of Claude LeBrun?'

This time Jean managed to croak out, 'Yes, my Lord.'

'Good, at least you are not dumb. You don't know me, do you?'

'N... no my Lord ... or at least I think...'

'You think what exactly, LeBrun?'

'I think you are my Lord Odo of Bayeux,' Jean blurted out, 'but your... your retainer, I'm sorry my Lord, I mean your...' he gestured to his escort, now standing respectfully away from the wall, 'said that I was to meet with the Earl of Kent.'

'That is because my Squire, Thibault, is privy to information that is not yet in your domain. I am, as you rightly say, Odo of Bayeux and the last time we met you were five weeks old. I was visiting my estates in Normandy and your good father handed you over to me for a blessing. You peed all over my tunic!'

'I'm sorr...sorry my Lord. I'm sure I didn't mean to.'

'I am sure you didn't but I trust it's a habit you've outgrown. To arrest your confusion, I am also the Earl of Kent, lately created so by Duke...I mean King William, and I have good reason to expect that this will shortly be my castle, inasmuch that I will be expected to hold and defend it in the King's name.'

Odo moved to the table on which he dropped an assortment of vellum, fragments of linen and thin, painted wooden boards.

'Recognise any of these?'

Jean gulped as Odo spread the pictures over the table, looking them over before picking one out and holding it up for Jean to see.

'You do recognise them, don't you LeBrun? Such movement, such sensuality and as a man of God I might add, such blasphemy. I am not mistaken am I, this is your work?'

Jean stared at his portrayal of a young and very naked peasant girl.

'My Lord,' he managed to whisper at last, 'how did you…?'

Odo picked up another drawing. Different girl, similar pose. Out of the corner of his eye Jean could detect Thibault crossing himself. Odo picked out another picture.

'How,' he said, 'is not important but let us say that your father found where you had hidden them and, considerably distressed, had them delivered to me. Perhaps it occurred to him, considering the seriousness of the offence that I might be better qualified to deal with it.'

Jean's knuckles whitened as they tightened on the edges of his cloak, as if he might become invisible if he could envelope himself in it. Blasphemy was punishable by death. Odo straightened up and smiled. Not a pleasant smile, his eyes remained cold. He pointed to the drawings.

'These are very good. Very good indeed but then, I expect you know that?'

He searched Jean's blank response, and then frowned.

'You don't, do you? This comes to you as naturally as breathing, doesn't it? I suppose we could view it as a gift. A gift from God himself, so we could say that dispenses with any charge of blasphemy. What do you think, Thibault?'

They both looked at Thibault. His eyes were almost closed. One hand was clenched around the crucifix while the other slowly massaged the side of his head.

He managed a tight smile and whispered, 'Indeed so, my Lord.'

Odo's features softened momentarily but reverted as he turned back to face a relieved Jean.

'Well, LeBrun?'

Jean mustered as much contrition in his voice as he could.

'I am sorry, my Lord, to have offended against you or my God. You have my promise that I will draw no more.'

'Yes you will, boy. Not this though.'

He dismissed the drawings on the table with an imperious sweep of his hand.

'From now on you will work for me, but first I have to be certain that you are as talented as I think you are. Thibault!'

His Squire, now more composed, bowed his head.

'Thibault, bring this boy to me tomorrow morning and I will set him an examination,'

He turned to Jean.

'You pass this test, LeBrun, and you will find yourself drawing history as it has never before been recorded.'

He nodded at Thibault, picked up the drawings and swept out of the room.

Odo made his way towards the King's chambers but, after a couple of steps, changed his mind. He stood for a moment before turning on his heel and walking back into the Great Hall. By this time, apart from scullions collecting pots and dogs scrapping over bones, it was empty. He walked up to the high table and stood behind the ornate chair, recently occupied by his step brother, the King. He ran his fingertips over the carved back, like a housewife testing for dust, and smiled to himself.

CHAPTER TWO

Dover, the same day

William and Mathilde retired to their apartments in the tower. Mathilde hated this cold and primitive castle but when William wished her to accompany him to England, she regarded the inevitable discomfort as yet another duty of state.

She sighed when they entered their room. Here, at least, the floor was clean and strewn with sweet smelling herbs. Her waiting women had put out clean linen, hot water and the braziers had been fired. In this room too, wall hangings of rugs and tapestries absorbed the worst of the damp and draughts. She sat by the fire, thawing out after the chills of the Great Hall. Perhaps William would stay tonight, they saw too little of each other these days. A servant brought in mulled wine and started to fuss with the drapes around the bed. Mathilde shook her head and he hurried from the room. William came to join her by the fire. They sat quietly, sipping their wine, until William casually said.

'Did brother Odo have much to say to you at table?'

Mathilde gauged the purpose of this seemingly innocent enquiry, thought for a moment, then said, 'Not really. He seems pre-occupied with the consecration of his new cathedral.'

William chuckled. 'His cathedral! I thought it was supposed to be God's cathedral.'

Mathilde smiled back.

'You know Odo. Never believes in selling himself short.'

'Yes, that's one thing of which you never could accuse him. By the way, I don't know if you noticed at dinner, one of his Squires, Thibault was having a word with some fellow at the bottom of the hall and dragged him off to one of the ante-rooms. You didn't recognise him I suppose?'

Mathilde pulled a loose thread from her sleeve.

'No, I can't say I noticed. Who was he, the man that Thibault took off?'

'I've no idea but I do like to know what Odo's men are up to.'

He swirled the wine in his cup.

'I have no real grounds for suspecting disloyalty but Odo...'

Mathilde wound the thread around her finger and looked at her husband.

'He is my kinsman too but, like you, I sometimes wonder. Do you think that your refusal to grant him Canterbury might have given rise to discontent? I can quite see why you didn't,' she added. 'He has far too much power, although as I said, much of his energy is taken up with Bayeux. Perhaps if he's going to cause trouble, it could be over there.'

William kicked a glowing ember back under the brazier.

'Possibly. God knows, we're surrounded by enough troublemakers in Normandy and our territories there are of more value than this island is ever likely to be.'

'I don't disagree William, but don't forget that here you are King and this conquest cost our people much in blood and sacrifice. I would hate to see it all go to waste.'

He rose and stretched.

'As ever, my love, you are right. May I stay here tonight?'

Mathilde dropped the thread into the dying embers and held out her hands to him.

'There was a time William, when you wouldn't even have thought to ask.' she paused, 'This mysterious man of Odos, point him out to me tomorrow and I will get Mirabelle to investigate. She can be very persuasive, as well as discreet.'

CHAPTER THREE

Dover

Jean had no brazier to keep out the cold. He was quartered with the clerks and messengers in a freezing dormitory. Not for them the luxury of beds or cots, only straw. Not that Jean did much sleeping. He tossed and turned wondering what it was that Odo said, something about drawing history. So, he passed a wakeful night knowing that, from daybreak, he would have to take up a prominent position within the castle so that Thibault, would be able to find him. Thereafter, his destiny appeared to be in the hands of the Bishop of Bayeux, Earl of Kent, whatever the latter title was supposed to mean.

As soon as dawn began to throw its pallid fingers of light through the unglazed holes in the walls and tentative birdsong made itself heard, Jean groaned his way out of the straw and, wrapping his inadequate cloak more tightly around him, walked down to the hall. As he made his way to where Thibault could find him, he slipped into the kitchens where he managed to scrounge a hunk of stale bread and a smear of honey. He was sitting by the main door watching a mouse scuttling along the wall when he felt the familiar sensation of the hand on the shoulder.

Thibault was dressed in what looked like a new leather tunic, dark red hose and square-toed leather shoes. Jean looked down at his own apparel, all wool, all brown and all a bit too small. Unwilling to appear awed, he stood up straight, brushed the crumbs from his chest, ran his fingers through his hair and looked Thibault in the eye. Thibault held the look then dropped his eyes and said.

'Come on. We'd better be going.'

This time, instead of taking Jean to the ante-chamber, he took him up to the tower. He pointed to the wooden construction.

'Within a few years there will be stone strongholds in every strategic point in this benighted country. That'll make it easier to control these rebellious Saxon bastards!'

Without thinking, Jean blurted out.

'Come on, it's their country. They were here before us.'

Thibault whipped round.

'Oh no it isn't, boy, it is our country now and if Harold had been a man of his word it would have been ours without us having to fight for it. God knows, we paid dearly enough for it so don't you ever let me hear you say that we haven't earned the right to be here. How old were you when it happened? Seven? Well I was there. I fought alongside my father and I saw him die. So not a word more, understand?'

Jean looked at him. Thibault didn't look that much older than he was himself but he could see steel in his eyes and an austerity that didn't quite go with the fashionable clothes.

He looked away and muttered, 'Sorry.'

Thibault's expression remained cold. 'Let's get a move on. If you find me intimidating, it's nothing compared with my Lord when he's been kept waiting.'

They mounted rough-hewn stairs to the second floor, arriving at an iron studded door on the north side. Thibault knocked and Odo's deep tones bade them enter. This time the chamber was better furnished and the air smelt aromatic from bunches of herbs that were hung from hooks or placed in earthenware crocks around the room. Once again Jean was conscious of his inferior dress and position. He looked around him, breathing in the unaccustomed fragrance. Odo, resplendent in a tunic worked with silk thread and fine cloth, was sitting behind a desk studying a document. Jean's drawings spread out in front of him. Thibault pushed Jean forward, where he stood doing his best not to look at what was on the table. It seemed an age before Odo looked up. Thibault made as if to leave but Odo waved him back. He leaned back in his chair.

'Stay Thibault. I want you to hear what passes between us because you are going to look after this young man. You will stay by his side and when he is in need of council you will council him. Despite his birth, you will instruct him in the ways of his betters, improve his manners and advise him in whatever matters are deemed necessary.'

Thibault moved towards the table and stood next to Jean.

'But, my lord…' He got no further.

'Those are my wishes, Thibault, and you will carry them out. I need this young man to do something for me which, unless I'm mistaken, will serve to remind future generations of Norman supremacy.'

Again, Thibault attempted to protest.

'My lord, you have already sponsored one of the most magnificent buildings in Europe. Why, your new cathedral will be an inspiration for hundreds of years and this… this boy is a mere…'

Odo regarded Thibault with amusement.

'My dear Thibault, I would hope that you have learned much while in my service. We have witnessed great events both as companions in arms and occupiers of a foreign land but there are things of which you appear to be unaware. Have you not noticed that here in England, unlike in our own country, it is possible for a man to improve himself. Here, by dint of effort or ingenuity or talent, an ordinary man may better himself, especially in the towns where greater opportunities present themselves. Small men are becoming shopkeepers, shopkeepers are becoming merchants, merchants may, in time, become owners of substantial properties and so it goes on.'

Thibault looked puzzled while Jean was beginning to look interested. Odo continued,

'The point I'm trying to make, my dear Thibault, and I must say I don't generally find you quite so slow on the uptake, is that LeBrun has talent. Whether he is also industrious and ingenious we have yet to find out but don't write him off as not worthy of your attention. Let's find out first shall we?'

Thibault looked uncomfortable. Perhaps, thought Jean, he was not used to being rebuked by Odo who continued, twisting the ruby on his finger as he spoke.

'LeBrun, can you read and write?'

Jean replied eagerly

'Indeed I can my Lord. My father had ambitions for me to enter the Church so I took my lessons from our priest and…'

Odo interrupted him.

'The Church! Your father never mentioned…but then, in the circumstances, I don't suppose that he would. Now listen to me very carefully, LeBrun. These images, pictures, whatever you want to call them.' he waved toward the table, 'are they copied from life? This bird, for example, about to leave its perch. Did you draw it as you saw it or was drawn from your imagination?'

Jean stepped forward to take the proffered sketch.

'I drew it as I saw it, my Lord. As you can see, the legs are slightly bent as it is about to push itself…'

'Yes, yes I can see that. You have caught the moment quite uncannily but do you have the ability to draw the same thing out of your head. In other words, is it necessary for you to have the subject in front of your eyes before you can reproduce it?'

Jean thought for a moment, then said cautiously.

'I don't think I have ever drawn that way my Lord so I don't know if I can or not'

He'd never before been called upon to talk abut his drawing – it was just something he did. Odo went on, 'What I want to know is this. If a particular action or event was described to you – do you think you could produce a picture of it?'

Jean thought for a while. He sensed that his reply was important and the answer might affect his future. He also realised that his answer had better be honest. After a moment's hesitation he said.

'I think I could my Lord. Why do you not present me with a subject of your devising and I will give of my best…but my Lord, I have no materials with me, unless you wish me to re-cover one of those.'

He pointed to the table but Odo quickly slammed his hand down on the drawings and kept it there.

'I think not LeBrun.'

Odo stroked his chin and turned to Thibault who was stifling a yawn.

'Yes I know, Thibault, you would rather be practising martial skills with the other young men. I promise you, you will soon be free of Master LeBrun but before that I require two things of you. Firstly, take him to your tailor and see that he looks less like a scarecrow and more like a junior member of the Court. Nothing too ostentatious, just enough to ensure that he blends in. I require him to talk to people, some of them of rank but the cost of this exercise must also be born in mind, and Bayeux is proving an expensive project. Is this clear Thibault?'

'Quite clear. You said there were two points my Lord?'

'Ah yes, the second point. The second point is to direct our young friend here to some of the people to whom I have referred. I'll furnish you with names. You will be familiar with them and if you mention that their co-operation is at my behest, I'm sure you'll find them willing to spare a little time with LeBrun. In fact, it might be best if you just introduce him as, shall we say, my protégée, no need for names and background. As ever in this shifting world, the less anyone knows of anything the better. So tomorrow morning Thibault! I've not quite finished with LeBrun yet.'

Thibault bowed, ignored Jean and said

'Tomorrow morning your Grace.' and left the room.

CHAPTER FOUR

Dover

O do regarded Jean.
    'Your materials! Judging by these' he indicated the artwork on the table, 'you have merely used whatever happened to be available. In order to achieve the degree of continuity I am after, that won't do. Vellum is out of the question. Too expensive for what I have in mind and totally impracticable.'

'But my Lord.' interjected Jean, 'How many drawings does your Lordship want and how large are they to be?'

Bishop Odo waved a hand. 'The actual size and number can wait. Let us first of all assess your ability to draw from scratch and transcribe words into pictures. Are you familiar with The Song of Roland?'

Jean nodded. 'Of course my Lord. From my earliest days I can remember the travelling jongleurs visiting us every year and singing it to the whole village. My father told me it was sung to our army before Duke William sailed for England. I can remember some of the most memorable verses. Would your Lordship like me to...'

Odo broke in swiftly. 'That will not be necessary. What is important is that you have the verses in your head.' he moved over to a press at the side of the room, opened it and took out a cloth bundle which he passed to Jean.

'Open it,' he said.

Jean unrolled the linen and found a bundle of fine charcoal sticks. He frowned.

Odo went on 'You have the materials in your hand. I want you to give me your impression of the death of Roland at Roncesvalles. Just as you see it in your mind. I suppose you can work on that piece of unbleached linen. Do your best because much depends on what you produce on that scrap of material. Bring it to me tomorrow. The day after, I am going to Normandy to oversee the next stage of the construction at Bayeux so it will be the last occasion, for a while, that you and I will meet. When you return tomorrow I will tell you more. Talking of Bayeux, it might amuse you at some time to let me have some drawings of gargoyles that I might incorporate into the buttresses of my new cathedral. I can think of one or two individuals that I would quite like to be caricatured in stone for all eternity. But go now and seek out Thibault. You'll probably find him at the stables.'

The interview over, Odo picked up the sketches and left the room with a flourish of velvet and silk. Jean, dazed and confused, followed him out like a sparrow after a peacock and set about finding Thibault who, he hoped, would help him to brighten up his own plumage.

#

On the other side of the Tower, in the Queen's rooms, William, who always rose earlier than anyone else in the castle, was sitting at his wife's desk in his nightgown and over-mantle. The feudalisation of England was an ongoing process and much of his time and energy was devoted to it. At first he had been patient with the defeated Anglo Saxon nobility and many had retained their administrative posts under the new regime. Things, however, were moving too slowly for William's liking. England was a rich island and it was important to his security that as much of this wealth as was possible be diverted into his own exchequer.

His current pre-occupation though, was with the Church. Again it was a question of power, always power and the Church was extremely powerful. It was important that this power be diluted and it was this problem that was engaging his attention now. Mathilde had been awake for some time but she did not disturb him while he was working. She knew he would share his thoughts and concerns when he was ready, so she lay quietly enjoying the warmth of the heavy furs that covered her. He had his back to her and she watched him as he ran his hand through his hair and drummed his fingertips on the tabletop. He then rose and walked to the window, pulled aside the hanging, looked out and gauged the time of day. As he turned back he noticed her looking at him. He smiled at her and said.

'I must go to chapel before morning council.'

She propped herself up on one elbow.

'I hope you will find time for breakfast my Lord, before meeting with your advisers?'

'Advisers! I don't know why I bother with them. It's always me who has to make the final decisions. Frankly I think you and I would be better off if we dispensed with everyone else and ran the whole thing between us. Here I am going off to chapel to pray and yet it's the very authority of the Church that is giving me concern.'

'The Church? But William, I thought that you'd replaced most of the Bishops with our own people?'

Mathilde reached for one of the fur covers and put it around her shoulders.

She went on, 'I suppose much of ecclesiastical authority lies in their courts, doesn't it?'

He nodded and she continued.

'Then why not bring the ecclesiastical courts under lay jurisdiction? That way you can ensure that their power is subject to common law, for which you are responsible.'

William shook his head admiringly.

'What have I just said, we could run this island between us. Anyway, it's time I was dressed and on my way. Thank you.'

He jumped off the desk, took off his nightwear and sluiced cold water over his face from the bowl on the stand. He called his page from the anteroom to help him get dressed and when ready, strode to the door. Before he opened it he stopped, turned towards the bed and said.

'That squire of Odo's, Thibault isn't it? Don't forget to have a word with your Mirabelle. See what she can find out about that young man he was talking to. We'll meet at dinner.'

She answered, 'My Lord.'

As the door closed behind him, she called for Mirabelle.

#

Odo, sitting at the council table, rose when William entered the room as did all the rest. The King looked relaxed and was smiling to himself as he took his chair, nodding pleasantly to the others to resume their seats. Odo thought to himself that William had just left Mathilde but, before doing so, had resolved the business of this meeting between them and it was she that was in his thoughts when he entered this room.

It was not for nothing that William respected Odo's political instincts!

CHAPTER FIVE

Dover

Jean watched Odo retreating down the corridor and panic set in. Somehow, by tomorrow, he had to sketch this scene from the Song of Roland and he couldn't remember it. When he'd said that he knew it, he had, but now perhaps Thibault could remind him although he didn't expect a lot of help from that quarter and why should he? Having to baby-sit some raw youngster from the depths of the Normandy countryside must have seemed like an intolerable imposition. He'd better get a move on. He sprinted along the corridor, out of the tower and into the bailey towards the stables, all the while trying to recall the stanza that was to be his inspiration. He was so concentrated on this that he charged into a couple who were talking outside the grain store.

'Watch where you're going you stupid… Oh my God it's you. I might have known.'

Jean started to apologise to Thibault and in doing so, fumbled the bundle that he had received from Odo. This became undone and Jean snatched at the linen. The last thing he wanted was to get that wet and dirty but the charcoal rolled out of the linen and across the ground. He bent to pick one up and found himself looking at a shoe, a ladies shoe which had imprisoned the crayon beneath it. His eyes were then drawn upwards past a fine blue woollen gown which covered a linen shift. A lady, a young and attractive lady, auburn braids hanging down beneath a raised veil, topped by a high round hat, twinkly eyes, not that much older than he was. The charcoal!!

'Please my Lady, don't break the sticks, they're easily broken and I can't…'

The foot lifted just enough for him to extract it but not without him brushing against an ankle. He picked up the rest and stood, blushing and stammering out apologies. Thibault was not smiling. She was though, well laughing actually, at his discomfiture but not he thought, unkindly. She spoke to Thibault.

'Are you not going to introduce this clumsy, pretty boy to me?'

Thibault looked at Jean, then at the girl.

'I think not Mistress Mirabelle. I cannot imagine that either of you would derive any benefit from it.'

Jean spoke before he could help himself.

'My name is Jean LeBrun, Milady'

She wrinkled her brow in his general direction. 'You are from where, Master LeBrun?'

'Normandy, Milady.'

She glanced at Thibault then back at Jean.

'Master LeBrun, we are all from Normandy. You, I imagine,' looking at his rough clothes, 'are from somewhere in the country. Had you come from Caen, I'm sure I would have recognized you.'

'No Milady I have only lately arrived from the estates of ...'

Thibault cut him off.

'You must excuse us Mistress Mirabelle, Master LeBrun and I have appointments we must keep.'

He bowed, grabbed Jean's arm and dragged him towards the stables. Mirabelle called after them.

'Master LeBrun, I hope that we will meet again.'

Jean twisted round and would have replied but Thibault's grip tightened and, for the second time in two days, Jean found himself steered in the direction of a door; this time the one that led to the stables. As they pushed their way into the gloomy, pungent interior Thibault eased his hold on Jean's arm and said,

'I suppose you can ride?'

Jean replied indignantly.

'I've been riding since before I could walk. Who was that young lady?'

Thibault busied himself with harness for a few seconds then said, 'The Lady Mirabelle, Lady in Waiting to the Queen and by definition out of your class. Never mind about her. We have to ride into Dover, get you dressed in something a little more suitable and get back so that I can carry on with my life.'

The stable boys brought out the horses, a handsome bay gelding belonging to Thibault and a rougher looking mount for Jean. They rode to the outer bailey, through the great gate and set off down the road to Dover.

They left the castle to scenes of frenzied activity; engineers measuring trunks of trees and masons supervising the areas into which stone blocks were to be taken. Droves of labourers were digging the new foundations inside the old walls of the outer bailey. Scaffolding was being erected everywhere and timber was being cut to size for framing, flooring and partitions. There must have been upwards of two hundred men milling about. As they trotted away, Jean inquired of Thibault how long would it take to complete the new castle.

'About ten years' came the reply. 'But this is one of the bigger fortresses, as befits the status of Lord Odo. I haven't seen it myself but they say the new fortress on the banks of the River Thames is nearly completed. As soon as it is, the King will take up residence there.' They rode on for a while in silence until Thibault said

'Here we are, we take this next street on the right. The tailor's rooms are at the end.'

The horses picked their way through the narrow street, their riders ducking to avoid the overhanging casements. There was a foul smell and Jean wondered how these people could live in a place that stank like the privies in the castle. The faces they passed were surly and unwelcoming and for the first time Jean was aware that he was part of an occupying power. At the bottom of the street they handed their mounts into the care of a grubby urchin and they entered the rooms of the tailor. It was the last house in the street and the end wall had large holes in it which had been covered in a translucent material that Jean had not seen before. He looked at Thibault who said.

'First time you've seen it? It's called glass and it means that the tailor can work for much longer without the need of candle or flambeau. I hear that some of the windows in the new castle might be glazed, as it is called.'

A small, swarthy man came down the stairs.

Thibault said, 'New customer for you Paul, his Grace is paying.'

The man looked at Jean and frowned. When he spoke, Jean was surprised to hear that he was Norman.

'Welcome Sires. What is the quality of this young man?' The question was addressed to Thibault who gave a short laugh and said:

'I'm surprised you feel the need to ask' then turning to Jean said.

'You do know that you are not supposed to dress above your rank? The rules are strict but I think on this occasion his Grace would not be unhappy to see them bent very slightly.' He turned back to the tailor.

'A tunic, wool of course but a fine cloth and I think green would suit him, don't you?'

The tailor was walking round Jean with a measure.

'Yes Sir, I have a bolt of fine green English wool, arrived this very morning. It pains me to say it but many of these English wools are better than anything we produce in Normandy.'

He looked up from his measuring and enquired, 'A surcoat? Might I suggest mid-calf. Any longer and we are into the realms of lower nobility. Perhaps a lighter green? The lichen dyes are very adaptable. A cloak?'

He removed Jean's cloak from his shoulders with the tips of his fingers.

'Yes, yes, black I think for the cloak.'

When he had finished, he turned to Thibault.

'Thank you Sire, tomorrow will be all right?'

'Tomorrow, I'll send a messenger to collect it, late afternoon'

'Very good gentlemen.'

Jean had been trying to pluck up the courage to say that he'd rather like his cloak in dark red but thought better of it, nodded to the tailor and followed Thibault back to the horses. They rode back to the castle without saying much. Jean was trying to remember the scene that he was supposed to depict and, as they entered the gate, he asked Thibault outright if he knew the Song of Roland.

'Of course I know it' replied Thibault. 'Everybody knows it we all learned it when we were small.'

'Yes' said Jean dismounting as he spoke. 'But do you remember it? I thought I did but there is one verse that I seem to have lost completely.'

Thibault threw his reigns to one of the grooms and gave Jean a quizzical look.

'Why are you worried about the Song of Roland? New clothes, new patron who is the second most powerful man in the land and you're fretting about some poem.'

Jean replied casually, 'Oh it's nothing really. It was just going through my mind as we were riding home and there was one verse which I just couldn't recall.'

Thibault thought for a moment and then said.

'Only one verse? The damn thing goes on for ever and you can't remember one particular verse.'

He stopped and frowned, 'Go on then, which verse is it?'

Jean regarded him innocently.

'The one about the Battle of Roncesvalles, the death of Roland'

Thibault immediately said.

'Oh! That one. Yes, I remember that one. We had to learn it by heart and recite it. Hang on, it goes...'

He thought for second longer then launched into

'Roland is dead, his soul to heav'n God bare.
That Emperor to Roncesvalles doth fare.
There was no path no passage anywhere
Nor of waste ground no ell nor foot to spare
Without a Frank or pagan lying there...'

He carried on until the end of the verse and had started on the next when Jean interrupted.

'That's it. That's the one, I remember it now. Thank you Thibault.' He turned to go but once more Thibault grabbed him by the arm, a habit which Jean was beginning to find tiresome.

'You don't realise LeBrun do you, the significance of The Song of Roland to some of us here in England?'

Jean shook his head.

'Well it's time you did. Before we went into battle in '66, Duke William, as he was then, had his jongleur, Taillefer, sing it to us. He rode up and down the lines singing those hundreds of verses while he juggled with his sword. The man was an idiot but some Englishman, equally mad, broke ranks and tried to kill him. Taillefer killed the Englishman instead. He then took off and charged the English lines all by himself. They cut him down in no time. "Song of Roland" though! I can tell you, that story of chivalry and bravery was a very inspirational moment for all of us. Still, I don't suppose you are really interested in any of this are you. Within five minutes you'll have forgotten it again so why don't you go and do whatever it is you have to do for his Grace.'

He released Jean, turned on his heel and waved a languid farewell as he walked away.

Jean turned to find some board. Time was pressing and he worried that he might not be able to produce anything that would satisfy Odo. Already, though, in his mind, a picture was forming. Charlemagne's dying knight surrounded by the debris of battle, dark skinned Saracens dead on the ground, armour. He needed a board, he needed to make a start. He approached a gang of joiners who were making up vast door frames under the supervision of one of the master masons. The mason, a large fierce man did not regard him too kindly and told him to make himself scarce, couldn't he see that they were busy. There'd be hell to pay if the necessary daily work quota wasn't fulfilled. This was the Earl of Kent's castle and the Earl himself kept a very close eye on the schedules and if…'

Jean broke in 'But that's who the board is for, Bishop Odo – I mean the Earl of Kent, I'm working under his orders and it's urgent.'

'Then why didn't you say so straight off' growled the supervisor. 'Hey Ranulph! Over here.'

A squat Saxon artisan in a leather apron dropped the length of timber on which he was working and came over. A rough thumb was jerked in Jean's direction.

'This young fellow's on an errand for the Earl, says he wants a piece of board. Sort him out and get back here sharply.'

He turned again to Jean, 'What's it for anyway, this piece of board?'

Jean shrugged his shoulders and said, 'Don't worry, I'm in a rush myself, I'll not keep him long.'

The mason watched him with interest as he accompanied the carpenter.

'This way Sir.'

The carpenter pointed over to a stack of wood piled up alongside the wall of the bailey and inquired exactly what it was that Jean wanted.

'A flat, smooth piece of board, about four spans square.' Jean displayed the required size with his arms.

'Smooth could be a problem. Got to be real smooth 'as it Sir?'

'Very important' said Jean.

When they arrived at the pile of wood, Ranulph clambered over it picking over and rejecting pieces as he went. Eventually he appeared waving a board.

'Old door panel. I'll 'ave to cut it to size Sir and if you can give me 'alf an hour with some water and sand I'll have it real smooth for you.'

Ranulph took himself and the board off to a nearby bucket of water and a pile of sand, took a piece of grimy cloth from his apron and got to work while Jean looked on. He was now impatient to start work. He'd never noticed it before but this was the sort of feeling he'd often experienced just before starting a drawing. Then he felt a tap on his shoulder; light, gentle so it wasn't Thibault. He turned to see Mirabelle standing in front of him, a finger stroking her lower lip and frowning, assessing him. Not for the first time that day he reddened and felt slightly foolish. He tried to hide his confusion by drawing himself up to his full height, a head taller than she was and gave her one of his instinctive grins. He must have got part of it right because her smile in response was warm, if slightly mocking.

'Thibault's pretty boy from the depths of Normandy, Master LeBrun, isn't it? One minute it's charcoal sticks and now it's cast-off bits of wood. Let me guess now… What would a curly haired youth from the French countryside want with wood and charcoal? Oh! I forgot. A square of linen as well, one I would say that is just about the size of that board the carpenter over there is taking such pains over. I must say he has managed to make it beautifully smooth. Don't you think so Master LeBrun?'

She looked at him, her head on one side.

'I would almost say that board is as smooth as my cheek, what think you?'

At which she caught his hand in hers and held it to her cheek, gently rubbing it along the line of her cheekbone.

'Well, Master LeBrun, wouldn't you say so?'

Jean pulled his hand away but slowly over her fingers, just lingering long enough over the tips to feel the shiver that ran down her arm.

'My lady,' he said quietly but with more confidence than he felt. 'I cannot dare imagine that anything as crude as a piece of polished wood could bear comparison with even the least smooth portion of your Ladyship's …person.'

She gave a hoot of laughter.

'Master LeBrun, we shall make a courtier of you yet.'

Her eyes flickered past him.

'I think your friend wants to give you that oh-so-smooth piece of wood Master LeBrun.'

'Thank you Ranulph, that's perfect'

Jean stood holding the board between himself and Mirabelle who laughed again.'

'You are an artist, I think Master LeBrun. How interesting. Tell me if you will, what is an artist from rural France, a rare breed I would imagine, doing in Dover Castle? I understand that this country is overrun with picture makers. Why, it's not that long ago when they were all painting each other blue with woad, so I've been told.'

Jean's self possession left him as quickly as it had arrived.

'Oh my God, I… Your ladysh… Must go. Sorry!' With which unpolished adieu, he turned on his heels and tore off across the bailey, the inner bailey and into the hall, from where he could still hear the echoes of her musically mocking laughter.

CHAPTER SIX

Dover

Jean's first task was to fix the linen. Since the whole place was a building site, tacks were lying about everywhere and stretching his canvas with those and a borrowed hammer was the work of minutes. He left the hall and stood on the top step, looking around the inner bailey and calculated he probably had about five hours of daylight left. For once the weather was fine so where to set up his makeshift studio? The walls! That was it, the walls. He ran over to one of the fortified wooden walls which formed a circle around the inner bailey attached to which, at intervals, were permanent ladders. Tucking the board under an arm he scaled one of them until he had hauled himself onto the platform that served as a gallery between the double wooden fortifications. Safe from prying eyes, he sat down with his back to the outer wall, the board on his knees and his charcoal beside him.

He worked tentatively at first, his strokes light and almost invisible. As he gathered confidence the lines became bolder and more defined. Everything was sketched in outline until his composition began to look like the picture he had been nurturing in his head. Then he shaded and graded the images. The Death of Roland began to emerge on the linen. Jean's concentration was absolute and it took him little more than a couple of hours before he relaxed enough to lift his head and indulge in a few neck rolls to relieve the tension. He held the picture at arms length; Roland's body under a tree on a hill overlooking the battlefield. His limbs at a grotesque angle, his sword and bugle lying by his side and around him the bodies of slain infidels.

Was there something he'd forgotten? Not that he could see although… He studied the picture again. The figures were stylised but Jean thought he had captured the essence of the occasion. He frowned, feeling that something was lacking but decided that further tinkering was unlikely to improve it, so he descended the ladder and started looking for a somewhere to hide the picture overnight. The dormitory was the last place, too many questions and too much pilfering. Where then? After rejecting various possibilities, he eventually found himself in the chapel where he chanced on a spot in which it was unlikely to be discovered, under the alter and behind the alter cloth. It didn't look as though it had been cleaned under there for years so the chances of some over-zealous skivvy doing it that night was unlikely.

As he closed the door to the chapel he thought he heard or rather sensed, a faint noise. He wheeled round and re-opened the chapel door. Nothing! He walked slowly inside and stood listening, again nothing. At last satisfied, he turned on his heel and started walking back towards the lavabo, set into the only part of the new stone curtain that had been erected inside the inner bailey. He turned on the bronze tap, shaped like a lions head, and sluiced his hands and face. He still marvelled at this innovation which the engineers had copied from ancient Roman buildings and when he had first arrived at the castle, the sheer novelty of it had caused him to wash several times a day.

Refreshed and quietly satisfied with his day's activities, Jean walked into the bailey where he could stand and chat with the few acquaintances with whom he had formed a loose friendship since being in England. They were mostly lads of his own class, sons of reeves, marshals and stewards. Not persons of blood but the offspring of aspiring men who, by sending their sons to the new colony, hoped they would make the best of their chances and rise in the world.

Soon the space was filling up. The Normans preferred to eat their main meal at lunchtime but because of the workloads associated with rebuilding and constant military training, it had been ordained by the King that no more than fifteen minutes be set aside for the midday break. Consequently, come the evening, appetites were sharpened to the extent that people wasted no time in getting to their tables and the noise soon rose to it's customary deafening level. The bailey was filling up but as nobody could take their place before the nobility, hunger sometimes gave rise to irritability, quarrels sometimes became violent and it was for this reason that everyone had to leave their weapons at the door.

Jean was chatting to one of the messengers, asking if he knew Thibault. The man said.

'Thibault? Yes of course I know him. Too good to be true, is Thibault. Nobody can understand why he hasn't taken Holy Orders. With Lord Odo as good as a father, he could go a long way in the clergy.'

Jean was about to agree that Thibault seemed an unlikely courtier when he froze. Idiot! What an idiot! Boudouin, the brother of Roland! That was what had been niggling at him. He'd forgotten Boudouin. The picture couldn't be a faithful representation of the death of Roland without his brother kneeling by his side, about to pick up the sacred horn and sword, before delivering them to Charlemagne. Jean didn't wait to finish the conversation. He pushed his way through the waiting crowd and once he found space, ran for the gate. In his haste, he noticed nothing. Not even The King, Queen Mathilde, Odo or Thibault whom he brushed in passing. William looked at Mathilde, Odo looked at Thibault. Jean flew towards the chapel.

William chewed on a piece of venison and turned to Mathilde.

'Did you notice him?'

'Who, my Lord?'

'The young man I asked you about this morning. He nearly knocked us over in the bailey.'

'Well, what of it.' Mathilde looked puzzled, 'People are always behaving strangely. Personally I blame it on this awful brew they seem to drink in such unnatural quantities. Have you ever tried it? So uncivilised.'

'Yes Mathilde I have tried it and I rather like it. I grant you it's something of an acquired taste but… That boy, Odo's boy, the one that you didn't notice, did you ask your woman to find out about him?'

'Of course William, I always do everything you ask me.'

'And?'

'I don't think her researches are concluded yet. She is a very thorough young lady. If there is anything to learn, she will find it out. More to the point William, I trust your time in Council was profitable?'

William looked pleased with himself and took a sip of wine.

'I think everyone present could see the advantages of what I suggested, at least, they all said they did.'

Mathilde looked at him and raised her own cup.

'Including my uncle?'

'Odo? He more than anybody and that's important. The Church will listen to him more readily than it will to me and he is going to set the necessary wheels in motion straight away.'

'They won't like it William.'

'Of course they won't like it but they'll have to cooperate in the end, powerful though they might be.'

Mathilde put her hand on his arm.

'If Odo has given his blessing to all this then he is obviously on your side. So why the concern with this mysterious young man of his?'

'It is vital that I know everything that goes on here and in Normandy, come to that. I have been harsh and sometimes even cruel but it's only been through necessity. Without order, imposed order, there is chaos and in order to survive I have to know what is going on. Paranoid perhaps but it's what keeps me on the throne here and secure in our Duchy in Normandy.'

Mathilde moved her hand down to cover Williams'.

'You will do whatever it takes to create a kingdom governed by laws but don't forget, force by subjection is only one of your weapons. You can also retain the loyalty of your vassals by granting them lands or properties but only for as long as they stay loyal. Should any choose to rebel you simply withdraw the right to these lands and pass them over to vassals whose fealty is absolute.'

The King sandwiched her small hand between his.

'As we have always done in France, my love?'

'As we have always done in France, my Lord.'

He pulled her towards him and whispered in her ear. She raised an eyebrow.

'Again, your Majesty?'

Laughing, they bade farewell to their fellow diners as they left the table and made for the tower. On his way the King stopped behind Odo's chair and clapped a hand on his shoulder. Odo made to rise.

'No, don't get up brother. Is all well?'

'Well enough, your Highness. I have delayed my trip back to France in order to meet with the Bishops. I have already intimated our intentions to subject the church to common law and since most of the English church leadership has been replaced by our own, I don't foresee any great problems.'

'With you in charge of our negotiations, I'm sure there won't be. Good night brother.'

Mathilde rested her hand on Odo's other shoulder. 'Goodnight Uncle'.

'Goodnight to your Majesties.'

As soon as they had left the hall, Odo signalled to Thibault to join him and said:

'LeBrun rushed away without his supper. What do you imagine that was all about?'

Thibault said 'Do you want me to follow him?'

'No. It's probably nothing or if it is, I'm seeing him tomorrow morning. It can wait until then.'

CHAPTER SEVEN

Dover

Jean charged into the chapel which was, again, empty. He made straight for the altar, knelt down, lifted the cloth and … Nothing! It had gone. True it was dark in there but it wasn't a large space and he felt and felt around and still… nothing. He sat back on his heels and put his hands in his hair, gazing up at the great cross as if seeking the answer there. A slight rustle behind him. His fingers froze in his curls.

'I had no idea you country boys were so devout. Hope I haven't missed a flagellation!'

Still on his knees Jean turned his body round. In the gloom it was difficult to see anything except the outline of a cloaked and hooded figure but the voice, mocking, lilting was unmistakable.

'Lady Mirabelle!' he croaked 'I've lost …'

'Yes I know. Don't worry, it's safe.'

He gave an exhalation of relief.

'Where is it? Can I have it? You see I suddenly remembered…'

'Boudouin! Yes I know. We women might not have the benefit of much education but the Song of Roland, well, you can't get away from it. Fathers, uncles, brothers going on about all that chivalry and fighting. I've heard it so many times and I thought to myself when I saw your picture, something is missing. Now what could it be? The sword is there, that ridiculous horn, all those dead, dark gentlemen are littering up the place…Oh! I know. It's brother Boudouin. He's not kneeling at the late Roland's side.'

Jean rose to his feet. 'Please, can I have it? It's important. Please!'

A braid was escaping from one side of the hood. It caught the thin ray of moonlight coming through the transept window. She looked at him. Again her finger was touching her lip.

'If you really want it Master LeBrun, that is, really want it, you'll have to come and get it.'

'Where is it, Milady?'

'My room.'

'Your room, Milady?'

'Shall we go?'

She turned round and skipped from the chapel. Taking a moment to collect himself and he followed along the wall of the inner bailey, both of them in deep shadow and unseen. They came to a door set in the wall. One he'd not seen before. She looked around quickly and finger to lip, but this time indicating silence, preceded him through the door and up narrow steps which terminated at another door which opened into a lower gallery between the walls. He hadn't known it existed but he calculated that he was only about six feet below the gallery on which he'd been working earlier. The only light was through arrow slits but she sped along, lifting her cloak and skirts to give her feet the freedom to do so. Another door, this time leading to a small solar situated, Jean guessed, in one of the corner watchtowers. Not a large room but comfortable enough with open windows protected by parchment, a bed, a chest and a small table with a chair. There were rushes, as opposed to straw, on the floor. Jean stood, slightly breathless and not certain what his next move was expected to be. She threw her cloak onto the back of the chair, turned to face him and giggled.

'Master LeBrun don't tell me that this is your first time in a lady's bedchamber. I do believe it is. Look at you, you have the look of a stag at bay. Aren't you going to ask me where your picture is?'

She gave him one of her mischievous looks which, try as he may, he was unable to return. He did manage to blurt out, like a schoolboy.

'Can I have my picture back please?' and then, a little more controlled, 'Where is it?'

'I think you're going to have to earn it Master LeBrun. Now, let us see what you're worth shall we.'

She came over to him, standing too close for his comfort. She smelled fresh, a new experience for him, reached up and gently ruffled his hair. He took a step back. She followed him and stood there for a moment, looking intently at him. He felt like a beast being appraised for slaughter, when she grabbed both his ears and pulled his mouth down to hers. She kissed him for a long time, long enough for him to get the idea of how to kiss her back and when he did she released his head and began to work on the rest of him.

Finesse hadn't figured too much in his previous encounters with the opposite sex and the act tended to be of a basic and uncomplicated variety; not this however. He obviously had much to learn but Jean was beginning to prove an apt pupil. She undid his belt and slipped her hand down the front of his hose. When she found what she was looking for, which was not too difficult, she let out an 'Ooh' of pleasure – as did he.

'Don't you dare be too precipitate Jean.' then she added with a smile, 'Do you know what? I think you're going to get your picture back.'

This wasn't all that Jean wanted to hear but it did wonders for his peace of mind so he pulled her hand from his clothing, picked her up and put her on the bed. He was just about to throw himself on top of her when she held up both her hands and shrieked.

'NO! No, the picture, under the mattress.'

He looked blank for a moment so she slipped off the bed, put her hands under the mattress and produced the "Death of Roland", together with the small bundle of charcoal. It didn't look too smudged although just at this moment he had other things on his mind and once again she had to hold him off.

'Goodness me, how impatient you are! Now come here and give me your hand.' Lifting up her skirts with her other hand, she took Jean's and guided it between her legs. When his fingers had found her she gave a little mew of pleasure and moved against him, pulling him down on top of her.

'You see' she breathed 'You're not the only one. Now fuck me gently... gently.'

She let out a long sigh. 'That's better.'

Afterwards they lay together, damply entwined and very still.

After a while, she moved away from him so that she could get him into focus properly. She pushed his curls back from his forehead.

'You are going to have to go.'

He made to move out of the bed but she stopped him.

'But first, what are you really doing here? No not here.' She giggled again as he snuggled back against her and brushed her nipples with the backs of his fingers.

'Here in Dover and how did you get to know Thibault.? No offence Jean but Thibault is – no Jean, no more, stop it – Thibault is a very proud young man and very particular of the company he keeps. I wouldn't have thought you were his type.'

Jean raised himself up on one elbow and grinned at her.

'Funny you should say that Milady. I wouldn't have thought I was your type!'

She grinned back.

'You're very good looking, young and male. That's precisely "my type", as you put it. You still haven't answered my question.'

Jean rolled over, leaned out of bed and picked up the picture, holding it up for her to see.

'This! This is apparently why I'm here. Bishop Odo found out that I could draw and had me brought over to execute some art for him.'

He slapped a hand to his forehead.

'Oh my God! This isn't finished yet. I'd forgotten all about it I must...'

She frowned as she interrupted him, 'That's all, that's the only reason you're hanging about Dover Castle with Thibault, and how does he come into it?'

'Well, he's the Bishop's Squire isn't he? So his Grace asked him to show me around, help me order new clothes and …' Jean's voice tailed off.

'And what? What else is Thibault going to do for you, apart from introducing you to his tailor?'

A sharper edge had appeared in her voice and her eyes narrowed. Suddenly Jean felt uncomfortable and on his guard.

'Well, he introduced me to you for a start – and look where that got us!'

His attempt at humour was not reciprocated. Her eyes had lost their mischief and taken on a more steely aspect.

'You forget yourself Master LeBrun, who you are and what I am. Anything that happened between you and me was not of his making or yours. If I choose you as an amusing diversion, you have little say in the matter.'

The steel in her eyes was matched by that in her voice. Jean felt he had been slapped in the face.

'You've outstayed your welcome. You'd better go. As you say, you have to finish playing with your picture.'

Angry and confused, Jean dressed without saying a word, collected his things and walked to the door. He was nothing more than a plaything. Mirabelle was right, he did have a lot to learn if this was how they carried on at Court. As he made his way to the bailey, his sense of unease returned. What did Odo really want with him and why was Mirabelle so interested. Too dark now to work on the picture, he trudged back to the dormitory where another sleepless night awaited him.

CHAPTER EIGHT

Dover

In his austere room, Thibault sat on the edge of his cot studying his feet, thrust into wooden pattens to keep out the pre-dawn chill. His head ached and he massaged one of his temples as he tried to fathom what it was that Odo was planning for young LeBrun. When Thibault's father had been killed at Hastings, Odo had been his chief source of comfort and had effectively taken on the role of surrogate parent. The fact that Odo had successfully shielded the youth from his own vices and excesses spoke volumes for the disparity in their two characters; Odo for whom deceit was second nature and Thibault who scarcely seemed to have matured beyond the innocence of childhood. Apart from Odo, with whom he had forged an obsessive emotional attachment, he shrank from any form of intimacy. His whole being was focussed on carrying out whatever duties were assigned to him to the best of his ability. He found this present role of nursemaid to an apparently talented but unmannerly youth, disturbing and Lord Odo's motives unclear. He sat there, fingertips moving in circles against his shaven temple, thinking…

#

In his large canopied bed, Bishop Odo, Earl of Kent and beneficiary of this castle, had the fur covers pulled up to his chin and slept like a baby.

#

Queen Mathilde, as cosily cocooned as her uncle, slept well too, smiling in her sleep, one hand caressed the warm linen where, until a short while ago, her husband had lain.

#

Three loud hammer-blows! Jean whipped round just in time to see the last of the three huge bolts being drawn on the oaken door which formed the entrance to the inner bailey. It was just after dawn and the first of the tradesmen and artisans were being admitted. The lower servants, skivvies and the like, were also drifting in, yawning, coughing and complaining, to commence the day's activities. Hooves echoed in from the outer bailey as horses were prepared for messengers, huntsmen and knights.

Jean had left his dormitory before the dawn chorus had even started. He needed to finish his drawing before appearing before Lord Odo but it wasn't working out as he had hoped. After half an hour of looking at his work, propping it up against a wall, standing back and squinting at it, he was still undecided. It wasn't too bad but if he added the kneeling figure of Boudouin, then it would unbalance the composition. If, on the other hand, he left it out it would not properly represent the "Death of Roland", as described in the poem. He wondered what to do. He sighed and absent-mindedly knuckled the bridge of his nose.

On the other side of the bailey he caught sight of Thibault, crossing the space towards the Great Hall, making his way through the crowd of artisans who were always hungry and anxious to get to their first meal of the day. Jean picked up his picture and tucked it under his cloak. If Lord Odo wasn't happy with it, the worst he was likely to do was to send him packing, back to his father in Normandy. Not a prospect to be relished. Not after last night, the memory of which brought a flush to his chilled cheeks, but why had Mirabelle's mood changed so quickly?

Again, he experienced a moment of panic, of being out of his element. He couldn't think of anything back home which compared with the Lady Mirabelle but had he done something wrong, of which he was unaware? With a sense of foreboding he elbowed his way into the Great Hall and onto the bench where he'd just have time for a bowl of the disgusting English porridge before he had to clean up and meet his patron.

#

Queen Mathilde was preparing for her day, assisted at her toilette by her ladies of whom Mirabelle was her favourite and confidante. This was not a protracted procedure, for the Queen was not a vain woman. She was though, always eager to hear what gossip was in the air and she used this period of the day to have her ladies bring her up to date on what was going on in the court. Few of her attendants realised how these snippets of information were dissected, analysed and combed through as thoroughly as her hair dresser was now doing to the royal hair. Information freely offered was seldom as valuable as that which Mathilde teased out of her waiting ladies and among that select number of four, three of whom were the wives of favoured Norman barons, Mirabelle had proved by far the most productive. Unmarried, attractive and blessed with a sexual energy that quite overpowered such meagre conscience as she appeared to possess, she was the one whom Mathilde employed where there were things to be learned from ambassadors or important foreign visitors.

Mirabelle was a daughter of one of Mathilde's father's vassals in Flanders and the Queen had taken no time to assess the potential value of this latest acquisition to her household. She quickly brought the eleven year old under her wing. Precocious and pretty, Mirabelle was quick to learn what was required of her and within a couple of years was proving invaluable as a source of information to the Queen.

As soon as her toilette was finished, Mathilde dismissed her women with the exception of Mirabelle who sat quietly in one corner of the chamber, eyes lowered to her inexpert embroidery but with ears pricked to gather any fragment of conversation which the others might have let slip. Once they had left the room she dropped her sewing and stood at the Queen's side. Mathilde looked at her, not directly but in her mirror.

'Well?'

'Your Highness?'

'The young man of Odo's, Mirabelle. What have you discovered, what have you to tell me?'

'Not very much your Highness'

The eyes in the mirror narrowed slightly.

'Not very much Mirabelle, you disappoint me. You must at least have emerged from the encounter with some notion of his virility, or did you not even reach that happy stage?'

Mirabelle, without even the faintest suspicion of a blush, returned the gaze of the Queen.

'I'm sure your Majesty has no wish for me to describe everything that passed between us. Suffice it to say that I did as your Majesty requested.'

Mathilde toyed with her comb for a moment and then, still conducting the interrogation through the mirror.

'Just tell me what this "not very much" was. My imagination is more than capable of dealing with whatever other activities resulted from your labours.'

'My Lady, he is nothing but an artist, a painter of pictures and he had just finished a scene of "The Death of Roland". Actually it was quite good, although I thought…'

'The Death of Roland?' interjected Mathilde. 'And for whom precisely was he painting this masterpiece that you thought was 'quite good'?'

'Your uncle, the Earl of Kent your Majesty.'

Again the eyes narrowed slightly and there was a pause.

'Anything else?'

'Nothing my Lady, apart from the fact that my Lord Odo's squire, Thibault, had taken the young man to be measured for apparel more appropriate to his present surroundings.'

'Tell me Mirabelle, when are you going to see this young artist again? I would imagine that his attentions were quite refreshing after some of the older interviewees you have been required to entertain in the past.'

Mirabelle looked down at her slipper clad feet before replying.

'I doubt if there will be another meeting with him my Lady.'

The Queen looked surprised.

'Indeed Mirabelle. Did he not please you or, and this I cannot imagine, did you not please him?'

'It's not that my Lady. It's just that I didn't think there was anything else of interest to find out. After all, he is only a peasant artist.'

The Queen dropped her comb onto the table and, turning on her stool, looked up at Mirabelle and took her hand.

'Whenever there are people connected to people in power, and next to my husband, Odo is the most powerful man in this Kingdom, there will always be something more to be learned.'

She squeezed Mirabelle's hand, just hard enough to make her wince and try to withdraw it but the Queen kept her grip and drew Mirabelle closer.

'I want to know everything. You understand? Everything.'

Again the grip tightened. Surprisingly powerful for so small a woman.

'Everything.' she repeated.

She released Mirabelle who took a respectful step backwards.

'Of course Ma'am. I am very sorry if I have disappointed you. You have my word that if there is anything else to find out, I will do it.' she smiled ruefully and went on, 'After all, I cannot pretend that the task is likely to prove arduous, rough though his manners are.'

Mathilde's expression softened and she half smiled at the unusually penitent Mirabelle.

'Go now and report to me as soon as you have anything you think will be of interest to me.'

She waved her hand in dismissal and Mirabelle backed out of the room, still massaging her fingers. The Queen plucked at an imaginary thread on her sleeve and murmured to herself.

'Probably nothing at all, but then again…'

CHAPTER NINE

Dover

The object of Queen Mathilde's speculation was waiting outside Odo's suite in the company of Thibault. No formal summons had been issued but Thibault had dragged Jean away from his half finished bowl of porridge with the advice that it might be as well for them to make themselves available at the earliest opportunity.

So they waited, each preoccupied with their own thoughts. Thibault leaning elegantly against the wall, wondering if this was going to take very long while Jean inwardly fretted about the inadequacy of his unfinished drawing. Occasionally he glanced at his companion, studying his languid pose and the care with which Thibault had dressed and couldn't help but wonder how Thibault would have handled last night's activities with Mirabelle although the thought of Thibault, folding his fine mantle and tunic with exaggerated care before submitting himself to the sport in hand, brought a smile to his lips. His speculations were interrupted by a flurry of activity at the other end of the passageway.

Thibault almost sprang to attention as two men-at-arms with shouldered halberds came into view. Behind them the burly figure of Odo accompanied by a man Jean had never seen before. An older man, not richly dressed as was Odo but nevertheless carrying an air of authority and obviously on easy terms with the Bishop since they were engaged in animated conversation. The door to Odo's chambers was opened by one of the men-at-arms and the two men entered, Odo disregarding Jean and Thibault as if they didn't exist. Jean frowned at Thibault who merely shrugged his shoulders and said.

'Take no notice, it happens all the time.'

He then moved to Jean's side and led him a little distance from the room, acknowledging the guards as he did so.

'You know who that was don't you?'

Jean clutched his picture closer and looked blankly at his companion.

'For God's sake LeBrun, don't you know anything?'

Jean, still anxious about the reception of his picture and tired from the stress of the previous night, was not really in the mood for another dose of patronage from someone not much older than himself. So looking Thibault straight in the eye he said.

'Sorry Thibault!. It's all very well for you to keep going on about this and that but no! I don't know him from Adam so why don't you just tell me.'

He indicated the closed door, 'Come on then, who is it?'

Thibault looked long and hard at him, a flush of anger tinting his pale skin. It faded as he got himself under control.

'Well, well. The boy has some spirit. That man, Master LeBrun, is Robert Beaumont and the deeds he performed during the battle for this island will go down in history. It is said that he is likely to be granted the Earldom of Leicester.'

Jean looked puzzled.

'What's Leicester?'

'A town, LeBrun, surrounded by thousands of hectares of land. I have not been there but I am led to believe that it's somewhere in the middle of this island. Oh, by the way, I meant to ask you. The Lady Mirabelle. After our chance meeting yesterday, did you happen to see her again?'

Jean managed a wry smile.

'Yes, we did… bump into one another.'

Thibault's response was sharp.

'Master LeBrun, you need to be careful. That woman is one of the Queen's spies. One of her most productive in fact so I do hope you didn't say anything which might compromise our Lord and Master. Of course we all are completely loyal to the King, but these are tricky times and it wouldn't do to drop the wrong word in the wrong place.'

Jean's reply was defensive.

'I didn't say anything I shouldn't have'

'I would hope not but did she not question you at all, why you were here, what you were doing with me for example?'

'Well, yes. She did.'

'And…'

'I told her that his Grace, his Lordship, whatever he is, had asked me to draw something for him. That was all. She did try to delve a bit deeper but she changed, her attitude. She became sharper, less friendly so I shut up. Then she got really nasty and I walked out.'

'Walked out or thrown out?'

'Well, thrown out I suppose. But, Thibault, I couldn't have told her any more if I'd wanted to because I don't know anything. Do you know why I'm here, because I'm blessed if I do?'

Thibault answered impatiently.

'I don't know either and for what it's worth it's as much a mystery to me as it is to you. All I know is that His Grace asked me to keep an eye out for you and I presume that means keeping you out of trouble although it looks as if I might have already failed in that regard.'

Hardly had he finished speaking when the door opened and the man Jean now knew as Robert Beaumont walked out. A few seconds later, Odo strode into the corridor and beckoned the two young men into the room, a man at arms closing the door after them.

Odo wasted no time in welcomes. He merely nodded to Thibault and turned immediately to Jean, holding out his hand for the picture. Jean handed it over and Odo studied it briefly, frowning while he did so.

'There's something missing. The picture is good but you've missed something out.'

Jean decided there was nothing to be gained from making excuses.

'Yes, my Lord. It's Roland's brother. When I first did the sketch, I forgot all about him and when I remembered, I decided to leave him out because I thought it would detract from the composition.'

Odo looked at the picture again and again he frowned.

'So you value your creative integrity above truth. Is that it?'

'Not always my Lord. It depends on the subject but had I remembered in time I might still have included another figure. It's just that there's so much going on here and…'

'Not so much going on, I trust, that you might be tempted to carry out your orders in a slipshod manner?'

The tone on this occasion was quite hostile and Jean looked to Thibault for help. Much to his surprise, help was forthcoming.

'My Lord' said Thibault. 'I think what Master LeBrun means is that his commission was not made easy by his unaccustomed surroundings. There is much activity here, what with the building works and the comings and goings of the Court. I think he found difficulty in finding a quiet spot in which to work.'

Jean was grateful that the exact nature of one of the these distractions was not made public Odo, on his part, seemed as surprised as Jean that Thibault had spoken in Jean's defence. He looked at both of them in turn and growled.

'The thing is LeBrun, you have, by accident or design, accomplished exactly what I hoped you would. You have produced a facsimile of an event without slavishly adhering to the truth. What I am about to say is not for the ears of the rest of the Court. You understand, both of you, the rest of the Court? Don't look so worried Thibault. I'm not planning treason or anything likely to prove detrimental to the interests of our monarch. It is only that I wish to keep this particular project of mine quiet until I deem the time is right for it to become public knowledge.

Thibault and Jean exchanged a glance before saying that, yes, they understood. There then followed silence while they waited for their master to throw more light on the business. For the time being they were compelled to remain in the dark since Odo seemed disinclined to satisfy their curiosity and was content to sit at his desk and study "The Death of Roland." It was as if he'd forgotten their presence and three sets of breathing were the only sounds to be heard. Eventually he looked up at them and beckoned them to sit in the two chairs that faced him across the desk.

He adjusted his heavy fur around his shoulders, cleared his throat, sat back in his seat and addressed his Squire.

'Thibault, you recognised the man who came in with me just now?'

'I did my Lord, although it is some time since last we met. It is said that military prowess and wisdom are seldom seen combined in one man as they are in Lord Beaumont.'

Odo glared at his Squire and growled -

'It has been suggested Thibault. It has been suggested.'

'I was not, my Lord, suggesting that you were not, indeed are not...'

'Yes, all right Thibault. You've made your point. The thing is that I want you to introduce our young friend here to this.... this paragon of yours.'

Thibault and Jean looked at one another.

'Why didn't I do it just now, when Robert was here, that's what you want to know isn't it? It's quite simple. He didn't have time. The King is seeking his advice on new fortifications in the middle lands of the island where there have been some signs of Saxon unrest. Since Lord Beaumont is shortly to make his way to Leicester and supervise fortifications for the region, the King has called for him to discuss the matter. He has, however, graciously agreed to meet you later in the day.'

Thibault looked at Jean, his hand moving to the crucifix.

Odo caught the look.

'Relax, my boy and let me finish what I want to say. Firstly, LeBrun's new apparel has been delivered so at least you need no longer be ashamed of appearing in his company.'

He held up an arresting hand.

'No need to argue my young friend. I know well how you feel but if I'm not very much mistaken, LeBrun's new wardrobe, such as it is, will allow him to pass muster anywhere. By the by, I did take it upon myself to change the colour of his cloak. I thought red more suitable. Don't look so worried Thibault. It is a suitably dull red, nothing aristocratic about it.'

Jean grinned at Thibault, who ignored him and continued to look perplexed.

'But the point of all this my Lord, if you don't mind me saying so, exactly what is all this for?'

'What is it for Thibault? Why, the project I have in mind is like nothing that has ever been attempted before. It will ensure our place in history. Nothing more, nothing less than that. Much will depend on you Thibault. LeBrun is in your care and although you won't always find it easy, you must look after him as if he were your own brother. Now, both of you, listen carefully.'

CHAPTER TEN

Dover

The large room was bare but for a long, high table and the two men standing at the table were clothed in similarly plain fashion. The contrast with Odo's apartment and his extravagant costume was stark. William and Beaumont cared little for outward appearance and the austerity of the Council Chamber was of William's choosing, because he considered that even the addition of seating might distract from the business in hand. The attention of the two men was concentrated on large maps spread out in front of them.

Robert Beaumont was to prove one of the most successful survivors of his age. He had outlived two Kings of England and sat in the French Parliament. He had amassed great personal wealth and this was one of the reasons that William trusted him. Beaumont's ambition was limited to the accumulation of fortune but unlike Odo, not power.

The maps being studied were those of Middle England. William as an able administrator, was well aware of the importance of good mapping and he enjoyed these sessions with one such as Beaumont, who also knew the value of strategic planning. He appraised his companion, watching him sip his wine. Sipped, not quaffed. Odo, he remembered, was a quaffer of wine. William took a sip from his own cup. Never out of control, William was uncompromising, could sometimes be vicious but his every action was dictated by logic. He placed his cup on the table and put an arm around Beaumont's shoulder.

'When will you start? The sooner the better, the year is running into spring and the natives will feel their blood getting warmer. These defences need to be in place before the warmth turns to heat and they have food from their harvests on their tables.'

'Quite so Sire,' replied Beaumont, 'before sun-up. If we are ever to get any sun in this fog-bound island.'

William nodded. 'Tomorrow, that is as I had hoped. What preparation for an occupying force. Not too many I hope. I don't wish to be left too exposed.' He held up a hand. 'Yes, I know, as well as my personal guard, I have the luxury of Odo's men and I shall have to leave him in charge when I return to Normandy.'

Beaumont smiled.

'My Lord Odo is a busy man these days. His new cathedral in Bayeux, his clerical duties, such as they are and the re-building of this castle which, I have to say, is coming along better than I expected.'

William smiled back ruefully.

'Yes, Dover is beginning to take shape but I can't help thinking that it would move at an even better pace if my step-brother had fewer projects to occupy his mind. I assume you'll recruit on the road? There should be plenty of willing hands between here and London.'

Beaumont nodded, 'That is what I have in mind, although it isn't easy to find willing hands in this immediate area. I regret to say that my Lord Odo has not helped to bring people over to our side. His methods have been fairly brutal and the local population has little love for us.'

William raised an eyebrow. 'Well, Robert, he has done little other than follow my orders. You, as much as anyone, must be aware that my policy has always been to bring these Englishmen to heel with the utmost speed. I well understand, my friend, that you favour a more subtle approach. We can all accomplish what we need to do in our several ways but what's important is that we end up with an island that we can govern without fear of rebellion.'

Beaumont looked doubtfully at his sovereign and for a moment there was a silence between them. When he did speak it was with some hesitation.

'My Lord, I completely understand that Lord Odo is following your orders in administering his authority in the way that he does but...'

William's eyes sharpened and the hand stayed the goblet before it reached his lips.

'But what Robert, is there something I should know?'

Beaumont too stayed his drinking hand and his brow furrowed.

'Nothing tangible Sire but I have just left his Grace and while in his company he did surprise me by asking the question, in a somewhat different form, that you have just posed.'

'Question Robert? The only question I think I raised with you concerned your proposals for a force to accompany you to the middle lands.'

'Quite so my Lord, as I say my Lord Odo put his query slightly differently in so much as he wanted to know if I was recruiting en route and, if so, were there likely to be any of my personal men at arms that I could turn over to him.'

William stroked his chin then took another sip of wine.

'Did he say why Robert? Why he could use an addition to his personal force?'

'No your Majesty but I have noticed that some of his retainers are no longer billeted here in Dover. I assumed he was looking for people to replace them.'

The King put his cup on the table.

'Thank you Robert. We seem to have a mystery here and mysteries worry me. Disappearing men at arms! Have they returned to France do you think?'

'I have no idea my Lord. To be honest with you I hadn't really given the matter much thought. Had I not been called to this council with you immediately after leaving Odo's chambers, it might have escaped my attention completely. Especially as I do have other matters on my mind.'

William smiled.

'Indeed you do Robert. Anything else?'

'Since you mention it my Lord, there is, although why it should or could be significant, I have no idea. Your step brother asked if I could spare a few moments with a… a protégée of his. Apparently this, this…Whatever he is, needs to ask me a few questions.'

'Questions again Robert? What about this time?'

'About my memories of the battle your Majesty. Oh yes, and of the events preceding it.'

'What events preceding it?'

'I'm not sure but I imagine those which precipitated our invasion, that is to say, Harold's repudiation of Edward's wish that you should succeed to the English throne but time is running out on me. With your permission Sire, I really must take my leave.'

Beaumont bowed and made to leave but William beckoned him to stay.

'A few moments ago I was the one anxious for you to be on your way but just minute longer if you will. This protégée or whatever he is, of Odo's. Who is he? What's his purpose?'

Beaumont turned from the doorway, his hand on the iron handle.

'I have no idea my Lord. All I know is that I have been asked by the Bishop to give a few moments of my time to − whoever he is and Odo's squire. Thibault isn't it?'

A slow smile spread across William's face.

'Ah, the mysterious young man from the Great Hall. My wife is, I believe, engaged in finding out exactly who he is. See him Robert, can't see that much harm can come from the meeting.'

He mused for a second.

'Thibault though! A straightforward young man I would have said. Not dissimilar to yourself Robert. Not had a lot to do with him myself but his father was a very worthy soldier and companion in arms. He is Odo's man though. Almost adopted by him, you might say and, unlikely as it may seem,

Thibault worships him and he Thibault. Always thought that strange. Send word to me of what you find out. Whatever, we mustn't allow this probably unimportant interlude to divert us from our present purpose.'

He turned back to the maps and Beaumont bowed for the second time taking himself from the room. Alone now, William sat himself on a corner of the table, drumming his fingers lightly on the edge and turning the conversation over in his mind. He then called for his servant and instructed him to find the Queen and ask her to wait for him in her apartments.

CHAPTER ELEVEN

Dover

Thibault and Jean stared at Odo who looked calmly back at them, toying with the seal nestling in his fur collar. Jean was the first to speak.

'How big, my Lord? Did you say...'

Odo nodded.

Thibault broke in –

'But my Lord you are talking about a length of embroidery in excess of 250 pieds and ...and'

'Approximately one and a half pied in width Thibault, yes. Do the dimensions alarm you?'

'Not alarm me my Lord but that is...' He stopped and thought for a moment.

'Would this be some sort of ...of hanging for your new cathedral, my Lord?'

Odo settled down in his chair, obviously enjoying the discomfiture of the two young men.

'Well done Thibault. I always said that you were quicker than people gave you credit for.'

Jean's mind was racing. When he did open his mouth he chose his words carefully.

'Your Grace then, is proposing to create or have created on your behalf, an embroidery two hundred and fifty pieds in length by one and a half pied in width and this work is to depict the events leading up to our invasion of this island, the ensuing battle and our role in administering justice after victory?'

Odo leaned forward. His small eyes narrowed and his reply came not in his customary growl but in a triumphant whisper.

'Exactly Master LeBrun. You have encapsulated the entire project in a single sentence. Well done. So!...' he beckoned Jean closer, 'Perhaps you can now tell me in the same simple terms, exactly how you intend to produce such a piece of work which, I hardly need tell you, is to be of superlative design and construction.'

He sat back and slammed the flat of this hand onto the table. Jean jumped and Thibault straightened up. This time no whisper but the old deep throated bass.

'It is by this that posterity will know and never, forget me. Who I am and what I did. So LeBrun, talk to me. Think how you intend to accomplish this masterpiece. Let me see. How old are you? Sixteen, seventeen? Strange isn't it, but you, a boy from the country and hardly educated, are going to make history but, make no mistake, you are making it for me. You do your work well and you will be rewarded. This work is to my glory so no self portraits. The only signature on this creation will be mine, do you understand?'

Jean looked at Thibault who shook his head and looked away. He moved back towards the table, no longer in awe of the great man but puzzled by what had just been said.

'But, your Grace, you must appreciate that I know absolutely nothing of embroidery. I have never handled a needle in my life, except to thread them for my mother when I was small. And the sheer size of the work. I wouldn't know how to begin or where to begin.'

He shrugged and stared at his patron, taking a pace back towards the table.

'All these events of which your Lordship speaks. I know nothing of them.'

He turned to elicit the aid of Thibault.

'Ask Thibault, he's always criticising me for not knowing enough of what was going on during the battle, let alone what went before.'

Thibault's expression was blank and Jean turned back to Odo, attempting to continue his protestations but Odo interrupted.

'LeBrun' Odo said sharply, 'I have decided that you are the man I need for this work. You have an unusual talent and are not without imagination, but remember both your talent and your imagination belong to me. Your task is to design the work and between you' he nodded to Thibault, 'to have the designs worked by embroidery of the highest quality. I expect a product that will outlive time.'

This time it was Thibault's turn to step forward but he was stopped in his tracks by an imperious hand.

'Thibault, I am only too aware that you are as loath to undertake this work as LeBrun here. You are however in possession of knowledge without which our young friend would not be able to function. I want you to take him to Robert Beaumont. Our friend Beaumont, as you so glowingly reported earlier, is a man of wisdom and experience and the ideal man to enlighten LeBrun on the events leading up to Hastings. Don't look so miserable Thibault. I have to have somebody of quality to introduce LeBrun. You know how it works as well as I do.'

Thibault looked doubtfully at Jean, then back to his mentor.

'With respect my Lord, would the introduction not come better from yourself?'

'It would not and I prefer to have others to provide the history. Anything I say might be construed as bias. There are, however, certain phases of the actual conflict of which I will furnish details personally, when that stage in the design has been reached. For the moment and for the events preceding the campaign, it would be better for the information to come from other sources. I am commissioning this project and it would be unfortunate if it was thought that it were little more than a vehicle for my own conceit. You understand?'

There was no response from either of them and Odo groaned impatiently.

'If you're to speak to Beaumont, you need to get a move on. He leaves shortly for Leicester.'

The two young men made to leave but Odo stopped them.

'Remember LeBrun, your job is to interpret what has gone before and design appropriately for the needle. As for you my dear Thibault, look after him and provide him with everything he needs. I know that your loyalty is unquestionable. I have to leave for Normandy but I expect to return within these next ten days. By then you will have formulated your proposals for the work.'

He pushed back his chair, glared at them from beneath his heavy brows and swept from the chamber.

Jean slumped onto a stool and ran his fingers through his hair.

'This is terrifying. He's mad! Stark staring mad! How can I …I know nothing about …did you have any idea what he was going to come out with?'

Thibault sat on the table and faced him, arms crossed, shaking his head.

'No, Master LeBrun. It's as much a surprise to me as it is to you and let's have a little more respect shall we, for the second most powerful man in England.'

Jean gave a snort of disgust, 'You can give him as much respect as you like Thibault. You're not the one who's supposed to undertake this stupid job. Your part in this is simple. All you've got to do is introduce me to your aristocratic friends. I'm the one whose job it is to come up with a picture that goes half way round Normandy. You can afford respect Thibault but don't expect me to have any.'

He concluded this outburst with another snort of derision and sat down. His brow wrinkled and he continued to ruffle his hair.

Thibault said nothing for a while and then, dryly, 'I do hope you haven't nits up there LeBrun or is it something you always do when you're worried? You might not like it and I'm not exactly thrilled myself but it's orders and the first thing we do is find Lord Beaumont. Before that though, we'd better get you into this new finery of yours. The hair, unfortunately, will have to wait.'

Before either of them could move, the heavy door swung open, hinges squealing and Robert Beaumont in full marching order, minus helmet, strode into the room. His clear eyes surveyed the ill matched pair.

'So! Thibault, you I know. How are you?' and without waiting for a response turned to Jean.

'You must be the young man our esteemed Earl of Kent wished me to meet. Well, here I am, so let's start. What is it you want from me?'

His voice was measured, authoritative but not unfriendly. Even so, Jean stared at him tongue-tied. Beaumont raised his eyes heavenwards and sighed. Thibault took command.

'My Lord, it seems that my master wishes this... this young man to have the benefit of your knowledge of the circumstances leading up to Duke..., sorry my Lord... King William's invasion of this island.'

Since Jean's impression of a village idiot seemed to have taken root, Thibault decided that more credibility was needed so he continued.

'My Lord Odo holds this young man's talents in very high regard and wishes him to create a pictorial representation of these events.'

Beaumont regarded Jean with interest.

'Your name, Sir.'

The unaccustomed title took Jean by surprise and he looked around for a likely recipient.

'Your name boy.' This was repeated quietly and not unkindly.

'Jean LeBrun sir.' Jean managed to stammer.

'Well Master LeBrun, I hope you have a good memory because, assuming you have the ability to write...' He paused while Jean nodded, 'I do not have the time to dictate. Therefore I must ask you to listen carefully to what I have to say.'

Jean, at last gaining control, nodded and Beaumont started his summary.

'This all started in 1051. The then King of England, Edward, who because of his piety was known as The Confessor, made an agreement with Duke William, as he was then, that William would succeed to the English throne on his death. Harold Godwinson was a Saxon nobleman, born of a princess of the Danes and a powerful figure in the English court. He was also something of a hero to the Saxon nobility of the realm because he argued against many of the Norman practices introduced by Edward who, you may or may not have known, spent much of his time in our part of France. Your father could well have met him Thibault.'

Thibault looked gratified, 'It was one of his most treasured memories, my Lord.' Beaumont continued, 'In 1064, Edward ordered Harold to make a journey to Normandy to pay homage to William and confirm his succession to the throne. Because he, Harold, had ambitions of kingship himself it might be said that he was far from willing to embark upon this journey. Edward, however, insisted and so he sailed for France. Unfortunately for him, a storm blew them off course and a landing was made in the territory of Guy of Ponthieu who promptly took Harold prisoner…'

Jean raised a hand

'Master LeBrun, I really do not have time for questions but what is it you need to ask.'

'My Lord, did Earl Harold travel with a large entourage?'

'Now you come to mention it LeBrun, he did. Local reports of the time suggested that he rather treated the expedition as a hunting trip. Now, if I may continue. To cut a long story short, as indeed I must, Duke William ordered his liege-man, Guy to release Harold into his custody which he did and then Harold accompanied William to Rouen. He was then at Duke William's side on his expedition to overthrow Conan of Brittany. I have it on good authority that Harold acquitted himself admirably during this campaign, personally rescuing some of our soldiers from the treacherous quicksands at Mont St Michel and in the pursuit of Conan through Rennes to Dinan. For his bravery and service, Duke William made a gift of arms to Harold.'

Beaumont turned to Thibault.

'The significance of this action will not escape you Thibault.'

Thibault, whose interest in the account was intense, was not slow to respond.

'No indeed, my Lord. By doing so Harold became vassal to The Duke.'

'Exactly. Anyway, if not quite bosom friends, our King and Harold became quite close and I have witnessed myself on several occasions, when hunting for example, that they were easy in each other's company. In any event, before allowing Harold to return to England, Duke William extracted a promise from him that he, Duke William, was the rightful heir to the English throne, as decreed by Edward. In fact Harold swore an oath to that effect, over holy relics in Bayeux.'

Jean was sitting on the edge of his stool, concentration etched on his brow.

'Then my Lord, what happened then?'

Beaumont, thought for a moment, then continued.

'Then Master LeBrun? Well what happened then was that Harold returned to England and in January of 1066 Edward died having, according to the English, changed his mind on his deathbed and making Harold his successor. It has to be acknowledged that Harold was much favoured by the English and the nobility of this island lost little time in confirming his succession. Harold lost even less time in accepting and was crowned on January 6th, the very day that Edward was committed to his vault. The service was carried out by Stigand, supposedly Archbishop of Canterbury whose appointment to that See was not recognised by Rome. That in itself perhaps would have cast considerable doubt on the legitimacy of the coronation.' He picked up his helmet from the table and looked in turn at Jean and Thibault.

'I'm sorry but that has to be all. I must leave you and I wish you success Master LeBrun in your endeavours. Goodbye to you both.'

As he passed Thibault, he laid a hand on his shoulder and said quietly.

'Out of the considerable respect I had for your father and for my belief in your honesty of purpose, do not let your loyalty to your Master, blind you to your loyalty to your King.'

Patting him on the shoulder, he passed out of the room. Thibault rounded on Jean.

'Look at the state of you. Still in the rags you came in, hair like a haystack. God knows what Lord Beaumont must have thought. Do you realise…'

Jean merely lifted a hand and said, 'Sh. Thibault. Be quiet.'

Thibault took a step towards him, furious. 'What did you just say?'

But Jean's eyes were shining with excitement. Thoughts were swirling around in his head and images already taking place in his imagination.

'I must have linen Thibault, now, this instant. This is brilliant. Don't you see. Don't you realise just how brilliant this is?'

Thibault's look of anger was rapidly replaced by one of perplexity

'Linen? What on earth… Oh yes, I see. Of course you need it to…'

'Exactly Thibault and I need it now.' Jean started looking around the room, then moving to chests and closets.

'Just a minute LeBrun, this is His Grace's apartment. You can't just…'

'Shut up Thibault and help me find something to draw on. I can't hold on to it for ever.'

Thibault started to say something else but the enthusiasm radiating from Jean stopped him in mid breath and he too was soon pulling open drawers and opening cupboard doors. Suddenly he stopped and rushed out of the door. Jean stared after him and had hardly continued with his search when Thibault returned, pushing in front of him a red faced peasant woman. She was carrying a bundle of linen cloth and was obviously not happy.

Thibault pointed to the table.

'Put it down there.'

The women did as she was told but not without a token show of resistance.

'I was taking this to the sewing room. This cloth was destined for the Earl of Kent's bedchamber…'

'Which is exactly where it is you silly woman. Just tell them I ordered you to leave it here.'

Thibault pointed her to the door while Jean started laying out strips of cloth on the table. He stopped and turned to Thibault.

'How did you know where to find this?'

Thibault sniffed.

'You may be the one with the talent LeBrun but one of my jobs is to minister to his Grace's every need, which means I keep my eyes and ears open. I just happened to remember when this lot was ordered. It's all right isn't it?'

Jean frowned.

'Yes, of course it is but charcoal. I'm going to need lots and lots of charcoal of the very finest quality.'

Thibault sniffed again.

'Do you know, LeBrun, I can help you with that too. His Grace's scribes ordered a new batch to be prepared about a month ago. I suppose you want me to look for it? You can see why his Grace ordered me to look after you. Without me you'd be running around like a headless chicken!'

Jean didn't answer. He was hand spanning measurements across the cloth.

CHAPTER TWELVE

Dover

William knocked on the door of his wife's apartments and walked in Mathilde took one look at his face and waved her ladies from the room.

'Well, my Lord, something has happened?'

He looked at her, fingers stroking his chin.

'No, it hasn't but it could be that your intuitive streak might be on to something.'

She beckoned him to take the stool beside hers.

'Odo? Something to do with this mysterious young man he's had brought over from Normandy?'

He took the seat and turned to her.

'It could be. It could also be something to do with the mysterious soldiers he seems to have sent out of the country. I've just been talking with Robert Beaumont.'

'And?'

'Apparently brother Odo has been looking for some extra men, possibly to replace some of his original force which, Beaumont thinks, have been sent to France.'

'Normandy?'

He patted the hand on his arm and shook his head 'No, not Normandy, I'm too well supported there. Brother Robert and our son keep things under control. No, definitely not Normandy.'

'Where then?'

'I've no idea. I never like to show my hand as you know but if Odo was here at the moment I'd be inclined to ask him myself. I wonder if this is something to do with Canterbury. Giving the Archbishopric to Lanfranc can't have pleased him over much'

The Queen thought for a moment.

'Obviously he is disappointed but he must be realistic enough to know that you were unlikely to add to his already considerable power by giving him something as important as Canterbury.'

William gently removed his wife's hand from his arm and rose from his seat. He walked a few paces, turned and faced her.

'I suspect that Odo's appetite for power is unlikely to be governed by realism.'

Taking another couple of steps, thinking he added.

'What about your woman. Any chance of her finding anything out?'

She shook her head. 'Not Mirabelle, no, not directly from Odo. I'd rather not say why but that seems to be one ... how shall I put it... sacrifice she would not be prepared to make.'

William looked at her.

'Really! Why is that? I thought she showed boundless enthusiasm for the work.'

She just looked at him.

He went on, 'Anyway, there's still this young rustic of Odo's. Any more news on that front? Apparently Beaumont's role was to be that of history tutor.'

'History tutor?'

'Yes. It seems that Odo wished him to teach the boy something of the events preceding our invasion. You know, The Confessor's role and Harold's escapades in France, that sort of thing. The boy is an artist of sorts but then, you'd already found that out. Perhaps Odo wants him to provide a pictorial record of our recent history. Nothing wrong in that I suppose. It's just that... can't put my finger on it really. The sums don't seem to add up, if you know what I mean.'

She stood up and joined him.

'I do know what you mean. Let us just keep an eye on things. Don't worry, I'll put Mirabelle to work again. One way or another we'll find out between us.'

He bent down and kissed her gently on her brow and left the room. Her brow remained furrowed as she thought over what he had said. She called her ladies back into the chamber and summoned Mirabelle to her side.

'Now, ma petite, we have to go to work!'

'Your Majesty?'

'The question we were discussing earlier, Mirabelle, has now moved on. We need to know what is happening in the entourage of his Grace, the Earl of Kent, and we require that knowledge sooner rather than later.'

Mirabelle's healthy complexion paled.

'The Earl of Kent, Ma'am. I thought you were only interested in Master LeBrun.'

The Queen drew Mirabelle closer to her.

'Master LeBrun, or whatever his name happens to be, is in the service of Odo is he not? That being the case, why would you wish to separate the interests of the two?

What LeBrun does is presumably at the orders of his master.'

'Yes Ma'am. Of course. I thought for one moment that you wished me to...to...'

'To what Mirabelle, to apply your talents to the appetites of the Earl himself?'

'Yes your Majesty.'

The Queen looked away for a moment, then smiled at her young charge.

'No Mirabelle, even I would not subject you to that. Surely though, LeBrun is not as frightening a prospect? In fact, after our last little chat, I thought you would already have some information for me.'

'The truth is Ma'am, I haven't been able to talk to Master LeBrun. Since your last instruction he has been closeted with my Lord Odo.'

The Queen nodded.

'Very well my dear. I understand that my uncle is preparing to leave for Normandy, if he has not yet already done so. So off you go and report back to me just as soon as you have something. Oh! Just a moment, there might be another avenue for you to explore. If LeBrun is not very productive, what about Thibault? He is as a son to his Grace. They are almost inseparable. He could be a valuable source of information. Why don't you try him?'

Mirabelle's colour returned and she grinned.

'I don't think so your Majesty. I'm not sure Thibault is very interested in... well, he could even be ...you know?'

The Queen raised an eyebrow.

'Another persuasion, Mirabelle. Is that what you're trying to say?'

'It would not surprise me Ma'am.'

She giggled.

'Indeed. Then I would have thought him an excellent challenge for you Mirabelle. Whatever, I need some answers. How you obtain them is your affair. Go now and return as soon as you have something.'

She waved a hand in dismissal and Mirabelle bowed her way out.

#

When Thibault returned to Jean, he found him surveying the strips of newly cut cloth laid out on the table. He had also changed into his new clothes and Thibault was surprised at how his appearance had changed from that of a rustic artisan to a presentable young gentleman. He also noticed that Jean's unruly mop of hair had been tamed into some sort of submission. It occurred to him that here was a young man with few inhibitions, who was, almost certainly, highly attractive to the opposite sex; someone completely different to himself. The only relationship he had ever sought was with his master, Odo of Bayeux, to whom he was devoted, together with his God, of course. He couldn't imagine that the Church had ever been a significant factor in the life of this young man he had been called upon to supervise.

He marched over to the table and deposited a bundle of charcoal stylus. He then turned and surveyed Jean

'Anything else?'

Jean frowned, 'What?'

'Is there anything else you'd like me to fetch and carry for you?'

Jean seemed to realise, for the first time, what had been going on and started to disarrange his newly tamed hair.

'I'm sorry Thibault. I didn't mean for you to…'

Thibault snorted. 'Yes you did. You've been giving orders as if to the manner born and I, like an idiot, have been carrying them out. Now, is there anything else I can fetch and carry for you?'

Then Jean became abstracted again, strode back to the table and started to sharpen sticks and fix down his cloth. Then he paused and turned.

'No, thank you Thibault, I'm sorry if I've offended you.'

Thibault shook his head

'For goodness sake don't start being polite. What with that and the change of clothes, I don't think I could take much more. You look very good in them by the way.'

But he'd lost Jean, who was once more engrossed in his preparations. Thibault was about to say something else but thought better of it and left Jean to his work.

The corridor outside Odo's suite was empty and, suddenly hungry, Thibault quickened his pace and, on turning the corner, nearly flattened Mirabelle. He managed to grab her to stop her falling over and in doing so pulled her to him. Once over the initial shock she recovered far quicker than he did. At the same time she thought much quicker than he did and still holding on to him, gave out a small squeal of pain.

'Oh! My knee, I think you've hurt my knee.'

Thibault continued to support her while stammering his apologies which, for some reason, caused her to bury her head in his cloak and start to shake, an action which he totally misinterpreted and the apologies became even more incoherent. Eventually disentanglement was accomplished and Mirabelle leant against the stonework looking at him as reproachfully as her amusement would allow. He, in his turn, looked at the ground and wished himself elsewhere. She continued to rub her knee and wincing, said.

'I suppose there's no way you could help me to my room is there?' I really don't think that I could…'

Thibault pounced upon this opportunity to be helpful and blurted out that it was the least he could do in the circumstances.

'Where um, exactly is your room Mistress Mirabelle?'

She leant heavily on his arm and pointed down the corridor.

'At the present time I'm using one of my companions' chambers. She's married and it affords me a more space while she's away.'

They continued slowly along the passageway, he awkwardly supporting her. He frowned.

'One of your companions? You mean another of the Queen's ladies-in-waiting?'

'That's right Thibault, one of those.'

'Which one would that be then? I presume if she's married, it is to one of our noblemen and I was not aware that any of those had left the court.'

'Oh, you didn't know, Thibault, that my Lord Granville had departed these shores?'

He looked perplexed, 'No I didn't and since he's one of my Lord Odo's knights I'm surprised that I knew nothing about it. Where has he gone?'

'They Thibault, where have they gone? His wife is involved as well. Actually, I'm not sure but I imagine they have returned to their estates in Normandy. Why, does it matter?'

Thibault made no answer but merely grunted as they stopped before a door. Mirabelle opened it and started to draw him in, her arm still firmly clutching his. He hesitated.

'Oh! For goodness sake Thibault, I'm not going to leap on you. Just help me to the bed will you?'

He supported her into the room and they stood for a moment, she making no effort to disengage her arm. Instead she looked up at him and said innocently.

'Tell me Thibault, are you a sodomite?'

He blushed and thrust her away from him. His reply was made with as much dignity as he could muster.

'As it happens, Mistress Mirabelle I am not but I would be interested to know exactly what it is that gave the idea that I might be.'

She shrugged and gave him a smile.

'Come on Thibault, many of the ladies of the court, oh yes and some of the girls who don't fall into that category, find you attractive. You are very good looking in a cold sort of way and yet, you have never been known to indulge in any of the amorous activities of the Court. I merely wondered if for you, the appeal might be something different. For example, Master LeBrun! After all, for the last few days, ever since he has been noticed here in Dover, you are seldom to be found far from his side. Mind you Thibault, I can't say I blame you. He is a very pretty boy and…'

'As I think you have already noticed Mistress Mirabelle, since you didn't waste much time in tempting him to your bed.'

Thibault was, by now, forgetting his embarrassment at the situation in which he found himself. He pressed his fingertips to a throbbing temple and went on.

'He is but an unsophisticated country boy and no match for your experienced ways.'

She laughed but not with humour.

'Oh come on Thibault. If you live to be a hundred, you'll never enjoy the favours of as many girls as Master LeBrun has. There's very little I could teach him, I can tell you.'

'That I can well believe Mistress, with your reputation; the whore of Dover. The Queen's whore isn't it? I tell you, I…'

The blow took him by surprise. Particularly as it was delivered by one so slight. In fact he was still coping with the shock when her small hands hauled on the neck of his cloak as she pulled his head down to the level of her blazing eyes.

'Yes' she hissed in his face. 'I might well be a whore and if I am, do you know who is responsible for it? Do you have any idea who it was that reduced me to the level of doing what I do. Oh yes, you smug bastard, I'm not denying I occasionally enjoy my work and young Jean was certainly no exception but does it never occur to you to ask yourself who it was that reduced me to this position?'

Thibault made a token show of resisting her hold on his collar but she tightened her grip.

'Well, Thibault?'

Still shocked by her anger, he made no answer but slowly shook his head.

'I thought not Thibault. You would always be the last to know anything wouldn't you? Well, for your information it was your esteemed and holy lord and master the Bishop of Bayeux, the Earl of Kent. He raped me. I'd been here no more than twenty four hours. Quite alone, no parents to look out for me and do you know how old I was when the Queen sent for me to come here. How old I was when he forced himself upon me?'

She didn't wait for an answer.

'I was eleven Thibault, eleven! Not one of those forward eleven year-olds, my life up until then had been very sheltered.' She shuddered, 'It wasn't just the once either. I just couldn't…'

Her voice faltered and she relaxed her hold. Thibault straightened up and gently removed her unresisting hands from his collar. She turned away from him, still shivering as if in the grip of a fever.

There was a long silence until, at last, he cleared his throat.

'Surely Mistress Mirabelle, surely the first person you told of this was the Queen? What did she say? What did she do?'

She slowly turned to face him again. Her expression was lifeless, cold.

'Do Thibault? Why, she did nothing. Actually that's not quite true. She did tell me that henceforth I would be under her protection. He would never touch me again.'

Thibault blurted out, 'And?'

'He hasn't, Thibault but the protection of which she spoke came with a price. Even to you, I don't have to spell out what that price was do I?'

Thibault appeared to be inspecting the toes of his boots and kept shaking his head in disbelief. When he spoke his voice was unsteady and he seemed to have difficulty in breathing.

'I just can't believe it. I mean, he has been like a father to me since my own...he is a man of the cloth. A senior and important spiritual leader 'It's inconceivable that he...' He shook his head.

Her voice was stony and matched her expression.

'Where have you been hiding yourself all this time Thibault? Don't you ever listen to what the rest of the world has to say? Everybody knew. How came it that you were the exception? Does nothing interest you Thibault but your own damned honour? What a good job it was that I never thought of asking you to revenge mine. My God! I cannot believe that you could remain so ignorant of what sort of man Odo is. Above all men on this island, he is the most hated and you never knew of it. Do you mean to tell me that he has never invited you to share in his vices, his cruelties? Why, they're legendary Thibault.'

She had to wait a long time for his comment and when it came it was delivered in a whisper; fingers of one hand kneading his temple, those of the other gripping the crucifix.

'No, I wasn't even aware that he... I swear. This is the first I have heard of any of it. Of course, I have been aware of rumours but I have always distanced myself from that sort of thing, especially at court where ambition and jealousies abound. I still cannot believe that he is anything but the father figure who earned my admiration for his feats at Hastings and who earned my gratitude after my own father was slain there. It cannot be possible that I should have had his confidence for all this time without my being ... without my knowing of...and yet...'

He started pacing agitatedly around the chamber, then stopped, saying as if to himself, 'Of course. It never occurred to me before but deep down... my memory... something...'

'What Thibault, what?'

'Hastings. It goes back to the battle. When I first observed my Lord Odo. Killing, killing...'

She went towards him, saying quietly. 'It was a battle Thibault. A bloody battle. What else did you expect?'

'NO! He was an ordained priest. He wasn't supposed to carry weapons, except for his staff. He was dressed in a white robe. It was billowing out all around him and he was riding straight into the heat of battle and smashing a mace into Saxon heads. It wasn't only that. He was laughing. He was enjoying it. Smashing brains out and his robe was becoming bloodier and bloodier. It sounds stupid but something just seemed to be wrong. I thought it was valour he was exhibiting but it wasn't. It was ... God knows what it was but it was horrible and I never thought about it until now.'

He turned to her, 'I need to know. What else has he done?'

She smiled sadly at him, 'I think you should ask elsewhere Thibault. I'm not exactly a dispassionate observer but you are right. You do need to know. Ask anyone. Ask Lord Beaumont, he's an honest man.'

'I can't, he's left for Leicester. Just before, he was giving our Master LeBrun a history lesson.'

He regained his composure, 'Talking of LeBrun, I must get back and organise some food or something. He's so wrapped up in what he's doing, he'll forget to eat.'

He moved towards the door but she ran up and stopped him.

'A history lesson Thibault, what about? Why should somebody like Robert Beaumont talk to Jean LeBrun? And why are you playing nursemaid to him? I would have thought you and he don't exactly move in the same circles. Not like you Thibault to lower your social standards.'

'Not now Mistress, I must get back to LeBrun.' He paused, then looked at her as if seeing her for the first time.

'I'm sorry.'

'Sorry?'

'For what I called you. You see I... I really am sorry.'

She returned to her normal self and grinned.

'Oh dear, and there was I feeling horrid for hitting you like I did. Let's start afresh shall we?'

She tiptoed up and gently kissed him on the cheek.

'Go on, back you go to our mutual friend.'

She giggled.

'Perhaps you'd like to give him a kiss from me.'

She took a step back and her hand flew to her mouth.

'Joke, Thibault...it was only a joke.'

He blushed half smiled back and turned on his heel and left. When he'd gone, she sat on the bottom of the bed and looked after him. Not smiling now but weeping quietly.

Just tears, no sound.

CHAPTER THIRTEEN

Dover

On his way to Odo's apartments, Thibault stopped a serving girl and ordered her to bring victuals and wine. When he entered the room, Jean was bent over his work, concentrating with his whole being. Thibault walked to the table and was brought up short by what he saw there. He whistled in admiration and came closer.

'This is brilliant, boy. Obviously my lord Odo wouldn't have dragged you over here for nothing but I had no idea you had this much talent!'

He was looking at a panel of cloth on which Jean had reproduced with uncanny accuracy, the story related by Robert Beaumont earlier in the day. King Edward instructing Harold to pay homage to William in France, his capture, his release, Edward's deathbed and Harold's indecently rapid coronation. All this reproduced in brilliantly executed cartoon and it had taken Jean no time at all. This raw youth, who hitherto he'd viewed as little more than a country bumpkin, had seemingly emerged from his grubby chrysalis and was due some serious respect and Thibault was man enough to acknowledge the fact. Jean cursed and Thibault hastily stepped back out his line of vision. Jean straightened up, stretched his back and turned.

'It's all right Thibault, it's nothing to do with you. All the same, we do have a problem or rather I have a problem. It's mainly a problem of scale and I don't know how to address it until I have some idea of how much material, narrative that is, not linen, there is to complete the story. What do you think?'

Thibault looked blank and Jean sighed.

'No, I didn't think you'd be much help. Come on, think! The preparations for the battle, you must have some idea of the space that'll take up. Then there's the battle itself, the victory celebrations, and the coronation. Think Thibault, I really need to know these things before I can go on. We have the dimensions of this damned thing and you're going to have to help me decide how much of what goes where.'

Thibault looked baffled.

'I'll do all the hard work Thibault but you're just going to have to give me a hand with the scale. Oh yes! Then there's the embroidery! I haven't a clue where to start looking for needlewomen. I don't suppose that you...'

Thibault immediately went on the defensive.

'What makes you think that I know anything about embroidery LeBrun, because let me tell you if...'

Jean held up both hands.

'All right, all right Thibault. Don't worry. I wasn't implying that you...but seriously, I need to know these things. When does his Grace come back.?'

Thibault shrugged and turned to look out of the window, saying casually.

'By the way, in the servants quarters, what do they say about him, what do they think of him? Have you heard anything, any gossip?'

Jean looked guarded for a while and then admitted that, yes, Odo was talked about by the lower orders. In fact they had quite a lot to say about him. Upon being pressed, he went on to say that much of what he heard could hardly be regarded as complimentary to his Lordship. Jean wondered why Thibault wanted to know about such things. Especially as it seemed that he was so attached to his guardian or whatever their relationship was supposed to be. Thibault made no reply and Jean looked at him in disbelief. 'Thibault, you didn't know any of this did you? You've practically lived with the man for how many years and you never knew of his reputation as one of the most vicious degenerates in Christendom? This is a man who is responsible for the deaths of countless people. Not just men and not just Saxons. Anybody that gets in his way and from what I hear an awful lot of people have done just that. What nobody seems to be able to understand is why the King allows him to get away with it. Come on Thibault, you must have some inkling of what he is like. You can't be that innocent, can you?'

Thibault made no reply. He turned and looked at Jean. He said nothing for a long time and Jean, sensing his confusion, turned away and pretended to embellish some fragment of his work. Eventually Thibault gave a cough to regain his attention.

'I think you ought to eat something LeBrun, you can't go on through the whole day without some sort of nourishment.'

Jean gave an impatient sigh and stretched himself from his work. He rubbed his charcoal stained hands on a piece of discarded cloth.

'All right, I could do with a break.'

He walked over to the platter and tore off a hunk of bread, stuffing it into his mouth as if he hadn't eaten for days. Speaking as he ate, his mouth full and spitting crumbs in all directions but mainly in that of Thibault, he couldn't refrain from a further dig at Thibault's dignity.

'Of all the things I suspected you to be, a mother hen was possibly the last. Why the change of character all of a sudden?'

Thibault fastidiously brushed some bread from his tunic and stepped away.

'For God's sake LeBrun. These new clothes might have smartened you up a bit but you still behave like an oaf. Incidentally, what else might you have suspected me to be, besides a mother hen as you so graphically put it? If I was anxious for you to eat it was solely in order that you remain capable of getting on with the work in hand. Anyway, come on, boy, tell me. What other characteristics would you assume me to possess?'

Jean continued munching and regarded Thibault thoughtfully as he did so.

Thibault raised his eyes heavenwards in exasperation and waited for his companion to swallow a particularly resilient piece of crust. 'Well, what else?'

Jean, having successfully swallowed, went to wipe his mouth on his new sleeve, saw the look on Thibault's face and quickly changed it to the back of his hand.

'Sorry Thibault, didn't want to say anything until I'd finished. Why this curiosity about what I might think? You're a Squire, I'm an artisan, what do my thoughts matter? Anyway, why this sudden interest in what other people think, and come to think of it, why this concern about our illustrious lord and master?'

He cut off Thibault's interruption, 'All right, for reasons which I can't even begin to imagine, you didn't seem to have any idea of what sort of man he really is but why the sudden interest. You've known him for years.' he paused for a second, 'But you haven't have you? That's the whole point but why now, why so bothered about it now?'

Thibault turned to the window again and with his back to Jean mumbled Mirabelle's name. Jean straining to hear, uttered an incredulous, 'What?'

Thibault turned to him and eyes fixed to the floor said.

'I bumped into Mirabelle!'

Jean smiled at his embarrassment.

'Did you now Thibault? Well, well! The Lady Mirabelle must be one of the most bumped-into ladies in the Court.'

Thibault looked at him but despite the lingering smile on Jean's face, could see that the remark was not intended to be offensive. Jean pressed him further.

'Well go on, what happened?'

Thibault studied his feet and continued.

'No. I mean it. When I left you to order up some food, I bumped into her in the corridor. So hard that I injured her knee... ' He tailed off.

'Then what?' Jean's interest by now fully aroused.

'Nothing. That is she asked me if I could help her back to her room, well, actually it wasn't her room it was the room of another lady in waiting who'd gone to...'

'Yes ,yes' interrupted Jean, 'Never mind whose room it was, go on, what happened then?'

'She told me all about Odo' Thibault replied simply, 'I'm afraid that I had made certain assumptions about Mirabelle and I said some things to her that were...well, rather ungallant, unkind if you like and she... she told me things which caused me to re-think many of my original ideas.'

He closed his eyes and shook his head as if trying to clear it. Jean brought him back to the conversation.

'About her, ideas about her?'

'Yes, about her and about Lord Odo and, if you really want to know, about myself.'

The smile had vanished from Jean's mouth but not totally from his eyes. He went back to the table, picked up his stylus and put it down again. When he turned to look at him, Thibault's head was still bent forward and he appeared to be scratching a pattern in the dust with the toe of his boot. When Jean spoke it was quietly, thoughtfully.

'Strange, isn't it? I thought I was the only one out of my depth. Insecure, worried about what's going to happen next and all the time...Oh dear! Looks a bit like the blind leading the blind doesn't it? Or rather the partially sighted leading the blind. At least I know what his Lordship is really like. No nasty surprises for me but it must have come as quite a shock to you. I'm sorry. No really, I am sorry.'

Once more Thibault turned to the window and spoke his thoughts to the Kent countryside.

'Why should you be sorry? Not your fault is it? Anyway, it's not just that. It's as if I'm orphaned again and I feel so stupid, so stupid, so unworldly, so... Oh! I don't know. So pitifully and inadequately fitted for this life.'

He took a deep breath of the misty air rising from the marshes and turned to face Jean with a new light of resolution in his eyes.

'We have a job to do. The fact that the job is the brainchild of Odo is neither here nor there so we might as well do it to the best of our abilities. Let's start afresh shall we? Now, tell me your problems again and we shall see how we're to overcome them.

CHAPTER FOURTEEN

Dover

Mathilde moved to one of the windows in her apartment and looked out. Dusk was just settling in and the continual daily clatter of stone being dressed, timbers hewn and shouted commands, was beginning to subside. The wind was freshening and, at last, the fogs and sea mists were clearing. Not so damp now but the rising wind carried the chill of March. She shivered and dropped the heavy woollen hanging back over the aperture. Through the open window this early spring breeze had penetrated the room and the rushes and dried herbs which carpeted the room had been stirred to release some of their herbal fragrance. Mathilde inhaled the welcome perfume and sat in her favourite chair, winged against the draughts, her face set and concentrated. This was her favourite time of day. No women's prattle in the background. Nothing to intrude on her thoughts.

One of her greatest assets to William was her reputed intuition and he seldom took a decision, political or military, without consulting her. What he didn't know was that her advice was not so much based on 'intuition' but on her ability to rationalise a situation. Mathilde was more than wise enough to know that her husband would be happy to humour a woman's 'intuitive' arguments but not to ones which might challenge his own intellect. That is why these private moments were so important to her and when William next visited, her thoughts would be in order and ready for him.

They had always agreed that Odo's restless ambition was likely to pose a threat at some time or other but, she reasoned to herself, Odo was no fool and he was unlikely to make an outright bid for the English throne. Denied Canterbury, might he be looking to Rome? Power over the whole of the Christian continent! William wouldn't like that one little bit and come to think of it, neither would Phillip of France.

Of course, if Odo fancied taking on Phillip…a smile touched the corners of her mouth. Normandy, then, was a distinct possibility! The smile disappeared and she sat up in her chair. Brother Robert of Mortain and son Robert, her first born, were surely trustworthy custodians of the Duchy but son Robert had lately come to her for funds and she had parted with a considerable amount. Why should not a mother spoil her favourite son especially as she had assumed the gift was to be used for purely personal reasons but …she plucked at her sleeve. Rumours had reached her that Robert was not satisfied with a mere Regency of the Dukedom. Supposing… she was still musing over this conundrum when a sudden blast of chill wind through the open door heralded William's entrance.

'William, what a nice surprise. I didn't expect you this early.' She started to rise but he motioned her to stay seated, came over and planted a kiss on the top of her head.

'Well, I felt like a chat. Beaumont's gone, Odo's disappeared, and the daily business is all dealt with so I thought we might have a few quiet moments together.'

He moved to the window, moved back the hanging and peered out. Mathilde shivered slightly but William never seemed to be aware of any change in temperature. Still with his back to her he said.

'Anything to tell me?'

So she related what had been going through her mind and she could tell that he was listening to her. The only thing she didn't mention was the gift to Robert. She was relieved that he wasn't looking at her as she delivered her thoughts.

#

Two days later Thibault stood and looked over Jean's shoulder as he worked. Again, he was impressed by the skill, dexterity and creativity of the young artist. He also noted that, when working, Jean had such confidence in his ability. Not that he ever expressed it in any way other than through his work. Thibault never heard him brag or exhibit any form of conceit. He just accepted it for what it was, a perfectly natural extension of his being. This was a revelation to Thibault who'd had to work hard to master his own accomplishments and if he did possess a gift, it was that of industry. As if he sensed what Thibault was thinking, Jean stopped what he was doing, which was embellishing the narrative by adding a hunting dog here and there, stretched and gave Thibault the sort of grin that, a few days ago, would have seemed unthinkable.

'You still here then?'

Thibault struggled with his dignity and with a resigned sigh, gave up.

'Yes of course I'm still here. Tell me, where did this talent of yours come from: father, mother, grandfather?'

Jean carefully sharpened another stick and said, 'I have no idea. If it was my grandfather, nobody's ever told me about it and as for my parents, my mother wouldn't have time if she wanted to and my father used to beat me whenever he caught me doing it – drawing that is. So, I'm sorry Thibault, I can't help you. All I know is that when I am drawing, nothing else seems to matter. I lose all sense of time or place and the beauty of it all is that it's so easy. It just happens.'

Thibault's laugh was bitter. 'I don't suppose you realise how lucky you are either.'

Jean shook his head.

'I just never think about it like that. That's your trouble Thibault, you think about things too much. Do you envy me this talent, as you call it? Do you wish you could do it? Is that it?'

Thibault signified his answer with another shake of his head but still faced with an inquiring look from Jean, said, 'No, LeBrun, I don't envy you your talent. What I would like however is a share of the self-confidence that your talent seems to give you.'

Jean hooted with laughter.

'Coming from you Thibault, do you realise how strange that sounds. When I first met you who had the confidence then? Don't forget, I'm the son of a servant. All right, we've never really wanted for anything but I was terrified of you. You represent all the things I've been brought up to respect and fear; birth, position, power. You have it all Thibault and yet, you turn round and tell me you envy something which I appear to have and I don't even recognise it. Funny old world isn't it?'

Thibault walked over to the table and picked up a stylus. Jean promptly took it from him and carefully placed it back on the table.

Thibault said, 'I don't believe you.'

Jean made to interrupt but Thibault held up his hand.

'I don't believe that you don't recognise your gift. For someone who doesn't appear to give a damn for his appearance and has some pretty appalling personal habits, you are very particular about the tools of your trade. I also don't believe you would want to be in my shoes. You have family. The fact that you don't get on with them particularly well is neither here nor there. You form relationships with quite uncanny ease but I don't. There is nobody on this island for whom I care or who cares for me and the same goes for France. Perhaps my Lord Odo does genuinely hold me in affection but knowing what I do now, I doubt it and in any case, I would not now find it easy to bind to a man such as he. This is all I have.' He touched his crucifix.

Jean cleared his throat.

'Thibault, I think we ought to be going back to this.' He gestured towards the table. 'If nothing else, it might take your mind off things…'

He didn't finish because Thibault swung round and snarled.

'How exactly is that,' he pointed at the design, 'going to take my mind off anything? You. Yes! You're the one that's doing it but me. How in God's name am I supposed to derive anything other than some …some voyeuristic entertainment from watching you exercising your damned creativity.'

Jean said simply. 'That's the whole point Thibault. I can't do this without you. I don't know my way around. I don't know where to find anything. I don't know anybody here except you. All I've done so far is a couple of panels. How on earth am I going to get the information I need to fill another seven or eight. I don't know how to source my materials. I haven't the remotest idea where these designs of mine are going to be made up, how or by whom. I thought that was the idea. We work with each other. Look!'

He took Thibault over to the table, 'this is one panel. I suspect that there could be months of work to get this project completed and I haven't a clue where I'm going from here. I can't carry on without your help and that's a fact.'

This time Thibault's anger had been replaced by bitterness.

'I understand that LeBrun; that you need me to fetch and carry, to make the necessary introductions, to make enquiries about embroidery schools and talk to needlewomen. To see that you don't lack nourishment when you are working and can't be bothered to look after yourself. Of course I understand all that. But please don't pretend that you need anything other than a servant with contacts. Don't pretend that I make any difference to what appears on that linen. This has nothing to do with pride, LeBrun. All I am is thanks to patronage and with my sort of patron I don't think I can afford the luxury of pride. Do you?'

Thibault hurled this final question at Jean, as if challenging him to make any sort of positive response. He then, slumped against the wall, while Jean, for once, seemed bereft of speech. He just leaned against his table and pretended to study a point of a stylus.

Eventually he said, 'Thibault, you are the one to be envied and I'll tell you why. You know how to behave. Important people like Robert Beaumont treat you with respect. Why do you think that Lord Odo saddled you with this task? Because you can open doors that I wouldn't have a hope in hell of getting through. Because you are good at organising things. Oh don't look at me like that. That's a talent. You were born and trained to do things I haven't even heard of and yes Thibault, I do envy you your birth and position and everything that comes with it. You might not have a family but how do you know that nobody loves you. Have you bothered to ask them? You might not be loved, whatever that is supposed to mean but you are respected. Whereas me! The Beaumonts of this world don't even know that I exist, so for God's sake stop whining and let's get some work done.'

'Whining! How dare you speak to me like that, how dare you…!'

Jean gave a whoop of laughter.

'That's better, that's more like it. Now we're back to normal perhaps we can move on. Now! What happened after Harold got himself crowned? What's the next part of the story because…'

He got no further because they were both silenced by the sound of heavy boots, outside in the corridor. When the boots reached the door, it was flung open and two fully armoured men-at arms, grim and unsmiling, stood on the threshold.

Thibault moved to Jean's side and whispered, 'The Queens men.'

Then, after an uneasy silence, another sound intruded, only this time it had none of the clank of metal and steel. More like the rustle of slipper and swish of a gown. Suddenly, framed by the metallic bulk of the two men-at arms, stood the Lady Mirabelle. Her auburn hair was braided and coiled under her cap but enough of it was visible for Jean to catch the rich chestnut tint, highlighted by the flame of the torch bracketed above the door. Her royal blue cloak was pulled across her body against the cold of the corridor and from under the edge of her cloak, her fine, soft leather slippers could just be seen. Jean glanced at his companion who stood with his eyes fixed on the guards. Suddenly and totally alien to the tension in the room, Mirabelle laughed. A typical Mirabelle laugh with the customary hint of mockery. When she spoke though, it was obvious t that she was making every effort to be serious.

'Her Majesty commands you to her presence.'

CHAPTER FIFTEEN

Dover

Thibault was the first to regain his composure. He bowed and greeted Mirabelle. Jean just stood there, turning his stylus over and over in his fingers.

Thibault turned to him and with no trace of his recent emotion said, 'It would appear, Master LeBrun that we must suspend our activities for the time being. Might I suggest that you do something about the surplus of charcoal about your person and try to get that mop of yours in some kind of order. Mistress Mirabelle, we will keep you but a moment.'

She turned to the escort and told them to wait outside the room. Once they were out of sight, she swept over to the table. She drew in a deep breath. When she turned to Jean, her eyes were sparkling.

'So this is what it's all about, Master LeBrun. This is the great mystery. Her Majesty will be disappointed, she was expected something a great deal more subversive than this.' indicating the drawing.

She inspected it in more detail.

'I don't think I've seen anything quite like this before. Of course I've seen your Death of Roland. In fact, if you remember I...' Her hand flew to her mouth.

'Oh dear, I'm sorry Jean I didn't mean to...'

Thibault broke in. 'Fear not Mistress, I already have some inkling as to what... I think we should go, don't you? We mustn't keep her Majesty waiting. Can you give us any idea why she called for this audience?'

Mirabelle shot him an uncharacteristically warm smile.

'I'm afraid not, although I think her Majesty would like to find out about Master LeBrun's presence here in Dover.'

Proceeded by the men-at-arms, they continued in silence until they reached the Queen's apartments. Sitting outside, at a desk with the implements of his profession, was a secretary dressed in the habit of his religious order. As he saw them approach, he raised a hand to halt further progress and knocked on the door, entering without an invitation. A few seconds later he re-emerged and ushered them inside. The two guards took their customary places on either side of the door and he resumed his seat and continued with his work.

Once in the presence of the Queen, Thibault assumed command of the situation. He took a few steps towards where she was seated, next to the fire, her furred cloak almost hiding her from view with only her head and an embroidered sleeve visible. Jean hung back and although somewhat nervous, he still retained enough awareness to note that she was extremely small and that the embroidered sleeve had several pulled threads on it. Obviously he had seen her before in the great hall but then she was seated at the raised table at the far end of the room. Thibault bowed and murmured, 'Your Majesty.'

Mirabelle took up her position behind the Queen's chair, standing with one hand resting on the top of one of the wings.

The Queen, when she spoke, had a surprisingly clear and strong voice for one so tiny. She returned Thibault's bow with an almost imperceptible nod but all the while her eyes were on Jean. Even when Thibault spoke again, this time to enquire after his Majesty's health, she still continued to look at him. Eventually she turned her attention to Thibault and said, 'Well Thibault, it seems a long time since we have had the pleasure of your company. Only the other day William said the same thing. He thinks highly of you, you know. Not just because of your valiant exploits in the field but he finds you honest, I think, and trustworthy; unusual but valuable attributes in this day and age. Still, I mustn't embarrass you with over-praise but I must confess that I cannot understand why some lady of the Court has not wooed you for these virtues, can you Mirabelle?'

All this was said without a hint of humour but behind the Queen's back Mirabelle was finding it increasingly difficult to cope with the picture of Thibault, red as a beetroot and stumbling to reply to the Queen's words.

'Your Majesty, it's most generous of you. I am pleased to hear that your Majesties think well of me.'

Even Jean was quietly revelling in Thibault's discomfort but the grin soon vanished when Mathilde renewed her inspection of him. Her eyes, he noted, were not cold but seemed to bore right through him. This, he thought, was not a woman to whom one lied. His charm would serve him no useful purpose here. Having quelled him with a look, she returned her attention to Thibault, still blushing from her compliments.

'Did the Earl of Kent give you any indication of his business in France?'

The question was brutally direct and the unexpected change of tone took Thibault by surprise, to the extent that he found it difficult to collect his thoughts.

'Your... Your Majesty? Why no. He didn't confide his intentions to me at all.'

He paused, 'He never does. That is, he never talks to me of state matters or his ecclesiastical concerns, anything of that nature.'

She leant forward in her chair.

'What sort of things does he discuss with you then?'

Thibault's open features clouded slightly but his voice was firm and he spoke with the confidence of one who had committed no offence.

'Ordinary, everyday matters, your Majesty. The rebuilding of these fortifications, the difficulty of finding competent artisans among the Saxons, the latest fashions, those sorts of things.'

'And this young man' she pointed at Jean. 'Does he fall within the category of 'those sort of things?''

Thibault's face cleared.

'Exactly your Majesty. This young fellow's skills became known to my Lord and he brought him over to carry out this project which, I believe, is very close to his heart. My role has been to introduce LeBrun, his name is Jean LeBrun, Ma'am, to individuals here in the Court who can describe the events of which he is to make a pictorial record. Also to find him suitable wear and ensure that his behaviour is in accordance with the accepted protocol of the Court. That sort of thing your Majesty.'

This time, when she fixed him with her keen eye, it was with just a hint of amusement.

'Would 'nursemaid' be too unkind a description for your relationship to Master LeBrun here?'

At this, Thibault's expression showed such obvious pain that she quickly continued.

'Oh dear, Thibault. I wish that we could surround ourselves with people of your integrity. I will not say innocence because that would be too unkind and untrue when one remembers the brave service you rendered our cause. Now boy!'

Another abrupt change of direction as her finger, pointing at Jean jabbed at him. Jean took a step back but now she beckoned him forward.

He took a tentative pace but it was as much as he could manage. This diminutive woman was almost more frightening than Odo.

'Now boy!' she repeated, 'tell me what exactly it is that you are doing here. Do not be afraid of upsetting his Grace, the Earl of Kent. He is our subject, just as you are and you will tell me the truth. Let us start with you though. Who are you and what is your background?'

She was no longer agitating at her sleeve but concentrating closely on whatever it was Jean had to say. What he had to say didn't take long because there wasn't much to tell. He related how he received a summons from his liege lord, when idling away his time on the estate. He told of his father's position, his own education, his journey to England and his reception by Lord Odo.

'Why you?'

Was the next question and again he answered as honestly as he could. She then asked the question which he knew to be the central reason for his summons to this room.

'Now, what exactly, Master LeBrun, is your commission here on this cold and unfriendly island. Surely not to record the local soggy landscape?'

He then, at first haltingly but then warming to his subject, told her everything about the proposed tapestry for the new cathedral at Bayeux. She listened attentively then nodded.

'I thought so. Why your presence among us should have been the cause of such speculation, I cannot imagine and I told the King as much. All right, how far have you succeeded in this enterprise of yours?'

Jean then told her that the first panel, depicting Harold's attempts to deprive William of his rightful succession had just been completed and he was ready to move on to the next phase, whatever that may be. Without a narrator of events he could go no further. Also, while he had the ear of her Majesty, he could do with as much help as possible with the needlework. The actual design was one thing but the end result was supposed to be embroidered. In order to bring the sort of life to his narrative that he judged proper, he needed to be acquainted with the actual process of embroidering his work.

To still his now loosened tongue, she held up her hand. Then she smiled.

'Do you know Master LeBrun, I think I may be able to help you. I don't think my esteemed uncle, The Earl of Kent,' she added in answer to his unspoken question, 'would object to my playing some minor role in this grand scheme of his, do you?'

Before Jean could frame any sort of intelligent reply Thibault, with a courtly bow said

'I think he would be honoured your Highness.'

She fixed him with a brittle smile.

'Yes Thibault, I think he would. Not perhaps pleased but certainly honoured.'

She turned again to Jean.

'Tell me Master LeBrun, where is this work in progress?'

Jean in his turn made a half decent bow which was not good enough to prevent Thibault from frowning and said.

'In the apartments of my Lord Odo, your Majesty. Would your Majesty like me to fetch it for you?'

'I think not Master LeBrun. I would like to talk more with you.'

She turned again to Thibault.

'Please fetch it for me would you Thibault. Oh! And take the Lady Mirabelle with you, I'd like a few moments alone with this allegedly talented young man.'

She dismissed them with a wave of her hand and they backed out of her presence. She beckoned Jean with a small but imperious forefinger.

'Now young man, stand there and listen to me. I am probably better qualified than anybody to inform you of our preparations for the invasion. In fact I even commissioned and had fitted out a vessel at my own expense to contribute to the invasion fleet. I can help you with the embroidery and might be able to point you in the direction of women capable of carrying out the work to your satisfaction. Now, listen.'

#

On their way to Odo's apartments, Mirabelle had to lift her skirts from the ground to keep up with Thibault. He was striding out, his face set and angry. When they reached the room, she brushed ahead of him and faced him with her back to the table and its contents. He barely looked at her but reached around her for the linen. She caught hold of his arm.

'Gently, gently. The Queen won't thank you if this gets spoiled. Nor will your friend Jean if it comes to that. Look, you stand back and let me do it.'

He offered no resistance but merely turned his back on her and walked to the door. She carefully folded the drawings, draping them over her arm and joined him in the doorway.

'Oh, for goodness sake Thibault, stop sulking. The Queen is in an excellent mood. This is the ideal opportunity to earn her favour.'

He grasped her roughly by the arm and turned her to face him. His grip was strong and his eyes blazed, then he released her, almost pushing her away. Mirabelle caught her breath. There was something about this man that intrigued her. His innocence was an obvious challenge and she still found it difficult to believe that he was so completely unaware of Odo's reputation. She stood looking at him, her head on one side, trying to read him. He was still looking down and a lock of his dark hair had fallen over his brow and she had an almost overwhelming urge to brush it out of his eyes for him but she restrained herself and halted the movement in mid air.

'Come along Thibault, we must get this back to the Queen' she gave a tiny gasp of exasperation, 'Don't look so mournful. You haven't hurt me, I'm fine so cheer up.'

Still he said nothing and she raised her eyes to the ceiling.

'Oh, please yourself!' she went on, 'You can stay here looking miserable if you like but I'm going back to see if there's anything left of Master Jean. For a small woman she can inspire an enormous amount of fear.' She expected him to share the humour of the remark but still he maintained his mournful demeanour and she began to loose patience.

'Do come on, let's go.'

He made to take the strip of linen from her.

'No, it's all right, I'll take it!'

He again offered no resistance and she gave a sigh of resignation but after a few steps, she stopped. He had been following on her heels but his head was still down and without looking where he was going he trod on the heel of her slipper.

She whipped around.

'For goodness sake Thibault do you have to keep barging...'

She took one look at his face and held back. Instead she reached out with her free hand and took his, lifted it to her lips and gently kissed it. For a moment she thought he was going to be overcome with embarrassment but instead he surprised her by turning her hand over and bringing the palm of it to his own mouth. She gave a little gasp but soon recovered herself and said quickly, 'Don't you dare apologise. Don't you dare say "sorry". Don't spoil it Thibault, please don't spoil it.'

His features relaxed.

'How did you know that I was going to...'

She shook her head.

'Not now Thibault, we don't have time.'

She patted the cloth draped over her arm.

'Let's get this to the Queen.'

They continued walking down the corridor, neither speaking, thinking their own thoughts. In a few moments they were at the doors of the Queen's apartments and admitted by the imposing and expressionless men-at-arms.

CHAPTER SIXTEEN

Caen/Dover

The weather in Normandy was dreadful, with howling gales and curtains of rain sweeping through the alleys of Caen. In the comparative comfort of his ducal stronghold, William stood brooding at one of the windows and watched as his minions, soldiers and clerics went about their various tasks, scurrying from doorway to doorway to avoid the worst of the weather. God knows why they always complained about the weather across the channel. It was just as bad here in Normandy but at least it was Norman rain and Norman wind. Anyway the weather was not the problem.

The problem or problems were his son and he suspected, although he had no proof as yet, his step brother. Son Robert, unkindly nicknamed 'Curthose' was nominally in charge of his father's Norman interests. Strong in battle but weak in almost every other respect, he had been a frequent cause of concern to William and was always harrying his father for more power that he, as the eldest son, considered his right. To keep him quiet, William had reluctantly granted him the Co-Regency of Normandy in partnership with his mother. Trouble was, if the normally dependable Mathilde had an Achilles heel, it was the regard in which she held her eldest son. In her eyes he could do no wrong.

William paced the room. It was ironic he thought. He placed so much reliance on his wife's instinct for political strategy and yet she had failed him in this one regard. Perhaps he should have left her here in Normandy where she might just have been able to curb the ambitions of their headstrong offspring. But she wasn't here in Normandy. She was still in England where he had thought she might serve him best. So! What to do? It was all so stupid and a waste of his valuable time. A sibling quarrel, that's all it was; a juvenile squabble between Robert and his brothers, who had subjected him to some childish indignity. Robert had turned to his father, asking him to punish brothers William and Henry for their behaviour. His father refused and the next thing he knew, Robert had gone off in a huff and was now preparing to revolt against his father by laying siege to Rouen.

William returned to the window and slapped his palm on the stone lintel. It was too bad he reflected . He had brought sons into this uncertain world to ensure succession and then they turned against him. He couldn't be in all places at once and what about Odo? He turned from the window. So far as he knew, Odo wasn't implicated in this latest fiasco but, with Odo, one could never be sure. He and young Robert had always been very close. His eyes narrowed. Was it for this that Odo had been marshalling a force in France? Before he had a chance to ruminate further he was interrupted by a knock on the door. It was a marshal and behind him, resplendently garbed as ever, stood the un-priest-like figure of his step-brother.

For a moment the two just stood looking at each other; Odo, massive in the doorway and William leaning against the wall opposite, born of the same mother but physically very different. Odo was richly apparelled, larger than life and swelled by his excesses and William, lean almost aesthetic in his plainness and simplicity. Odo was the first to break the silence.

'My Lord, I have just heard. Your son! You must be furious with the young fool.'

William moved away from the window and beckoned Odo to enter the room. William gestured to a chair and Odo sat, William remained standing. He had still not spoken. He waved a hand to dismiss the Marshall from the chamber and then sat himself on the table, one foot on the ground, facing his kinsman. He spoke quietly but with unmistakable authority.

'Well, brother, I think it's time we had a filially frank discussion, don't you?'

#

When Mirabelle and Thibault entered the Queen's chamber they found, surprisingly, a scene which was almost cosy in its domesticity. Mathilde was talking to her scribe, who had moved to her side, together with his table and accoutrements. She was dictating and he was taking notes. Far from being cowed as they had expected, Jean was pacing about the room, stopping the Queen in mid-speech from time to time to ask a question and even stepping in front of her, the better to see what the scribe had written. This drew no rebuke from her Majesty, rather she smiled at Mirabelle and Thibault, holding a finger to her lips. They were not kept waiting for long because, after a few moments, she said, 'Well Master LeBrun that, I think, is as far as I can help you. I hope you agree that some record of events leading up to the actual embarkation is of importance to your document?'

She turned to Thibault and Mirabelle, who were standing just inside the door. She beckoned to them.

'Come along then you two, let us see what this young magician has conjured thus far from his enquiries. Incidentally, Mirabelle, Master LeBrun is not a man to be taken lightly when he warms to his theme. He was most insistent that I clarify certain points to which he felt I had not given sufficient thought. I rather had the impression from you that he was little more than an untutored farm hand. He is highly articulate and intelligent, are you not LeBrun?'

Jean, now far from being awed, looked up from the scribe's writing which he had been studying carefully, oblivious of anything except translating words into the pictures of his imagination, and replied abstractedly.

'I beg your pardon your Majesty?' Mathilde repeated what she had said, whereupon Jean, instead of lapsing back into the persona of an untutored farm hand, gave one of his spontaneous grins.

Mathilde held out a hand for the drawings and Mirabelle stepped forward, laying them out on the floor in front of her. The Queen leaned forward and inspected them carefully. She then sat back and looked at them from a different perspective before addressing, not Jean, but Thibault.

'Thibault, how long did it take Master LeBrun to complete this work?'

Thibault stepped forward.

'Something in excess of two days Ma'am.'

She looked at him disbelievingly and then turned to Jean.

'Is that correct LeBrun, that's how long it took you to do this?'

She gestured to the drawings. Jean shrugged and said that he wasn't sure. He glanced towards the window and, noticing the light fading, said that he would go away and assimilate the information he had just been given. He reached out for the vellum on which the scribe had made his notes but Mathilde leant forward and stayed his hand.

'Just one moment Master LeBrun, we haven't quite finished our conversation. What you have accomplished thus far is all well and good but where do you go from here?'

Jean shook his head and shrugged. She continued, 'Your designs have to be worked by needlewomen. Have you given any thought as to where or how this might be done. Has his Grace, my Lord Odo, not given you any idea?'

Noticing Jean was looking to Thibault for help – and Thibault was deliberately ignoring him, she went on.

'I thought as much. Men tend to be much the same, whatever their station. They get a good idea and launch it on an unsuspecting world in the hope that it will take care of itself. I'm sure that Mirabelle here will agree with me. Life is not like that is it Mirabelle? All ideas need nudging in the right direction if they are to succeed and this one is no exception. You are faced with a multiplicity of problems here. Firstly there is the size of the commission by which I mean the actual dimensions. Have you any idea how long it will take to undertake a piece of work like that? You might be lightening itself with charcoal but working with a needle is a slow and painstaking business. It will need doing a panel at a time although given sufficient hands, there is no reason why different teams could not be simultaneously employed on different panels. Provided, of course, they were adequately supervised for continuity. Then how do you propose to have this design transferred to a suitable fabric for the needlework. This material is not at all suitable. Hang that up around the nave in his Lordship's beautiful new church and it'll be shredded within the month.'

Jean took a step forward but Mathilde went on.

'Colours! Would you wish to oversee a system of co-ordinating colours for the different elements of your drawing?'

Jean tried to get a word in again but the Queen carried on remorselessly.

'Have you given any thought to where this might be done? Do either of you know where to find teams of needlewomen capable of carrying out this ambitious project?'

The two men looked at each other and then at her. She sighed.

'I thought as much. As I say, it's all very well getting this far.' She leaned forward. 'Master LeBrun, I would strongly advise you to forget about the rest of the history for the moment. There will be Hastings veterans a plenty, for a good many years to come, to give you more information about the battle than you'll ever be able to use. You need to find your needlewomen first and establish what problems they are like to face.'

This time it was Thibault who attempted to speak and he too was halted by an imperious hand.

'Although this enterprise is nothing to do with me, I will give you one piece of good advice. Have the work done here in England. Ah! I'm sorry. From the way you both groaned I imagine that you had hoped this would prove your passport back to Normandy. No gentlemen, the needlework in this island is far superior to anything we can produce at home and the wools are infinitely finer. I can only suppose that the perpetual damp must prove beneficial to the sheep or something. Now you must leave me, all of you. I have matters of state to consider.'

She terminated her audience with a wave and they all made to back out of the door, except for Jean who stood his ground. He ventured to ask, if her Majesty, who had been very helpful and whose advice he would certainly take, might suggest where he might find these excellent craftswomen of which she spoke. Thibault and Mirabelle moved forward to drag him away from the Queen's displeasure but she halted them.

'You have two possibilities Master LeBrun, Winchester and Canterbury. Both have renowned schools of needlework and associated crafts. You can of course take your pick but I would remind you that the town of Canterbury is in this Region of Kent and I don't have to tell you who is the virtual ruler of the Region. Not only will it be more convenient for you but using his own facilities, so to speak, will be pleasing to my uncle, something which should stand you in good stead. Now be off with you.'

Once outside they all started talking at once. So animated were they that Mirabelle and Jean took little notice of a royal messenger, lightly armed for speed and bearing the King's emblem on his sleeve, rushing by them and heading for the apartments that they had just left. Thibault not only noticed him but marked the urgency with which he went about his business.

Meanwhile, his two companions were still unburdening themselves of the tensions of their audience with Mathilde, although both agreed that the ordeal was less traumatic than Jean had expected. As they spoke Jean was unfolding a section of the cartoon to point out some unflattering expression he had given to King Harold and Mirabelle was laughing with him. Thibault's attention was still on the messenger's back as he hurried down the corridor. He watched him until one of the guards ushered the messenger into the Queen's apartments. Thibault's two companions were oblivious of everything but their shared mirth until they felt Thibault roughly propelling them down the corridor. Jean wrenched his arm from Thibault's grip and carefully re-folded his designs.

'What's the matter with you Thibault, are you incapable of laughter or what?'

Mirabelle, sensing Thibault's mood, shook her head at Jean to be quiet.

Seeing he had their attention, Thibault said urgently.

'Let's get out of here, I've a feeling there's something going on and until I find out what it is, I suggest we keep out of everybody's way.'

Jean was not satisfied with an explanation as incomplete as this and once more attempted to stop and argue. So far as he was concerned, he had the commission from Odo which had received the Queen's blessing herself, so what was the problem? Again though, Mirabelle's look cautioned silence so he unwillingly allowed himself to be ushered back to Odo's chambers from which they'd been summoned a couple of hours previously.

It was getting late and the room was in darkness when they entered. It wasn't until Thibault had lit a wall sconce that they noticed the figure emerging from the shadows. The figure was quite unmistakably that of Odo, Bishop of Bordeaux and Earl of Kent. For once his overwhelming personality seemed somewhat diminished and his dress less immaculate than normal, Mirabelle gave a small gasp of alarm when she recognised who it was and instinctively took Thibault's arm. Jean, by now tired after his labours and the excitement of the day, leant against a wall, clutching his drawings and hoping he wasn't going have to go through them all over again with Odo. Thibault made no effort to remove Mirabelle from his arm but drew her quietly and protectively behind him and kept his gaze firmly fixed on the rush matting under his feet.

CHAPTER SEVENTEEN

Dover

Because of the semi-darkness, the change in Odo's appearance was not noticeable but the voice was unmistakable.

'What a pretty scene' he rumbled, 'The lovely Mistress Mirabelle sheltering behind her protector. Are you her protector Thibault? I must confess, I never thought I'd see the day when you…Well! No matter. And you Master LeBrun. Is that part of my commission that you have under your arm? Again, no matter. I've been travelling, I'm weary and I'll thank you all to get out of my sight.'

They looked at one another and turned to go… 'Until the morning, that is. First thing Thibault, if you please.'

Thibault merely nodded his head before leading the way back out into the corridor.

When they had descended the stairs they entered the great hall as it was filling for the evening meal. Thibault turned to Jean.

'LeBrun, take that creation of yours and stow it somewhere safely in our quarters. Then get back here and we'll find something to eat.'

Mirabelle, appearing pre-occupied, excused herself and they all went their separate ways.

For the last two nights Jean, out of respect for his new found status, had been elevated from the lower dormitory to Thibault's room, with the promise that new quarters with better light for his activities would be made available to him in due course. He'd thought about making some sort of flippant remark about sharing a room with Thibault then, quite wisely, had reconsidered. He still had to make do with a straw mattress laid on top of the bare boards but at least he was in better company. He made his way from the hall and entered a narrow passageway from which doors opened into small rooms. Finding theirs, Jean entered, climbed onto a rough table which, apart from Thibault's cot, was the only furniture and stowed the rolled-up linen on the wooden beam which supported the roof boards. Tomorrow's meeting with Odo weighing on his mind, he made his way back to the great hall.

Thibault had not forgotten him and had not only managed to get him a reasonable meal but had stayed his own supper in order that they might eat together. Another advantage of being in Thibault's company was the improved quality of the food. He wearily dropped on to the form and was about to remark on Mirabelle's absence then thought better of it. As though he had anticipated the question, Thibault reported that Mirabelle had excused herself on account of the messenger they had seen.

If the Queen was in receipt of urgent despatches from her husband in France, it could well be that Mirabelle was required to attend upon her Majesty. Jean then enquired if they were likely to encounter problems when they met with Odo the following day. Thibault replied that he didn't see that there could be any in view of Jean's progress and the Queen's interest in the work. There was of course the fact that Odo had ordered the project be kept secret but since they were commanded by one to whom even Odo was subservient, he was not likely to make too much fuss about it. So all in all, there was no reason why they should not enjoy a good night's sleep and worry about the morning when it came. Jean doubted if he would enjoy a restful night. Things were moving too fast for his liking and he felt his life was spinning out of control and although he was trying hard not to show it, Odo frightened him. He worried that his work might not be acceptable. If so the meeting could prove a disaster. Perhaps this whole silly idea was little more than a whim on Odo's part and likely to be cast aside. That being the case what would become of him then? Sent back to Odo's estates to suffer the wrath of his own father was not exactly a recipe for a good night's rest but he could hardly convey his worries to Thibault who, he felt, also had things on his mind.

In spite of his reassuring words to Jean, Thibault was also contemplating an uneasy night and again, it was Odo that was on his mind. This was to be their first real meeting since LeBrun and Mirabelle had confirmed what he had sometimes suspected of the man. Odo had always been as good as a father to him and had appeared to fulfil the role in an exemplary fashion. These new reports of Odo's veniality and cruelty threatened the relationship between the two men which was central to Thibault's very existence. As if that wasn't worry enough, there was something else on his mind. He felt his self-sufficiency, for which he was so often scorned, was being undermined and he couldn't say why. Was it Jean, he wondered.

He had to admit to quite liking the boy, but it wasn't that. Mirabelle then. His fingers carefully massaged his aching temple and his lips moved in a silent prayer. Still unhappy, he resolved to take himself off to the stables to check on Nero, his gelding. The horse had been sadly neglected since Thibault had been forced to spend so much of his time with LeBrun and although he would have been exercised by the grooms, it was no substitute for his master's attention. Typical, he thought. He was so pathetic an individual that he found the company of a horse preferable to that of anything else.

He rose from the bench and without acknowledging the few remaining diners, left the hall and made his way across the bailey and towards the stables, where the comforting smell of horse and warm straw mingled sweetly with the night air. It was colder and as a result the ubiquitous fog had dispersed and stars could be seen in the clear sky.

That was something he must remind young Jean to include in his designs, the huge shooting star with the long tail which had been witnessed by the English in the April of 1066. It was seen by them as an ill omen and considering the invasion that followed in September, they were probably quite justified in this view. Thibault couldn't remember if Jean had portrayed the event or even if Robert Beaumont had mentioned it in his summary. He must check with Jean tomorrow because Odo, who missed nothing, would be sure to see it as an omission.

Before entering the stables, he stopped and looked around him. It had been a long time since the moon had been bright enough to throw up the tower and the surrounding buildings in such clarity. The sight pleased Thibault who, unlike so many of his countrymen exiled to this island, quite liked Dover. He looked up towards the pharose, the lighthouse which had been there since Roman times. It had one of the best views of the area so Thibault decided to make the most of the unaccustomed light and walk up to it but first he must look to the welfare of his horse.

There were the customary stable noises when he entered. Soft shuffling of hooves and gentle snorting accompanied by the not so gentle snoring of some of the grooms who slept in the same straw as their charges. With so many of the knights and men-at arms in France or on duty elsewhere in England, the number of stabled mounts was not large and Nero soon recognised his master's scent and footstep. Careful not to wake the groom, Thibault carefully stepped around him and between Nero and the other horse that shared his stall. Holding his hand over Nero's muzzle to prevent a whinny of recognition, he ran his other hand through the horse's mane to make sure that he was well groomed. Next he ran his hands expertly down the four quarters and found the animal to be in fine condition and the moonlight, which shone through the holes in the walls, was reflected in a shiny and healthy coat. Thibault was satisfied. The boy that looked after Nero had always been thorough in his work and cared well for his charge. In fact his section of stabling was always better maintained than any other in the castle. Many of the Saxon menials did as little as they could for their Norman oppressors but he put the welfare of his horses above any such feelings. Thibault gave the animal a farewell pat and quietly left the stall, wrapping his heavy cloak against the chill of the night outside.

He stood for a moment, undecided, before walking up the hill. His mind was still full of unresolved thoughts so his bed was the last thing he wanted. No, he'd walk up to the lighthouse and along the cliffs a way and perhaps, by doing so, clear his head enough to snatch a few hours sleep before facing Lord Odo in the morning.

The lighthouse was within the castle boundaries, near to the church where Jean had met with Mirabelle. In order for it to fulfil the purpose for which it had been built, it was situated on one of the highest spots on that part of the coast which overlooked the sea and the port. As he climbed, he checked for the dagger in his belt because a lone Norman, particularly one of quality, was still a tempting target for a vengeful Saxon. Once there, he walked around the base of the lighthouse, the better to view the harbour and the town. The sea was calm and the moonlight picked out the ripples as they softly rolled back and forth. The town was almost in darkness but the harbour was unusually active for this time of night. Seamen were scurrying on and off the boats, Norman boats, still modelled on the old Viking designs, had changed little from those used for the invasion. How many vessels had there been? Near enough five hundred or more. Thibault shuddered at the memory. Why this activity though? It was unusual for the harbour to be so busy at this time of night. True, there was always plenty going on during the day because of the constant traffic between here and Normandy, but something must be happening to justify all this activity. It looked as though this was no ordinary embarkation. Difficult to see from this distance and in this light but one of the vessels looked far too well appointed for ordinary cross-channel traffic. Not the ship that sailed William's messenger over either. He could see that one. It was easily identifiable by it's racier lines and multiple oar banks to assist a speedy passage. It almost looked, in fact, like the ...A voice cut through his train of thought. He spun round, hand on dagger.

'Where have you been Thibault?'

'Mistress Mirabelle? Wha...what are you doing up here?'

'I could ask the same question of you, Thibault I've been looking everywhere for you.'

'Where have I been? Oh, I've just come from the stables but...'

'Dear Thibault, I might have known. You have been talking to your horse again. You find animals easier than people don't you? Especially people like me!'

Thibault hugged himself in his cloak and managed to keep his fingers from soothing the sudden flash of pain in his head.

He said, 'How do you mean, people like you?'

She grinned at him and her white teeth gleamed out of the cowl which still covered her head.

She said, 'I've come to say goodbye.'

The silence between them was only broken by the faint sounds of the sailors as they worked far below them, then Thibault said, 'Why, where are you going?' His voice was steady and gave nothing away. She let out a sigh and turned her back on him

'I'm sorry Mirabelle but…'

Still facing away from him she said quietly

'I sometimes think Thibault that 'sorry' is the only word you feel comfortable with. I never want to hear you say it again but then, in the circumstances, I'm not likely to am I? I didn't want to leave without saying 'goodbye', that's all.'

She started to walk down the path towards the bailey but he caught her arm and turned her round to face him and said 'I wasn't apologising, I was saying I'm sorry that you're leaving here. Truly I am but what is this all about? Why and where are you going?'

She gave him sad smile but said nothing. He asked her again.

'Mistress Mirabelle, what's happened?'

'Come on Thibault, can't you guess, you saw the messenger and urgency of his arrival.'

She moved a step closer to him and said, 'Oh dear! I thought this was going to be easy. I have to accompany the Queen to France. We sail on the morning tide. Look, they're already making preparations.'

She indicated the activity taking place below them. He didn't even turn to look but frowned at her and questioning her further. He learned that the King was facing a crisis in his own dukedom in Normandy and needed his wife's presence to take over the administration of the region while he dealt with the problem. Bishop Odo had been sent back here where, together with William FitzOsbern, Duke of Hereford and Robert Beaumont, he was to act as Co-Regent for the Kingdom.

Thibault's frown deepened. He stood thinking, brow furrowed and apparently so far away from her that she thought he'd forgotten she was there. She turned from him again, her head held high and started down the path. He called her name and once more she turned and looked up at him. She couldn't help but smile. He looked like a small lost boy. Perplexed and completely overcome by everything that was going on around him.

'I'm…' he started to say but she raised a warning eyebrow and he made a mock defensive gesture with raised hands.

'It's all right, I wasn't going to say it.'

She waited expectantly. He took a deep breath before continuing.

'I was going to say what a ridiculous situation this is. Here we are on an island, peopled by natives that hate us, which is in the care of the one man most responsible for creating that hostility and over there,' he waved a hand vaguely in the direction of France, 'our native Normandy is apparently under threat so King, or Duke, William has left it at the mercy of another Regency in the form of his wife. What in God's name is supposed to be going on?'

His manner was almost petulant and again, Mirabelle couldn't help but smile. She wanted to hug him and tell him everything would be all right but she didn't quite dare, so she said, 'Come on Thibault, you know very well that is how it has worked ever since we came to this island. The King has always spent more time looking after his ducal possessions than he has his royal ones and the Queen has always proved herself a shrewd and able steward of his affairs when he's been forced to defend Normandy against external threats. In the same way Lords Odo and FitzOsbern have spent most of their time acting as his representatives in England. It's nothing new so what is the problem?'

Thibault responded with a rueful smile and he offered his arm. Companionably, they talked as they made their way back to the castle.

'So', he said, 'What time do you expect to sail tomorrow?'

'Today, Thibault. It must be after midnight by now. In answer to your question, I think the tide is favourable about nine.'

He stopped and looked at her. 'As early as that?'

'Yes, I think that's the time that was mentioned. Why?' and added mischievously, 'Will you miss me?' She was not expecting him to say anything at all and was not surprised by his neutral 'Of course.'

She looked at him for a moment, her head on one side, then said.

'Would you be kind enough to see me to my room?'

'At this time of night Mistress Mirabelle, I could not possibly allow you to make your way there alone. You took a grave risk walking up here by yourself'

'Yes I did, didn't I Thibault and do you know why I did?'

'No, of course I don't. Why did you?'

She squeezed his arm and said resignedly 'It doesn't matter Thibault. It really doesn't matter.'

On their way back they saw nobody apart from the occasional guard who, because he was so well known in the community, didn't even bother to challenge Thibault. They did not, however, see the dark be-cloaked figure that, from the shelter of a doorway, monitored their progress across the bailey. One of Odo's creatures, he was employed to live in the shadows and keep his eyes and ears open. Odo needed to keep one step ahead of any plots that may be simmering against him. Thibault's natural fastidiousness had kept him aloof from these activities but even he would have to acknowledge that the young lady on his arm, to which she clung with surprising warmth, was herself no stranger to these sordid goings-on although, in her case, it was on behalf of the Queen.

When they entered the hall it was almost empty, except for some of the lower servants who had no where else to sleep and seemed to live on whatever scraps they could find from the tables. Scavenging, they took no notice of the tall Squire and the muffled form of the young lady as they progressed through the length of the building and out towards the suites, rooms and chambers of the court.

Thibault started to walk to the room where last he had escorted Mirabelle but she stopped him.

'Sorry Thibault but it's a different room again, I'm afraid. I went in there this evening before going to her Majesty, only to find that Lady Granville had reclaimed it.'

Thibault frowned. 'Lady Granville? Has her husband returned with her?'

She shrugged. 'I suppose so, although I didn't see him.'

The frown deepened. 'Well! That was a quick trip wasn't it? They must have turned around as soon as they landed in France.'

Again she gave a shrug.

'I don't know but if you think about it, so did your Lord and Master and we know that he came back post haste because King William's crisis in Normandy meant that William had to stay there. Lord Odo has returned to assume his duties as Regent which, as I said, is the role he's assumed for most of the time that we've been on this island. That being the case, I suppose that Granville, who after all is one of Odo's men, has returned with him.'

'Yes but why did they sail to France in the first place? That's what I can't understand.'

'Oh! I don't know Thibault. Everybody who's anybody over here has interests over there and vice versa. Life is complicated enough for me at the moment without agonising over the travelling arrangements of our leaders.' She gave him a weary smile. 'I'm tired Thibault and in five or six hours I'm going to be making the journey myself so...'

He took her arm again.

'Of course I'm s... '

He swallowed the word and she patted the hand that held her arm.

'There's a good boy.'

'Yes, all right, all right. Let's get you to your old room.'

When they arrived at the door she turned and looked up at him and said hesitantly.

'Thibault, I know I said I was tired just now but, I wonder, would you come in with me for little while?'

He looked at her enquiringly so she went on, 'You know what it's like. I haven't used the room for a few days and I'm always a little concerned at what might have taken up residence in there, especially in this ghastly old place. It's teeming with wildlife. Please!'

'Well, yes I suppose…'

'Thank you Thibault'

She led the way into the room and smiled apologetically.

'Not much is it?' He looked around.

'I don't know, it's … well, it's quite cosy – if that's the right word.'

'Cosy will do nicely Thibault. I suppose it's not unlike your room actually, although yours would be much tidier of course.'

He took a step away from her.

'How do you know what my room is like? When have you been there?'

His voice suddenly took on an edge.

'Not with LeBrun in my room, not that.'

She moved towards him, both hands held out and said, so softly he could hardly hear her.

'Oh dear! What am I going to do with you Thibault? You are so intelligent yet you just can't see. Do you remember what you called me not so long ago? That particular incident which has since prompted nothing else but a string of apologies. Do you remember?'

He nodded dumbly.

'Yes of course you do. It's probably scarred you for the rest of your life but it was true, what you said, about me being the Queen's whore.'

She dropped her eyes from his miserable expression.

'But being the Queen's whore doesn't mean I'm lacking in those feelings which decent and ordinary women experience. It doesn't mean I can't want someone just for their own sake or for my own sake.'

She took his hand and led him to the bed where they both sat facing each other.

'When I said a little earlier tonight that my life was complicated enough without all this politicking that's going on around us well, you happen to be that complication Thibault. There! Now you know and I'm sorry. Yes, this time it's me that's sorry because I quite understand that it's the last thing you wanted to hear.'

He rose abruptly, his back to her. He was shaking his head and moaning, as if in pain. When he turned, she saw tears in his eyes.

Her first instinct was to offer him words of comfort, for whatever it was that was causing him distress, but something held her back. Instead he came over to her and said.

'Help me.'

He then dropped on his knees in front of her.

She giggled and said, 'At last I've brought you down to my level.'

She ran her fingers through his hair and gently pulled his head to rest against her breast. Her hands moved from his head to his neck and she increased the pressure of her massage until she felt him move restlessly against her. She stopped what she was doing and put both her hands on his shoulders willing him to look up at her.

'Yes' she said, 'Of course I'll help you but firstly you have to agree to one or two very simple conditions.'

She moved her hands and cupped his upturned face in them.

'Do you agree?'

He covered her hands with his and said,' I agree.'

She gently leant forward and kissed him on the brow.

'Now,' she said, 'You promise not to say that word. In fact you must promise not to say anything at all.'

Her hands restricted his head but he managed a nod.

'And' she went on 'you must do exactly as I say, without question or disagreement. All right?' Again he nodded.

She released his head and stood up, raising him up at the same time. She unclipped the clasp of his cloak, sliding it from his shoulders and laying it on the bed. Then article by article she removed the rest of his clothes, each time kissing the part of his body that they had covered. When she had finished she retrieved the cloak from the bed and replaced it around his bare shoulders. Last of all, she knelt down in front of him and took him in her mouth. Before she had taken him too far, she stopped, stood up and whispered.

'Now, it's your turn. Undress me.'

At first he fumbled then, with increasing urgency he reduced her to the same state of nudity as himself and like her, he replaced her cloak around her shoulders. She drew him to her bed and guided him into her.

#

She pushed herself a little way from him, walked her fingers over his chest and whispered.

'You must go. Go now, back to your room.'

Thibault shook his head but then moved away from her. He began to dress, all the time keeping his eyes averted from her tear streaked face. He paused, holding his crucifix before clipping it back on his belt. As he pinned his cloak he, at last, looked at her and said, 'I shall be back shortly, before you go. If we have to say "goodbye" it will be then, not now.'

She sat up and shook her head at him in exasperation.

'Oh Thibault, you are such an idiot. Don't you realise that I have loved you ever since I clapped eyes on you. Now go! For God's sake go.'

She threw her pillow at him. He picked it up from the floor, carefully brushed it down and replaced it. He then walked out of the door, shaking his head and frowning. When he reached the door to his own room it was as though he had forgotten Jean's existence. He threw the door open and slammed it behind him and leaned back against it. His tousled room-mate was glaring at him through sleep drugged eyes. Once fully awake, Jean realised that Thibault was laughing to himself. Jean said, 'What the …you've been drinking! What's the time?'

Thibault continued to laugh which Jean found quite unnerving. He rubbed his eyes and peered at Thibault through the gloom.

'You have, haven't you? You've been drinking, I didn't even know you liked that rubbish they serve up here – or have you managed to get your hands on some of the good…'

'No LeBrun, I have not been drinking and in answer to your other question, I have no idea what time it is and what is more I don't care. I'm sorry I woke you. To be honest I'd forgotten you were here. Go back to sleep, I'll try not to wake you when I go out.'

Jean stared at him. 'Go out! What do you mean 'go out'? You've only just come in…'

Thibault cut him short.

'Yes I know I've only just come in but there is something I have to do. Don't worry I won't be that long.'

Jean frowned, 'Thibault, are you telling me that you don't intend to go to bed at all tonight? What the hell is going on? You're different you've gone all…I KNOW…'

Jean stared in disbelief until his features dissolved into a grin.

'I know, you've been with a woman! No don't lie to me Thibault, I can tell the signs. You've just had a woman and it's your first. Who is she then? Not that Vicompte Aimery's wife that was talking to you the other day in the hall? The one that dropped her kerchief so that you could pick it up for her. Bit old for you isn't she?'

Thibault pushed him back on the mattress and told him to shut up. He looked down at him.

'LeBrun, I wonder, would you do me a favour?'

Jean thought for a moment and drew in a mock, deep breath.

'I don't know about that Thibault. It depends doesn't it.'

Thibault and told him to be quiet for a moment and try and be serious.

'The thing is LeBrun, I wonder if you wouldn't mind meeting with Lord Odo on your own. Just to start with. Perhaps you could make some excuse for me, say I'd been called away on some important court business. I know, say that I've been summoned by the Queen to accompany her and her train to the port.'

Jean assumed a pious expression which was anything but convincing.

'You mean to say Thibault that you want me to lie for you. The ever-so-honourable Thibault wants me to tell a lie so that he can plough some other man's wife? Oh dear, I don't know about that. Hardly ethical is it? I mean to say…'

Thibault leaned over him.

'Please Jean , just this once.' The sincerity of this plea impressed Jean who was pleased to find that the noble Thibault was displaying some signs of human frailty. He decided that further teasing would be going a step too far so he said, albeit reluctantly, 'All right Thibault but for God's sake don't leave me alone with that ogre a second longer than you have to. I hope she's worth it, this lady. It is that one I said, isn't it?'

Thibault shook his head.

'Sorry Jean. You'll never know how much I appreciate what you're going to do for me but no names. Not yet. Later I promise but not now.'

Jean looked keenly at him from under a furrowed brow. 'If I do this for you Thibault, does that mean you owe me a favour?'

Thibault laughed.

'There are few things in this life, LeBrun, of which I am certain but one is that you will never make a gentleman. Gentlemen do not barter and bargain over such accommodations. Anyway, thank you again. Now I shall take a walk to the stables. There are things I need to clarify in my head.'

Jean curled up in amusement.

'You can't go to the stables.'

'Why not?'

'You can't go courting your ladylove, smelling of stables. Honestly Thibault, it's easy to see you're new to this sort of thing. Now, if you want my advice…'

'Oh be quiet and get back to sleep. When I want your advice I'll ask for it but I imagine it's not likely to be in this lifetime. I'm going but I'll be with you just as soon as I can.'

He gave a careless wave of the hand and was out of the door. This time closing it gently.

CHAPTER EIGHTEEN

Dover

The sound of the Angelus woke Jean with a jolt, although after his disturbed night it was a while before he was awake enough to register his unfamiliar surroundings and find the wash bowl. Already he was regretting the promise he'd made to Thibault. He dressed and flattened his hair as best he could. Then he carefully retrieved his artwork; whether or not it would meet with Odo's approval, remained to be seen. The Queen had thought it good but she wasn't the commissioning agent.

The Angelus stopped its leaden pealing. Jean hoped Thibault would not leave him alone with Odo for long. He took one last look at the drawing, carefully rolled it in his cloak and made his way down to the great hall which was already witness to a steady stream of people breaking their fast. Usually the artisans and workmen had to spend a few hours at their occupations before taking their break but there were still a number of clerks, pages, and people of that sort, who were obliged to eat early in order to be in attendance when their masters surfaced. No sign of Thibault though and he dare not leave it any longer so, brushing the crumbs from his tunic and gathering up his bundle, he slowly made his way to Odo's rooms.

When he arrived at the heavy, oaken door, he stood there for a moment, undecided. He raised a knuckle to knock and lowered it again, taking one last look along the corridor to see if Thibault was anywhere in sight. Not a sign. He groaned to himself and tapped gently. The familiar bass told him to come in. One last look around for the absent Thibault and he was committed. He pushed on the board and entered the room. He was not surprised to see that his master had recovered from his travels, looked fresh as a daisy and much more dangerous. It took a few seconds before Odo glanced up from the papers on his desk and his first expression was one of surprise.

'Where's Thibault?'

Jean had already made the decision that if he was forced to lie on Thibault's behalf, he would keep the invention to a minimum. He therefore bowed before his Lordship and said that the Squire would be with them within the next few minutes. Odo grunted but much to Jean's relief did not enquire into the reasons for Thibault's absence. Instead he beckoned for Jean to come forward.

'Right boy,' he growled, 'Let's see what you have to show me thus far. By the way, I hear the Queen has already had a preview of your work; I thought I asked that this project should be kept between ourselves? Until I decided otherwise that is. How did that come about?'

Jean affected some surprise.

'I'm sorry my Lord but her Majesty commanded us.' He then thought for a second.

'But how did your Grace...?' Odo gave a short laugh.

'It is my business to know everything LeBrun. However, on this occasion I was informed by the Queen herself. She commanded me to her presence last night after you left me and I can tell you, I was not best pleased. All I wanted was my bed and she kept me from it for a good half candle in order to tell me how much she admired your talent and how little thought, in her opinion, I had given to the execution of this project. Anyway it's in the open now so no pleasant surprises for my royal kinsman. Let us see the fruits of your labours then, boy.'

He held out his hand to Jean for the work and Jean had only taken one step forward in his direction when, with an enormous bang, the door was thrown open, hitting the wall from which Jean had stepped a second earlier.

He whirled round, protectively clasping his work to his chest and saw Thibault standing there. His initial feeling of relief at seeing him was immediately supplanted by one of anxiety, then fear. Thibault appeared to have difficulty in breathing and seemed to be gasping for air. His eyes were unfocussed, his normally immaculate appearance, dishevelled and careless but what Jean noticed most of all was the blood with which his hands were covered and the dagger tightly grasped in one of them; so tightly that the white of his knuckles gleamed through the shining crimson.

Turning his head to gauge Odo's response to this apparition, Jean was amazed to see that the customary set, hard features of his patron had dissolved into a look of sadness. A look that was so alien on that face that for a split second, Jean was more intrigued by that than he was by Thibault's dramatic entrance. It was brief however because Thibault let out an anguished roar and dagger raised, launched himself at Odo.

Instinctively Jean thrust out a foot and Thibault was sent sprawling, the dagger clattering across the boards and under the table. At the same time and with incredible speed for a man of his bulk, Odo was out of his chair, around the table, kneeling and cradling a sobbing Thibault in his arms, murmuring comforting and reassuring phrases to him, as a mother might to a child who had fallen and hurt himself.

Thoroughly confused and not a little embarrassed, Jean mumbled an excuse and started to back out of the door but Odo, still rocking Thibault in his arms told him to stop where he was. After a while Thibault, though still distressed, was quieter. Odo continued to talk soothingly to him but, so quietly and in Latin that, Jean could not really follow much of it.

Suddenly, Thibault thrust Odo away, sprang to his feet and rushed from the chamber like a blind man with arms outstretched, almost knocking over Jean as he cannoned out of the doorway and down the corridor. Again Jean made to go after him and again, he was pulled up by Odo's command to stay where he was.

What came next was almost more of a mystery than what he had just witnessed. Odo rose to his feet, brushed down his knees, sat behind his desk and as if nothing had happened in the interim, ordered Jean to hand over the drawings. Still mesmerised, Jean flung out an arm in the general direction of the doorway and Odo, anticipating the unasked question, barked out, 'No, stay where you are LeBrun and hand over those drawings that you're clutching to your chest. You look like a virgin protecting her breasts. You have heard and seen nothing. Do you understand? Nothing.'

Jean who, by this time, had lost any capacity for intelligent speech, nodded and placed the drawings on the table. Odo gave one of his usual grunts, turned them around, unrolled and started to peruse them. After a brief inspection, which seemed to Jean to last an eternity, he sat back and steadily regarded the artist.

'The Queen was right. These are very good and what is more to the point, exactly the sort of thing I was hoping you would produce. Her Majesty has informed me that you already have details for the next panels; the preparations for the invasion in '66. Get on with those straight away and then I'll have you pointed in the direction of people who will tell you everything you will need to know about the battle itself. Understood?'

Again Jean nodded dumbly.

'In the meantime', Odo went on, 'you will be required to find needlewomen who can reproduce your work to your satisfaction.'

Jean looked blank.

'Your satisfaction,' Odo repeated, 'I'm now leaving you in charge of the whole project.'

At last Jean found a voice.

'But, your Grace... I'm not... I mean, what about Thibault, what about...'

Odo slammed a hand on the table.

'Damn you boy, just do as you are told. Thibault, at this moment in time, is no longer at your disposal.'

Again he anticipated Jean's question and this time Jean managed nothing more than 'Bu...'

'No 'buts' LeBrun, just get on with it. Don't worry your head about all the business of finding things, materials, people, that sort of detail. I'll furnish you with a helpmate to look after all your practical needs. While we're about it, you'll need money'

He turned and unlocked a small chest which stood under the window behind him. Having shut the lid and locked it he turned with a leather pouch which gave a metallic ring as it landed on the table in front of Jean, who stood looking at it but made no move to pick it up.

Odo smiled grimly, 'Take it! It's not a fortune but it's almost certainly more money than you have ever seen and you can take that look off your face. There won't be any more where that came from so manage it carefully.'

Jean tentatively leaned over and took it, weighing it in his hand. He then made to take back the drawings with his free hand but Odo stopped him.

'Not yet LeBrun, satisfactory though this is, there are one or two additions I would like to see included.'

Jean raised an eyebrow, as Odo continued. 'Don't worry, nothing really significant but tell me, why have you left borders and not drawn right to the edges?

Back in his comfort zone, Jean assumed some of his assurance.

'Well my Lord, since it has to be embroidered, I'd assumed that there would need to be a surplus of cloth to allow for stretching over a frame or whatever it is they use for the needlework.'

Odo stroked his chin then nodded and said.

'Yes, well done for thinking of it and since we are about it, it would leave room for an inscription, some sort of text describing the events your are illustrating. Might give it a little gravitas, what do you think?'

Jean, who hadn't given it any thought up until that point, considered his work and eventually came out with 'Good idea my Lord.'

Odo nodded again and then said, 'Yes. It might render it something more than just a picture book but something worthy of more serious consideration.'

Jean pretended to consider for a moment.

'I don't see why not your Grace but rather than incorporate it into the design as it stands, I think I would rather have it superimposed at the embroidery stage. That is, of course, if your Grace is agreeable.'

Odo merely nodded, 'LeBrun, before you go. That unfortunate scene you witnessed just now. Thibault! He is a good young man.'

Jean frowned.

'Yes my Lord but I never thought him anything else. That blood my Lord. How did...?

Odo levelled him with one of his penetrating looks.

'I have no idea LeBrun.

Jean felt emboldened enough to hold Odo's gaze.

'But, my Lord. Thibault! We, he and I that is, have had our misunderstandings but I have learned to like and respect him. Am I never to see him again?'

Odo shook his head thoughtfully. 'I don't know. I honestly do not know. Enough of that. You have work to do. How do you intend to proceed?'

Jean pointed at the work he had already done.

'I shall think out and then draw the next phase, as related to me by her Majesty, then I suppose I'll…'

For the second time that morning the door was flung open with the same force. Jean turned and instead of Thibault in the doorway, there stood an imposing man-at-arms in full battle order, his hand on the hilt of his sword.

Jean instinctively turned to Odo who had sprung to his feet. The sound of footsteps could be heard in the corridor. Light, feminine steps and a moment later Queen Mathilde had swept in the room, dressed for travelling and, by the look in her eyes, ready to do battle. She was furious. Jean stepped away from the table and was pleased to note that it was not him against whom her fury was directed but Odo.

Huge though he was and tiny as she was, when she confronted her uncle he seemed to visibly shrink in the face of her fury.

She positively hissed at him when she spoke, pointing an accusative finger in his direction.

'You evil bastard! Why?'

He quickly regained a measure of composure and gave a perfunctory bow.

'I, niece? Why what Madam? I have done nothing.'

She lowered her arm and pulled agitatedly at a thread on her mantle.

'Oh yes you have and this time you've gone too far. Our relationship cannot excuse this act. She was my creature, not yours. I warned you before. How dare you. You know I am about to take ship to France and you know that I cannot tarry here and miss the tide. You are also aware I imagine, that as co-Regent, you are too valuable at this time to be disposed of. But that time will come Uncle. Oh yes! That time will come. Whatever her faults, she did not deserve this and whoever was responsible will pay for it, that I promise you.'

She paused and glanced round the room.

'Where is Thibault?'

Odo, looking straight at her, merely lifted his arms and shrugged his massive shoulders to indicate that he had not the remotest idea of the whereabouts of his Squire. Jean started to croak and the Queen wheeled round and seemed to notice him for the first time.

'Well, young man. Do you know where he is?'

Jean looked mutely at Odo but Mathilde interposed herself between the two.

'You answer to me, not that, that …

Well?' Jean gave a pale imitation of Odo's shrug and also managed a barely audible, 'Don't know your Majesty.'

Her look at him intensified, boring right into his brain and he said, more loudly this time, 'I don't know your Majesty, really I don't know.'

She relaxed a little and turned back to Odo. Calmer now, she said, 'I suppose it doesn't really matter where he is at the moment. Whatever power you exercise over him my Lord, it would not be enough to induce him to an act of this brutality. I sometimes think that you retain him as your conscience, the one thing that is so noticeably lacking in yourself. Yes I know, I know.'

She turned to the man-at-arms who had moved to her side and murmured a reminder of the need to leave.

'Regretfully I have to leave without any answers. But then, I imagine it was unrealistic of me to expect to find any in this depraved animal's den. William will be informed. In the meantime, we will expect you to carry out your duties here without alienating more of our subjects than you can help.'

Without even a nod at Jean, she turned and together with her escort and train, who had been waiting for her outside in the corridor, she left them but had barely exited the room when she returned and stood in the doorway from where she regarded Jean with a puzzled look.

'You don't know do you?'

Jean, who thought that he was being asked the same question, repeated his previous answer.

'No Ma'am, I honestly don't know where he is.'

She gave a sad shake of the head.

'No, young man, I don't mean Thibault, I mean Lady Mirabelle. You and she spent some time together. I hope the memory was a good one for you because it won't happen again. She's dead. Found in her bed this morning, stabbed through the heart and then…well, no matter.'

She turned to give a last dismissive look at Odo and left the room for France. As the footsteps echoed away down the corridor, Jean felt his knees turning to jelly. He was brought back fully to his senses by Odo's terse command to pull himself together. He was then told to sit himself down on the bench and stop looking like a whey faced wench about to faint. This he gratefully did but Odo was far from finished with him although the question, when it came was almost casual.

'I didn't know you knew the Lady Mirabelle. See much of her did you?'

Jean suspected that much might depend on his answer and took a deep breath.

'No, my Lord, I just happened to meet her around the castle once or twice. Squire Thib...

Odo's voice was strained, 'She was with Thibault, was she?'

'No Sir. What I mean is... Thibault was with me ...Sir.'

Odo let out a large sigh and sat down at the table, rolling out the designs as he did so.

'Very well LeBrun. We can't waste any more time over that. Now the next...'

Jean broke in, forgetting in his anxiety that an interruption was unlikely to win him any favours. 'But my Lord. How did Lady Mirabelle... I mean... What about Thibault, what happened to...'

Odo smashed his huge fist down onto the table.

'I said that is enough. No more. Do you hear? Everybody is expendable in this world and you are more expendable than most. So shut up.'

Employing a more reasonable tone, Odo continued.

'Listen boy. If I have to find another artist, so be it. Whatever else, this project of mine will be brought to fruition. Time is pressing and I have much to do. As I said, I will furnish you with as much help as you may think necessary but we or rather you, need to get on. You understand me? If not, your return to my estates and your father can easily be arranged.'

He then drummed his fingers on the table awaiting his reply and Jean, on this occasion, did not keep him waiting.

'Yes my Lord. I'll straight away get on with it but I do need...'

'I'm not interested in what you do or do not need LeBrun. I'm not going to fetch and carry for you. I have said I'll find you a new helper and I will. He'll contact you in the hall, at dinner this evening. Remember, this entire business is now in your care. Not just the design, everything including the needlework. There are enough people around the place of whom to make enquiries. They'll all soon know who you are and more importantly, who you work for. You will find them falling over themselves to be helpful. Now, take this,' pointing at the work on the table, 'and be off. I've a country to run and I don't want to see you again until the work is near completion.'

CHAPTER NINETEEN

Dover

Jean couldn't remember taking his leave from Odo. It wasn't until he reached the door of his room that the full reality of the situation hit him. He was just about to throw open the door when it occurred to him that, lurking on the other side, could be a deranged Thibault poised to spring for his throat or maybe as he'd seen him in Odo's apartment, curled up on the floor, stripped of his self assurance. He tentatively pushed the door open and the room was empty. No Thibault. He let out a loud sigh of relief and entered.

Jean threw the drawings on the table and sat on the edge of the cot, trying to get his thoughts in order. The leather purse was beside him, invitingly showing contours of coin. He picked it up and weighed it in his hand. It didn't occur to him to open it and count its contents. He'd never had money before. Perhaps the odd coin or two but that was about it. Even his travel and passage money to England had been in the care of that miserable toad Gaston.

He put the purse on the bed beside him and looked over to the now rumpled pile of linen which constituted his recent labours. This seemingly endless drama was all getting a bit too much and what was this business with Thibault all about? Where was he now? Despite all his adolescent bragging, Jean had depended on him rather more than he cared to admit. It was all very well being told that he was to be granted another assistant or whatever term the position warranted but he had become used to Thibault and, to be honest, he had grown to like him.

Then there was Mirabelle. Stabbed to death, the Queen had said. Whatever she was, she hadn't deserved that. Obviously the manner of her death and Thibault's bizarre behaviour were in some way connected. The Queen had said as much but like her, Jean found it difficult to believe that Thibault was guilty of the crime. To top it all, Odo had now made him responsible for the production of this monstrous wall hanging. At least, when Thibault was around, that responsibility was shared but not any longer apparently.

Jean heaved himself off the cot and peered out of the window, which was enough to remind him that the day was passing and he hadn't made much of breakfast. After the scene he had witnessed he was surprised to feel hunger but he was starving. He looked at the drawings and wondered about restoring them to their hiding place in the roof, then decided he couldn't be bothered. If anyone thought they were worth taking, they were welcome. He could always replicate them if he had to but there was no way he was going to carry them down to the great hall again.

The purse though, that was a different matter. The tailor responsible for his new garments might have been good at his job but he hadn't seen fit to provide him with pockets. Probably because he thought he wouldn't have any use for them. He did now though. He looked around the bare cell for something which might serve and discovered, under Thibault's bed, a box containing various oddments of clothing, neatly folded, among which was an old belt. With the makeshift blade he used to sharpen his sticks, he hacked a strip of leather from it and carefully threaded it through the drawstring holes in the top of the pouch. He then tied it securely to his own belt and moved it around where it was hidden from view by his cloak. That problem being solved he took himself down to the hall.

It was noon, and the place was bursting at the seams. The fine weather of the last few days had changed during the morning and once more the eternal mist was blowing in from the sea. In fact it was so thick it might as well have been pouring with rain. Consequently, all the labourers, land workers, masons, in fact everyone who worked outside had come inside to escape from the damp and bring their picnic lunches with them. Those who had managed to evade the eye of their overseers and skipped early from their labours were bunched around the huge central fire where they steamed and stank. Since his new wardrobe entitled him to more elevated company, Jean made room on a bench between a master mason and a clerk and he called to one of the servers for food. As bread and cheese was put before him, the master mason, a big fellow with huge scarred hands, leaned forward and addressed him.

'Seen you somewhere before haven't I, young fellow?'

Jean thought for a moment and then realised that this was the man who had been supervising the construction work at the castle and who had ordered Ranulph, the carpenter, to find and prepare a suitable board for him. Then he hadn't seemed quite so jovial but now that seemed a long time ago. Jean grinned back at him and reminded him of the occasion. The man furrowed his brow in thought and then remembered. He then gave Jean a friendly pat on the arm and introduced himself as Guy of Falaise.

'I've overseen Duke William's construction work since he came to power' he said.

'Well' he went on, 'You've come up in the world I must say. It hasn't taken you very long either has it? You must be in favour with the powers that be. My Lord Odo perhaps?'

Jean nodded in affirmation and Guy looked at him through narrowed eyes.

By this time the server had left the table and he leaned closer.

'You'll know something about this if you're that close to the great man. He had a squire, Thibault by name. Been with Lord Odo ever since the battle. This morning, earlier…' he leaned closer and dropped his voice, 'He was seen running across the bailey as though the very devil was after him and some said that his hands were bloodied. Now, what would that all be about then? You would have known him I don't doubt.'

'Really!' Jean said, feigning astonishment, 'Well, I haven't heard anything. Obviously,' he added, 'I did know Thibault. Not well but we have spent some time together.' Then feeling that he owed Thibault some sign of loyalty he went on 'and I have to say, I always quite liked him, found him a straightforward, honest sort of person.'

The mason nodded.

'I've never heard a word said against him, I must say but…' and here he pulled Jean even closer to him and cautiously looked around before saying, 'One of my carpenters was ordered to make a coffin first thing this morning and it was taken into the castle by Lord Odo's men. They brought it out a few minutes later and when we asked them who was in it, do you know what they said?'

Jean shook his head.

'The Lady Mirabelle, that's who. One of the Queen's ladies. Died suddenly apparently. Funny that because I only saw her yesterday and she looked fit as a fiddle and pretty as a picture.' his eyes held Jean's, 'But then, you've met her haven't you? I spotted her talking to you when Ranulph was dealing with that piece of board you asked for.'

Jean, with his mouth full, mumbled, 'Sorry, I hardly knew the lady and as for Thibault…' then with a cautious note of interest, 'Who was it exactly that ordered the coffin?'

This time Guy pulled Jean close enough to whisper directly into his ear.

'The man that's standing right behind you!'

Before Jean had time to turn round, he felt a hand on his shoulder and he knew it wasn't Thibault. Not this time. Thibault's grip was firm, authoritative. This was more in the nature of a caress and he felt a shiver of unease run through him. He shook off the hand and turned. The man was of average height, probably aged some thirty summers. Not muscular but sinewy. His hair was very fair and he was beardless. His skin unnaturally white, his features faintly pocked. The hand that had just rested on Jean's shoulder was now clasped in front of him by his other hand and Jean was amazed by how incredibly clean they were. Not a speck of dirt visible, even under his immaculate fingernails and his eyes? So blue, they were almost opaque and totally devoid of any emotion or interest. Again Jean shuddered but this time inwardly because otherwise the fellow was unremarkable. His dress was that of a superior servant, of similar quality to Jean's newly acquired costume but more sombre and contrasting dramatically with his pallor.

He bowed and when he spoke it was a strange, high pitched voice that emerged from his bloodless mouth. His accent too, was strange. He obviously had not originated from Normandy.

'Master… LeBrun I believe?'

Jean finished chewing the mouthful that had remained unswallowed since the Master Mason had first spoken to him.

'Yes, who wants to know?'

The stranger thrust out a pristine hand.

'My master, the Earl of Kent, has instructed me to…' a minimal pause ensued as if he wanted to be very precise in his choice of word, 'attend upon you. I am to place myself completely at your disposal!' There was an imperceptible stress on the word 'completely.'

Because of what he had witnessed that morning, Jean was feeling more than a little vulnerable. Normally he took things in his stride and confronted problems only when they occurred and it became a matter of self preservation. With Odo, the feeling of fear was ever present but with most other people, no matter what their rank, he soon became relaxed and at ease but with Wulfric Aronnson for that, it transpired, was the man's name, a sense of disquiet never left him. He later learned that Wulfric was the product of a liaison between a Saxon mother and a Norse father although the instinctive dislike that Jean felt for him had nothing to do with this pedigree. The fact remained that, from this first meeting, Jean's guard was up and he took great care never to drop it in Wulfric's presence. It was then the turn of their neighbour, the Master Mason, to feel the hand on his shoulder. Wulfric wanted him to move over so that he could sit down beside Jean but the craftsman was used to exercising his own authority and made it quite clear that there was no way he was going to move over for some mongrel upstart. Added to which, he was twice the man's size. Then Jean noticed the hand on Guy's shoulder stiffen.

No words passed between them but Guy stifled a cry of pain and quickly dropped his challenging stare. He also shuffled himself along the bench without another word and Wulfric insinuated himself in his place. He turned to face Jean and waved a negative hand at the offer of food. His eyes never wavered from Jean's face and Jean couldn't help noticing that he never seemed to blink.

CHAPTER TWENTY

Dover

'Well, Master LeBrun, as I say I am at your... service, so what is it that I can do for you?' Jean started to say something but Wulfric Aronnson held up his hand and went on in his curiously high voice with it's singsong cadences.

'I know of your commission and I think I can say that The Earl, my Lord Odo, has enlightened me as to your progress to date. I know you will forgive me for saying so but it appears that you have much to do and ...' one of his pauses which apparently indicated his search for the right words, 'Perhaps due to your inexperience and youth...' here he bared a set of perfect teeth in what Jean imagined, was meant to be a smile, 'You have no ideas on how to proceed further in your... endeavours.' Once more he used a restraining hand to prevent Jean from speaking.

'Naturally, we are not impugning your artistic ability. That is beyond question, judging from some of your work which I have been... privileged to view.'

Another smile, this time more distasteful than the last and from it Jean guessed the nature of the drawings Wulfric had been shown. Before Wulfric could elaborate further, Jean forestalled him.

'The girls?' Jean said. 'You mean my nudes. You liked them? Are you a follower of the arts or only of that particular sort?'

He held Wulfric's eerie, unblinking stare. He was beginning to feel it was time he asserted himself. He had been promised a servant, or at least an assistant and he was not going to be cowed by a slimy specimen like Wulfric.

'Tell me!' Jean continued, 'I've spent quite a lot of time just lately with Lord Odo and I've been in this freezing castle for two months. How come I've never seen you before.'

Wulfric dropped his head in an obsequious bow. 'I like to keep a... um... low profile, shall we say Master LeBrun. The work I do for his Lordship is sometimes of a ...a ...delicate nature and although I have been in his service since before the Conquest, I ...'

'Before the Conquest? But you're not one of us. I mean you are not

Norman. How did you know Lord Odo before…'Wulfric's eyes locked into Jean's again.

'I was a minor, very minor part of King Harold's retinue when he visited Duke William's realm and Lord Odo found me…useful.'

'Useful! How do you mean useful?'

'I was able to furnish him with … information.'

'About?'

'Oh! Many things. The disposition of Saxon property, the various entertainments our island had to offer and…'

'And what?'

'Oh! This and that. It's not important now. It was a long time ago. Anyway, when Harold was released and returned to England, I stayed in Normandy to serve my Lord Odo. I even accompanied him into battle although not, of course, in any significant role.'

Jean snorted. 'I suppose you're going to tell me that you fought valiantly at his side.'

For a few seconds Wulfric said nothing but his fingers were clenching and unclenching on the table top until his knuckles were even whiter than the rest of him.

'No Master LeBrun, not that exactly. It was not my job to …engage the enemy as such. I had other …responsibilities…'

Another snort of derision from Jean, 'Since you were of Saxon descent, who exactly did you identify as the enemy, or had you so completely changed your colours?'

Wulfric digested this for a moment, running a tongue over his compressed lips.

'Master LeBrun. I think our mutual master would imagine that an… harmonious relationship might be …beneficial… to our… enterprise. We are of different cultures but we all have to make our way in the world by employing such talents as we possess. I am sure you would agree?'

This time it was Jean's turn to think. He had no doubt that Odo had encumbered him with this unpleasant individual in order to keep an eye on him and Jean would be expected to be seen to co-operate. That being the case, so be it. He knew of nobody else in the place that was likely to be of any use to him. On the other hand, it was rapidly becoming clear that he, Jean, was possessed of one weapon against which even Odo was powerless, his talent. It was the one commodity that Odo and Wulfric needed. They might call the tune but without a willing piper, they had nothing and Jean thought he must keep this idea in his mind if it ever got to the stage of Wulfric proving difficult. So he nodded and offered up a friendly smile to which Wulfric responded with one of his own. Again a shudder ran through Jean. What was it about this man? As it was, he held out a conciliatory hand which Wulfric took. Jean was surprised. He was expecting a limp, cold hand but it wasn't like that at all. His hand was as warm as Jean's, a great deal cleaner and his grip was firm. There was an impression however that, had he wished, he could have applied enough pressure to cripple those extremities that Jean relied on for his work. More worryingly, Jean sensed that Wulfric wanted him to know that. Wulfric gently wiped his released hand on a spotless square of cloth that seemed to have materialised out of nowhere.

'To business Master LeBrun. Our time is limited and if we are not to displease our master we must progress. What is it, exactly, that you …want from me, how can I …assist you?'

Jean quickly tried to get his thoughts in order. He needed information, he needed materials, he needed some knowledge of how his work would translate through the medium of the needle. That was all very well. No doubt this Wulfric had the ability to find 'things' for him but he needed more than that. He needed to know where to go and how to get there, who to ask – for God's sake, he was so unprepared he didn't even know what questions to ask. Wulfric was looking at him with expectation mingled, he fancied, with a measure of contempt. Damn the man. He was not going to be intimidated by him. He drew a deep breath and matched Wulfric's faintly supercilious stare with one of his own spontaneous grins. He then started to state his demands in a way that would leave Wulfric in no doubt who was in charge of this operation. He ticked items off on his fingers.

'One, I need to identify and negotiate with the best needlewomen that can be found on the island.

'Two, I need introductions to people of note, who can give me first-hand accounts of those aspects of the battle that need recording.

'Three, I need more canvas and materials with which to make designs. Not that I've used that much up to now but the linen I'm using is not of the necessary quality. It needs to be woven as closely as possible and of good weight.

'Four, I need some form of transport so that I can maintain communication with and oversee work done by the needlewomen. I can't imagine that you know of any suitable embroiderers within the precincts of this fortification, so extensive travel could be involved.

'Five, I need the necessary authority, in writing or by seal, to proceed wherever and whenever I choose in the furtherance of my work.

'Six, I need you to ensure that I am kept sustained in such a way that my abilities to work in a creative and efficient environment are not threatened.

'Seven…'

Jean thought Thibault would have been proud of him. By the time he had finished, Wulfric had actually dropped his eyes and was inspecting his faultless fingernails, spread out on the table in front of him. Over his shoulder, Guy of Falaise flashed Jean a brief admiring wink. Without turning or looking up, Wulfric put out a manicured hand and grasped the neck of Guy's cloak.

'Get out!!' he hissed 'and have a care Master Mason.'

Guy went without even bothering to finish his meal.

Wulfric's eyes came up to meet Jean's, he was smiling again and wiping his hand.

'Really!' he said, 'the sort of people with whom we are expected to mix.'

Jean was, by this time, totally composed, so was his answer.

'Too true, Wulfric, you get all sorts in here.' was invested with just the right amount of irony and whether Wulfric noticed or not didn't bother Jean in the slightest.

'Where would you like me to start Master LeBrun?'

Jean let him stew for a moment.

'I'll tell you where I think we, or rather you, ought to start Wulfric. I think you ought to start by getting me the authority I'm going to need to travel, to interview the nobility and to requisition whatever I think I might need.'

'Whatever Master LeBrun? And what sort of...authority would that be should you think?'

Jean grinned again.

'That's for you to find out my friend. Your job is to serve me is it not? But would you be good enough to inform our Lord and Master that without such authority any further progress will be impossible. I feel sure that you will be able to make him understand, don't you?'

Wulfric didn't move but sat there, his eyes boring into Jean's but his were the first to give way. He was breathing heavily and obviously making a massive effort to retain control. Eventually he slid along the bench, away from Jean, swung an immaculate boot over and slowly rose to his feet. Again he smiled and such was the nature of it that Jean wondered if he had gone too far, especially as Wulfric was lovingly caressing the hilt of his dagger. Jean turned to face him.

'Oh yes Wulfric, there is one more thing I would have you procure for me.'

For the first time Jean detected a slight flush of colour to Wulfric's face and his breath quickened even further.

Eventually he managed to spit out, 'And that would be ...what, Master LeBrun?'

'A dagger Wulfric. I think I ought to be armed, don't you? Particularly as I shall probably be travelling through some potentially hostile parts of the kingdom.'

Wulfric's cheeks had now returned to their customary pallor and he might have been wrong but Jean swore that he could detect a tiny upturn at both sides of his mouth.

'An excellent idea Master LeBrun, we live in …dangerous times do we not?'

'Indeed we do Wulfric, indeed we do. Now be off with you and see about that authority.'

Their eyes locked and again it was Wulfric who looked down first. Without a further word or sign, he turned and walked away. Jean had been so engrossed and concentrated on winning this contest of wills that the hubbub and myriad distractions of the great hall had not existed for him. Now they assaulted his senses and he found himself looking around him to see if his victory had been noticed by any of his neighbours but apparently not. The rest of the world seemed unconcerned by the drama that had been enacted before them but then the thought occurred to him; perhaps they knew something of Wulfric that he did not.

He eased himself from the bench and made his way to the doors. The sun was making a late and watery appearance and the diners were starting to thin out. He blinked at the light and thought to himself, it would be interesting to see if Wulfric could comply with the catalogue of demands he had made. He wondered how he would frame his report to Odo. The grin faded and he trailed back to his quarters, turning over in his mind the information he had gleaned from Queen Mathilde and how he could best dramatise the story in pictures. The passageway leading to his, or as he still thought of it, Thibault's room was the same as all the others in the fortification. Narrow, ill-lit with the occasional alcove set into the walls to facilitate the passage of people coming from opposite directions. It was while passing one of these that he was seized roughly by an arm and dragged into the dark, confined space.

CHAPTER TWENTY ONE

Dover

It was fear that lent him the strength to twist out of the grip and, for a moment, nothing could be heard but his laboured breathing and that of his assailant. He turned slowly and found himself face to face with his recent companion at the table, not Wulfric but Guy of Falaise. The big man whispered his apologies and asked if Jean knew of anywhere quiet, where they could talk privately. As this corridor was one of the main conduits in the castle it was too public for whatever it was he had to say. Still unnerved from the encounter, Jean led Guy to his door and ushered him inside. Guy carefully looked around the bare chamber, tapped the side of nose saying, 'These are fearful times Master LeBrun. It doesn't do to be seen talking in dark corners.'

Jean was about to ask why Guy had chosen to initiate this meeting in precisely that sort of place but Guy continued.

'That Saxon or Norseman or whatever he pretends to be. He was the one that ordered the coffin and the removal of the body of the Lady Mirabelle?' he went on, 'As you know, I've been responsible for much of the rebuilding of this castle, after it was destroyed during the great battle.'

Jean nodded and said, 'Yes, you told me that, what of it?'

Guy looked thoughtful. 'That man, what did I hear him say his name was, Wulfrun?'

'Wulfric' Jean corrected him.

Guy nodded. 'As long as I've worked here, that Wulfric has surfaced every time there's been, how shall I put it, an unaccountable mortality. It's always to bully witnesses into "not seeing anything" or to clear up any mess that might have arisen from the accident because that's what he always calls these deaths, "accidents". These are the only times I've clapped eyes on him so where he hides himself the rest of the time, God only knows; probably under some stone or other.'

'But why are you telling me all this?' Jean asked. 'Just now, in the hall, was the first time I've set eyes on him.'

Guy looked at him from under his bushy eyebrows.

'Look Master LeBrun, Jean isn't it? If I'm not much mistaken, you have just made an enemy. A dangerous one too. I saw how you handled him and, correct me if I'm wrong, but you did it because you enjoy the favour of powerful men, perhaps the most powerful man at present in the Kingdom. Now, if that powerful individual is the one I think he is, don't bank on him being able to prevent you having an "accident". Wulfric may be his man but Wulfric, mongrel cur that he is, has engineered many an "accident" that my Lord Odo neither sanctioned nor indeed knew anything about.'

Jean rubbed his arm. Guy's grip was that of a big man used to handling heavy timber and stone. He nodded as Jean massaged.

'You see lad, I am no weakling.'

Jean nodded his appreciation of this undoubted fact as Guy continued, 'When that worm did that to me down in the hall, I don't mind telling you, I've never felt such agony. I've only just got the feeling back.'

And as if mimicking Jean's action, he massaged his own shoulder, wincing at the memory. Jean looked up at him, still puzzled.

'I don't understand. Why frighten the life out me just to tell me all this. I might look a bit green but it doesn't take a genius to realise the man has some nasty habits. You didn't have to tell me how horrible he is. I mean why bother, we don't really know each other so what's it to you?'

Guy took another look around before sitting himself down on the bed. The flimsy platform sagged under his weight.

'Well,' he said, 'setting aside the warning I've just given you, there is something else I want to talk to you about. You see, I think you might be able to help me.'

Jean groaned aloud at the thought of another complication being added to his life. Guy shook his head and said that he quite understood if Jean felt that he was making unreasonable demands on his time.

'You want me to help you?' Jean asked, omitting any hint of enthusiasm from his voice.

'Yes! Correct me if I'm wrong lad but you are an artist, are you not?'

'Yes.' Jean replied guardedly. 'How did you know that?'

Guy gave a sniff.

'It wasn't too difficult really. You needed a board smoothed. You had linen and charcoal with you so I thought to myself, that young man's going to make a picture and I was right wasn't I?'

He pointed to the roll of linen that Jean had had carelessly thrown into the corner.

'Is that what that's for then?'

Jean nodded and then explained what his commission entailed.

Guy exhaled a sympathetic breath.

'You won't have a lot time to spare then?'

Jean sighed and told him that not only did he have an enormous amount of work in front of him but he had very little idea how to accomplish it. Guy looked slightly bemused.

'Didn't Lord Odo bring you over here especially for this particular job then?'

'Yes' Jean said, 'And believe me, I'm beginning to wish he hadn't.'

Guy still looked perplexed. 'But if he did that, he must have known that you were capable.' Jean nodded.

'Well then, what's the problem. Doesn't he like your pictures or what?'

Another negative shake of Jean's head, 'No, it's not that. The designs aren't a problem for me or at least they're not if someone explains the stories to me that I'm supposed to be illustrating. No it's not that side of it. My problem is getting the designs made up into embroidery.'

He went on to tell Guy about Thibault and about the Queen's interest and her confrontation with Odo just before she sailed to Normandy. Throughout all this, Guy listened carefully and Jean rightly assumed that Guy had a better knowledge of the protagonists in this business than he did. After all he'd been here for years and Odo's reputation would certainly not be a revelation to him. His next words though did surprise Jean.

'Embroidery eh?' he said thoughtfully.

'Yes, embroidery. Why, do you know anything about it? Can you help?'

Guy gave a deep chuckle and held up his meaty hands in front of Jean's face.

'Just take a look at these. Come on lad. Does it strike you that these great appendages of mine are on speaking terms with anything so dainty as a needle? 'Course I don't know anything about it but, ' he gave Jean a wink, 'I might know a man who does.'

Jean's 'Oh yes?' signified that any favours Guy was likely to do him, would be conditional on him helping with Guy's problem, so he asked what it was exactly that Guy wanted from him. Guy merely repeated his last action and once again Jean found himself looking at a pair of powerful hands, the palms of which were scored with years of manual work.

'You know what lad? I can do anything with these. I can build you anything you like, from a monastery to a privy. I can do it in stone, that's what I do really well, or I can do it in wood. I know what to build and where is the best place to build it so that it's still standing in hundreds of years to come. I can look at a plan and tell you how much stone you need and how much it'll cost you and how many men it will take you to do the work. I'm good, I'm very good and the King himself would be the first to tell you that. But there's one thing I can't do and without that one thing all these talents of mine are useless.'

He stopped, lowered his hands and waited for Jean to say something but he didn't because he wanted to see where this was leading. Guy went on.

'I can craft with the best but I can't design to save my life. I can calculate stresses, quantities, load bearings and costings. I can know what it'll look like but what I can't do is make a good representation of it. I can't produce anything like a sketch of a proposed construction I…'

Jean broke in, 'So how do you manage? How do you get all this important work if you can't give your client some idea of what a building is going to look like?'

Guy grinned.

'I get somebody else to do it for me of course but, don't fret, that's not why I need your help. Well, it is actually but not like you think.'

'Go on' Jean said cautiously.

'Well, this is where I think we might be able to help each other,' Guy said. 'You see, my old friend Lanfranc wants me to put some finishing touches to his new cathedral…'

'Whoa!' Jean said. 'This "old friend Lanfranc", as you call him. Isn't he the head of the church over here, the Archbishop of Canterbury or something like that? What's all this "old friend" business? Bit out of your social sphere isn't he?'

Guy had the grace to blush slightly but then he laughed and explained to Jean that although the Archbishop wasn't a friend as such, he had known him a long time, long before he held his present office. Apparently, back home in Normandy, Guy had been commissioned to do some work for him when he was Master of the Cathedral School at Avranches. Later, when he opened a more ambitious school at Bec Abbey, Guy had been responsible for building the necessary extensions to the monastery which, such was Lanfranc's reputation, housed gifted pupils from all over Europe.

Before he could go on Jean interrupted him again to ask him about Duke William because he seemed to remember that, when they were together in the hall, Guy had said something about working for the King. Guy nodded and explained that it was King William who'd introduced him to Lanfranc in the first place. Even later, he worked for both of them at the same time when William built St Stephen's in Caen, of which Lanfranc became the first Abbot.

'Oh yes!' Guy went on enthusiastically. 'That was the year of the great conquest but when the old Archbishop here, Stigand, a Saxon of course, was kicked out and Lanfranc got the job, it was rumoured that your current lord and master was highly displeased that he didn't get it. Anyway, the first thing they both did was to start rebuilding their churches. Lanfranc here in Canterbury and your man back there in Bayeux. From what I hear, Bayeux has fallen a bit behind but considering the amount of time the sainted Odo spends throwing his considerable weight about terrorising people over here, it's not surprising. Give me Lord Lanfranc any time. He really is a man of faith. Whereas the other one...' He snorted derisively and left the sentence unfinished.

Jean, anxious for Guy to get to the point, asked him again how it was that he and Guy could be of service to each other.

'Right,' Guy continued. 'As I've just explained, Lord Lanfranc has just about finished his church, not that I've had a great deal to do with it. The King was more interested in getting this place back into good defensive order and at the end of the day I didn't have much choice in the matter. I'd much sooner have been working on the cathedral but orders are orders and like you, I just have to do as I'm told.'

He shook his head and sighed. By now Jean was starting to run out of patience and not in the mood for a prolonged Master Mason's lament so he repeated his question. What was it exactly that Guy thought they could do for each other?

'Right!' Guy began again. 'The Archbishop has asked me if I would go over to Canterbury and finalise some work on his new church there. You see, I had a lot to do with St Stephen's back home and Canterbury has been more or less built to the same design, that's why I haven't been needed, except in an advisory role. The fact is though, these new churches of ours do require much more engineering expertise and that's where I come in. The weight bearing calculations have to be much more precise and whenever there's been a problem of that nature, they give me a shout, I nip over there, sort it out and that's why I'm needed there at the moment. Although it's not so much the actual church that's the current problem. It's the proposed monastery and associated buildings. Lord Lanfranc is even talking about having to demolish one of the streets in the area and moving it back to allow for these extensions. In fact...'

Jean felt he just couldn't let him go rambling on so stopped him.

'For goodness sake' he said. 'Interesting though all this is, what about me? You said you could help me if I would help you. I'm running out of time here. Just keep to the point.'

Guy gave him a somewhat injured look.

'I'm coming to it,' he said. 'The point is I've been asked to submit some decorative designs for the stonework and, like I said, it's something I'm not very good at. All the designers who've been working on the main church have gone back to Normandy. I could call someone back but, like you, I don't have a lot of time. Now...'

'All right' Jean interrupted, 'I can see why you might need my help with your problem. How exactly do you think you can help me with mine?'

'Well...' he began and to forestall another long explanation Jean held up a warning hand and said.

'Please keep it short.'

Guy shook his head sadly, as if wrongfully denied a possible treat, but said.

'I just happen to know the man who is sort of responsible for the School of Needlework at Canterbury. Now, I couldn't possibly be expected to understand anything about this sort of thing, the sewing and what not but it strikes me that my man, if I introduce you to him, might be useful to you. At least it would be somewhere for you to start. How about it then? If you give me a few hours of your time and that's all it'll take, I promise you, I'll get you an introduction to the School of Needlework.' he clapped Jean on the shoulder. 'Come on, what have you got to lose?'

Jean sat there looking at him for a moment. It was certainly the best, indeed the only, offer of help he'd had so far and he had a rough idea that it was likely to be as good as anything he was likely to get. It also, he recalled, was precisely where the Queen had recommended he looked for the best needlework in the Kingdom. Before committing himself to the arrangement however, he needed to find out a little more about his side of the bargain. Guy assured him that all that would be required of him was to come up with some designs for column bosses and drainage spouts and that sort of thing. Jean need only to spend a couple of hours on site at Canterbury in the company of couple of stone carvers and draw directly onto the dressed stone. Guy, on his part, would introduce him to this contact with the Needlework School.

Jean had to admit that the idea appealed to him, not least because it would get him away from Dover and all the unhappy memories and associations the place held for him. It would be a breath of fresh air to put some distance between him and Odo and with luck it would make it easier for him to give Wulfric the slip should he feel the need to do so. Then there would be a new town to explore. Guy held out his meaty paw.

'Deal, is it then? I shall leave at first light tomorrow so we can travel together if that suits you. It's hardly to the ends of the earth but even with a journey like this, it's as well to have company.'

Jean took the proffered hand and after no more than a seconds thought agreed to meet Guy at the main gate tomorrow at sunrise, in the unlikely event of the sun actually putting in an appearance.

As soon as Guy had left him, Jean wondered about the practicality of this arrangement. He couldn't go anywhere until Wulfric had fulfilled the tasks he'd allotted him. Suppose Wulfric had just gone off in a huff at being treated like an ordinary servant? Suppose he'd taken his complaints to Lord Odo? Well, if nothing else the next few hours would determine how much priority Odo was giving to Jean's work. If he thought it that important, there shouldn't be any trouble but promising Guy a departure on the following morning might prove to be an ill-considered move. Only time would tell.

He looked around the cell for his other belongings. There wasn't very much but he felt that he couldn't afford to throw anything away at the moment. Consequently all his discarded old clothes were bundled up together with what remained of his working materials and the oddments that Thibault had left behind. They didn't amount to very much but then Jean supposed that Thibault hadn't perhaps owned very much. Whatever he had in the way of clothes though, he must have washed frequently because he never stank like most people did in this place, apart from the pristine Wulfric of course. Pity that, because if he had given off an offensive odour Jean might have detected his oily presence before hearing his falsetto tones. He certainly hadn't heard Wulfric enter the room and as he had his back to the door and was busy bending over the bed, tying up his possessions, Wulfric could, had he so wished, have planted his dagger between Jean's shoulder blades and his assassin would not even have been known to him. As it was he nearly brained himself on a beam by leaping up in fright.

'Don't do that!' Jean glared at him.

'I'm so sorry Master LeBrun, did I …frighten you?'

'No you didn't frighten me' Jean snapped back, 'You happened to surprise me, that's all.'

He gave Jean an ironic smile and an even more ironic bow. The man exuded insincerity from every odourless pore. Jean shook his head in exasperation.

'All right Wulfric, what do you want now?'

Wulfric eyed the hastily packed bundles.

'Would you be…leaving us, Master LeBrun?'

'Yes, Wulfric, I would be.'

Wulfric appeared to be pondering this unexpected turn of events and before he could say anything, Jean went on the offensive.

'Come on then! Have you managed to get everything I asked for?' Thinking to himself that in the time he had available it wouldn't be possible to find all the items he'd requested. However, Jean had miscalculated.

Another chilling smile and, 'Indeed I have Master LeBrun.'

Jean said to Wulfric, genuine surprise in his voice.

'Everything! You've found everything, including the authority I asked for?'

Wulfric rubbed his lips with his spotless fingers. 'That was not…easy but, yes you have your authority. Our master is most anxious that nothing, that is…nothing, should stand in the way of this …enterprise. Here!'

He held out a small roll of vellum, through which Jean could detect the outline of a seal. Jean took it and Wulfric cleared his throat.

'Um, when I say that I have everything. There is one item that has yet to be brought to a happy…conclusion.'

Good, thought Jean. 'One item eh? And what might that be? Nothing important I trust?'

'The… er… matter of the…needlewomen. I have not yet had sufficient time to make the necessary enquiries although my Lord Odo…'

Jean did his best not to appear too smug.

'Really Wulfric. Well I should have thought that you of all people … As it happens, I know exactly where to go and I even know who to ask about the necessary work. In fact I'm on my way there tomorrow and I'm…'

'Tomorrow?'

The word came out like a strangled croak. Jean was about to indulge in a smirk of pure delight until he noticed the look of venom in those pale opaque eyes. He decided not to push this one too far. Accordingly Jean made a crude effort at placating him by saying that he was sorry if he'd pre-empted his labours but such was his anxiety to get moving with the project, he felt he ought to make some enquiries of his own. Wulfric said nothing but toyed with the hilt of his dagger while overcoming the anger which Jean had obviously aroused. When he did speak, he reverted to his usual adolescent timbre.

'I'm afraid it's impossible to leave tomorrow. You see, Master LeBrun, I have another…errand to perform for Lord Odo which will keep me …occupied for at least two days and then, of course, I will be happy to…accompany you on your journey to…Where was it you said you were going?'

'I didn't Wulfric. I didn't say where but if you really want to know. And I think you do don't you…?'

Wulfric nodded cagily.

'I'm off to Canterbury' Jean continued, 'And I'm off tomorrow, whether in your company or not, first thing in the morning in fact. All right?'

Again Jean had the distinct impression that Wulfric was struggling to keep control of his emotions. Also he conjectured that Wulfric was trying to work out the effect that this piece of news would have on Odo. It wouldn't have surprised Jean if Wulfric only reported news that he thought Odo wanted to hear and he could well imagine that Odo would not be too happy to think that his artist, together with his purse, might be sloping off, unattended and unsupervised. Just at that moment though, Jean couldn't have cared less. Again he took the view that if his esteemed patron wanted his new cathedral to be adorned with this work badly enough, then he would have to let him get on with it in the way that he, Jean, thought best.

Since his meeting with Queen Mathilde and receiving Lord Odo's subsequent approval, he had stopped worrying about his ability to provide designs which satisfied his remit. These important people might have the power of life and death over him but if he had something they wanted – and it seemed to Jean that he had what they wanted – they would at least tolerate him until they got their hands on it. With this comforting thought in mind, he told Wulfric to run back to Odo and report what he had just been told. He reasoned that if his explanation for travelling to Canterbury the following day was properly articulated he'd probably get away with it. He therefore looked Wulfric straight in the eye and suggested, if Wulfric preferred, they could both make their way to Odo's quarters at this very moment. This, apparently, was not a suggestion that Wulfric favoured.

He failed to return the direct look and studied his boots instead as if trying to spot a stain upon the spotless leather. How on earth he managed to keep himself so clean in this pigsty of a community was a real mystery to Jean. Anyway, after clearing his throat and still intent upon his footwear he eventually said

'Not possible I fear. His Lordship is engaged on important …state business. Um…'

Now that he'd taken his hand away from his dagger, Jean felt emboldened to take a step towards him and decided to press home this uncertain advantage, saying.

'In that case Wulfric, I suggest that you make an appointment for us both to see him as soon as he is free. But I shall have to inform him that the inevitable delay was not of my making but yours. You see Wulfric, I'm not sure you understand the difficulties I'm facing here. I've only just started on this thankless task. There is a long, long way to go before I can finish it and that's just my part of the work. I have absolutely no idea whatsoever how long it is going to take to convert my designs into the finished embroidery and if our esteemed employer wants it in time for the consecration of his new church then he might just be unlucky. All you know about me are from those pictures of girls you've been slavering over. Well it's not as easy as that. This, so far as I can make out, is supposed to be a record of a tremendously significant historical event and that is why it is so important to him. So, Wulfric, if you want us to stand in front of him and say – you can do the talking Wulfric, I'm not going to – "sorry my Lord, we haven't been able to finish it in time because I didn't want Master LeBrun to go scooting off to Canterbury on his own. You can have it next year – or the year after that." Do you really want to have to tell him that Wulfric?'

Wulfric looked at Jean. Confusion all over his face and it occurred to Jean that he might be scary but he probably wasn't very bright. He took a deep breath.

'But… I was ordered not to let you out of my sight. I…'

Jean didn't let him finish.

'For God's sake Wulfric. Canterbury's only just down the road isn't it? Less than a day's ride so I'm told. With your talents, I'm not going to take much finding am I? All I'm saying is that, at long last, I have some idea where I can get this done. I don't know why you're fussing like an old woman, I'm the one with the problem not you.'

Odo's man stood there scuffing his boot into the floor. Eventually he looked up and although he was shaking his head, Jean knew that he'd won when, after some throat clearing, Wulfric announced, 'I shall have to report to Lord Odo. That is as soon as I can. When he is… available. Are you intending to travel…unescorted?'

'No' Jean said. 'I've Guy for company.' Wulfric looked at him sharply.

'Guy,' Jean said patiently, 'the Master Mason whose shoulder you nearly dislocated.'

Wulfric thought for a moment then nodded.

'Yes, of course, I remember the…gentleman.'

'That's all right then,' Jean said, 'because he certainly remembers you.' then added, 'I think he might be useful to us.'

Again Wulfric nodded.

'While you're still here,' Jean said, 'What about the rest of my requests. You said they were all resolved, with the exception of the most important one which I think I've sorted out myself. Transport for example?' he pointed to his pile of belongings, including the all important canvas.

'I'm not walking to Canterbury carrying that lot.'

Wulfric waved a pale hand.

'I have arranged a mount for you. Called Nero, he's in the stab…'

'Nero?' Jean was genuinely surprised. 'Why that's Thibault's horse isn't it?'

Wulfric smirked. 'Not exactly Squire Thibault's horse, Master LeBrun. Squire Thibault owned nothing, hardly the…clothes he stood up in. If it hadn't been for Lord Odo…'

Jean asked, disbelievingly, 'You mean to say that Lord Odo is giving me Thibault's horse?'

'No, not giving Master LeBrun. You have the use of it. The stables will be told to…prepare the animal. It's some time since he's been exercised. I'd better advise them that you will be riding him on the morrow.'

'At sun-up Wulfric. First thing.'

'Just so…Master LeBrun. Oh! The other items you requested… the er…

linen and so forth. I will have it left in panniers at the stable and so far as ...
persons who can help you with your er...story, his Lordship's authority need
only be shown to any suitable veteran of the ...campaign of '66 and you may
be assured of their...co-operation. His Lordship would prefer you to employ
noblemen as your ...source. The common sort can be ...unreliable.'

Jean couldn't resist saying, 'And that would be persons such as yourself,
would it Wulfric?'

He received another icy smile in return.

'Indeed it would Master LeBrun. My participation in the...battle was...
inconsequential.' Upon which, Wulfric made one of his funny little bows
and said that he would find Jean in Canterbury. He turned to leave but Jean
stopped him before he reached the door.

'You've forgotten something.' Wulfric raised his eyebrows, then shook his
head.

'I think not Master LeBrun.'

Jean held out his hand and all Wulfric said was 'Ah!!' as he reached into
his black doublet and drew forth a plain dagger in a leather scabbard. He
meticulously turned it around and handed it to Jean hilt first. For a moment
he retained his hold before releasing it into his custody. A quick nod and he
turned and left.

CHAPTER TWENTY TWO

The Road to Berham

Jean was up the next morning long before daybreak. He'd hardly slept for all the things that were going on in his head. Now that he had a possible introduction to the means of producing the completed work, the embroidery, he was quite pleased that the responsibility for the entire operation had been placed into his inexperienced hands.

He pulled aside the hanging and looked out into the blackness. Well, not complete blackness. There was a good moon and clear stars. At least it looked as though the day might be free of rain which would make the journey a more pleasurable experience. In the pre-dawn gloom, Jean grovelled about, locating and collecting together his property. The purse, which had spent the night under his old, folded cloak which served as a pillow, was re-tied to his belt. The rest of his discarded clothes were added to the few garments that Thibault had abandoned and tied into a bundle. His completed panels were carefully folded, even though he was well aware that they would have to be re-drawn on more suitable material. The only thing which he didn't seem able to find was the dagger. He had no intention of leaving without it because if he was going to be travelling it made sense to be armed. He felt around on the table, where he thought he'd last seen it but it wasn't there. Nor was it lying on the bed so that only left the floor. Down on his knees he crabbed about in the straw until his fingers walked over it, lying under the table. He picked it up, took it to the little window and examined it then gave a low whistle of recognition. The last time he'd seen the weapon was on the floor in Odo's apartment when he had tripped Thibault. So! Thibault's horse and now Thibault's dagger. He pursed his lips. He wasn't sure that he altogether liked being the beneficiary of Thibault's confiscated possessions. He sat on the bed and then reasoned that if he wasn't using them somebody else would be so what difference did it make.

It was beginning to get light and not the usual cold, grey, damp laden light either. The sun had yet to put in an appearance but the reluctant dawn definitely showed more promise than of late. One last look around to make sure that he hadn't forgotten anything, then he hefted his bundle and walked out of the door.

When he reached the bailey, it was filling rapidly with the usual mob of artisans, servants and hangers-on. Most of them were bleary eyed and foul breathed so Jean gave them as wide a berth as possible while he made his way to the tap to wash the sleep from eyes. As he anticipated from this lot, there wasn't much competition for it. There would be for breakfast though. The smoke told him that the kitchen fires had already been set so rather than wait his turn in the hall, he headed straight for the smell of new baked bread in the hope that he might be able to scrounge a crust. His smarter clothes seemed to work in his favour and when he emerged from the kitchens, bread in his free hand, the eastern sky was just starting to fulfil its promise and Jean made his way over to the stables with more optimism in his step than he had felt for a long time.

He hoped that Guy would be waiting for him and indeed he was. What Jean didn't expect was that he was sitting on a cart, behind two ill-tempered looking mules and he wasn't alone. Sitting beside him on the plank seat was Jean's old carpenter friend, Ranulph, whittling on a piece of yew. Guy spotted him and called him over, indicating his companion.

'Remember him Master LeBrun? He's coming with us because Lord Lanfranc wants a new pastoral staff and Ranulph here is the best wood carver this side of the Channel.

When he's done in Canterbury he'll bring this cart back, unless he's wanted over there for anything else. I need it to carry over some local stone to see if we can match it with our stuff from home. Not that I fancy working with it. Too much chalk. Give it a few years there's be nothing left. Got yourself a mount have you?'

Jean said, yes he had and he was just going to the stable for it. He walked to the outer bailey where the stabling was located and stood in one of the doorways, adjusting his eyes to the darkness after the unaccustomed sunlight. One of the grooms approached him and asked his business. Horses were valuable and Jean obviously didn't have the look of someone important enough to lay legitimate claim to one. Jean told him his name and mentioned that Wulfric had made arrangements with the stables for Nero to be made ready for him. At the mention of Wulfric's name, the level of noise subsided and quite a few uncomfortable glances were shot in Jean's direction. The lad still looked suspicious but led him to a stall where he immediately recognised Thibault's gelding. Chomping on the bit, shaking his head and pawing at the straw he was in the process of being saddled and showing some displeasure at the prospect.

Having tightened the girth to his satisfaction, Nero's groom turned to

Jean and spoke to him in Saxon. Jean still hadn't been there long enough to understand anything but the odd word but, to his relief, the lad then addressed him in extremely bad Norman, from which Jean deduced that, although the horse had been exercised around the bailey that morning, he was still full of himself so the young gentleman would need to proceed carefully until Nero quietened down. Jean then asked him when Thibault had last ridden the animal, to which the lad said that it hadn't been for a couple of days but that Squire Thibault had called in at the stable the other night and spent some time with the horse.

The boy went on to tell him that when Thibault left the stable, he had followed him to the door and watched him walk up towards the Pharoes. Apparently there were lots of rumours flying about concerning Squire Thibault. Did the young gentleman have any idea whether these were true? Jean, eager to be off, ignored the question and said that some panniers should have been left at the stable for him and could the lad find them. He had people waiting for him, anxious to be on their way to Canterbury, so if the boy could look sharp.

The groom ran off, reappeared seconds later with the panniers, led Nero outside, slung the bags over the horse's withers and helped Jean to mount. He looked worried and stood ready to grab Nero's bridle and although the horse wasn't too happy with Jean's inexperienced hands, he calmed down when coaxed over to join Guy, Ranulph and the depressed looking mules. The sun was now well up on the horizon. Guy gave a huge wink to Jean on his precarious perch, whipped up his own miserable looking animals and they made their way to the great gate. At the gate the porter demanded his pass and Odo's seal worked like a charm. In fact Jean got an obsequious bow out of it and that was a first!

Guy, whose position constantly required much coming and going on his part, merely had to nod his way through. As they exited the gateway Jean turned in the saddle to see Nero's groom watching their departure. He waved, although whether it was to Jean he was waving goodbye, or Nero, Jean couldn't be sure, although he suspected the latter.

Leaving the precincts of the castle behind him, Jean felt a sense of elation and freedom that he hadn't felt since leaving his home. Guy and Ranulph grinned up at him from their creaky cart, the sun was breaking through the morning mist and even the normally taciturn locals nodded a greeting as they passed. When they came closer to the town though, Nero seemed to find the noise, bustle and foraging pigs too much for his nerves and Jean needed all his inadequate skills to stay in the saddle. Guy called a halt to their progress and instructed Ranulph to take the animal's head until they reached the outskirts on the other side. Once there, he advised Jean to give the horse his head for a mile or two. Then Jean could turn Nero round, come back and rejoin their more sedate pace.

Ranulph obligingly put aside his knife and wood, jumped down and guided them through the narrow alleys, shouting out a warning when he spotted some late-rising householder about to empty the contents of their piss pot from an upper story. Once they were through the worst of the urban squalor, Jean thanked Ranulph, who resumed his place and whittling, and enquired of Guy how long the journey to Canterbury was likely to take. Pointing to Nero, Guy replied.

'With that animal under you, you should be there by noon but us...' he indicated the unenthusiastic mules, 'It'll be more like sundown. Tell you what, why don't you do as I said? Ride some of the steam out of him, come back to us and I'll tell you a place where we can stop and have a break. It's a place by the name of Berham but don't worry about it now. For God's sake, see to that horse before he has you off.'

Since Nero was so obviously impatient to get moving and Jean's arms felt like they were being pulled from their sockets, he was more than happy to take Guy's advice so he pointed the horse's head in the right direction and dropped his hands on his neck.

It was exhilarating for both of them to be galloping along the verges, passing all sorts of people including a group of brightly dressed men leading donkeys, piled high with household wares. There were artisans on foot, identifiable by the tools they carried, the occasional cleric mumbling a psalm, soldiers mounted on heavy horses and many others travelling in both directions and all clearly grateful for what appeared to be the onset of spring. Sheep too. Jean hadn't seen many sheep in his life but here, hundreds of them seem to be driven along the road. All these they re-passed as they trotted back to the small cloud of dust that signified Guy and his team.

As he turned and fell in beside them, Jean noticed that the Mason was sweating heavily and seemed to be expending more energy on getting his mules to move than they spent in pulling the cart.

'Better?' enquired Guy, setting his whip aside.

'Much, thank you. I have to say, I never imagined there would be so many on the road.'

'Well, Master Jean, this is an important thoroughfare. There's a lot of trade between Dover and Canterbury. Dover, as you know, is where we bring in much of our materials and so on from Normandy and the rest of France. Canterbury is a thriving city for commerce so you're bound to have a lot movement between the two. I dare say you'll have passed all manner of trade's people. You see, it's not like it is at home where we all owe our living to some master of other. Here folk trade on their own account and are answerable to nobody but God – and the King.' he added as an afterthought.

Jean nodded thoughtfully. 'This village you mentioned, Berham wasn't it? Look, why don't I go on ahead now and find some tavern or other. Then by the time you get there I can have a drink waiting for you. By the look of it, you could do with something to cool you down. How do I get to it?'

Guy nodded his agreement. 'You can't miss it. Just keep to the road. You have to ride through it to get to Canterbury. Plenty of alehouses just find us one that's reasonably clean.'

Jean waved and once more pointed Nero in the direction of Canterbury and off they went at a comfortable pace because, this time, Jean wanted to observe, a little more closely, the phenomenon of men who were answerable only to themselves and their wits.

CHAPTER TWENTY THREE

Berham

It wasn't long before a church spire, then outlying farms and cottages of a village, came into view. He made enquiries of a fellow traveller and was told that the village was that of Berham.

It appeared to be quite a prosperous looking settlement and, as Guy had told him, there certainly didn't seem to be a lack of available hostelries. Apart from the occasional pig scuttling across his path, Nero was much more placid here than he had been in the chaos of Dover. Many of the inhabitants were intent on their daily tasks and the more industrious goodwives were making the most of the improved weather by attacking winter dirt with fearful looking besoms. Jean couldn't help but notice that some of the women wielding them were possessed of equally fearsome looking bosoms and the sight of a handsome young man astride a handsome young horse riding past evoked some coarse comments and laughter from them. One or two ran a suggestive hand up and down the staves of their brooms and it struck Jean that perhaps these sturdy Saxon women might not be quite as solidly bovine as they first appeared.

He started to look for a suitable venue to meet up with Guy and Ranulph, looking over three or four possible contenders before settling on an establishment at the far end of the village. It looked clean enough from the outside and it had a bench in the sun and a hitching rail for the horse. He could therefore enjoy his drink and keep an eye on Nero at the same time. He tied the horse to the rail and sat on the bench, leaning against a wooden fence and stretching out his legs. He slid the purse around his belt so that he could reach inside it and extract a couple of coins. He had no idea what the refreshments were likely to cost because he had no idea what anything cost but if it wasn't enough, then Guy would have to help him out. That done, he kicked a couple of curious chickens out of the way and started to relax. A few minutes later, a decrepit looking peasant, wiping a continually runny nose on the sleeve of a filthy, ragged jerkin, emerged from the rear of the ale house and Jean wondered if he'd made the right choice after all. Apparently he was only the odd-job man who'd been sent to attend to the horse. Jean made him understand that Nero's only requirement was water which he duly fetched in an old bucket which was leaking faster than Nero could drink it.

The next servant was a distinct improvement and spoke both Norman as well as his native tongue. It then transpired that he was the owner of the place and since most of his customers were Norman he deemed it sensible to learn to speak the language. Having mastered it, he enjoyed most of the trade that passed through the village although, as he explained, business today was on the slow side. His words were drowned by a sudden excited whinny from Nero who became restless, stamping on the ground and throwing his head about as much as his tether would allow. Then the insistent drumming of hoof beats was heard, heavy hoof beats and, on looking back in the direction from which he had come, Jean saw a cloud of dust which, as it got closer, revealed itself as a group of mounted soldiers. One of whom was holding a pennant. They came into the village at a steady trot.

As they drew closer, Jean could see they were a lightly armoured troop of men-at-arms, six in number. They were led by a man who clearly out-ranked them. His head was uncovered and he looked familiar. They rode past the ale house, obviously not intending to take refreshment and it was not until they were some hundred paces clear of the dwellings that their commander held up his hand and brought them to a halt. He then made some gesture with his gloved hand, indicating they should wait for him. He turned and slowly rode back towards Jean and the host, to the accompaniment of more excited neighing and head shaking from Nero.

The ale-house keeper took a step back into the doorway and Jean stood up, automatically going to Nero's head and stroking his muzzle to calm him. When he was about ten paces away, the soldier stopped, dismounted and led his horse towards him, his hand on the hilt of his sword. Jean felt in his doublet for Odo's authority which, he hoped, would prove to be his passport should this encounter prove hostile. As it happened he had nothing to worry about because, as soon as the soldier was close enough, it took him but a second to remember who he was and where they had last met.

Robert Beaumont tied his mount to the rail next to Nero. The two animals were obviously not strangers to each other either and nuzzled each other's necks. Lord Beaumont gestured to the bench for Jean to resume his seat and sat himself next to him, regarding him gravely through narrowed eyes before indicating to the host to bring them refreshment. Beaumont continued looking at Jean until he clapped his hands together in recognition.

'Of course! It's Master LeBrun. I recognised the horse' nodding towards Nero, 'but I couldn't quite place you.'

That's nice, Jean thought, to be considered less memorable than a horse but he instinctively took to this man who, from Thibault's description, was reputed to be trustworthy and honest.

'My Lord' was the best response he could muster before managing to come out with, 'I'm happy to see you my Lord.'

The ale-house owner then appeared with two cups of ale and Beaumont took a long, thirsty pull at his, before continuing.

'I take it LeBrun, that you are still engaged on the Earl of Kent's business; his ambitious enterprise for his new cathedral in Bayeux?'

Since it appeared that everyone now knew of this project, there was certainly no need for secrecy any more.

'Yes, my Lord' Jean replied. 'In fact that is why I am on my way to Canterbury at this moment.' The obvious thought then came into mind. 'My Lord!' he tried to introduce an appropriate note of hesitancy into his voice. 'Would it be at all possible... I mean would it be too much of an imposition if I were to ...'

'Ask me to provide you with the details of our deeds at Hastings so that you might continue with the next episode in your illustrated history?' Beaumont, swirling dregs of ale around, pre-empted Jean.

Jean looked at him, 'But how, my Lord...'

Lord Beaumont thoughtfully rescued Jean by answering the question.

'How did I know that LeBrun? Ah well! I have to make it my business to know a lot of things. Sometimes they are things of great moment and sometimes things of ...' he thought for a second, 'no importance whatsoever. Your business...' he continued, 'would fall somewhere between those two extremes.'

He smiled at Jean.

'Now, finish your beer and tell me how you come to be riding Thibault's horse. I assume, of course, that it is you that has the use of the animal?'

Jean frowned. Something was not quite right. From the very beginning there were lots of things that hadn't been making sense but Beaumont's presence here. Jean thought he was supposed to be up in the middle of England or somewhere equally vague. He thought he would tread warily for the time being so instead of answering Beaumont's question he thought he'd risk asking one of his own.

'I am surprised to see you here my Lord. Last time we met, when you had the goodness to allow me to ask about the events leading up to the battle of Hastings, I, that is we, thought you were headed north.'

Beaumont raised a quizzical eyebrow. 'We?'

'That is my Lord, Thibault and Lord Odo and...'

His Lordship ran his finger around the top of his cup and looked back up the road, to where his followers had dismounted and were resting their horses. When he turned back to Jean it was to look at him thoughtfully again.

'Just tell me how you come to be riding Thibault's horse.'

So Jean did. He decided that he had nothing to lose so he told everything that had happened since last they had met. He told him all as it had happened; his audience with the Queen, Mirabelles's death and the subsequent bizarre behaviour of Thibault, Odo's reaction to it and Wulfric's appearance on the scene. His meeting with Guy of Falaise and his hoped for resolution of the embroidery problem.

'So my Lord' Jean concluded, 'That is how I come to be in the possession of Thibault's horse and on the way to Canterbury.'

Beaumont re-assumed his study of his distant companions before he spoke.

'Yes, lad' he said. 'I know. I know everything or that is, nearly everything.'

'You know... my Lord. But then why...'

'Why ask? Oh! Come on boy. You're not that innocent. I asked because I needed to hear it from you. Do I know you? Of course I don't. The fact that I've met you doesn't mean to say I know you. You are in the service of the Earl of Kent, our Lord Regent. His interests and mine do not always coincide and I'm sure he would be the first to agree with that sentiment, if you have the courage to ask him that is. So I need to hear every side of a story. Who's lying, who is not.'

He leaned towards Jean. 'In a shifting world such as we inhabit, the only real stability and security is to be found in the truth.'

He gave a short laugh.

'You don't know what I'm talking about do you boy? Why I should bother myself with telling you this I have no idea but for your information, I did ride northwards with my small army but I arrived there at the same time as the King's messenger, who delivered urgent despatches into my hands. What those despatches contain is my business but let us say, my recall to this region is regarded by his Majesty as imperative.'

Jean looked down into his empty jug. That answered one of the questions that had been gnawing at him. He decided to ask another.

'My Lord, forgive me if I'm being a nuisance but if you know all about my business here and Thibault's horse and everything, do you know where Thibault is and how he is. Is he all right?'

Beaumont laid a hand on Jean's shoulder. 'Sorry lad. That is one thing I can't tell you. Believe me, if I could I would but I honestly do not know where Thibault is.'

He must have sensed Jean's disappointment because he went on.

'When I saw the two of you together, albeit briefly it occurred to me that you were closer to breaking down Thibault's reserves than most other people.

I know of nobody who could actually claim to know him completely, with the exception of my Lord Odo, who has known him longer than anybody else and treats him as a son.'

Jean nodded gratefully.

'Thank you my Lord, I like to think that we were beginning to get to know each other but did you learn the truth of what happened, with Mirabelle I mean?'

Beaumont shook his head. 'You were probably more privy than anybody else to the circumstances leading up to Thibault's disappearance. You are an intelligent lad, what theories have you come up with?'

This time it was Jean's turn to shake his head. 'I've been thinking about it on and off for the last twenty four hours but I can't remember anything that might throw any light on it. I mean Thibault's behaviour the last time I saw him was sort of odd but...' Beaumont interrupted

'Everybody seemed to vouch for that fact. The fact that he was seen running out of the place, dishevelled, bloody and sobbing like a child. That's certainly not the Thibault known to the occupants of Dover castle.'

'No, my Lord, I didn't mean then. I mean the last occasion when we were alone together. He was strange, for Thibault that is. He was excited, emotional. As you say Sir, he was always so contained but that night, it was as if he'd been drinking or...something.'

A smile flitted across Beaumont's face. 'Thibault, drinking?'

'That's what I mean' Jean said. 'It wasn't the way he behaved normally.'

'Ah!' mused his companion. 'Could it have been on account of the girl then. They obviously knew each other. Perhaps he'd become ...well, you know...smitten. I didn't have much to do with her but from what I can remember, she was a lively young woman, pretty and did the Queen's bidding when Her Majesty thought it might be useful. Perhaps she'd ensnared him and he'd been made aware of the fact. That might have just pushed him over the edge and, well, we all know how it ended for her.'

'The Queen's bidding my Lord, useful...I'm sorry my Lord I don't quite understand. In what way could she...'

Jean didn't need to finish what he was saying. Robert Beaumont could hardly fail to notice the glimmer of understanding in Jean's eye as it turned into a fully fledged fire of comprehension. For the first time Jean began to understood why she had treated him as she did. She was only doing her job for God's sake. What he took for arrogance and upper class snobbery was only her way of dealing with the duties imposed on her by the Queen. Whatever, she certainly didn't deserve to die for it. This new found sympathy for her was now being accompanied by a new found anger with Thibault. Jean made his face a blank when he turned to Lord Beaumont.

'Not Thibault my Lord. I've seen them together on more than one occasion and there was never anything between them. She teased him because, well, you know Thibault? His attitude towards her was never less than proper, as you would expect.'

Beaumont glanced up at the sun.

'Perhaps LeBrun, perhaps. In any event, I must be on my way. As to your original question which I have been skilfully avoiding, the answer is 'yes'. I will be prepared to give you an account of that famous battle but it will have to be at a time to suit my convenience. You will find me lodged at the castle and before you ask, yes it is in the Earldom of Kent and therefore in the gift of Lord Odo. He seldom visits because Archbishop Lanfranc is building his new cathedral in the city and this displeases Lord Odo, who is of the opinion that the cathedral should be his to build and not Lanfranc's.'

He forestalled Jean's next question by telling him that Lanfranc was a favourite of King William and quite beyond the vengeful reach of even the Lord Regent. Then, shading his eyes, he looked back down the road to Dover.

'It looks as though your friend Guy of Falaise is coming to join you.'

Jean followed his arm and indeed saw the dust raised by Guy's cart as it rumbled towards them. The next question was inevitable.

'My lord, how do you know it's him, Guy I mean. Do you know...'

'I've just told you lad, I make it my business to know everything.'

Then he laughed at Jean's perplexed expression.

'I've known Guy of Falaise for years. All of us who are close to the King know him. Like the Archbishop he's a great favourite of William and has worked with him for as long as I can remember. Brilliant engineer and mason; can't draw a plan though to save his life. He has to build miniature models to show to his patrons. Takes him ages and makes him very bad tempered. If you're tied in with him you'd better watch it. He'll be after your skills and if you're not very careful you will find yourself working for two masters.'

'As a matter of fact...' Jean started to say then thought better of it. He stood at Beaumont's horse's head as he mounted. Beaumont waved and rode off.

Minutes later, Guy and Ranulph, both hot and covered in dust, drew in and gratefully stepped down from their hard seat and joined Jean on the bench. Guy called for beer and soon they were slaking their thirst. By the time some bread arrived and Jean's coin had been deposited in the hand of their host they were ready to talk.

'So, young Jean, you've had a meeting with the illustrious Lord Beaumont? Known him for years I have and I have to say, a nicer man I've yet to meet, for a nobleman that is. Waved to us, he did, as he rode past. I expect you bought him a drink?'

It had just occurred to Jean that that was exactly what he had done and he frowned. Guy continued, 'Because it'd be a miracle if he'd bought you one. A fine man and an honest one but it has to be said, a close one. What did he have to say to you then?'

Jean told him of his previous encounter with Lord Beaumont and also that he was hoping to talk further with him when they were in Canterbury. Guy replied it would do Jean no harm to have someone of Lord Beaumont's importance to call on, should he feel the necessity. He placed his empty vessel on the ground, nodded to Ranulph and rose heavily to his feet.

'Come on then, young Jean. Time we were going.'

Jean mounted Nero and, accommodating his pace to that of his companions, continued to Canterbury in a more stately fashion.

CHAPTER TWENTY FOUR

Canterbury

A couple of hours later they were picking their way through a market, the like of which Jean had never seen before. He looked at Guy.

Guy said. 'One of the biggest in the region.'

The Walls of the town loomed high above them as they made their way towards a gateway, around which peddlers were thrusting their wares at disinterested customers who just pushed their way past ignoring them. Occasionally a couple of burly looking men carrying stout staves would clear the way, allowing citizens to enter or leave without molestation. Guy, Ranulph and Jean had to queue until their turn came to enter the city and as soon they we were inside the walls, Guy pulled them over, stood up on the cart and looked around to orientate himself.

'What next then?' Jean asked.

'Stick close together' was Guy's response. 'And if you've any money left about you after treating Lord Beaumont, keep it hidden.'

Jean dismounted, took Nero's bridle and walked behind the cart as Guy led them through the bustling throng. Jean was interested to see that, compared with Canterbury, Dover was little more than a village. There was so much going on that Jean had a job to know where to look next and the noise was almost deafening as people shouted to one another to make themselves heard above the din of livestock. Nero was not at all happy and Jean was glad that he was leading rather than riding him. Apparently, so Guy yelled at him, the livestock market, held outside the walls, had just finished and those husbandmen who lived west of the city, were taking the shortest route through the centre, emerging from the West Gate on the other side. The three of them pulled into a side alley and sure enough, within a short space of time much of the hullabaloo had died down. Leaving the cart in Ranulph's care, Guy walked over to Jean, acknowledging the greetings of one or two local people on the way. Apparently his boast that he was known here in Canterbury was not an idle one.

He dropped a huge hand on Jean's shoulder.

'First time you'll have seen anything quite like this, I'll wager.' he said, grinning.

'Don't worry, it might all seem a bit strange and foreign to start with but you'll soon find your way around and when you do, you'll be grateful to me that I brought you here. This job you're doing for Lord Odo! That won't last for ever and unless you want to return to your former life in Normandy...' he studied Jean with a pair of shrewd eyes, 'and I've a feeling you don't, you've a good a chance of making your way here in Canterbury as anywhere else on either side of the water. Believe me young Jean, you'll thank me for this in years to come.'

For the moment though, Jean was mesmerised by what he saw around him; many houses, most of them poor in appearance. For the most part plain timber frames filled with wattle and daub. The smell was pretty dreadful and not unlike that in the castle but very different from the rural estate back home. It was inescapable and it was everywhere. Since it appeared that, as in Dover, many households kept a pig or other livestock, most of the stench could be put down to animal and human excrement but there were other smells hanging over the place as well. Guy laughed at him holding his nose and said that he would soon get used to it. A lot of the less identifiable odours resulted from some of the trades that were beginning to spring up. Brewing, dying and tanning being some of the worst offenders according to his guide who went on to say that the castle was at the southern end of the town which was relatively fume free. Just for the moment though, why didn't Jean forget about Lord Beaumont and the castle and at least spend the first night at a refuge which was equally comfortable and secure. Jean agreed, happy to let himself be guided by somebody who knew the town. Ranulph having taken the cart off to some unspecified destination, the two of them made their way towards the huge stone edifice which had been visible from way outside the town walls. It was truly enormous and the closer they came to it, the more awesome it appeared to Jean.

It soon became obvious that there was much building work still in progress. The activity here, although just as intense as that in the crowded alleys they'd walked through, was more ordered and disciplined. Jean was thankful for the chance to stop and admire this magnificent building which, to his artistic eye, fulfilled every possible feeling for proportion and beauty. Guy sensed Jean's admiration, said, 'All right, young Jean, when you've had your fill of looking at the cathedral, we'll sort out some lodgings but you're quite right, this building is quite something to behold. I must confess I wish I'd had more to do with it than I have but I'm still proud of my input. As I told you, I was responsible for most of the engineering calculations for St Stephen's back home from which this was copied.'

'Who actually designed it then?' Jean queried.

'A man called Gandulf designed it. A very clever man in that department as you can see from looking at his creation there but he needed me, or somebody like me, to calculate that his ideas were practical. It's all very well thinking up a pretty idea but no one thanks you if it's going to fall down on top of the congregation, are they? We've worked a lot together and we've got a lot more to do I hope but he's not easy. For a man of God he's got one of the worst tempers I've had the misfortune to deal with. Not unlike your Odo in a way although Gandulf is a real man of God, not a pretend one like him.'

'Will I get to meet him?' Jean asked eagerly. 'I could learn a lot from someone who could dream up something like that.'

'Don't know about that,' Guy replied. 'I understand he's moving near to London. Got his own mitre I believe. Could have left by now though I should think, with all this going on…' he indicated the building sites 'Lanfranc will still want to use his expertise. Anyway, you'll see it again tomorrow, we'd better get on.'

So saying he took Jean's arm and to Jean's surprise, started to guide him and his horse towards the city walls again, only this time towards a gate further along. When Jean asked him why they were leaving the city, having only just entered it, Guy merely said that he wanted him to see the new church first because he knew he'd be impressed. That was a good enough explanation for Jean and shortly after exiting the walls, they turned towards a large enclosed complex of stone and wooden buildings which Guy introduced as the Priory of St Augustine.

Jean eyed the collection of ecclesiastical buildings with some misgiving.

'I'm not sure I want to be locked up in a monastery.' he said. 'Not even for a night. Anyway, what makes you think they'll let us in?'

The gate was well barred, the only opening to the interior being a small grill half way up. Guy snorted.

'Course they'll let us in, we're travellers aren't we? They have to give us a bed for the night and even if they say they're full, that magic parchment of yours will get us in anywhere.'

Jean started to make a further objection but Guy stopped him.

'Just listen lad. For God's sake just listen. This place has walls and locks and a big, hefty gatekeeper.' He pointed at Nero. 'You don't want him disappearing in the night do you and you're carrying money. I don't know how much and I don't want to know but, if you think the countryside is full of thieves and vagabonds, a town is ten times worse so take my advice and don't fret, they're not going to be preaching at you all night'

Jean apologised and Guy banged on the door with the end of his measuring rod, an oaken staff he always carried with him. A voice at the grill enquired who they were and within seconds the door was opened and they were welcomed inside by a burly, black bearded man who loomed over Guy by a whole head and made Jean feel like an undernourished midget. As it had taken Jean the best part of a day to get on good terms with Nero, he was slightly piqued to see him nuzzle the boy sent to stable him, with instant affection. Then it was their turn to be looked after and this was the duty of a jolly looking Benedictine monk, well gone in years, who said the Abbott would be having words with them in the morning when they were well rested. This seemed ominous to Jean and he began to doubt the accuracy of Guy's prediction that there would be no sermons.

They were led to a row of featureless cells, not unlike the one he'd shared with Thibault but dry and fairly sweet smelling and he was relieved to see that they were of individual occupancy. Much as Jean trusted and respected Guy, he would not have been surprised if, like many big men, he wasn't possessed of a phenomenal snoring repertoire. He had the feeling that tomorrow was going to be a long day, even allowing for a short session with the Abbott and he didn't want to risk any chance of Guy's snoring keeping him awake. Before bed, however, they were urged to partake of a supper of bread and gruel washed down with a jug of surprisingly good ale. They then took their leave of the other guests, the monks apparently dining in their own refectory, and made their way to their respective cots.

It was a long time before Jean got to sleep. Too many questions were turning around in his brain but it had been, he thought, quite a good day. One of the best since he'd come to England and if it was to be a foretaste of similar times, then life was beginning to assume a rosier aspect. The only thing that didn't occupy his thoughts, was the job that he had come here to do. That made a change. The whereabouts and fate of Thibault was another matter. There was too, a vision of Mirabelle, not as he remembered her, flighty and full of vitality but cold, lifeless and bloodied, which threatened a twinge of remorse which he wasn't quite able to subdue before the onset of sleep.

After a series of sleepless nights, Jean had hoped this one would be better but it was not to be and, by the time he'd clawed his way back to semi-consciousness, he felt lethargic and listless. In spite of this, he was looking forward to getting on with whatever the day had to offer and once Guy had steered him to the trough in the courtyard and he'd sluiced his head with icy water, he began to feel slightly more human. Guy then took him back inside and guided him to the room where they had eaten on the previous evening. Here they broke their fast in the company of many other men, and a few women, of the older sort, all dressed in black but cheerful and friendly.

Guy explained to Jean that these were not incumbents of the priory but travellers, like themselves. Unlike them though, these were pilgrims who'd made their way from all parts of the kingdom to worship at the tomb of Saint Augustine. Holy they might have been but they were a jolly bunch of people and all of them made a hearty breakfast consisting of more gruel, only this time with vegetables, bread and more of their excellent beer which, as Guy informed Jean, was brewed there in the priory. To Jean's relief, the Abbott failed to make an appearance.

After eating they all started to disperse and make their separate ways. Guy counselled leaving Nero in his stable but Jean insisted that he check on his horse's welfare before he left the abbey. The animal seemed happy enough and Jean was pleased to see that the boy who had charge of him the previous evening was there grooming him and making soft whistling noises to keep him calm. Thus reassured, he rejoined Guy, who had been making enquiries about his priestly architect friend, Gandulf. It appeared that Gandulf had yet to leave for his new appointment which, as Guy informed Jean, was that of the Bishop of Rochester. Guy said that he hoped for a meeting with Gandulf before he left but Jean was quick to remind him that his first priority was to establish contact with these needlewomen, who or wherever they may be.

They re-entered the town through the gate they had used on the previous evening, Burgate, as Jean now knew it to be, and made their way through the various construction sites towards the cathedral. Once again the day promised some spring sunshine and even the re-awakened town smells, less obvious here than in that part of town they had walked through yesterday, failed to dampen Jean's sense of excitement and anticipation of what might lay ahead. Once again they found themselves standing some hundred paces from the new church which dwarfed all else surrounding it.

Guy led the way over to a spot where excavations were in progress. Jean supposed they were footings or foundations for some building or other. There was so much going on it was difficult for him to know where to look next but this was something that Guy was particularly keen for him to see so Jean followed his example as he knelt on the ground. Guy then started to pull away some loose soil with his hands although why he should do that when they were surrounded by shovels and trowels, Jean couldn't imagine. Soon though, Guy straightened his back and pointed to the spot where he had been gently digging. Still kneeling Jean leaned forward to follow his pointing finger and to his surprise saw flashes of colour emerging from the soil and dust.

'Know what that is Jean?'

Jean shook his head and scraped a little more soil away, revealing tiny tiles laid in a pattern. They were exquisite and for a moment he was utterly seduced away from all the activity which was going on around them and about which he had so many questions.

'That my boy, is a piece of history. Any ideas?'

Again, Jean shook his head and Guy continued.

'It's been there close on a thousand years probably, although nobody can be sure exactly how long. It's Roman. You know about the Romans?'

Jean scratched away, uncovering more fragments. He settled back on his haunches before he answered Guy somewhat impatiently.

'Of course I know about the Romans. Back home we often dug up odd bits of pottery and the occasional coin which my father said had lain hidden since those early days. But I've never seen anything like this. It's beautiful. What was it?'

Guy let out a regretful sigh. 'There again, nobody knows exactly but Prior Gandulf reckons it's a piece of pavement or perhaps the floor of an important man's villa or home.'

Suddenly a shadow loomed over them and they jerked their heads round, shielding their eyes from the sun to try and make out who or what it was. Jean felt uncomfortably vulnerable when he was on his knees. A voice said, 'That is indeed what Prior Gandulf thinks.'

The figure moved into their line of vision and Guy, moving faster than Jean had thought possible, sprang to his feet with Jean not far behind him. Facing them and smiling, stood a man of middling age, sombrely dressed in a Benedictine habit. It was not, however, coarsely woven, as with those Jean had seen at the Priory but fine and tailored to fit. He was about Jean's height, with fine features, an aquiline nose set below his tonsured head which was uncovered. When he laid a hand on Guy's arm as a gesture of friendly greeting, Jean noticed that he wore a large ring on his wedding finger. His eyes were grey and alive with intelligence. At the same time they possessed an almost mischievous twinkle as Guy and Jean bowed their submission to his obvious authority; an authority, which he wore with dignity rather than arrogance. While he spoke their language perfectly, it was with an accent that Jean couldn't quite place. The tone was, however, melodious and pleasing to the ear, 'Welcome back Guy, it is good to see you again' his hand still clasping Guy's elbow. He turned to Jean. 'And you, I imagine, are Master LeBrun. You too, are most welcome to Canterbury.'

Guy bowed his head again and said. 'My Lord, it is good to be back here and I am most happy to see your Lordship but how…?' gesturing to Jean.

The cleric waved his free hand heavenwards and laughed.

'No divine intervention, I assure you, Master LeBrun. No wizardry either.' He moved his hand from Guy's arm to Jean's and Jean's immediate impression was that he had never yet met a man like this. One who radiated this uncommon combination of authority, humility and intellectual power. The noble cleric smiled.

'Robert Beaumont was my informant. On his arrival in Canterbury, he came straight to me with...' he paused momentarily, 'Certain dispatches from the King that would brook no delay. The business of state concluded, he mentioned he had passed you on the road. I was therefore expecting you, therefore no mystery and no need for introductions. Except of course, Master LeBrun you probably have no idea who I am!'

Guy started to repair this omission but Jean stepped forward.

'You are the Archbishop, my Lord. Lord Lanfranc.'

As he said it, he hoped that he had not been too presumptuous. Lanfranc gave another of his warm chuckles.

'Beaumont said you were a bright young man. That is good. I like to have bright people around me. Guy here can vouch for that, can't you Guy?'

Without waiting for an answer, the Archbishop turned to Jean again.

'I also hear that you are a gifted draughtsman and artist. As such you are presently engaged on a project for my noble brother Lord Odo. I hesitate to use the word "commission" for I also understand that you are the son of the steward of one of his estates in Normandy. Therefore you are compelled to do what he orders you to do – whether you like it or not.'

His keen eyes twinkled as Jean nodded his acknowledgement of this accurate summary of his relationship to Odo. The Archbishop continued while Guy looked on as if he were a proud parent.

'Time did not allow me to learn of this project in any great detail but perhaps a little later on in the day,' he frowned, trying to recall his commitments, 'Say, towards the end of the afternoon, you might care to discuss it with me. I imagine that is why you are here, as part of your work. You never know, I may be able to assist you in some other way. What do you think Guy?'

Guy eagerly nodded his agreement.

'That's why I brought him here my Lord. He is going to help me with some designs – he's very good my Lord, as you shall see and I promised to introduce him to you because Jean has a problem which, if your Lordship pleases, you might be able to help him solve.'

This, Jean found a little confusing. Although Guy had made mention of the Archbishop he'd said nothing about Lanfranc being the one to help him to the School of Needlework. It all seemed very unlikely to Jean and his old suspicions re-surfaced. Had Guy got him here under false pretences? Was it just a ruse to use him and he gain nothing in return? The two older men looked at him with mild amusement.

Guy patted his shoulder, 'Don't worry, boy. I haven't misled you. I promised I would find someone in Canterbury who will help you and I have'

Lanfranc then said, 'To be plain, my son, until you tell me what it is that you are seeking here, I cannot tell if I can help you or not but you heard me just now when I said I liked to surround myself with gifted people?'

Jean nodded, 'Yes my Lord'

'My other proviso is that they be honest as well. Be assured, Guy here is an honest man and he would not have brought you here if he thought he could not further your interests. You and he are artisans and if your work is to be exemplary you must needs be true to your calling or your art. Now politics…!' he turned the ring around on his finger and looked towards his church for a moment. 'Sadly, politics are a different thing altogether and calls for different skills; skills that are not always as praiseworthy and laudable as those possessed by yourselves.'

He smiled ruefully at Jean.

'I am sometimes called upon to practice those sorts of skills. I only wish that I could restrict myself more to the honest kind but as well as a man of faith, I am a man of State. Sometimes the conflicts with which I am faced cannot be resolved by fair means so…' he raised his hands heavenwards. 'We can only do the best we can.'

He smiled at them both.

'So if I can be of any assistance to you Master LeBrun, it will be to the best of my ability but this one…' putting his hand on Guy's shoulder, 'This one, you can depend upon. Until later then.'

He turned and walked towards another group of clerics who were standing further off and Guy said.

'Well?'

Jean watched Lanfranc's retreating back disbelievingly

'So that is the man who is going to help me?'

He turned his gaze back to Guy.

'Why should he. Why someone like him should bother to spend his time listening to my problems, especially as I'm here are at the behest of Lord Odo. According to what you say the two of them have little reason to love one another. Why is he going to want to bother with me?'

Guy, who had also been watching Lanfranc engaged in conversation with this other group of monks, didn't even bother to return his look. He just gave a 'humph' of indignation saying, 'Come on lad, they're chalk and cheese those two. My lord there.' pointing at Lanfranc's back… 'Is a saint compared with your man. I'm not saying that he'll put himself out for you because he likes you, he's far too important for that but if he thinks you might be useful to him, that's quite another matter. He's told you, he's heard from Lord Beaumont that you seem a bright young man and he and Robert Beaumont see eye to eye on many things, so I've heard. He values intelligence and quickness of wit because he can use them to his own advantage, not only his own advantage, mind you. The advantage to the Church and State are equally important to him. That's the big difference between your man and mine. One does nothing that doesn't further his own ends, the other sees his own interests as inseparable from those of the King and country he serves.'

'I hope you're right Guy' Jean said.

He took another look around him.

'Now what are we going to do? What about this work you have for me? The sooner I have finished with that, the sooner I can make a start on my own work.'

Guy pushed his cap to the back of his head and scratched it.

'That's fair enough but I need to make contact with some of my people first, to see exactly what it is they're working on at the moment. Tell you what, stick with me for a while, get a feel for the place and as soon as I can find Etienne I'll introduce you and he'll be the one show you what's wanted.'

For the next few hours Jean trailed around the complex of building works, following Guy and standing by while he talked to various craftsmen, none of whom seemed to go by the name of Etienne. While it was all quite interesting to see the work that was going on and the sheer scale of the operation; footings being dug out, ground levelled, walls going up and in one place what looked like the beginnings of cloistered walk, Jean was getting impatient to see what his side of the bargain was going to entail. After, what from his point of view, was another pointless meeting, he suggested that since they were right under the shadow of its great walls, he would quite like to enter the cathedral and have a look around. Guy agreed that was probably a good idea and that as soon as he had located Etienne, he would bring him to meet Jean and they could talk inside.

Accordingly Jean left him talking to yet another artisan; he seemed to know every one of the hundreds of them working on the site, and took himself off. He liked Guy who was easy company but felt he needed some space to start to get his own thoughts in order. How he was going to handle the meeting with the Archbishop for example, and initiate another get-together with Lord Beaumont.

When he entered the great doors of the church, he became immediately aware of how different it was from the churches that he had hitherto entered. Not only the scale, it was far, far larger than anything he'd seen before but the detail and most of all, the light. All places of religious houses in his experience had been ill lit and dark. Even the abbey where he'd spent the previous night was no exception but this building seemed to attract light into its interior like nothing he'd ever seen before. Not only because of the use of openings in the fabric of the building, many of which appeared to be glazed with that miraculous glass material to which he'd been introduced at Dover but the soaring stonework seemed so light in comparison with anything he'd ever seen before. It was, without a doubt, the most beautiful building he'd ever seen.

Religion was not something that Jean thought a great deal about. The 'hereafter', whatever that was supposed to mean, was far too remote for him to contemplate and he had always questioned the 'logic' of religious belief, ever since he'd discovered that his village priest possessed appetites which hardly matched the liturgy he rammed down his congregation's throats. This first introduction to the interior of the new cathedral at Canterbury almost caused him to reconsider. Not quite though. For him this was to experience the beauty and ingenuity of man's work, not God's. He thought this building wonderful and was quite happy just to be seduced by its very magnificence.

As he strolled around the great space and breathed in the detail of the construction his attention was suddenly drawn to a figure emerging quickly and silently from a side chapel. It was too far away for him to determine, it's sex or it's occupation but there was no doubting it's sense of purpose as it moved out into the Nave, away from him and towards the Choir. The church was by no means empty and many craftsmen were still occupied with the interior of it. Other visitors and clergy were in attitudes of prayer and there were plenty of people, such as himself, who were merely there to stare and wonder.

Why then, should this brief shadow fleetingly crossing his vision as it did, engage his attention as it did? That was easy. Wulfric! This time though, Jean thought he'd spotted him first and that idea pleased him no end; his turn to surprise Wulfric. Perhaps nonchalantly tap him on the shoulder and ask him if there was anything that he could do to help him or even just to creep up behind him and yell in his ear. That idea he rejected as soon as he'd thought of it. Knowing Wulfric as he did, he was just as likely to end up with a dagger in his ribs.

As Jean moved quietly towards the choir he automatically felt for his own dagger, still at his back, hidden within the folds of his cloak. As he moved, he tried to keep the figure within his sight but it wasn't easy. People walked in front of him all the time but he could still just distinguish the dark shape as it appeared to move through the choir stalls, stopping at frequent intervals and crouching down. Whatever it was that he was doing, his behaviour was somewhat bizarre even for Wulfric.

As Jean moved closer, he kept the huge, ornately carved pulpit between them so, for a moment Wulfric disappeared from his view but Jean was determined to keep the element of surprise if he possibly could and having rounded the pulpit and having the choir stalls in view, Wulfric was still there with his back to him. Better and better! Again he crouched down and then Jean was behind him. It was probably the darkest part of the church, with only a few sconces at intervals along the stalls so it wasn't until this point, after Jean had administered a sharp tap on Wulfric's back, that he realised his pathetic blunder.

The figure gave a most un-Wulfric like scream, reared up or tried to for it appeared to have it's foot caught in it's black gown and after grabbing unsuccessfully at a choir stall, it fell back on it's backside, making the most unchristian like comments as it did so. Then it was Jean's turn to jump out of his skin when he felt a heavy hand land on his shoulder. Caught between the desire to investigate the apparition that sprawled in front of him and protect his own back, self preservation won out and it was Jean's turn to swing around on his assailant. In doing so he lost his own balance and fell back on the girl who, unfortunately for her, had all but regained her own feet. They went down together in an undignified heap and all Jean could hear was Guy saying,

'This is a church Jean, you're not supposed to be larking about like that in a church!'

The girl, on whom Jean had just fallen, was far less decorous in her choice of words and it occurred to him that it should have been her that was more deserving of Guy's admonition. Eventually they both scrambled on to their feet and ignoring Guy which, for Jean, was not difficult, he turned again and got his first good look at her. Headdress awry and almost purple with indignation, she was not quite as tall as him, with turned up nose and fair complexion. The disordered headdress revealed wisps of blond hair and dressed in black as she was, Jean was again reminded, perversely, of Wulfric.

Her blue eyes blazed out at him in fury and her language, incomprehensible but leaving Jean in no doubt as to its meaning, was little short of a physical assault. In fact, had they found themselves on unconsecrated territory Jean had little doubt that she would have caught him a fairly hefty thwack around the head with one if not both of her delicate hands. As it was she turned away with as much dignity as she could muster and swept out of the choir stalls and through a door behind the alter.

Jean turned to Guy and asked,

'Who on earth was that?'

'Haven't a clue' Guy said. 'I thought from the way that you were fooling about, you might have known each other.'

'We were not fooling about, we were…it was an …Oh! Never mind. What on earth was that language she was using and what was she saying.'

'Anglo-Saxon, lad' Guy replied. His seamed face cracked even more with the broad grin that it wore. 'Very expressive isn't it? Called you all sorts of things she did.'

He reflected for a moment. 'Even I hadn't heard of some of them before but I dare say you got the gist of it all. Anyway, if you've quite done with making a spectacle of yourself, I've found Etienne so come on, he hasn't got all day.'

CHAPTER TWENTY FIVE

Canterbury

As they walked out of the church together, Jean again asked Guy what precisely it was that Etienne wanted him to do. Guy dropped his massive paw on Jean's shoulder, in what had now become a familiar gesture and said,

'It's ever so simple and it isn't going to take you long, I promise you. Reckon you'll be done in a couple of hours.'

They threaded their way through the various construction gangs working in the precincts of the cathedral, eventually finding themselves in an area at the southern end of the church which, as Guy explained, was the site for the new Priory that he had mentioned. Here there was an enormous pile of blocks of white stone of all sizes but still requiring their final dressing. As they walked through them, Guy caressed them as if they were his favourite children.

'Lovely, aren't they?' he said. 'Quarried and rough cut to size back home, then shipped over here for finishing, carving and assembling. Nothing like it, this Caen stone. Lovely stuff to work with.' Guy was beaming with pride. 'All numbered and identified, every single one of them. It was me that thought of that. Well, me and Gandulf and it works a treat and now we don't even have to bother to transport all the workforce over here. Most of these men are native artisans and very good they are too. Learn quickly and most important, they respect the stone. Ah! Here we are. Meet Etienne. He's the mason in charge of this project and he'll explain what it is he wants from you.'

Etienne, much to Jean's relief, turned out to be a Norman and typical of those who worked on the estate back home. He looked slightly wary of Jean but on being assured of Jean's credentials by Guy, he soon warmed and started to explain what it was that he wanted doing.

He led Jean over to another pile of some fifty stone blocks of equal size. About two pieds square. They were better finished than the rest and quite smooth.

Like Guy, Etienne obviously felt some empathy with his native material and continually stroked the blocks as he talked. This stone was to be the material for a large cloister for the exercise and meditation of the brethren, some of whom were presently housed in the old Priory in which Guy and Jean were presently lodged. The blocks that now surrounded them were to be the bosses for the columns that would form the inner square of the cloister and apparently it was Gandulf who had ordained that each boss should be carved with a different design. That was where Jean came in. Etienne assured him that there was no reason why the designs could not be repeated on the opposite sides of the square, the distance between being far enough from each other for any duplication to be noticed. All he wanted Jean to do was to mark up the blocks that sat in front of them so that his masons could commence the carving.

Jean thoughtfully looked the blocks over and said that he'd do his best but he would require materials on which and with which to sketch. Etienne didn't let him finish. Instead he guided him over to a trestle on which were to be found, among the various chisels and hammers, a bundle of charcoal, conveniently cut or broken into equal lengths. He presented them to Jean and said that if he would draw his designs directly onto the faces of the stone blocks, his masons would carve them out, giving them whatever relief they deemed necessary. He suggested that Jean might like to try one and see how simple it was. To which Jean replied that if it was all that simple why did they need his help. Etienne and Guy exchanged rueful looks and Guy explained, 'I've already told you lad, the actual masonry work, the carving of the stone isn't a problem. You draw your design on the side of the block and our lads will chip it out in no time at all. What they can't do, or me and Etienne, is to come up with a whole lot of different designs for each boss. We've tried and after about a dozen we just run out of ideas. That's where you come in. Come on Jean, I thought I'd told you all this.'

Jean still wasn't totally happy that he was the right man for the job but decided that the sooner he started, the sooner he could discharge the obligation. He collected the charcoal and told them to leave him to get on with it. They nodded happily and having solved one problem, they started to talk about the next one as they wandered off to look at another part of the project.

Jean watched them go, turned to the stone, ran his fingers through his hair and started thinking.

In the event he really didn't have to think all that much because it was very simple. Within the space of a couple of hours he'd finished about a third of the available blocks. He only drew on the one side because he'd assumed that the masons would be able to copy their work on to the other three. As usual he didn't know where it came from but out of his head there emerged so many different shapes and patterns that by a process of permutation he was able to achieve a huge variety of styles and configurations. Loops, whirls, petals and geometric shapes flowed effortlessly and it was only the physical discomfort of having to lay flat, in order to deal with the blocks at the bottom of the piles that presented any problem. As usual, he was so engrossed in his work that the return of Etienne and Guy went completely unnoticed. It was only when he rose stiffly from finishing one of the lower stones and was stretching that Guy's whistle of appreciation made him aware of their presence.

Etienne walked around his work and Jean could see that he was pleased by the way he was nodding to himself. Occasionally he called over one of his masons to illustrate with his hand the depth of relief he thought would be applicable to a particular design. As soon as Etienne had rejoined them, Guy looked at him.

'Told you didn't I! Told you he could do it. Well, what do you think?'

Etienne rubbed his square unshaven jaw.

'Well!' he said eventually. 'Yes, I think that might do. Do quite well as a matter of fact.' his face then relaxed into a genuine smile. 'I'll get them working the stone right away. Give us a couple of weeks, lad and you can come round and see what they look like when they're finished.'

Jean picked up a discarded hank of material and wiped the combination of charcoal and stone dust off his hands. 'Thank you' he said 'I'd like that.'

He'd already put that behind him though. He didn't want to be late for his appointment. He turned to them both, 'Look, I have to go. I have to see the Archbishop. Where am I likely to find him, Guy?'

'In his smart new palace I should think.' he replied, 'We passed it earlier on today, you must have seen it, it's big enough.'

Jean looked around him, 'You mean that huge stone building over there, is that it?'

Guy told Etienne he'd be back in a few minutes and Jean was led to the large building, still unfinished, which stood but a short distance away. Again there was the activity of construction work and the air was filled with the shouts of workmen, the ring of chisel on stone and the creak of pulleys as they raised blocks to the higher elevations. Guy took him through a yard to a door in the building, of which the ground floor was obviously in use. A guard, on hearing of Jean's appointment, shouted to a colleague inside. Guy said.

'Find your way back to the Priory can you?'

He gave Jean the, by now, customary pat on the shoulder and Jean was left standing, waiting to be summoned into the great man's presence.

He didn't have to wait long and soon found himself being ushered into a room which looked like a combination of library, architects office and workshop. Books, charts and plans covered every available surface and, like the cathedral, the atmosphere was light and airy. The Archbishop was talking to a monk so Jean just stood to one side of the doorway until Lanfranc had finished his business. That done, Lanfranc accompanied his clerical visitor to the door and indicated that Jean enter the room. He gestured to a large desk and Jean walked in and stood by it. The Archbishop waved a friendly farewell to the monk, then joined Jean at the desk and busied himself for a few moments with a pile of documents. Having found the one for which he had been searching, he scanned it briefly, returned it to the table and gave Jean his full attention.

'How do you like this town of ours, Master LeBrun. Found anything to engage your interest?'

Jean answered that he thought His Grace's cathedral was most impressive and that the bustle of the city very much to his liking. Again, that steady look.

'Ah! Yes Master LeBrun. You are young and so is this city although, as Master Guy has told you, it has a long history. What you see now though, is a new and vibrant city. Not only the buildings, which will of course transform the look of it from what it once was, but there is also an energy which derives from its developing commerce and its relationship with the outside world. It is quite exciting so it is only natural that someone of your years should sense that excitement. To practical matters however, I have some prior knowledge of your current occupation and as I understand it, you have come here to locate a centre of needlework.'

'Yes my Lord' was Jean's instant reply. He continued slightly self defensively, 'Due to happenings over which I have had little control, I regret that I am falling somewhat behind in my work. I really must start. That is, Lord Odo, he...' his voice trailed off. The Archbishop gave him another long look.

'Ah yes, Lord Odo. I can quite see why you should not wish to displease him. In my experience, he is not a man who keeps his displeasure to himself. Yet, I understand that while you have been here, today is your first day I know, you have spent much of your time assisting one of my masons. If your work is so pressing how come that...'

Jean rudely butted in. 'I had promised Guy, your Grace. He said he would introduce me to someone who had knowledge of an embroidery centre in the town if I could help him with one of his problems. So I did.' he finished somewhat lamely.

Lanfranc's smile put Jean at his ease.

'So you have fulfilled your part of the bargain and Guy has not.'

Jean dropped his eyes downward.

'Yes my Lord. I...well I trusted Guy. I think Queen Mathilde might have helped me but she sailed off to ... Guy was my only chance.'

The gentle smile graduated to a gentle chuckle. 'Do not worry Master LeBrun, you did quite right to trust Guy of Falaise. As I told you this morning, he is a good man and will not let you down. Your instincts on this occasion were good and I am a great believer in instinct.'

He paused and looked again at the document he had found. Once more he replaced it and continued.

'Guy was telling the truth when he said that I am the man you seek, Master LeBrun and I can indeed obtain an introduction for you.'

This time the silence was of Jean's making. Eventually he found his voice.

'You, my Lord? But you are the Archbishop... I mean you're close to the King himself... How is it that you... embroidery is not...'

Lanfranc chuckled. 'Oh but it is Master LeBrun. It truly is. The church, my palace here, the priory. Not just stone and mortar. Clothes, vestments, alter covers, wall hangings, these are all the things that follow the building and to have those of the quality that we seek, we must have needlewomen of the highest order and that is exactly what we have here in Canterbury. Historically, the weavers have always had an important place here in the town and now we have a school of needlework to rival anything else in the known world. I am patron of that school Master LeBrun and if I so instruct them, they will work with you.'

Jean started to say something but Lanfranc went on.

'I should perhaps warn you that they may not do so happily. The school is controlled by a Saxon noblewomen and most of her pupils are of her race although she does use a few Norman ladies, albeit grudgingly.' He gave a melancholy smile. 'The Saxon tradition in this art is superior to anything we have in France although in Italy...but that is another matter. The fact is that I have established a good working relationship with the Lady Beornwyn and as her school is dependant upon my patronage, she is usually happy to accommodate my requests – for a fee. I prefer this type of arrangement. Unlike some of your Norman brethren, I have a respect for the culture and traditions of this island's people. Not better than ours necessarily, but different.' he then continued, almost to himself. 'The fact that I have been responsible for replacing most of their senior clergy with our own nominees is quite another facet of my role here.' another melancholy smile. 'Nothing to do with your problem, Master LeBrun although Lady Beornwyn might disagree with me.'

He walked around to the other side of his work table, resting his hands on it, fingers splayed so that the ring became even more prominent.

'I will give you a letter of introduction which should be sufficient.'

He took a small piece of vellum from the table, together with a stylus and began writing. He looked up at him momentarily.

'You might wonder why I am taking this trouble over a project initiated by my Lord Odo, my fellow Regent in the King's absence. One who, I might add, has little regard for me. Well, young man, to be honest with you, I am taking a leaf out of your book and working on my instincts. That and the recommendation of Lord Beaumont, he thinks that once you have finished this work for your liege lord, you might be of use to me. Would you mind that?'

He looked at Jean, head on one side, still with a half amused expression on his face.

'Would you?' he repeated.

Jean did not need long to think about it and told Lanfranc, quite unguardedly, that he would be happy to carry out any commission for him that The Archbishop thought fit. He then added the hasty proviso that he should be allowed to complete his present task before he undertook anything else and even then he would require Lord Odo's consent to such an arrangement. Lanfranc nodded his agreement then looked at Jean seriously.

'A warning, Master LeBrun. Wulfric is in Canterbury.'

That brought Jean back to earth with a bump. 'Wulfric, my Lord. But I only arrived...'

'Yesterday, yes I know. So did he. He will know your every movement of course. I would suggest that you make it your business to know his. That is all. I will arrange for one of my servants to take you to the School and I wish you success in your dealings with the Lady Beornwyn.'

Before he had finished speaking, a manservant had entered the room and stood waiting for Jean at the door. Jean stammered out his gratitude to Lanfranc and found himself ushered out of his presence.

He was led through the courtyard and back to the cathedral from where they turned west and made their way through a wide thoroughfare thronged with people. The servant was hurrying him along at a brisk pace and much as he would have liked to have questioned the man about what was going on around them, he needed all his breath to keep up with him. Soon though, they arrived at a large building which stood in the angle created by two roads.

'You would like me to announce you, I suppose?' The servant looked bored.

'Well, yes,' Jean said. 'if it isn't too much trouble.'

The man appeared to think for a minute, then walked up to the oaken door and banged on it, hard. Nothing happened. He gave a resigned sigh and repeated the action. This time footsteps could be detected moving behind the door and after what seemed like a painfully long time, it started to creak open. A small but powerful dwarf of a man was revealed in the opening. From under bushy, grey eyebrows he studied them each in turn, eventually resting his gaze on Jean's guide who, in the ensuing silence, uneasily shifted from foot to foot. Eventually Jean's guide coughed nervously and asked if it would be possible to disturb Lady Beornwyn for a few moments as Lord Lanfranc had sent this young man, here he waved an apologetic hand in Jean's direction, to seek her advice. The eyebrows shifted to him and then back to his guide.

'No!' he growled and slammed the door shut.

The servant, who Jean learned was called Christian, only shrugged his shoulders and turned away.

'Just a minute' Jean said, stopping him. 'Is that it? Lord Lanfranc has given me his letter of introduction to this Lady Beo… thingy, whatever it is. Are you going to leave it like that, without trying again? Just on the say-so of some idiot doorman?'

Christian shrugged again and said, in a voice that was far from apologetic.

'If Warin won't let you in, that's it. Believe me, young sir, nobody, not even the Archbishop himself, can get past Warin to see the Lady Beornwyn if Warin so decrees. If I might be permitted to advise you! Try again tomorrow and if you are not successful then, the next day. At least you know where the School is. I shall, of course, tell the Archbishop but as I say, he can do little more to help you. Now sir, if you will excuse me.'

A nod of the head and he was off, back in the direction from which they had come. Jean just stood there, watching Christian's departing back and swearing mildly to himself, partly at Christian but mainly at the wretched doorkeeper who had denied him entry.

What a let down. All right, he thought as he pushed his way through the crowded streets, I will try tomorrow. And the next day and if necessary, the day after that and the day after that. He was not going to be baulked by some venomous gnome and his, oh so high and mighty Saxon mistress, He patted the pouch hanging at his belt. Not only did it contain money but written authorities from the two most important men in the realm. Saxon noblewomen indeed. Who'd won the damn war anyway? He was so engrossed with these ungenerous thoughts that he failed to see Etienne and Guy, until he bumped into the substantial form of the latter.

'Watch what you're doing, cretin…' Guy began to remonstrate, until he registered who it was that had barged into him. 'Hello, young Jean. What's upset you? You look as if you've just come from a meeting with Wulfric.'

At the mention of that name Jean automatically looked around and hissed back.

'Sh. He's here somewhere.'

Guy grinned. 'I've no doubt he is but you won't see him. Not until he wants you to that is. Anyway, who told you he was here. It's not that that's put you in a bad mood is it?'

Jean explained that it was Lord Lanfranc who had warned him about Wulfric. Then he went on to tell Guy and Etienne of his fruitless visit to the School of Needlework and how he was refused entry by some dwarfish clown called Warin. Guy and Etienne looked at each other then at Jean. Not, Jean thought, too seriously.

'Oh dear, oh dear.' Guy said. 'I didn't like to say anything but...' he looked at Etienne and winked.

Etienne shook his head in mock despair and said.

'I didn't like to say anything either but...' he shook his head again and he could see that they found his predicament amusing so Jean chipped in.

'Look you two I don't know what is so funny about this. It's serious. I desperately need to get this business ...' he struggled for the right word.

'Sewn up?' interjected Guy and they both fell about laughing.

Eventually Guy stifled another guffaw and said, 'Sorry, Jean, sorry but...'

He took a deep breath and Etienne took up the explanation.

'The thing is this Master LeBrun. Warin and Lady Beornwyn have something of a reputation in this town. Saxon they may be but she is a really high born lady and despite efforts to convince her otherwise, she won't concede that she has ever been conquered by anyone. She's never even taken up with a man for that very reason although there was talk that there was someone, a nobleman of her race who was killed at Hastings.'

Guy then took up the narrative.

'King William reckons that if she'd been in charge instead of King Harold, she'd have won and we'd have all been back in Normandy licking our wounds.' he leaned forward confidentially, 'I've even heard that William has purposely kept Queen Mathilde from meeting the Lady Beornwyn in case she became tainted by her Ladyship's bloody-minded attitude towards all men in general but husbands in particular.' he looked at Jean reflectively for a second and then, more seriously, 'Really though, she's a good women is Lady Beornwyn and our people think a lot of her, despite her awkward ways. She worked hard to establish some sort of community in this city, where Saxon and Norman both work together for the common good and I can tell you that because if I don't Lord Lanfranc will. He reckons as much of the success of this region is down to her as it is to our people. The trouble is that so many folk have a claim on her time and charity that she needs someone to protect her and that's where Warin comes in. Don't underestimate him either. He might not be very big and getting on a bit but he's one of the strongest men I've ever met and he's devoted to her Ladyship. If he thinks she's doing too much or is too busy, nobody gets passed him. You can wave as many authorities as you like in front of his face but if the time's not right or he doesn't consider it to be right, you haven't a hope in hell. So you'll just have to keep trying I'm afraid. Sorry but that's the way it is, eh Etienne?'

Etienne nodded in agreement and Jean began to feel marginally better but still frustrated that he'd been denied a quick resolution of the embroidery problem. So much so that he thought that for what was left of the day and it wasn't that much, he would collect Nero and give him a good gallop.

He took his leave from the two masons and walked away from all the dust, rubble and noise to the comparative sanctuary of the area just outside St Michael's Gate and on to the abbey.

Since the day was by now fading fast, he wasted no time and went directly to the stables. He decided to let tomorrow take care of itself and for the time being look forward to feeling the wind blowing the stone dust out of his hair and clothes. This time Nero was only too happy to be saddled up and led to the block in the yard where Jean mounted. They left the Abbey gate and turned for the open road on which a marker pointed towards some town called Deal.

Suddenly the horse was spooked by something. Jean calmed him down and looked around but couldn't detect anything untoward. By this time the sun was well down in the sky and the Abbey walls at that point were pocked with alcoves but it was impossible to see anything or anybody lurking in their shadow. Jean's first thought automatically centred around Wulfric but ...so what? Even so, he dug his heels in and Nero, just as keen to get moving, took off at a good gallop towards the setting sun.

As soon as they both started to blow, Jean reigned in and turned Nero's head back towards the Abbey. Dusk had settled in but there were no more alarms. With Nero safely back in his stall, Jean repaired to the guest refectory where he found Guy well into his supper. They chatted lazily for an hour then made their ways to their allotted cells. This time Jean was asleep almost before his head had landed on his rolled up cloak.

CHAPTER TWENTY SIX

The School, Canterbury

He was woken in the early hours of the morning by a noise of banging and drumming. It took a few moments for his sleep sodden brain to register that it was a thunderstorm. The banging was no more than thunder and the drumming, rain pounding on the roof. He stuck his head under his makeshift pillow and groaned.

When a watery dawn made its reluctant appearance, Jean wandered to the refectory and broke his fast with a dish of equally watery gruel. There were only a few about at that time of the morning. Most, he imagined, were sensibly catching up on a disturbed night's rest. He needed to get on though so he took himself off to the overflowing trough, ducked his head in it and revived himself sufficiently to take on what had every appearance of an unpromising day. His hair, now sticky from a combination of the remains of yesterday's stone dust, was hastily combed through with his fingers and he returned to his quarters to grab the bag with the drawings and made his way back through the town walls to those of unwelcoming doors.

This time, rivulets of water were running down the streets and instead of the activity which had marked the building sites on the previous day there were now only a few labourers and even fewer craftsmen, standing about in white puddles looking as though this was the last place on God's earth that they wanted to be. Although it had stopped raining by now, underfoot there were the usual nasty things to be avoided and he carefully picked his way through the thoroughfares which suddenly seemed to have lost much of their original charm and interest. When he arrived at his destination, he was not surprised to find that there was no sign of life.

He had thought that, if he was there early enough, he might at least have the first call on Lady Beornwyn's attention but it was beginning to look unlikely. Tired and irritated, he turned from the doorway, nearly falling over something, or to be strictly accurate someone, and that someone was Warin!! Before Jean knew it, he was spun around and pinned, face against the wall, by a man half his size and twice his strength. God, Jean thought, was he strong.

In a split second Jean's dagger had been whipped from his belt and the point of it tantalisingly positioned against the side of his neck. He hardly had time to experience any fear and panic when he was surprised by another assault, this time on his senses, rather than his person. Warin seemed to be surprised as well, for the voice that came from somewhere in the region of Jean's left ear, the one nearest the doorway, would have done much to bring a legion of dead and buried Romans scurrying to the surface.

'WARIN!!!' was all the voice uttered but the tone of it and the sheer volume of it left Jean's assailant in no doubt that his action had incurred displeasure.

Warin whirled him around again, dusted him down and replaced his dagger. There then ensued a dialogue of which Jean understood hardly a word. He imagined that it was conducted in the old language of this island, of which some of the less complementary expressions were beginning to become familiar. The eventual outcome was that the owner of the voice, a dame as tall and angular as Warin was short and squat, inquired of Jean what his business was with her establishment. This enquiry was made in faultless Norman and Jean realised that this was the lady of whom he had heard so much and upon whom his hopes depended.

Looking at her or rather up at her for she bested him by a good head, Jean found himself in the company of someone who positively radiated nobility. Not that she was handsome! Any flattering adjectives, normally descriptive of women were, in her case, so inappropriate that handsome was about as charitable as Jean thought he could get and, it had to be admitted, she was not even that. No, this lady was no beauty. Her shapeless gown of some depressing rusty material cloaked, so far as Jean could judge, a masculine rather than feminine frame. An abnormally high forehead jutted out over deep-set eyes which, in their turn, surmounted an aquiline nose of alarming proportion and her teeth, when she opened her mouth, were yellow and uneven. Yet there was no mistaking her authority and her breeding.

It flashed through his mind that there were some, like Odo, who imposed their will on other people; as often as not finding conscious pleasure by doing so. Some, like Lanfranc and Beaumont, wore their nobility more lightly. But this woman was noble in a way that anyone meeting her would instinctively have known it. Not something to be bought or even earned. You either have it or you don't and she, Jean surmised, the Lady Beornwyn, was obviously pickled in it.

Not for the first time, Jean felt himself under prepared and inadequate for an encounter with the higher social orders but he was learning and he sensed that here, obsequiousness would not help his cause, so he made his self-introduction quickly and without embellishment. The presentation of the Archbishop's letter did much to ease the process but if he was going to impress this woman, it could only be with the single talent to which he could lay claim. If she could be persuaded by that, then he might stand a chance.

The Lady Beornwyn had lost all the male line of her family at Hastings. Similarly, the family estates and fortune had been quickly assimilated by the conquerors and while she had been left with little in the way of material wealth, one or two of the Norman nobility, of whom Odo was not one, recognised that she was a remarkable woman.

First and foremost she possessed an awesome intelligence. She also had a well developed sense of the reality of her situation and she immediately recognised that rebellion was pointless, a fact which the rest of England was rather slower to acknowledge. One of the first acts of Lanfranc, when he arrived in England, was to seek her out and look for her advice on many matters concerning the assimilation of the two cultures. She was not, however, easy to deal with and Lanfranc was often left with the feeling that the conquered, rather than the conquerors, had profited from whatever negotiations had taken place. He had, though, to acknowledge that without her help, Canterbury would not have become one of the most prosperous boroughs in the realm.

Then there was her incredible talent as a supervisor of needlewomen. Her request to be given the necessary means to expand and develop a School of Embroidery was one to which he was only too happy to accede. Not only was there his new cathedral and its needs to be taken into account but the School was providing something of a focus for the town as a centre of cultural excellence whose reputation had spread far beyond these island shores. This was good for commerce and that which benefited the community of Canterbury could not but benefit the new cathedral and its prelate.

There were also cultural advantages since many of the issues that arose, from time to time, involving the two races were resolved with the help and advice of Lady Beornwyn. Between her and the Archbishop there existed a respect which, if it did not quite extend to close friendship, became over the years an easy and companionable association.

There was however, one permanent cause of discord between them and that was Warin. Her personal servant, groom, lackey and above all, bodyguard: Warin never learned to adopt his mistress's philosophical acceptance of the Norman occupation. Despite her frequent orders to the contrary he, whenever the opportunity presented itself, carried on a continual campaign of hostility towards the enemy. He went out of his way to pick quarrels with soldiers and when he found himself in that happy situation, he set about causing as much damage as he could. This was invariably considerable and Lady Beornwyn was always having to intercede on his behalf. Possibly at Odo's instigation, several attempts had been made on her life and on each occasion Warin had intervened to save this mistress on whom he expended a dog-like devotion.

He reputedly slept outside her door every night and guarded her throughout her daily activities.

None of this was known to Jean when, having rescued him from her bodyguard, Beornwyn wordlessly ushered him inside the great double doors of the School and into an ante-room which evidently served as her office and place of business. Jean, who managed to get this far without dropping his saddle bags or tripping over the steps, at last found himself face to face with the person on whom all his hopes rested.

They regarded each other for a few moments, neither saying anything. Both seemed happy by what they saw and Beornwyn was the first to make a gesture by holding out her hand for the letter which Jean offered. There was no invitation to sit down although she assumed the rather unladylike posture of perching on the edge of her desk while he shifted from foot to foot and looked around the room. Not that there was much to look at. There was no indication of her business or interests. He had supposed there might be a crucifix or other religious items on display or perhaps wall hangings and samplers from her pupils but nothing. Bare walls pitted with high barred windows. Lots and lots of windows, through which the fresh breeze stirred the letter which she held in her hand.

She read it quickly and having done so, concentrated her gaze once more on Jean's face. She gave a small sigh, whether of irritation, boredom or contentment, he couldn't tell. She then left the table and walked past him to the door. She beckoned Warin inside and proceeded to talk to him quietly but commandingly in their own tongue. He left the room, almost immediately re-entering it bearing a tray containing pewter mugs, a jug of small beer and from the smell of it, fresh bread.

For the first time Beornwyn's face bore the trace of a smile as she observed Jean's appreciative reaction to the offerings. With the same hand, the one still holding Lanfranc's letter, she dismissed Warin with a wave and gestured Jean to the table then, for the first time since they had come into the room she spoke to him, again in his own language. It was almost impossible for him to detect a trace of accent and he was surprised to note that her voice was probably the most attractive part of this woman. The stentorian bellow that had nearly deafened him outside was now replaced by something that was quite beautifully modulated and instead of assaulting it, pleasing to the ear.

She waved the letter at him.

'My Lord Archbishop seems quite anxious that I should listen to whatever it is you have to say to me although I cannot imagine why. You are not a military man, too young to be an advisor or counsellor and not, if you will excuse me saying so, of obviously high birth. Tell me then, what is it that so commends you to the Archbishop and why should he commend you, in turn, to me? Would you like some breakfast? I seem to remember my young brothers when they were your age. Always hungry and from the way that your nose wrinkled as the bread passed beneath it, you are not so very different.'

So many questions in the one speech left Jean confused. He was on the verge of extracting the drawings from the saddlebags but at the mention of the food, his eyes automatically veered towards the platter. Again the half smile appeared on her thin lips. She waved the letter towards the table.

'Why don't you join me for breakfast or have you already breakfasted?'

At long last Jean felt able to speak.

'Yes My Lady, that is, well I did have a small, a very small bowl of gruel at the priory.'

She had already broken off a piece of the loaf and poured the beer into the cups. She handed him one and he dropped the saddlebags on the floor and moved forward to take it.

'Thank you my Lady.'

She looked at him speculatively again.

'At least you have manners Master…' she glanced at the letter and shook some crumbs from it. 'Master LeBrun. Now, perhaps you would like to tell me something about yourself and what this letter is really all about. First of all though, be under no illusions. My time is valuable, too valuable to expend it on projects or propositions that are outside my sphere of activity or interest. By the time I have broken my fast, I expect you to have explained what it is you want with me. So speak up and speak plainly.'

She then placed the letter on the table, thus leaving both hands free to attack the loaf and pour more ale. His first thought was to take out his drawings and place them in front of her on the table and go on from there. That though, was not enough so he didn't so much as bother with an introductory cough. Making sure that he was directly in her line of vision he firmly stated that he was looking for a centre of needlework capable of working a tapestry, the dimensions of which were something in the region of two hundred and fifty pieds long and…

As he reeled off the dimensions, Jean found his voice almost failing him, as if even he found the project too ridiculous to recite aloud. The Lady Beornwyn halted the crust that was destined for her mouth and looked at him in astonishment. At least this legendary gentlewomen was capable of surprise but not for long apparently. She dusted off her mouth and robe and looked up at the ceiling.

'Repeat that please' was all she said.

Jean did so and she left her perch on the edge of the table and started to pace slowly around the room. Brow furrowed, her hands were clasped together at her mouth as if in prayer. After a few moments she stopped in front of him and appraised him anew, as if she were seeing him for the first time.

'Well, Master LeBrun. I have to admit that you have surprised me. A piece of work such as that is not impossible. The fact that it is highly unusual does not make it impossible. Difficult, yes but not impossible. What is the subject of this disproportionate frieze, for that is what your dimensions suggest it is, a frieze and not a commonplace wall hanging or decoration.'

At least, Jean thought, I have her interest. Now I must try to build upon it.

'The great Battle of Hastings, my Lady. The events leading up to it, the battle itself and events subsequent to the conquest.'

She gave a short, mirthless laugh. 'You jest of course! You actually expect me to execute a work of Norman propaganda. Long on legend and short on truth? Why, in God's name should I, of all people, help you with something like that? Do you know nothing of my background?'

Jean thought furiously. 'No, my Lady. But the Queen herself suggested that your school might...either your workshops here or failing that, the one at Winchester which...'

'WINCHESTER !!!'

Jean flinched before another vocal onslaught and then flinched again as Warin came charging into the room, seemingly intent on damaging somebody.

She waved a calming hand at him.

'It's all right Warin, you are not needed. This young man hardly presents a physical threat to our person, which is more than one might say for his lamentable lack of sensitivity.'

Warin grunted and backed out of the door. She turned back to Jean.

'Tell me, what exactly is your part in this affair? Who is it that you represent?'

Jean answered immediately and directly. 'I am the designer of the work my Lady and I am in the service of Lord Odo, Earl of Kent who is ...'

She gave another dismissive laugh.

'We are all only too aware of who Lord Odo is and more importantly, what he is. Probably the most evil misrepresentation of the Mother Church it has ever been my misfortune to meet, which makes it even more remarkable that you should seek my help. I suppose this frieze is intended to decorate his Lordship's new church in Bayeux. Why is it that you Normans seem to have this habit of desecrating and destroying existing churches which are in a perfectly good state of repair and replacing them with new buildings of your own design and construction? You all seem to be endowed with a peculiar sense of your own superiority which, I might add, is seldom borne out by your loutish behaviour over here.'

Jean broke in, not because he felt any need to defend the reputation of his fellow countrymen but because he suspected that if Lady Beornwyn was allowed to continue in this vein, his chances of making his own case would be considerably reduced. It would have to be a matter of treading a fine line between humility and assurance.

'My Lady!' Again, he spoke out clearly and directly. 'My Lord Lanfranc's new Cathedral, here in Canterbury, is probably the most beautiful building I have ever seen. Its proportions are pleasing to my eye and I would go so far as to say that it represents, as far as it could, man's ability to create a structure to the greater glory of God. Not only that but…'

'Just a moment young man. Are you presuming to lecture me? You have chosen a singularly odd way of petitioning me for my help.'

She re-assumed her seat on the table's edge before going on.

'I do not disagree with your assessment of our new church and the Archbishop, I would be the first to acknowledge, has done much for this city and his useful work continues, but Odo, and I personally do not feel the need to adorn that ugly name with any sort of title, is quite another matter. I am truly thankful that this region of our poor overrun country is not in his sole charge. Therefore, since you represent this obnoxious creature, why should I waste my time on you any further?'

Her fingers tapped the table and Jean took another deep breath.

'Very well my Lady. You are quite right of course.' He started to repack his drawings which she still hadn't seen and continued, 'I shall take the alternative advice of her Majesty and offer the work to the school at Winchester.'

Her hand came down on the table so hard he was surprised the board didn't splinter! As it was, it brought about a further entrance by Warin who was immediately waved out again by his mistress.

'You obviously have no thought for the fate of your work, Master LeBrun. It is conceivable that Queen Mathilde and myself might see eye to eye on many things but not, I think, on this. I wonder if her appreciation and knowledge of the art of needlework is by any means comprehensive. Try Winchester by all means but I very much doubt if they will fulfil your commission to the satisfaction of yourself or your infamous master.'

She eased herself off the table and folding her arms, looked down on Jean. The look was not unfriendly and all he could do was to sit through her inspection, busying himself with the fastenings on his saddlebags. Eventually she came to the point.

'Presumably your designs are to be found in those bags with which you are so obsessively fiddling. Since you have come this far and the Archbishop advises it, I had better look at them. I have to say you don't look particularly artistic but then, neither do many of the Norman masons that work here and I am happy to admit that they can do things with a block of stone that I wouldn't have thought possible. So let us look at what you have brought.'

Jean undid the ties and unrolled his drawings on the table. He then moved over to the wall and stood there, fingers crossed behind his back. Lady Beornwyn flattened the drawings out carefully and moved her eyes along the narrative in front of her. Occasionally, she cast a brief puzzled look in his direction before continuing with her inspection. Having got to the end, she started again, this time stopping from time to time, apparently making calculations in her head and on her fingers before moving to the next segment.

While she was thus engaged, Jean stood very still, determined that the next move should come from her. He waited patiently while she went over it a third time and then a fourth. He hadn't the faintest idea what she was doing but he reasoned that the longer she took over it, the better his chances of her accepting the work. Eventually, she straightened up.

One hand smoothing down the linen as she still looked at it, she said, 'I do not know how you have managed it Master LeBrun. Your technique is untutored and extremely basic but somehow, just somehow, you have contrived to catch the essence of this particular story. I would go further and say your work here is more meaningful than it might have been had it been more strictly representational.'

She turned to him.

'The really extraordinary fact though, is that your designs are ... how shall I put it...uncannily suited to the discipline of embroidery. Might I ask if that was deliberate, the technique you have employed here?'

Jean scratched his head and gave a short embarrassed cough.

'Yes, my Lady, but not for the reason you have just given. I can make much more detailed and illustrative drawings but Lord Odo impressed on me that he wanted this finished as quickly as possible so I...'

She finished the sentence for him.

'So you adopted the cartoon form of illustration. Well, that was lucky wasn't it? That is not to say, young man, that I accept the commission. Have you any idea how much this is going to cost? Fine dyed wool is not cheap and I don't have to tell you that this establishment does not exist on air alone. I hope that your illustrious patron is prepared to make adequate funds available. Money, Master LeBrun, do you have the wherewithal to fund this expensive folly? Because without it you can take your designs to Winchester and your master can take himself to hell, a place for which I imagine he is predestined anyway.'

Jean reached under his cloak and fumbled with the drawstring of the purse he'd attached to his belt. He dumbly held it out towards Lady Beornwyn, who moved towards him to take it. Before her hand had closed on the leather however, she stopped and looked down on him with something akin to amusement in her eyes.

'You don't know, do you? You have no idea how much money you are carrying in that pouch, have you?'

Jean frowned up at her. She was close enough to him for him to be able catch the scent of her gown which appeared to have been brushed with herbs. The smell was fresh and it was surprising on her person. Bony and over tall, she certainly didn't display many overtly feminine traits and for a moment Jean was confused. His stuttered protestations were smothered by her unexpected throaty chuckle. Another surprise. He hadn't associated this rather awesome woman with a sense of humour. Gently, she disengaged his hand from the purse.

'Fear not, Master LeBrun. I will not cheat you. Just as I will not, on my part, be cheated. Come here.' He followed her to the table where she re-folded the linen before emptying out the purse onto the board. The pile of silver pennies moved seductively through her fingers as she almost caressed them. She split the silver into two separate piles. As with the drawing, her attention was fully engaged on the task and she spoke without taking her eyes off the table.

'How long did you say the completed work should be?' He repeated what he had told her earlier and she re-adjusted the two piles of money. The larger of the two, she left on the table and slipped the remaining coins back in their pouch.

'Presumably, you have to live as well, young man. I will keep this' pointing to the silver remaining on the table. 'Until I have decided how we are going to go about this business. There are technical problems associated with a frieze of this size and I need to consider the best way of transferring your designs onto embroidery frames. Is there anything else I need to know? Because now is the time to tell me. Should I find out that you are contemplating different dimensions or designs to those we have discussed, I shall not be happy' she threw him a sharp look. 'Well, is there anything else I need to know?'

Again, Jean resisted prevarication and came straight to the point.

'Yes, my Lady. Although nothing very difficult' he added hurriedly.

Her eyes narrowed. 'Go on.' she said. 'What else?'

'I thought my Lady, that is, Lord Odo thought…a written narrative of the events portrayed. He thought that…'

She interrupted him.

'I see. In the unlikely event that this work should ever come to fruition, Odo thought that history would better be interpreted through a combination of pictures and words. Is that right?' Jean merely nodded.

She continued, 'Thus posterity might be in no doubt, who was the chronicler of these momentous events?' Again Jean nodded.

'Hardly momentous to the peoples of this island though. Calamitous might have been a more apt word.' She placed a hand to her back and stretched, looking at Jean as if challenging him to disagree. He didn't. He rolled up the linen and made to replace it in the leather pannier.

'Back on the table, if you please Master LeBrun.'

The command was not to be denied and with feigned reluctance, he replaced it where she indicated with an imperious finger. Although still rolled, he could see that she was looking at it, evaluating it and registering all the detail in her mind that her eyes had taken in a few moments earlier. He had done his best and it was now down to Lady Beornwyn to make her decision. Eventually, she turned to him.

'Master LeBrun, you have undoubted talent. Why I should even think of taking this commission when it depicts events that for me and my countrymen meant nothing but defeat and subjugation, I cannot imagine. But it is a challenge and you may or may not know that I relish a challenge. We are not short of work here. Our good name is beginning to make itself known through many countries but something like this...' She ran her long bony fingers over the fabric. 'Something like this could be part of our heritage as well as yours. Well executed and carefully preserved, there is no reason why it shouldn't last for many years to come. I am prepared to help you but I warn you it will not be easy and should any of the difficulties that I envisage prove insuperable, then I will withdraw from our contract.'

Jean started to express his gratitude in a suitably fulsome form when she interrupted him again.

'I also impose conditions to which I must have your absolute agreement.'

'Conditions, my Lady?'

'Yes, LeBrun, conditions. Firstly, you confine yourself to the graphic portrayal of the events in question and I have the final word on what is and what is not acceptable. Secondly, should it be considered necessary I, or somebody else of my choosing, will design some upper and lower borders and thirdly, I alone take responsibility for the written commentary. In other words, you continue with what you are already doing and leave all the embellishments to me and my ladies.'

Jean broke in. 'But, my Lady, I am quite capable of supplying a text. I might look a fool but I can write and I can read. Not only...'

'Whatever else you may be, Master LeBrun, you are patently not a fool but I will brook no debate on these matters. These are my terms. Take them or leave them. I would only add that in the event of any interference from your patron, any attempt on his part to impose constraints of any conceivable nature, time, content, whatever, I wash my hands of the whole business.'

She looked hard at Jean, in the expectation of some sort of hostile response. She looked in vain. Truth to tell, Jean was thinking furiously and beginning to wonder if Canterbury was such a good idea after all. It was rapidly becoming evident to him that he was between the devil and the deep, a rather apt description of the two people he was most anxious to please. He scratched his head and toyed nervously with the edge of the cloth which still lay on the table together with the piles of silver pennies.

Then came the moment for which he had, quite sub-consciously been waiting. It appeared that the rain had stopped and through a high window of the room, a beam of sunlight suddenly flashed across the linen panel on the table and he could see the fair hairs on the back of the hand that held it reflect the light. He had not been waiting for an omen but it suddenly occurred to him that this was just what he needed to make up his mind. He moved his fingers and watched the sunbeams dance across them.

He turned and faced Lady Beornwyn who raised a masculine eyebrow at him. He nodded slowly and said that he would agree to her conditions but that she must remember, he could not possibly speak for Lord Odo, who would have to be informed of any arrangements that had been made.

She gave one of her short snorts of uncomplimentary laughter.

'Tell him what you like, young man. He and I are old enemies but if he is looking for a work, the quality of which will glorify his name for generations to come, he will raise no serious objections. Just do not expect him to be overjoyed at the prospect of working with me, albeit at a distance which, for me, cannot be far enough. Now, let us discuss these intriguing little piles of silver, shall we?'

The drawing now rolled up, she beckoned Jean to join her at the table where she indicated the pouch of coins that she had offered to him earlier. Still he hesitated and she immediately understood his predicament.

'You don't understand money do you? For goodness sake, boy, stop rifling through that unruly mop of yours and pick it up. Let me explain something to you. Correct me if I am wrong but I assume that you are in thrall to that odious cleric. Am I right?'

Jean cleared his throat and at the last moment, remembered not to run his hands through his hair. She nodded encouragingly at him. 'Well, are you or not?'

'My father is Lord Odo's steward of his estate in Normandy, my Lady so, naturally I do whatever he tells me. Should I not obey …'

'The consequences do not bear thinking about?' Her voice was quiet and again, he was struck by the pleasing timbre of it. She went on.

'Odo needs you, young man, because you have something that he cannot ever hope to own. You have a talent and without your talent, Odo could not embark on a project such as this. There are other artists. Of course there are, the world is full of them but you are different and like all people gifted with your sort of creativity, it is beyond me to try and explain exactly what it is that makes you so special. I could never replicate what you have done, working as you have from the reports of third parties. Like most people I need to see something before I can reproduce it. You don't and that is precisely why you have earned that silver. You have never needed money have you? Well, here in Canterbury, things are different. Artists, artisans, tradesmen, even people like me work for money. We still trade and barter goods but more and more people are selling their labour, their skills and their produce. With the money they earn, they, in turn, pay others for their services. It is proving very successful and without it Canterbury would not be the centre of excellence that it is.'

She leaned closer to him and he could catch once more the herbal scent of her gown.

'It appears that you have the goodwill of Lord Lanfranc. Earn my goodwill as well, Master LeBrun, and you could be your own master. A free man – insofar as any man is completely free. You will still have obligations but they will be of your own making. Now, what I...' Before she could finish, the door burst open and Warin made his third unannounced entrance.

This time, he made straight for Lady Beornwyn and started gabbling away in that gobbledegook of his. Whatever it was he was saying though, seemed to have captured her attention for she bent almost double, the better to hear him. As it was, despite his natural disadvantage, there was one word which Jean could not have missed had he tried, especially as it seemed to be repeated, each time with all the renewed emphasis that Warin could express through his whiskers. That word was 'Wulfric' and the mention of it caused the Lady Beornwyn to look very thoughtful indeed.

Eventually she held up her hand to put a stop to Warin's news which increasingly seemed to include more words with which Jean had become acquainted while on the building sites. She turned to Jean and said.

'I suppose you know of the existence of one, Wulfric, a creature of the night and it goes without saying, a creature of your master.' Jean replied that, yes he not only knew him but was served by him, under the orders of Lord Odo.

She gravely shook her head. 'But were you aware that he is a serial assasin? I believe that he could even teach your master a thing or two about cruelty and viciousness. I cannot say that I admire the company you keep LeBrun!'

Jean smiled bitterly. 'Wulfric has good reason not to love me, my Lady. At the time, my usefulness to Lord Odo was rather greater than his and, I have to confess my Lady, I played on that fact somewhat but yes, I have been warned that he is here in Canterbury. At Dover, with my Lord in residence, I don't think he would have dared harm me but here… '

'You do well to be on your guard, young man. Wulfric is a master of "accidents". I think I might have to lend you Warin for a while. Not a luxury I can allow you for long though, I depend on him too much myself. Where are you staying? The priory did I hear you say?'

Jean signified his assent so she then advised him to make his quarters at the castle and throw himself on the protection of Lord Beaumont. The manner with which she spoke Beaumont's name indicated that she viewed him in much the same light as Lanfranc. Not perhaps close friends but having respect for each other. Jean was more than happy to take this advice and for the time being, not too uncomfortable at the thought of having a bodyguard to look after him. He explained though, that he had first to collect Nero and his belongings. Lady Beornwyn told him that Warin would walk at his stirrup, if so ordered.

She then explained to Warin, in their own tongue, what was expected of him. Without another word, he hefted Jean's saddlebags on his shoulder and motioned with a nod of his head to follow him to the priory. As he was leaving, she called him back.

'One more thing, Master LeBrun, you will have to transfer your designs onto a better quality linen than that, something altogether heavier.' She pointed to the length he had left on her table. 'That will have to be re-drawn.'

For the first time, Jean felt that he could risk a grin.

'That's all right Milady, The Queen has already told me that.'

Beornwyn nodded thoughtfully. 'Has she indeed, Master LeBrun. Perhaps she and I might meet some day. Now be off. We will meet again at the Castle and discuss our work further.'

Reassured by the possessive pronoun, Jean happily took his leave and followed Warin to the Priory.

CHAPTER TWENTY SEVEN

Canterbury Castle

Insomuch as the basic design was of the motte and bailey type and constructed largely of earthwork and wood, the castle at Canterbury was not dissimilar to that of Dover. Where it differed, however, was that, whereas Dover castle was built outside the town, that of Canterbury was incorporated into the city wall and was surrounded by the mean dwellings of what had once been a hamlet on the outskirts of the town itself. Since the Roman wall of the city formed one side of the fortification, one of the gateways also served as an entrance to the bailey.

This gateway was presently guarded by two muscular men-at-arms and when they saw what was heading in their direction, they exchanged glances and tightened their grip on their weapons. Since the subject or rather subjects of their concern appeared to be no more than a squat, hairy Saxon leading a handsome bay on which sat a young man in a muted red cloak, their fears would appear to be groundless yet as the couple approached, the guards moved closer together, their swords now in complete readiness. None of this show of strength and purpose seemed to impress Warin who, with Nero in tow, hardly seemed to register that any guards existed.

As soon as he was close enough however, he started to harangue them so loudly and aggressively that Nero would have unseated his rider had not Warin's grip on the bridle kept his head down. As it was, he tried to skitter away from the noise but Warin pulled the horse after him as if he were pulling a toy pony on wheels. He continued until he was almost nose to nose with the guards who, as he moved up to them and despite their obvious superiority of physique and arms, backed away until they were up against the huge castle gates. What exactly it was that Warin was saying, or rather shouting at them, Jean could not precisely interpret but he felt it incumbent on him to try and calm Warin down before any real mischief occurred.

He managed to slither over Nero's sweaty flanks to the ground where he made signs to Warin to be quiet while he explained his presence to the guards. With much ill-tempered mutterings and rude gestures, Warin reluctantly handed over the reigns to Jean, gave Nero a pat on his rump, a friendly gesture which surprised the horse as much as his rider, and started to make his way back to the city centre. He was still muttering and the words 'shit-faced Norman bastards' were delivered over his hunched shoulder in such perfect Norman that Jean was left to wonder if, in fact, he had mastered the language of his enemy or only those bits of it which left them in no doubt that they had been comprehensively insulted. Jean shook his head apologetically at the guards and explained who he was, who had sent him and would someone be good enough to take him to Lord Beaumont who was expecting him.

Not only was Lord Beaumont expecting him, he was walking down the steps of the keep as Jean was escorted to the middle of the bailey. What Jean did not expect was to see the bleak figure of Wulfric, descending from the Keep, a few steps behind Beaumont. Typical, thought Jean, to be chaperoned to his destination only to be confronted by the very man from whom he was supposed to be protected.

Robert Beaumont, as ever, was courtesy itself and greeted Jean most civilly. Wulfric hung a few paces behind, head down and feet shuffling uncomfortably. He doesn't like being in the light, thought Jean. His host complemented him on Nero's excellent condition which, as Jean tried to explain was less to do with his temporary owner than the lad who looked after him at the Priory. Once Nero had been led away to his new accommodation, Robert Beaumont indicated the black clad figure lurking behind him.

'The Earl of Kent has sent over Wulfric here with some despatches newly arrived from France. While he was here he asked if he might have some time with you.'

He then motioned to Wulfric to stop where he was and stepped down to Jean. He spoke softly.

'I understand he is at your service should you have need of him but frankly I would prefer that he was back in Dover. Perhaps you could conduct your business with him now and when you are done, contact one of my men and they will bring you to me.'

He cast a glance over his shoulder, in the direction of Wulfric and added.

'It's probably better that you have your conversation here, in full view of everyone. I look forward to seeing you when you have concluded whatever it is you have to discuss. Later, I will have you shown to your quarters.'

He nodded briefly to Jean, ignored Wulfric and turned on his heel, walking back up the steps in the company of one of his lieutenants'. Jean watched them depart and then, still determined to take the lead in their relationship, walked over to Wulfric who was watching Beaumont's retreating back. Jean tapped him on the shoulder and Wulfric immediately spun round, his hand on the hilt of his dagger. Jean again noticed that the man was uncomfortable in the daylight. He squinted against it and was also unhappy to be in the centre of the Bailey, in the open. His eyes kept darting around him, seeking the sanctuary of stone or wood. Jean actually felt the stirrings of sympathy for him, until he remembered the things for which Wulfric was said to be responsible. Important, he thought, to retain the upper hand so he said brusquely, 'All right Wulfric, say what you have to say and be gone. Lord Beaumont wants to see me and I don't fancy keeping him waiting.'

Wulfric's shoulders dropped and the knuckles on his hand grasping the dagger hilt, whitened. Jean kept a close eye on that hand as Wulfric sidled closer, eyes firmly fixed on the ground although he lifted his head to speak.

'Master LeBrun. May I ... respectfully ... remind you that Lord Beaumont is here in this castle as a... guest of our lord and master, the Earl of Kent.'

Jean, to whom the fact had not occurred, quickly broke in.

'Yes, well never mind all that. What is it you have to tell me? Just get on with it and be on your way.'

Wulfric inclined his head and drew a black gloved hand over his bloodless lips.

'Our master is anxious to know whether or not you have succeeded in finding a workshop prepared to undertake the embroidery of his, that is... your...masterpiece. He also would like an ...assurance ... that the ... purse with which you were entrusted is still...'

'Yes it is Wulfric, although I have obviously had to dip into it to secure the services of the embroiderers. In fact,' he went on, thinking on his feet, 'you might tell his Lordship that the funds allocated to me might well prove insufficient for the work in question and that I, or they, could be asking for more.'

Wulfric's eyes flickered uneasily around the courtyard as if the wrath of Odo might suddenly appear from somewhere out of the walls.

'I'm not sure that his Grace...'

'Just tell him Wulfric. Tell him that the work is being graciously undertaken by the Lady Beornwyn and her team, here in Canterbury. Apparently it is not going to be cheap but her School was personally recommended to me by the Queen so if he wants the best he'll have to pay for it. Anything else?'

'No Master LeBrun, well, that is...there is something. The horse, Nero. His Lordship wondered if...'

'Still necessary I'm afraid Wulfric. Who knows when I might have to get back to Dover in a hurry and I have still many arrangements to make here in Canterbury that involve travelling about. Oh, and by the way, I understand that you are known to Lady Beornwyn and more particularly to her servant, Warin. Friends were you?'

He could have sworn that Wulfric's pale eyes were suddenly animated with red sparks.

'Yes Master LeBrun' he hissed 'I know Warin. He slowly drew his dagger from it's black sheath and just as slowly pushed it home again before going on, 'He killed my father.'

Jean thought he'd taken things far enough so he refrained from expressing surprise that Wulfric actually had a father, especially one that he knew, so he contented himself with a nod.

'Right then' he said. 'If that's all, you best be back to Dover. Just assure Lord Odo that everything is going according to plan. Take care Wulfric.'

'Oh I will, Master LeBrun…I will.' Was the reply as he turned on his heel and stalked out of the gate, the guards following him, weapons a little more to the ready than was strictly necessary.

Jean shrugged off Wulfric's presence and, before he had time to consider his next move, a servant ran across to him and led him into the tower and to the door of Beaumont's suite. The door opened immediately on the knock and Beaumont himself ushered Jean inside the room. Again, Jean was slightly mystified at the attention he was receiving from those so much his superiors in rank. Beaumont's attitude was as ever, courteous and warm. Jean was invited to be seated at the desk opposite him and drinks of wine, not ale, were brought in and placed in front of them.

'Now! To business.' was Beaumont's opening.

Jean breathed a sigh of relief. At least he wasn't going to have to try and make polite conversation about things he knew nothing about. Beaumont continued in the same straightforward manner.

'While you are here in Canterbury, it will probably be as well to take your lodgings in the castle. Fortunately, the garrison is well below strength. In fact, to be honest with you, there are none of Lord Odo's men here at all, only mine. He has seen fit to move them elsewhere and if you should, by any chance, hear anything that might throw some light on their whereabouts, I would be interested to know of it. For whatever reason, my erstwhile colleague in arms no longer appears to take me into his confidence.'

He regarded Jean for a moment, as if expecting him to require some clarification on the point he had just made. Jean thought it safer to stay quiet for the moment so Beaumont continued.

'I will of course be here to give you an account of the great battle and answer any other questions.'

Again, a pause to give Jean the opportunity to speak and again Jean contented himself with a nod. This time the pause was accompanied by the offer of more wine, which Jean declined. Beaumont took time to refill his cup while Jean patiently awaited his next pronouncement.

'I think you will approve of the accommodation to which I referred earlier. This is a rather more agreeable fortification than Dover. Of course, in time, it too will be replaced by more permanent stone buildings some of which are nearing completion. These wooden walls were not intended to last for ever. I have arranged for you to have one of the south facing rooms, that way you can enjoy the maximum amount of light for your work. It will also serve as your sleeping quarters. Now is there anything you feel you need to ask me?'

Before he could stop himself, Jean blurted out 'Why?'

Instead of being affronted, Beaumont regarded him with his usual tolerant amusement.

'Why what, exactly, Master LeBrun?'

'I'm sorry my Lord. I don't mean to be stupid but none of this makes sense to me. I mean I appreciate your kindness and thoughtfulness but I am supposed to be working for Lord Odo and as I understand it you and he...'

'Are not of one mind, LeBrun? Is that what you're trying to say? Well, we do have a slight problem at the moment with Bishop Odo. Not me personally, although I have not always approved of his suppressive methods. No, he created his own problems when he supported young Robert in his rebellion against his father. Of course, he denies it and the King has, for the moment, allowed him to retain the power of Regency, albeit reduced but he has lost the confidence and support that he enjoyed only a few months ago. I don't imagine for one moment that I would be lording here in one of his castles had his Majesty not specifically requested me to do so. Together with Lanfranc, who by the way, seems to have taken to you, we have been granted a greater responsibility for the security of the southern territories of the island. Fortunately, I appear to have succeeded in gaining the support of the Saxon barons in the Mid Lands, otherwise these added duties would be difficult to shoulder.'

Jean toyed with his empty cup.

'My Lord, I can understand why what you have just told me might explain your presence here in Canterbury but what I really meant was...'

'Why are we all being so uncharacteristically kind to you? Especially as you are directly in thrall to Odo who has just incurred the King's displeasure. Is that what you are trying to say?'

Waiting for an answer, Beaumont studied Jean and saw, sitting opposite him, a young man much matured since their first meeting. There was something about him that commanded respect. Perhaps it was the way in which Jean steadily returned his gaze and the naturally keen intelligence that was revealed behind his eyes. Perhaps it was the reports that he'd received from Lanfranc. Whatever, he decided that it was only fair to inform the young artist of his present position, so this he started to do.

'LeBrun, while you are and I suppose always will be, a servant of Lord Odo, the commission on which you are presently engaged has been adopted, yes, I would say adopted is probably the right way to put it, by another party. Why? Well, although Lord Odo, still remains your original mentor and master and the design on which you are working remains his property, this other party to which I refer wishes to register an interest.'

Jean had the grace to look puzzled. 'Interest, my Lord. In what way exactly?'

Beaumont took a thoughtful sip of wine.

'That I cannot say. All I do know is that this person is interested in seeing your work reach a successful conclusion. What happens after that will, I imagine, be a matter between them and Lord Odo.'

'But does Lord Odo know about this other party, my Lord? As it is, I don't feel very safe with Wulfric on the prowl and if my master were to get wind of another...'

This time it was Beaumont who rose from his chair and cup in hand, moved to Jean's side of the table on which he sat and looked down at Jean's anxious frown.

'Yes, LeBrun, Odo is aware of this other person's interest and things being what they are, he is extremely unlikely to do anything about it. Indeed, in view of his recent ill-advised excursion into the realms of treason, I don't think he would dare to incur further displeasure.'

Jean didn't really need to think about it.

'Are we talking about the Queen, my Lord?'

'Exactly so, LeBrun and we need not delve too deeply into the whys and wherefores of the matter. Whatever her Majesty thought of the recent events in Normandy, and it has to be said that the activities of Duke Robert did meet with a degree of maternal tolerance, Odo's part in the affair left him with no alternative but to agree to almost any demand she, or the King, might make of him. It is, therefore, in Lord Odo's interests to lie low for a while. I'm not sure how you do it but you seem to have the knack of gaining the attention of those in high places and you can't get much higher than the Queen of England.'

Jean nodded. 'Yes my Lord. It was she that recommended I came to Canterbury for the needlework. She was most gracious when I met her with...' he faltered for a moment, 'with Thibault and Mirabelle. Does this mean that when it is finished she will take it from my master?'

Beaumont returned to his seat.

'No, I doubt that very much. I think she is more than happy for Odo to hang it in his newly consecrated cathedral so long as she can claim some of the credit for its existence. Who knows, perhaps she will put it about that the whole idea was hers in the first place. I can't quite see why it should be so but there seems to be a general consensus that this scheme of yours, when completed, is likely to confer some sort of immortality on its patrons. Just think LeBrun, if it doesn't catch fire or get lost at sea, this hanging of yours could make you famous for centuries to come.'

Jean caught the flash of amusement on Beaumont's customary sober countenance and was quick to reply.

'I don't think so my Lord. I am far too insignificant to enjoy that sort of fame. I very much doubt if masons, such as Guy for example, will be remembered for the magnificent buildings on which they have worked but Archbishop Lanfranc will forever be in people's thoughts when the cathedral here in Canterbury is mentioned.' Beaumont smiled.

'I have no doubt that you are right in that regard Master LeBrun, regrettable and unfair as it may seem. Now, I will have you shown to your quarters. What are your plans for the morrow?'

'Well, my Lord' answered Jean enthusiastically. 'I would like to return to the embroidery school to discuss further Lady Beornwyn's ideas for the work; colours, commentary and so on. Later, if your Lordship agrees, I would like to spend some time with you to talk about the battle and how best to illustrate it. There is one more thing, if I might be so bold.'

'And what is that LeBrun?'

Jean thought for a moment before asking. 'My Lord, you seem to know much of what is happening here and in the court and in Normandy. I just wondered, my Lord, if you had any further news on the whereabouts of Thibault?'

Beaumont stroked his chin. 'The short answer LeBrun, is that there is nothing of any substance I can report. I have little doubt that your Master is also pursuing similar inquiries and I assume, and it is only an assumption, that if Thibault is still at large, he is making some effort to remain undetected. Can't say I blame him either. Is that all then?'

Jean nodded, 'Yes my Lord. I'm sorry.'

Upon which Beaumont nodded his head and called for his aide, instructing him to conduct Jean to his quarters and went back to studying the maps and scrolls on his table.

Beaumont's lieutenant was a man of few words and judging from the easy relationship he seemed to enjoy with his master, one who was well used to being in his company. A sturdy Norman of military bearing, it came as no surprise to Jean to learn that Josclin, for that was his name, had spent all his life in Lord Beaumont's service, as had his father in the service of Beaumont's father. That was all that Jean was able to elicit from him, although from the warmth of the man's few words it was not difficult to imagine the affection in which he held his Lord.

The accommodation far exceeded Jean's expectations. For a start he had it all to himself and although, from the outside, it appeared to be little more than a stable, the inside was clean with a good beaten-earth floor, a solid roof and furniture enough for all his needs.

It backed onto the city wall so the south facing wall of the habitation was stone with a high barred window, large enough to light the room but not quite enough to work by. There was a roofed lean-to which fronted onto the bailey and Josclin explained that it would provide cover for working outside in daylight, providing, thought Jean ruefully, it was warm enough to do so. When he enquired about meals, he was told that he could take them in the central hall or if he wished, they could be brought to him here. Again, that feeling of surprise that so much attention should be given to him and his needs. What he really wanted was to use the castle as a place where he could eat and sleep.

He hoped that, so far as work was concerned, Lady Beornwyn would provide him with facilities. It would be so much easier to work at the School, where he could also keep an eye on the progress of the embroiderers and, if necessary, make last minute improvements to the design before it got to the frames. As it was, he thought himself lucky. Not only did he appear to have won the protection of someone as exulted as the Queen herself but at long last it looked as though he was going to be able to get on with his work.

Once Josclin had left, Jean brought out the second panel, the one depicting the preparations for embarking the invasion fleet, and laid it out on the table. It would have to be drawn again, as would the first panel since his material wasn't considered robust enough and that was another thing: he would have to ask Lady Beornwyn to procure a supply of suitable linen or would she expect him to do that himself? Not that it mattered having to re-draw the episodes. In some ways, the longer the job took, the more secure he ought to be because once he had finished, he stopped thinking about it and within moments was immersed in sketching in some improving details.

CHAPTER TWENTY EIGHT

Caen

Mathilde glanced at her husband across the table, watching his face for some sign that he might be relenting. Apparently not, because on meeting her eyes he quickly vacated his stool and walked to the window, his back to her. She sighed to herself, more in exasperation than unhappiness and returned her attention to her embroidery frame. He would come round eventually, he always did. This time though, he was just that little more intractable than usual but then, things hadn't quite reached this stage before.

She sensed that, as the problem was of her making, it would have to be up to her to make the first move. Even if she felt herself to be in the right, it didn't alter the fact that he saw things completely differently and, although he had not actually accused her of treason, she knew that he had felt her disloyalty very keenly. The strange thing was that she had not been disloyal. She had not even acted impulsively, as any mother might have done under similar circumstances. Her decision to help Robert had been carefully thought out and William should have known that.

She gave another inward sigh and put her work on the table. She would not get up. She had always used her tiny stature as a defence against William's anger and she was happy for him to tower over her. The lower she was the more helpless she appeared so she would stay seated. The next thing was to bring him over to her. He was drumming his fingers on the stone and still pretending to be looking at something down below. She gently plucked at the thread of her sleeve and careful not to allow the slightest hint of command in her voice, called to him.

'William'

Nothing! No, she reflected. It was never that easy. He was silhouetted in the window, his chin jutting obstinately from his lifted profile. She tried again.

'William! Please let us stop this. Please.' She looked at him at the window, struggling with his pride and his love because he did love her. She was in no doubt about that. She wondered for the hundredth time whether or not she loved him. She thought so. She certainly loved the power that he brought to her and he was head and shoulders above any other man she had ever met, in every sense of the word. His fingers stopped their tattoo on the window ledge. She waited. He half turned and shook his head sadly, speaking from where he stood.

'Why? You are his mother but you are also my wife and not just any wife; a Queen and a Duchess. Between us we rule a small empire and what you have done does no credit to either title. We cannot afford insurrection, filial or otherwise. God knows there are enough forces ranged against me everywhere I look without you aiding and abetting our idiot son in his ineffectual attempts to overthrow me. You disappoint me Mathilde. Not only do you support him but you send him funds. Why? Why did you do it?'

She looked down at the plucked threads of her sleeve. He was not angry. Just sorrowful. Anger would have been easier. His rages were legendary and people feared them. For her though, it would have been less difficult to cope with than this. He was right, of course. She had been uncharacteristically silly but there was some rationality in her actions. The question was whether this was a good time to say so. She smiled at him but he did not respond. Instead, another shake of the head and another turn of the back.

'William, the fact is…no you are quite right, it was inexcusable of me but my actions were prompted by much more than mere maternal bonds. If you think otherwise you do me a gross injustice. You know that I have long argued for you to give Robert more authority. He is of age, no fool and with the right counsel, well able to superintend our affairs in Normandy. No please, let me finish. We are no longer young and it is becoming more and more important for you to delegate…'

Again William shook his head but she continued. 'Who can you really trust William, if not your own family?'

This time he broke in. 'What about Odo? He's family. You think I would trust that rapacious uncle of yours?'

She raised a hand and he noted the threads hanging from the sleeve of her gown.

'He is your half-brother too, William and no, I don't think you should trust him but we have no proof that he was guilty of putting Robert up to this escapade of his. Although like you, I would not have been surprised if he hadn't had something to do with it.'

William snorted. 'Of course he had something to do with it. Why do you think I have sent him back to England with reduced powers? One day he won't be able to help himself and he will overstep the mark enough for me to be able to deal with him properly but, in helping Robert, you have weakened my position here in Normandy. Louis of France is rubbing his hands at the thought that this ridiculous family feud will leave Normandy his for the taking.' He shook his head again and gave her a look of such reproach that, just for the briefest moment, she experienced the novel sensation of remorse. At last, he sat opposite her and she ventured one of her hands on his.

'I am sorry William, if you feel that I have betrayed you but it was solely to mend this…this feud, as you put it, that I acted in the way that I did. Think about it. If I had not supplied Robert with funds, from where else would he have obtained them? Louis, Odo, my brother in Flanders? Either way, he would have bound himself to them and away from us. We… You have two fiefdoms to defend, one of which is a hard won foreign kingdom. We cannot afford any family squabbles William. You and Robert must effect a reconciliation.'

He relinquished her hand and started to rise again.

'Please listen William. You know what I am saying makes sense. As you rightly point out, you have problems enough without allowing your eldest son to add to them. He is a good young man at heart, you know he is but do you really think that I would have helped him if I thought you would be harmed by it? We have been through too much together. We have made history William. Do you honestly think that I would be prepared to risk all that for some weak, maternal gesture?'

He sat down and did nothing for a moment. Eventually, he gently engulfed her hand in his and gently stroked the back of it with his thumb. When he looked up he was smiling.

'Why do you do that?' he said.

'What? Oh, my sleeve! It's a silly habit. For as long as I can remember, since childhood. It sometimes helps me to concentrate although. If you must know, I'm not always aware that I'm doing it.'

He teased out the threads as if examining the individual reds, greens and golds.

'I doubt your ladies love you over much for it.'

She smiled and her smile reflected the relief at having him back with her.

'Oh, I don't think they mind too much. Mind you, Mirabelle used to…'

She paused. 'I shall never forgive Odo for that. For me, that was when he overstepped the mark.'

'Was it him, do you think. Are you sure?'

She nodded and he could see the steely glint in her eyes which had the effect of adding to her stature.

'Yes, of course it was him. Oh! He might not have slit her throat himself although I wouldn't put that past him. No! In all probability it was that slimy madman Wulfric but it would have been at Odo's command.'

She withdrew her hand and crossed her arms about her chest.

'Why should he?' William's tone was genuinely puzzled. 'I mean why should Odo want her harmed? We all knew he'd raped her when she came to the court and he knew that we knew, so there was nothing to hide there.'

Mathilde teased at the threads again. 'I don't know for sure but I have a theory and it concerns Thibault's relationship with Mirabelle rather than Odo's.'

'Thibault! Thibault and Mirabelle?' William gave a disbelieving grimace.

'Yes William, Thibault and Mirabelle. I know it seems, well..., unlikely. Although Thibault was never a womaniser, I have never heard of anything which might suggest that his tastes tended to the opposite sex and don't forget, shortly before she was murdered, I saw them both together in my chambers and there was something in the air...something different about Thibault.'

She stopped as William smiled at her and said, 'Oh God, Mathilde, not your intuition again.'

'All right William, scoff if you like but I think Odo treated Thibault as his alter ego. He was everything that Odo was not and Odo didn't want Thibault's purity, his natural goodness, tainted by association with a girl of Mirabelle's reputation. A reputation which, as you have just said yourself, Odo was responsible for creating in the first place...'

Here William interrupted, 'Oh come on Mathilde. Her reputation, or lack of it, was in no small measure down to the way in which you manipulated the poor girl. Using her ...talents shall we call them, to obtain information didn't exactly cast her in the role of a vestal virgin and anyway, if Thibault was as pure as we all thought him to be, he was hardly likely to be drawn to a girl like Mirabelle was he?'

His wife gave him the look which, through their years together, he had learned to interpret as faintly patronising.

'My dear William,' she said softly, 'for a man who knows so much about the world and how to govern it, you are surprisingly ignorant of what makes people behave as they do. The fact that such a liaison seems unlikely makes it all the more credible. Yes, my dear. I expect you have a problem with the logic of that remark but believe me, I am right.'

All William replied was a disbelieving 'Humph', although he then went on to say, 'When you spoke of Odo and Thibault together, your reference to Thibault was in the past tense. Is he dead?'

She shook her head, 'More or less. He is at present, so far as I know, recovering in the Abbey of St Stephen's, just down the road.'

'Might one ask how you know this?' he said.

'Because I put him there' she replied. 'He sailed over with me and I don't think I have ever seen anybody so stricken. He thought his head was splitting asunder and was barely conscious for much of the journey. More evidence of his feelings for Mirabelle perhaps. Anyway, when we landed, I had him taken to Saint Stephen's with instructions that he should be given the same care that would be accorded to any one of my own sons.'

William took a moment to digest this information. He then left his stool and walked back to the window and asked, 'Will he recover do you think?'

She shrugged her thin shoulders. 'He is young. I have no doubt that time will heal. Why do you ask?'

He evaded the question but instead enquired, 'The lad that Thibault was supposed to be looking after, the artist fellow, what was his name?'

'Jean LeBrun, son of one of Odo's stewards. A boy blessed with considerable talent in my opinion.'

'Yes' he mused. 'I gathered as much when Robert Beaumont told me that he was taking him under his protection, at your specific request. Why would that be, I wonder? You have a reputation for many things but a patroness of the arts…! Well as I thought I knew you, this is a first is it not?'

She had stopped worrying at her sleeve and having diverted William from his original mood was now happy to indulge him. 'I decided that this project of my uncle's, this incredible frieze intended for his cathedral, would be better supervised by someone who understands about these things. It is my intention to divert the design of the piece away from Uncle Odo's ego to the greater cause of trumpeting our own achievements.'

William sat down again and before he could make any comment, she continued, 'I am quite serious about this William. This piece, executed properly, could be our legacy to posterity. Reports from Lanfranc and Beaumont, concerning the LeBrun boy, are extremely encouraging. Not only because of his talent, which is undeniable but also his character. They like him and so do I. I think he can do a great deal to ensure that our conquest of England and events leading from it will be remembered.'

William looked at her doubtfully and said, 'I would not, indeed could not, take issue with you in this matter. Putting it how you have however, it might not be such a bad thing for Odo to be brought down a peg or so. He won't like it though. Everybody in Canterbury will have to watch their backs, your young man in particular. I take it that Beaumont has taken over the baby-sitting duties from Thibault?' She nodded and he continued, 'Just so long as it doesn't interfere with his State duties. Why Canterbury? I can understand why you would want to get your artist away from Odo's clutches at Dover but couldn't you have got him further away from Canterbury?'

She shook her head. 'It had to be Canterbury because of the needlework. The school there is the best. It was me who suggested it to LeBrun.'

He frowned. 'Needlework school, isn't that run by that Beornwyn woman. Poor lad, she'll scare the life out of him.'

She gave him a rare grin, 'I don't think so William, he wasn't scared of me and anyway, she will put her pet bulldog to guard his back. If Odo's odious toad tries to get at LeBrun, he could well find himself squashed under Warin's Saxon boot.'

William gave an equally unusual guffaw. 'My God, Mathilde you are priceless.' The laugh faded away. 'You still shouldn't have done what you did though. In future, leave son Robert to me.' He turned to go.

'By the way, I'm back to England, the Northern rebels there have to be put down, once and for all. You are in charge here. Not Robert, you. Can I trust you Mathilde?' Without waiting for an answer he again made to leave. At the door he stopped.

'One more thing. Keep an eye on Thibault. As soon as he is recovered, get him away from those monks and make him get into training again. I think I might be able to use him.'

He left without further word or gesture and she thoughtfully resumed her seat and took up her frame – but not her needle. She now had one of the most powerful dukedoms in France to administer and much to think about.

CHAPTER TWENTY NINE

The School of Needlework

It was early morning and Lady Beornwyn leaned on her table, her large hands splayed on the board, her attention once again focussed on Jean's design. She turned to her companion.

'Well! What do you think?'

It was some time before the girl made any reply and, when she did, her fingers were skittering over the figures in front of her as if she were already working them in stitch. She spoke without raising her eyes.

'How long did you say?'

Beornwyn repeated the dimensions that Jean had given her. Again, it was some time before the girl spoke and, young as she was, it was with the confidence of one who enjoyed the respect of this Saxon noblewoman.

'I don't see why not. The design is perfect for our sort of work and the scale of it is not important.'

She looked squarely at Beornwyn.

'So long as the client is not in any hurry?'

Beornwyn shook her head and waited for the girl to continue but she just stood there, frowning at the picture. 'I say the scale is not important but we would have to obtain the right framing for each panel. 'This...' she pointed at the panel on the table, 'is not suitable for stretching. No allowance has been made for extra material for that purpose. How do you think we can overcome that? Presumably the designer can be instructed to remedy the fault for future panels – or have they already been completed?'

Beornwyn shook her head again.

'The honest answer is, I don't know. Anyway it isn't important because I have already instructed that whatever has been completed will have to be re-drawn on a more suitable fabric.'

She gave a rueful smile.

'To tell the truth niece, I was so taken by the quality of the artwork and the challenges presented by it, that some of the practical issues slipped my mind. Thank goodness one of us has retained some common sense. But you do think it fine, the work that is? Forget the practical issues for the time being.

All I want to hear from you now is what you think of the design and whether, in principle, we accept the project.'

The girl stepped back from the table and gravely regarded her aunt. Although only seventeen, she was astute enough to appreciate that Beornwyn, usually the most outspoken and straightforward of women, had not perhaps told her everything and she had no intention of getting involved in something that might have unforeseen consequences. She tucked an errant blonde lock of hair back under her coif, moving the finger to her lip which she stroked as she considered her reply.

Beornwyn noticed this unselfconscious, girlish gesture and smiled. She allowed few weaknesses into her austere life but Alysoun, her niece, was a notable exception. Indeed Alysoun was quite an exceptional young lady in her own right. Educated to a standard to which few of her sex could lay claim, she was also strong willed, awkward and difficult. To those few fortunate enough to have access to this relationship between aunt and niece, it was amazing that the two of them had not created hell from their shared existence but no! They seldom had occasion to differ but when they did, they argued their respective positions quietly, respectfully and without any hint of rancour.

Alysoun turned her attention from Beornwyn, back to the panel.

'It is clever, is it not, the way that the artist has captured the essence of the story and yet retained the simplicity of the design. It is as though it was drawn for children but there is an underlying sophistication to it... I can't really explain it but it almost tells the story verbally as well as visually – which I suppose to be the intention of...of ...who exactly is the artist?'

Beornwyn waved a large dismissive hand.

'At the moment I don't think we need worry about that. All I wanted to hear from you, was your opinion of what you see before you and whether or not you think it suitable for our ladies to embroider.'

This time it was the turn of Alysoun to be dismissive.

'Yes, yes. Of course it will be suitable. Just tell me again, how big?'

Beornwyn repeated the dimensions.

Alysoun's fingers moved back to her mouth.

'Of course we must do it. Otherwise your artist will take it off to Winchester and they'll jump at it, you know they will.

They'll make a mess of it, of course, but something like this is far too interesting to turn down. I wonder what the rest of it is like. Since what is depicted here,' she indicated the length of the panel 'relates to events preceding the battle, I assume the other panels continue with the story, the actual invasion and so forth.'

She stopped for a moment and when she next turned to her aunt, her eyes had taken on a mischievous twinkle.

'There is no way is there, that we could…well… turn this piece of work to our advantage. You know what I mean? Alter things just a tiny bit. Not much but just enough to sow one or two seeds of ambiguity into the story of the great Norman victory and occupation. I know it wouldn't mean a lot to most people but we would know wouldn't we? I take it that this is destined to be a record of their heroic achievement. Could we not, well, you know…'

Beornwyn took both of Alysoun's small hands in hers and gave a resigned shake of her head.

'Too dangerous my dear. I haven't yet told you who is behind this, this …Oh! I don't know what to call it. This illustrated history of our decline, this frieze, this… Look the power behind this idea is our old enemy Odo of Bayeux. He is certainly the man financing it and I am not, I repeat not, going to do anything which might even remotely put you in danger from him.'

Alysoun attempted to pull her hands free but Beornwyn kept them tightly within her own and when the girl tried to speak, she was hushed by her aunt.

'I mean it my dear. My brother, slaughtered by the Normans along with the rest of our family, left you under my protection and if there is one person in this world I would keep you from it is that awful man. His pet toad, Wulfric has been seen in Canterbury and if Odo even remotely suspected that our centre was compromising his intentions, I would be the first to suffer and Odo knows only too well that the best way to bring me down would be through you. I could not bear to see that happen. It would…'

Alysoun wrenched her hands free at last but only to reverse the hold and prevent her aunt from further speech.

'Does Odo even know of my existence? I thought I was your best kept secret. I thought that was the reason why I was never allowed into your circle and meet interesting people like Lanfranc and Gandulph, even if they are Norman.'

'Italian, dear'

'What?'

'Lanfranc, he's Italian by birth and yes, of course Odo is aware of your existence. He knows everything. Especially so far as his enemies are concerned and be in no doubt, I am his enemy and he will be well aware that you are the chink in my personal armour. Nothing would give him greater pleasure than seeing me destroyed, as I would be if you came to any harm at his hands.'

Alysoun gave an irritated shake of her head, causing the lock of hair to escape its confinement again.

'You won't always be here to protect me, Aunt. Anyway Warin would never let anyone within miles of me. Oh! You don't think I notice but wherever I go he's never far away. He wouldn't let anyone talk to me let alone threaten me.

I would have thought he was more of a match for Odo, let alone Wulfric – or whatever his name is.'

Beornwyn immediately became very serious.

'Listen carefully Alysoun. This is not the first time we have had this discussion and, knowing you, I very much doubt that it will be the last but I don't only protect you because you are my niece and I have sworn to do so. You have many talents my child. You are possibly the best needlewoman in Europe. Yes, even at your age, I can think of none better. You are clever and when you chose to be, wise. I have impressed upon you from the very start just how important it is to retain some vestige of power and influence. We can't do anything about The Conquest. It is a fact and we unfortunately have to live with it but we can, providing we have the respect of the Normans, have some influence on the future. Time will bring about total assimilation of both Norman and Saxon but it is only by earning their respect for our talents that we can hope to retain any vestige of our own culture. Lanfranc sees our value, as does Robert Beaumont. I think that even William himself realises that it is only by harnessing the energies of both our races that his rule and that of his successors can be assured but brutes like Odo expect nothing more than the total subjugation of the Saxon peoples, not for reasons of State but for his own ends. His must not be the view that prevails. So you see my pet, it is vitally important that rare blooms such as yourself be protected. Now, tell me you do understand and you must promise me that if we undertake this work, you will not attempt to sabotage it in any way that will antagonise Odo.'

She gently disengaged her hands and pushed Alysoun out at arms length, the better to focus on the girl's response. In the event, Alysoun merely nodded her acquiescence but the hint of a furrow on her smooth brow indicated a thought that was formulating but was not yet to be given voice. She nodded again and suggested that they return to the matter in hand.

While they were discussing the practical aspects of the embroidery, quantities and quality of wools, dyes and tensions, Alysoun suddenly turned to Beornwyn and again asked about the designer; if it was a Saxon in the employ of the Earl of Kent or one of his own countrymen. Whether it was a woman or a man and what else of note the artist had done.

Beornwyn pretended to be concentrating on the drawing and it was some time before she answered her and when she did so, she took care not to look at her niece.

'Does it matter? We are always undertaking commissions involving anonymous artists and designers. Why so interested in this one?'

She kept her voice casual but for the second time that morning, Alysoun felt that something was being held from her and being Alysoun, she was not prepared to leave it at that. Her tone was reproachful.

'Please, Aunt. This is different, you know full well it is. This is no ordinary commission for a wall hanging or a cushion cover. This is enormous and it is exciting.'

She waved her hand over the panel.

'This is a challenge such as we have never before undertaken and it is important to understand the mind of the designer if we are to do it justice.'

Her aunt remained silent, then turned unwillingly towards her niece, noting her youth, the strand of hair, her figure hidden under the shapeless black habit she wore, her beautiful blue eyes and clear complexion. She coughed.

'Well, of course there is no reason why you should not know. It isn't a secret. It…it is a man. There. Now, where were we?'

Alysoun giggled but seeing her aunt's expression, suppressed it immediately.

'Just a minute Aunt. What sort of man. Is he one of us, one of theirs. Old, young?'

Beornwyn sighed. Alysoun had no intention of letting her guardian recover her customary composure.

'Well. Why won't you tell me?' She had a sudden impish thought. 'He's not… surely not… not a special friend of yours is he? I mean a special friend. Really, Aunt. I never knew that you…'

'Of course he isn't, you silly girl.' broke in Beornwyn roughly. She, who had never in her life known a man in any sense of the word was, nevertheless, not unhappy to be teased occasionally. 'I thought I'd brought you up to be more sensible than that. Special friend indeed. I might have expected that remark from one of our more foolish needlewomen but from you…'

She sighed again, knowing that she was going to have to be a little more informative before Alysoun would let the matter rest.

'If you must know, he, yes it is a 'he', is a son of one of Odo's stewards in Normandy and if the Archbishop had not been so particular in his recommendations, I might well not have given him any of my time which, by the way, you now seem intent on wasting. As it happens, I also think he has great talent. Like you, I cannot quite put my finger on it but there is something about his work which is very compelling. It might only appear to be a simple representation of events but he has somehow captured the very essence of the history.'

Alysoun looked interested. 'Have you seen anything else of his?' Beornwyn shook her head.

'No, nothing, only this but I seem to remember Robert Beaumont saying something about his life drawing, whatever that is supposed to mean. According to him it is quite extraordinary, if unusual. Perhaps I should ask LeBrun if he has anything else here in Canterbury that we can look at.'

Alysoun frowned again, 'LeBrun! Is that his name?'

Suddenly her aunt seemed abstracted and again retreated into her inspection of the design. Alysoun was about to push the conversation further but had the feeling that this was not quite the right time. Not now but perhaps later. She was intrigued. Usually so open with her, Beornwyn had never before prevaricated in this way. Never mind, she could wait. She returned to discussing the matter of leaving sufficient width for borders and stretching. Beornwyn nodded her approval.

'Very well,' she said, 'I will make it my business to talk to LeBrun as soon as possible. As I told you, the murderous Wulfric is in the area. It appears that LeBrun has no great affection for Wulfric but then, who could have, the creature's not human but LeBrun seems to have gone out of his way to make an actual enemy of the man. That being the case, I have seen to it that Warin's protective duties have been extended to LeBrun. Another reason why you should have particular regard to your own safety.'

She shot a sideways glance at her niece. She expected to see another frown, accompanied by another question and was not disappointed.

'But Aunt, I thought you said that they were both working for Odo. Surely that puts them on the same side. Why would this Le…LeBrun go out of his way to antagonise Wulfric who is presumably here to look after him?'

Beornwyn sighed, 'Not look after him Alysoun. At least not in that sense. Odo has given LeBrun the silver to pay for our work. Wulfric's task, I imagine, is to make sure that it is not spent on anything else. No! Of this I am sure. LeBrun sees Wulfric for what he is. A particularly nasty creature that prefers to carry out his foul deeds in the dark. Whatever else he may be, I am certain that LeBrun is an artist first and foremost and as such, is an unlikely bedfellow of either his master or his minder. Warin will see he comes to no harm, at least until he has completed his work. After that it is not really our concern is it?'

'No, I suppose not, Aunt.' came the reply. 'But I think we should resolve these matters we have been discussing as soon as possible because…'

'Not we, dear.' Lady Beornwyn broke in. 'Any future discussions that are required between the designer and our school will be conducted by myself. There is no need for you to be involved although, naturally, that does not exclude you from raising points that you feel necessary to be brought up at such meetings. But you can do that through me. No!' She raised her hand to forestall the inevitable argument. 'There is no more to be said on the subject.

Alysoun shrugged her shoulders and just for a moment, allowed a shadow of a pout to appear on her lips but it quickly disappeared, as Beornwyn knew it would. Then, relenting slightly, she thought that the girl deserved to take something away from this meeting, so the raised hand was lowered onto that of her niece.

'What you said just now, you know about including, shall we say a hint, of the Saxon participation in this work? Well, I have informed the artist that a condition of my accepting the commission is that I have control over the design of the borders and the accompanying text…'

Her next words were lost in the shriek of delight from the girl upon whom her aunt gripped her shoulders so tightly the shriek ended in an involuntary 'ouch!' and Beornwyn continued seriously.

'It will have to be subtle and ensure that there is no way Odo can perceive any slight or Saxon bias but believe me niece, when I have done my work there will be no doubt as to the origin of the embroidery. Sneaking regard that I have for William's consort, I will not have her claiming it as Norman work.'

She stood back from Alysoun and awaited her response. The girl looked back at the design and when she returned her eyes to those of Beornwyn, they twinkled mischievously. She stretched up onto her toes and gave her aunt's cheek a resounding kiss and then, without saying another word, whirled around, black habit flying and skipped out of the door.

Beornwyn smiled indulgently at this undignified exit but almost immediately composed her features into their customary severity.

Alysoun would have to be the one to oversee the actual application of thread to cloth. She would bring vivacity, echoing that of LeBrun, to the finished embroidery that Beornwyn, for all her skills, could not hope to match. Sooner or later, she pondered, the two young people would have to meet but not just yet. No indeed, not until it was absolutely necessary and even then…

Alysoun's carefree mood accompanied her out into the sunlit, now busy, street as she made her way to the dyers. She chuckled to herself as she spied Warin inexpertly following her progress but she had not seen the other one, the one that kept to the shadows, out of the way of the townsfolk and so quietly as to be almost invisible.

As she walked, she thought over what she had just seen, the image of the panel firmly fixed in her mind. It would need fine wool, expensively dyed, if the embroidery was to remain true to the artist's intentions but with a work of this incredible length, continuity of shade would be difficult. She needed to talk to the designer if she were really going to do him justice. She wondered, again, what he was like and why it was that her aunt seemed so reluctant to have her meet him. True, Beornwyn took her responsibilities as a guardian very seriously but she, Alysoun, had never given her cause to feel protective so far as men were concerned. Especially since things had settled down in the region and Lanfranc had imposed a more disciplined regime on the occupying forces. She turned a corner, once more catching sight of Warin as she did so. No, she felt safe here now. It would take a particularly talented individual to penetrate the protective screen provided by the over-tall noblewomen and her over-short servant. Certainly, she had no need to worry on that score.

CHAPTER THIRTY

Canterbury Castle

Jean opened his eyes, stretched and blinked at the drifting dust motes revealed in the ray of watery sun that pierced the missing thatch in the roof. He then became aware of the noises. Quarrelsome birds, people talking, utensils clanging and animals whinnying, bleating and snorting. He shot upright. He was late! Late for what? He lay down again.

Now that it had been decreed that his designs required a better quality linen, there wasn't much he could do until better quality linen had been made available to him. He then reflected that the time since leaving Dover had probably been the best that he had experienced since arriving on these shores. This project was to be taken up by the best schools of needlework to be found anywhere. He now appeared to enjoy the protection of, not only Lord Beaumont but also the personal bodyguard of Lady Beornwyn. The detestable Wulfric had been sent packing and best of all, it seemed that the power of Lord Odo was, for the moment, neutralised.

A cloud must have drifted across the sun because the thin shaft of light disappeared. There was a knock on his door and a gruff Saxon voice announced something or other. Jean pushed himself upright and opened the door, only to find that the owner of the voice had gone but on the bench outside his hut was a hunk of fresh looking bread, some yellowish cheese, a pitcher of weak beer and an earthenware bowl of cold water. He took a deep breath, ducked his head, shook the water out of his hair, dried his hands on the cloth which had also been left on the bench and wondered how long this favoured treatment was going to last. Then, as he made his breakfast, thought what did it matter, he'd just enjoy it while it did.

Having wandered off to use the jakes, he returned to the bailey which, despite Beaumont's comment of the previous evening, seemed to be quite busy. He was pleased to notice that most of the occupants, of all stations, greeted him and each other with a civility which was noticeably lacking at Dover.

He re-entered his refuge and rummaged about in his bag until he found the notes that had been made for him during his audience with the Queen.

Such a short time had elapsed since then and yet so much had happened. He shook his head and went back outside. Everything he drew now would have to be redone on new material but he couldn't just sit and idle away his time. Anyway, he felt the urge to start drawing again so he looked at the notes on the scenes for the preparation of the invasion. Very soon his fingers were itching to translate the words into pictures so he mounted a length of linen on his trestle and started to sharpen some charcoal. The first specs of charcoal dust were still floating down when he heard the bugle at the gate.

The Lady Beornwyn, accompanied by two servants tottering under heavy loads, registered her noble presence as she entered the inner bailey. All the Saxon workers immediately stopped what they were doing, the women curtsying, the men bowing deeply and the Normans, even those of quality, dipped their heads as the lady passed on her way to Jean's ramshackle shelter. Out of the corner of his other eye Jean could see Lord Beaumont and the ever present Josclin, making their way down the steps of the keep in order to make their own welcome. It so happened that Jean was situated half way between the entrance to the inner bailey and the keep so it was at his table that the two parties converged.

Jean hurriedly rose to his feet, brushing crumbs from his tunic with one hand and failing to smooth down his hair with the other. Beornwyn gave him a nod of recognition and formally greeted Beaumont who responded equally formally. She then turned her attention to Jean.

'Well, Master LeBrun, I am gratified to see that you are prepared for work.'

She indicated the servants.

'I have brought you a bolt of unbleached linen of the required weight and a supply of the finest charcoal to be found in this region.'

She instructed her servants to deposit their burdens onto the trestle. She dismissed them and they took their leave. Again she addressed herself to Jean.

'The charcoal, as I have mentioned, is as fine as you will get anywhere but I would urge you to use it lightly and wherever possible, avoid smudging. Do not forget that borders, top and bottom, are to be added at a time to be specified by me and that I will also be responsible for deciding the content of those borders…'

Jean started to interrupt but she raised her hand and continued, 'Although you will still be required to draw them in when the time comes. Did you wish to say something?'

Jean looked from Lord Beaumont to her and asked would it not be possible for him to make his studio somewhere in The School of Embroidery because… Before he could give his reasons for the request it was most firmly nipped in the bud with a resounding 'NO!' which had the effect of even making Lord Beaumont and Josclin take a step backwards. She went on more quietly but equally firmly.

'That I will not allow but should you wish to confer with me or I with you, I have no doubt that a meeting can be arranged. Your commission is one of design, mine is one of needlework. When we come to the matter of the borders, as I have intimated, collaboration will of course be necessary but I will decide how, when and where that collaboration will take place. Is that understood?'

Jean started to look rebellious and was about to ignore Beaumont's warning look when, for the second time that morning, there was a clamour at the gatehouse and any further conversation was halted by the sound of hoof-beats in the outer bailey and the entrance of a hard ridden horse, the rider of which threw himself at the feet of Lady Beornwyn, almost before the animal had skidded to a halt in front of her.

She immediately hauled him up and dragged him to one side where, with a voice verging on hysteria, he imparted whatever the message was that he'd raced to deliver. When she turned from him towards them, her face had drained of all it's natural colour and her hands were tightly grasped together in an unsuccessful attempt to stop them shaking. Lord Beaumont was at her side in an instant, leading her to Jean's bench.

Josclin had called for water. She took a sip, spilling more than she was able to swallow and just sat there. She was not in shock but she was fighting to control her feelings as well as her hands. The three of them kept a respectful distance to allow her time to recover her composure and Josclin impatiently waved away the curious crowd that was threatening to gather. The messenger, or whatever he was, had his face buried in the sweat flecked mane of his horse. His shoulders were heaving, whether from shortness of breath or emotion, it was impossible to say.

Beaumont gently nudged the beaker closer to Beornwyn and indicated that she take another drink but this time she shook her head. She was not and probably never had been a woman of beauty but when she raised her face to them it was as if she had, in those few moments, aged a decade. She had not, however, lost one ounce of her spirit. Her eyes gleamed with a fierceness and her angular body was tense with anger. She spoke quietly but in a tone that was not to be questioned.

'Beaumont, come with me. Josclin, horses and some men. You,' pointing at Jean, 'Stay here.' Jean started to protest but she stopped him. 'Stay here LeBrun and get on with your work. We will talk later. Here, mark you, not at the school.'

Her look brooked no argument whatsoever. Jean bowed and she nodded. Horses appeared from the stabling. She shrugged off offers of help and unaided, mounted the biggest horse there, rearranging her robes and riding like a man. She was the first to leave the gate, the rear being brought up by five armed soldiers wearing Beaumont's colours.

Jean walked over to the messenger who was just about to remount and follow. He waved him away and spurred his mount after the others. It was ages before the dust settled again and the silence which had accompanied the frenetic activity of moments before was replaced by a buzz of conjecture. Small groups were gathering and voices were raised, speculating on the events just witnessed. Among them Jean caught sight of his erstwhile companion Ranulph, the carpenter. Ranulph saw Jean wave. He waved back and came over to him. He nodded towards the gate.

'What was all that about then?'

Jean had to confess that he had no idea.

'All I know is that somebody galloped in, spoke to Lady Beornwyn and off they all went like they were chasing the devil.'

Ranulph stroked his stubbled chin. 'Funny old business! Not like his Lordship to take off in a hurry like that. Must be something serious.'

Jean sighed. 'Yes, it must be but at the moment I have my own problems.' Ranulph nodded sympathetically. 'The pictures not going well then?'

'Not going anywhere Ranulph, that's just it. As soon as I think I'm up and running, something or more likely somebody, comes along and puts a stop to it.'

They sat on the bench together and Jean told him all about having to start again because of the linen, the borders and the stretching. About not having enough say in the finished work and generally, how totally pissed off he was with the whole thing. Again a sympathetic nod, then a thought seemed to have occurred to the carpenter.

'Stretching you say. I take it you mean like embroidery frames?' Jean nodded, still concentrating on his own concerns.

'I think I can help you there,' Ranulph continued. 'I've made frames since I was old enough to cut myself. For me Mum, me sister, sister in law, lady up at the manor and I can tell you why they liked 'em!' Jean made no comment, still frowning at the dust thrown up by the horses.

Ranulph went on. 'Well, do you want to know or don't you?' Again there was no response from Jean so he just continued.

'Thing is, most frames lay flat and you have to lift them up to get the stitches round the back. You with me?' At last Jean nodded, wondering where this seemingly pointless conversation was going.

Ranulph took an exasperated breath.

'Well, I mounted them on an easel. Easy! Couple of good leather hinges which you can fold down if you want the frame flat or stand it up if you want to work both sides and keep both hands free. Good innit?'

At last he seemed to have Jean's attention.

'Sorry Ranulph, can you just go through that again?' This Ranulph did with the barely suppressed patience of a craftsman talking to an artist. Jean thought for a moment longer then said reflectively, 'Suppose I could introduce this idea to the Lady Beornwyn that is if she hadn't already heard of it, it might well work in my favour. Wouldn't be exactly teaching her job, that would be more than I would dare do but still…' Then Jean appeared to think of something else. He turned to Ranulph, 'I imagine that the important thing is to keep the fabric stretched. How would you do that.?'

Ranulph tapped the side of nose and grinned. 'Ah well, that's the other thing. See,' here he started to warm to his subject. 'There are two ways of doing it. The first is to fit the first frame with the cloth stretched over, into a second frame, just big enough to take it and hold it securely…' Jean broke in.

'Yes I know, my mother uses one but it's only small, not nearly big enough to cope with something like this.' He waved to the panel on the trestle.'

Another grin. 'That brings us to the second way. You'll never guess…'

'Oh stop fooling about Ranulph, just tell me.'

'Well!' Ranulph said, 'You could fix a roller on either side of the frame and stretch it over those. All you need to do is to be able to anchor the rollers to get the right tension.'

Jean tried to visualise what exactly he was talking about. He thought he'd got it but if he was to present a possibly radical idea to the school of embroidery, he needed to make sure he'd got it right.

'How many of these have you made?' he asked, 'The ones with these rollers?'

'None.' Ranulph said, still grinning.

'None!' Jean groaned. 'Look Ranulph, I haven't time for this. If you really want to help me you can find me some really smooth board. Like you did last time only this one as big as this trestle top.'

Ranulph whistled through his blackened teeth, 'I'll 'ave a go but it might 'ave to be two pieces. Suppose I could butt up the joints so's you'd 'ardly notice. I'll 'ave a look. Meantime, I'll see if I can't experiment with this frame thing.'

'You do that,' Jean said 'But a really flat top is the main priority. Is that all right?'

Ranulph started measuring up the worktable, while Jean was still visualising how best to interpret Mathilde's record, when Josclin's harsh tones brought them both back to reality

'I would have thought you both had enough to do without gossiping like a couple of nuns in a cloister. On your way master carpenter. Go about your business.'

Jean nodded farewell to Ranulph and mouthed that he'd see him later, then turned to the grim faced Josclin.

'Josclin, I thought you'd gone with…'

'I did but I turned back. Sit down!'

Jean gave him an enquiring look.

'SIT DOWN' he hissed 'And listen carefully. Don't bother to ask me questions because I don't have answers. All I know is that I was ordered by his Lordship to return and make sure you are still in one piece and ensure that you stay that way.'

He took Ranulph's place on the bench and turned to face Jean. His mouth was set in a tight line and his fists were clenched. Eventually he told Jean everything that he knew and although it didn't amount to much in the way of information, the content hit Jean like a blow from a cudgel.

'Warin is dead' Josclin said simply. That was all. He had no details because it appeared that on route to wherever it was they were going, Robert Beaumont suddenly reigned in his horse and ordered Josclin to return. Josclin took the order without question so here he was and as much in the dark as Jean. Jean regarded the table in front of him and the panel that lay on it. Josclin must have picked up Jean's thoughts because he said.

'You'd better forget that for the time being' he nodded in the direction of the table. 'I think I'd sooner have you in the keep instead of wandering about in the open.'

Jean protested. 'But I've only just moved in here, what…'

Josclin clutched Jean's arm like a vice.

'Didn't you hear what I just said LeBrun, Warin is dead. Have you the remotest idea what he meant to Lady Beornwyn. He wasn't just her bodyguard. He was…Oh! It doesn't matter, you wouldn't understand, but this,' waving dismissively at the panel. 'Can wait. Now, let's get up into the keep and we'll see if we can't find you a room with half decent light. Obviously it won't be as good for you as here,'

He looked up at the cloudless sky which had promised so much for Jean at the beginning of the day.

'But needs must. I was ordered to see that you came to no harm and that is all that concerns me. I can watch out for you in there, here in the open, there are too many distractions.'

Glumly Jean packed up his bags and Josclin ordered a couple of young menials to carry the bolt of cloth and they followed Josclin up the steps. After throwing open several doors, he eventually grunted. 'See if this one is any good.'

Actually the room didn't look too bad to Jean, at least while the sun was shining. It had two uncovered windows looking out on to the bailey and at this time of day he would have plenty of light with which to work.

What he didn't have was a trestle long enough to take even half of one of the panels. Although he had been given an arbitrary length from which to work and he assumed it had something to do with the space in which it was going to be hung, he still had not been given the full catalogue of events that were to be portrayed. Therefore he had divided the lengths into the length of the table on which he'd had first worked in Dover. This was twenty seven pieds and if he had to condense or stretch the narrative to fit this size, it really didn't matter too much. The actual size of the worktop was of no importance. The excess length of linen could drop over the ends but he resolved, for no very good reason, to retain the panel size on which he'd first settled.

He was, however, beginning to wonder if it was all going to happen anyway. If Warin had been killed by Wulfric, whether in revenge of his father or by orders of Odo, would Beornwyn still want to continue with the work? Would she in turn feel threatened enough not to carry out a commission which appeared to be slipping out of Odo's sphere of influence into that of the Queen? Odo had laid great store by this work. What was it he had said? 'My passport to posterity' or something like that. It was beginning to look as if the Queen was looking to grab this particular piece of posterity for herself and Odo wouldn't like that, especially as he was funding it. That thought prompted Jean to check his pouch and yes, the remainder of the silver was intact.

He went to look for a servant to tell Ranulph where to find him in his new quarters. Then to work.

His latest orders had been to start again, leave borders at either end and top and bottom of the panels and redraw everything he had thus far done and that is what he would do. This was assuming that Lady Beornwyn was still interested in taking on the project. Jean could see that keeping up his initial enthusiasm was not going to be easy. Fortunately, Beornwyn only had the first panel and so vividly was the image of every line of it etched on Jean's memory that he would have little trouble in reproducing it on the new linen without recourse to the original.

He managed to catch up with one of the boys who had carried up the linen. Saxon and not over-bright, he was eventually made to understand that he was to find Ranulph and inform him of Jean's new whereabouts. Jean also instructed him to find the longest trestle in the castle and have it brought to the room. Jean watched him meander off down the passageway, shrugged and thought he'd be lucky if what he'd said had filtered through, taking into account the language and the apparent dimness of the lad but he was wrong.

Within the hour, the boy had returned with a companion, carrying between them the trestles and the board which Jean had left in the bailey. The message to Ranulph had also been delivered.

He wasn't sure how long he had been bent over the table but he was certainly aware of the ache in his back so he imagined that it must have been for four or five hours. That was the trouble. Once he started, he seemed to lose all track of time or things that were going on around him. It wasn't until he had unfolded himself and was painfully stretching his back that he became aware of somebody else in the room. He whirled around, hands still firmly pressed into his spine and saw, with much relief, that it was Robert Beaumont standing in the doorway. From arching backward he leant forward in a clumsy bow and Beaumont smiled. It was a sad smile which soon faded. He placed a hand on Jean's shoulder and said.

'I see you haven't wasted any time. You look tired, let us be seated. I need to talk to you.'

They both found stools and Beaumont looked at him seriously, brow furrowed. Josclin entered the room and took his master's position in the doorway. Eventually Beaumont, indicating Josclin, said 'Josclin tells me that he has informed you of the reason for our precipitous departure.' Jean nodded.

'Well!' he went on. 'The first thing you need to know is that Lady Beornwyn wishes you to continue with your part of this commission and she will be here within the week to discuss the matter in more detail. She is much affected by the death of her servant. I think it fair to say that the absence of Warin in her life will mean her own safety is considerably more at risk than when he was alive. I have as you would expect, offered her an escort, bodyguard, call it what you will, from my own resources, even Josclin here, but she has declined. She is a lady of courage and fortitude and as such, has made enemies as well as friends in this region. You have, I think, been made aware that the more, shall we say, enlightened among us Normans, see her collaboration as essential to our successful government of south eastern England and I would include the King himself in that number.'

He paused for a moment.

'Warin was murdered and it will not come as much of a surprise to you that Wulfric is the prime suspect. Warin killed Wulfric's father, himself a distinctly unpleasant individual, and Wulfric has long sworn to have his revenge.'

Jean started to say something but he went on.

'I think, however, it goes deeper than a matter of mere revenge. I think, as does Lady Beornwyn, that there are political implications here. I think The Earl of Kent sees his power here eroding. I have already discussed with you the recent developments in Normandy which might have led me to this conclusion and somehow this work of yours has become almost symbolic of this struggle. Her Majesty's interest in it and the corresponding protection which this lends you and for that matter anyone connected with it is being seen by your Lord as a challenge to his authority. The same could be said for my presence here in Canterbury.'

He looked at Jean as if expecting some kind of comment on his observations but Jean couldn't think of anything intelligent to say. All these matters of intrigue and politics were so far removed from him and his experience that any contribution from him was not going to be relevant. Beaumont drew a deep breath and continued.

'LeBrun, I fully understand your reluctance to get involved in something which is quite beyond your understanding but you have no choice! The Queen is particularly keen for this embroidery to be satisfactorily completed and since she wishes it, so does the King. Between you and me, His Majesty will be here within a few days and will doubtless be looking for some reassurance on this point. So, we mustn't disappoint him, must we? With Wulfric on the loose, many from this garrison will be focussed on the protection of those engaged in the production of this work so I don't think you should have too many fears from that quarter. He is though, and I don't have to tell you this, a practised assassin and I do not imagine for one instant that Lord Odo has him under tight control so, it won't be easy. Protecting Lady Beornwyn, without her knowledge, is going to be particularly difficult, however, that is my problem, yours is to get this work completed as soon as you can. Any assistance that you might need will be forthcoming. Perhaps you would like a little time to assimilate all this, in which case I will leave you to your thoughts and return later.'

'That won't be necessary my Lord.' Jean spoke quickly because his mind was already made up. He went on, 'If I am to finish this design then so be it. I will do my best but if you remember, my Lord, I need to know in detail the story of the battle and what happened immediately afterwards, if I am to complete it to the original specification that is.' Beaumont nodded his acknowledgement of this fact and said that other duties allowing, he would put himself at Jean's disposal for as long as it took to give him the information he needed. Jean, however hadn't quite finished.

'There is one other thing, my Lord. What is to become of me once this commission is completed? Until that time I might well be under the King's protection but afterwards? Another thing, my family is still in thrall to my Lord Odo on his estates in France, what of their future?'

Robert Beaumont rose to his feet and smiled before answering.

'That is two 'other things' LeBrun, but so far as the latter is concerned, Lord Odo's reliance on your father's stewardship is such that he is unlikely to do anything which might jeopardise it. As for you…well, time enough for that when the moment arrives. You are too young, I think, to give much thought to the future when the present offers you so much.' he swept an arm around the room. 'You are comfortable here and I will tell your old friend Guy of Falaise to make some improvements to the light in here. It is too difficult to protect you in the bailey. Too many comings and goings but then, I think Josclin here has already made that fact known to you.'

Jean, who stood up with Beaumont, wandered over to his table.

'The liaison between myself and the school, my Lord. There will need to be much consultation between us if my designs are to be interpreted in such a way that both of us are satisfied. Is it not going to be at all possible for me to work at the school, next to the embroiderers?'

'Not a chance, according to Lady Beornwyn.' Beaumont replied 'and I would strongly advise you not to alienate that lady. Believe me, we have all tried and she has always succeeded in getting her own way. Anyway, as I told you, she will be here within the week, when she will certainly tell you what exactly it is that she wants from you. Take my advice and give her whatever that might be and don't ask for more. Tell Josclin here when you are ready to resume our discussions and I will do whatever I can to accommodate you. Good afternoon.'

CHAPTER THIRTY ONE

The School

Beornwyn stood facing a shocked Alysoun, her heavy hands enclosing the more delicate ones of the girl and a look of compassion marking her heavy features. The voice was as melodious as ever but the tone was compounded of sorrow and anger. It was the girl who broke what had been a long silence when she whispered, as if hardly daring to give voice to what was in her mind.

'It must have been just after I left the dyers. It is horrible, just too horrible. The master dyer had accompanied me onto the street and instructed his people to have their breakfast. They all came out too, to enjoy the sunshine and eat their bread away from the smells of the vats. He walked with me a little way and I remember, I looked around for Warin,' she gave a sniff and a faint smile 'You know what a terrible job he made of shadowing me. I suppose it was because he dare not let me out of his sight. I couldn't see him and it must have been then, about that time, while the vats were unattended. What......what happened exactly Aunt. I have to know.'

'I don't know child, exactly what happened.' was the response. 'The first thing I knew was when Ward, one of the senior dyers, fetched me from the castle. He was, for a time, quite bereft of speech. Eventually I managed to elicit from him that the body of my trusted friend had been found in one of the vats...I...'

Her voice tailed off and she turned her face from that of her niece. Her hands, still holding those of Alysoun, trembled very slightly. When she turned back, her voice and eyes were steady and strong.

'It appears that Warin was stabbed from behind, expertly of course, and pushed into the vat. I think, that is I hope, that his death resulted instantly from the stabbing rather than from drowning in the dye.'

Releasing Alysoun's hands she took a deep breath and continued.

'Of course it had to be the madder vat in which he was found. When we arrived on the scene he had been hauled out and because of the red, it was a little while before Beaumont located the actual wound but you don't need to know any more of that.'

She stopped and looked at Alysoun who was standing there trembling, a fist to her mouth. Beornwyn hugged her and spoke over her shoulder.

'Child, I cannot understand it. I had always assumed that Warin was indestructible. He had always been so much a part of my strength. Whenever, after the conquest I felt that things were slipping away from me, I only had to clap eyes on that squat, ugly, unlovely man, still waging his own private war and winning his own silly little battles and it gave me the impetus to carry on. Now I shall worry about you more than ever, without him to look after you.' She released Alysoun and turned her back on her, her defeated posture echoing her distress.

Alysoun moved over to her.

'What about you Aunt. You have lost your bodyguard. Few people know that I exist, thanks to you. But you, how will you fare?'

Beornwyn snorted, 'Me child! I'm more than a match for any of them. Besides, Beaumont and Lanfranc will, between them, see that I come to no harm. Oh! I told Beaumont that I didn't need his protection but he will see that I am looked after. It is you that concerns me. I'm afraid that, from now on, you will not be out of my sight for longer than I can help. If Wulfric...'

'Is that who it was Aunt?' Alysoun broke in.

'Yes, I have no doubt of it,' came the reply. 'He has always sworn to avenge his father's death but,' and here her voice took on a more thoughtful note, 'It is just how much the act was influenced by his master. I find it hard to believe that at this moment Odo would want to take that sort of chance with William on his way here. He is not in favour at the moment and William would not be kindly disposed to one who was responsible for sabotaging a project which, if what we are led to believe is true, has been adopted by his wife. No, I think this was a pure act of revenge on the part of Wulfric but we must continue to be on our guard.'

She took a deep breath and became more businesslike.

'It is my intention to meet with the designer later this week at the castle. Against my better judgement I propose that you accompany me. I believe we should make a start on this embroidery with the least possible delay. It will do our cause no harm if, when he arrives in Canterbury, Duke William is able to see for himself that we have made progress although I do not intend starting on the borders and the text until he has left the city.'

She gave Alysoun a conspiratorial half smile, the first time that she had allowed the grief on her face to be lightened. Alysoun's tear marked cheeks did not respond to this slight change in mood. In fact it seemed to intensify her own sadness but she quietly moved to Beornwyn and hugged her, hanging on to her as if her life depended on it. When she raised her face to her aunt's it was to say.

'Whatever you want of me Aunt, I will do your bidding. I know that when we spoke of it earlier, you had your own reasons for not wanting me to meet this artist. Are you sure you want me with you when you see him because I have plenty to do in the school and locked in here I will be quite safe.' Beornwyn gently disengaged herself.

'No, I will feel happier if you are with me. Beaumont will be only too pleased to provide us with an escort to and from the castle. Yes, yes, I know child, I told him in no uncertain terms that I wouldn't tolerate his help but he will arrange it somehow and have the grace to ensure that it is unobtrusively done. In fact, I think he will be quiet pleased to discover a vulnerable side to my nature. I think, like most people, that he is under the impression that I don't possess one but at times like this...' she gave a deep sigh.

Alysoun took one of her hands and kissed it.

'I know you do Aunt. I also know that although you have seen many horrific things in your lifetime, Warin's death has been an enormous sadness to you but just think, we will make a big, big success of this work and I am so excited at the thought of meeting the artist. Why do you look so worried Aunt? We will be all right. From what I have heard you say, Lord Beaumont is a good man. He will keep us safe and if William and Mathilde are on our side, what can go wrong? You have the best school of needlework in the world and it will be a triumph.'

Beornwyn smiled at her enthusiasm but there was a reserve behind the smile. This, narrow, over length and totally bizarre piece of embroidery might well be a wonder of the age but privately, she wondered at what cost.

She took a deep breath, straightened herself and clapped her hands. 'Now,' she said briskly, 'We must get on. How are the women getting on with the kneelers for the choir stalls? They should be nearly ready by now.'

'They are ready Aunt' was the equally brisk reply from Alysoun, pleased to take the cue that business was now back to normal although, as she reflected sadly to herself, it never would be quite the same again without Warin. Even she would miss his perpetual scowl and bad tempered over-protectiveness. Beornwyn had lost too many loved ones over the last decade and she could ill afford to lose one who on whom she had come to depend so much. Alysoun repeated her last statement.

'No they are all finished and ready for the cathedral. I think the Archbishop will be delighted with them. Do you wish to inspect them before they leave the school?'

Beornwyn shook her head.

'No, if you are happy with the quality they will serve well and I would hope Lanfranc will be pleased with them, he'll not find finer anywhere though I have no doubt that we will have the usual argument about the cost.'

She sniffed and Alysoun grinned.

'You know very well Aunt, there is nothing you enjoy more than arguing with the Archbishop.'

She turned back to the drawing on the table.

'When can we go to the castle? Soon please, dear Aunt.'

'Patience child, in a few days, a few days,' came the measured reply.

CHAPTER THIRTY TWO

Canterbury

Jean was just sketching in Harold's battle helm when, with a cheerful slamming of the door, Ranulph burst into the room. He came across to the table and stood there for a moment looking at what Jean was doing and gave a whistle of approval.

'That's really good that is. How many of those did you say you 'ave to do?'

'I didn't,' Jean replied, 'But for your information it's about another seven or eight.'

This time his whistle was more of disbelief than approval.

'You have got your work cut out then 'aven't you lad. Right, that idea I was telling you about, 'ere it is.'

He started to put a parcel on the drawing before Jean stopped him with a yelp of alarm.

'Oh! Sorry Jean, can you roll that up a bit so that I can put this down somewhere. It might not be very big but I've had to cart it all over the castle to get it inside the keep. All the guards seem to be very jumpy and when I said it was you that I was after they called for that officious sod Josclin. He wanted to know what I had in the parcel and when I told him it was for you he made me hand over my knife. First time for years I've been separated from that blade, and I 'ad to explain what exactly it was that I needed to see you for. When I told him it was an embroidery frame, he said he didn't know what the castle was coming to. One minute it's home to a military force and the next it's been taken over by men who walk funny. Anyway, here it is, that idea I was talking to you about.'

What he proudly unwrapped in front of Jean was a complicated combination of wooden bits about two pieds long and half a pied high.

'That's it?' Jean exclaimed, 'I told you how big these panels are. What's the use of something like that? You couldn't embroider a kerchief on that.'

Ranulph looked slightly hurt that his idea had not met with a more enthusiastic response but very patiently went on to explain that it was a model. Another blank look from Jean prompted Ranulph to remind him that, because Guy was rubbish at draughtsmanship he always had to make models.

Still Jean remained doubtful and was made only slightly happier by Ranulph's assertion that, if a model could be shown to work, then so should the full sized version. He shook his head sadly at Jean's obtuseness.

'You honestly think that I was going to build a full size working frame in me lunch hour? I might be good but I'm not that friggin' good. Course it'll work. Mind you, I'm not saying we might not have to tweak things a bit but no, it'll work fine. Give us a length of that linen, the same size panel that you're working on, and I'll have a go at sorting out the proper tensions and that sort of thing. Mind you,' he went on, 'I'll have to get the go-ahead from his nibs. I can't just drop everything else without his say-so.'

Jean assured him that, if this project was as big as everyone seemed to think it was, then Ranulph's doors or whatever he spent his days working on, would have to wait. The carpenter seemed more than happy to think that his humdrum door-making days might be suspended for a while but Jean felt it only fair to mention that he would have to convince other people of the effectiveness of this idea. While he was trying to explain this to Ranulph, Josclin walked into the room.

'Humph' he grunted at Ranulph.

'You found your way here then? All right, LeBrun, this artisan has already confused me with science, perhaps you can explain what this…this "thing" is that he was so anxious to see you about.'

'Well Josclin,' Jean began, 'It's a model for an embroidery frame.'

Josclin shook his head impatiently, 'Yes, yes lad, I know all that, he's already told me what it's supposed to be. What I want to know is, how does it work and what is he doing, spending his time on this sort of…. toy, instead of making sure this castle stays in one piece. He's here to do Lord Beaumont's bidding, not yours.'

Jean was saved from having to think up an answer because, at that moment, Beaumont himself entered the room and on hearing Josclin's comment asked what it was that he was talking about. Jean then went through the whole business again, explaining how the frame was supposed to work. When he'd finished, Beaumont stroked his chin thoughtfully before delivering his verdict that perhaps it would be better to await the arrival of the Lady Beornwyn and let her decide whether or not Ranulph's invention was worthy of further investigation.

If she decided that it was, then he would be willing to release the carpenter from his normal duties. He then went on to say that men would be dispatched to escort the lady to the castle at her pleasure, whenever that may be. He also added that perhaps they should all be prepared to suffer at the hands of her legendary ill humour at having her wishes disregarded concerning the safe conduct he had provided for her.

'I dare not risk her coming to any harm.' he said. 'Too much depends on the goodwill of the native people of her calibre.'

Josclin, whose mockery of Ranulph's idea had been effectively suppressed, then spoke up and introduced a subject with which he felt much more familiar.

'My Lord, why do you not allow me to carry out a search for Wulfric. With him safely out of the way, surely the chances of her safety would be much improved. A few good men, that's all I would need to catch the man. After all, he is but an animal like any other and can be hunted as such.'

'It is not as easy as that.' replied Beaumont. 'To begin with, I have my doubts that he can be found still here in Canterbury and if not, he is likely to be under the covert protection of the Earl of Kent. We have to tread warily in that area. Odo might not currently enjoy the confidence of The King but he is related to him and to cross him openly at this stage could be counter productive to our plans for this region. The other thing is that Wulfric is not like other animals, although you would be quite correct to assume he shares the morals of the lowest. He is clever and he is a creature of darkness. He would smell a trap a furlong away and you probably wouldn't be able to get within striking distance of him, no matter how good your men may be. It's all right Josclin, we are all aware of your talents and in the field there is nobody I would not sooner have at my side but this is different. This is a sort of conflict of which you have had no experience and I hope to God that you will end your days without having to.'

Josclin, who was at Jean's shoulder and a little removed from his master, murmured something but his attitude showed that he had accepted Beaumont's compliment in the right spirit and was not prepared to argue his point further. As for Jean, it did seem strange that people tended to imbue Wulfric with powers that were almost superhuman. He shuddered slightly to think of the liberties he had taken with him but that was when he was under the direct protection of Odo and he and Wulfric were supposed to be on the same side.

Even so any further thoughts on the subject were dispelled by Robert Beaumont who now seemed to be intrigued with Ranulph's idea. He wandered across, picked it up and inspected it.

'All right... er'

'Ranulph, my Lord.' interjected Josclin. 'He's one of the carpenters over here to work on the renovations. He's one of Guy of Falaise's artisans,'

He went on in an effort to place Ranulph more precisely in Beaumont's memory.

'Ah! Yes. I think I passed you and Master Guy on my way here from Dover.'
He turned to Jean.

'Shortly before you and I shared a cooling ale, LeBrun. Well now, Master
Carpenter, explain to me again how this is supposed to work?'

Ranulph eagerly went through the whole process again and Jean could see,
from Beaumont's expression that he was engaging with the idea.

Eventually he turned to Jean and asked him what he thought about it. Did
he think it would work, would it save time and so forth. Jean had to admit
that he had not the faintest idea of how useful it would be, assuming, of
course, that Ranulph could come up with a full sized version.

'Well then,' said Beaumont cheerily to Ranulph, 'So be it. You will be
released from our service and temporarily put at the disposal of Master LeBrun
here. If this business becomes much more fascinating to their Majesties, we
could all end up by working for him. I would imagine that's a thought which
holds enormous appeal for you Josclin?'

His man-at arms attempted a smile which quickly faded.

'So!' his Lordship continued, 'how long will it take you to have a full sized
frame completed?'

Ranulph thought for a moment, grabbed one of Jean's charcoal sticks,
jotted down some undecipherable hieroglyphs on a scrap of linen and said he
thought it could be done in a four or five days, providing he could find the
rollers and perhaps borrow the blacksmith to make the rods to go through
them.

Another grunt from Josclin indicated that the addition of a blacksmith to
the team had not gone unnoticed. His Lordship, waving an airy hand, told
Ranulph to carry on and do whatever was necessary but to make the best
speed he could with the work.

'I want you here to explain that,' pointing at the model, 'To the Lady
Beornwyn. I am not certain that LeBrun here or myself are sufficiently
qualified to do so unless, of course, you Josclin feel that...no I thought not.
Now, Master LeBrun, let us see what progress you have been making.'

He walked over to the table and peered at the scene.

'Quite remarkable, I have to say but...' He indicated the scene on which
Jean had been working, or rather re-working in charcoal; Harold's coronation
tableau. He turned to Josclin.

'Do you remember hearing of some sort of celestial event occurring at the
time of Harold's quite indecently hasty coronation... if such it really was?'

Josclin stepped forward, much more at ease with a straightforward question
which involved neither art nor mechanics. He too looked at the drawing and
then back to his Lordship.

'Some sort of shooting star, if I remember rightly my Lord and yes, I did hear that the superstitious Saxons blamed the star for them losing the battle. Some sort of ill omen.' he gave a short snort of derision, 'Trust them to look to the supernatural than their own military incompetence for losing.'

Beaumont laid a placatory hand on his lieutenant's arm.

'Steady Josclin. The battle could have gone either way if you remember but you are quite right. It was some sort of comet that appeared at this period.'

He looked back at Jean and once again indicated the drawing.

'Might not hurt to include it somewhere at this time of the narrative if you want this to be an accurate historical record.'

Jean poised the charcoal over the linen strip and in the sky, sketched in a star. 'Like that?' he asked.

'Bit bigger!' Josclin interposed, 'And it had a tail, a sort of trail of light coming out behind it. That's it, that's better.' and then realising he'd actually made a contribution to Jean's artistic creation stepped back to the doorway, mumbling something uncomplimentary about time being wasted on this sort of girlish nonsense when there were dangerous lunatics at large that needed hunting down.

His observations, which somehow amused Lord Beaumont to the extent that he gave Jean a comradely wink, were interrupted by a large shadow appearing in the doorway, dwarfing even that of Josclin's ample frame and which materialised into Guy of Falaise

He bowed to Beaumont, slapped Josclin on the back, waved a ham like fist at Ranulph and joined his Lordship and Jean at the table.

Robert Beaumont leaned across and told Guy that Jean was now working under Lady Beornwyn's instructions. At the mention of her name, Guy's normally cheery face lost its smile and he nodded sadly.

'Ah! Warin. Bad business that. Talk of Canterbury of course. Got all of us looking over our shoulders. Never forget when you and me first met at Dover, Jean. That nasty little mongrel nearly broke my collar bone. Anyway, you're safe enough here and you'll need to be 'cause if I remember rightly, you took one or two liberties with Wulfric and he won't forget that, you mark my words.'

Guy had been called to look at the possibility of creating a large window in the room in order that Jean might have more light to work. What Jean was not expecting was that this aperture was to be glazed, like some of the windows in the cathedral and the tailors he had visited in Dover. When Jean raised an eyebrow at the thought of the cost involved, Beaumont dismissed the unspoken question by saying that this work was to be carried out at the instigation of the Archbishop.

Jean shrugged, as much as to say that all these decisions, emanating from all sorts of high places, were not really his business and all he really wanted to do was move on with his own work. Accordingly he applied himself to his canvas sketching in a few suitably stupefied Saxon idiots pointing up at the star thing he'd just drawn. Another panel nearly finished. What came next? Oh yes! The preparations for the invasion.

He stood up, trying to ignore the noise going on all around him, Beaumont was muttering something to Josclin about how best to arrange an unobtrusive escort for Lady Beornwyn while Ranulph was explaining his idea to Guy, Jean walked to the small hole in the wall, soon to be enlarged and tried to imagine the scene on which he was about to embark.

The activity would have been tremendous and he felt the importance of conveying that sense of urgency; villagers harvesting timber and preparing it for the shipwrights. They would, he imagined, also be wondering how much of their own meagre resources, livestock, produce and so forth, they would be expected to contribute to the war effort. One thing would have been certain, they would have put a lot more into it than they would ever have profited by it. But then he supposed, it was ever thus.

As Jean looked down onto the bailey something caught his eye. A momentary glint of something, a shadow shifting in the breeze. Hardly anything at all but just enough to distract him from his thoughts and the general activity going on below. He thought for a moment of drawing Josclin's attention to whatever it was but soon decided that it wasn't worth it. After all, how likely was it that Wulfric would have penetrated the castle in daylight? In any event, it was Lord Beaumont who broke his reverie by joining him at the window and quietly saying.

'I can see you have come to the end of another panel, LeBrun. Perhaps it would suit you if we repaired to my quarters for some refreshment and we continue with the history which you are interpreting so creatively. I do have some little time at my disposal so if it is convenient?'

'My lord,' Jean said, turning to him, 'it is much easier for me if you just give me orders rather than extend to me courtesies to which I am not accustomed. I appreciate what everyone is doing for me but I am what I am and I have no desire or ability to find myself playing a role to which I have no right.'

Beaumont gave one of his quiet smiles as they left the others, still looking over the design.

'LeBrun,' he said gently as they walked the stairs to his chambers, 'If I thought that for one moment you were likely to be the sort of man to abuse the opportunities that you have been granted, I would not begin to indulge you in the way that I do but believe me, you are different from most other young men of your background and station. You do not realise it I think and it is that very fact that makes it easier for us to treat you as something other that an ordinary servant. Your talent has been recognised by all and sundry, including your own sovereign and his consort. It is a thing of rare value and it is a thing to be envied.'

They reached the door of his rooms and Jean stopped for a moment, thinking, remembering.

'What is it LeBrun, have I embarrassed you again?'

'Not at all my Lord. It is only that what you have just said reminds me of something very similar that was said to me by Thibault shortly before he...'

He paused while Beaumont opened the door and invited him to follow him inside where a servant stood waiting with a jug of wine and some sweetmeats. Beaumont gestured him to a stool and handed him a mug.

'You two got on well didn't you? You and Thibault?'

Jean said that the two of them had seemed to strike up some sort of friendship but went on to say that he doubted if anyone would ever get to know Thibault that well.

'Yes, I remember you saying. Well now, we had better get on. Where are you up to in your quest for information?'

Jean told him of his meeting with the Queen. How the force was assembled, of the men and a fleet with which to convey them. How various nobles (Beaumont included) had contributed to the enterprise, both in terms of equipment as well as vessels.

'So, you know nothing of the conflict itself?' Beaumont asked.

'No, my Lord, apart, that is, from stories I half remember being told as a boy and, of course, the odd snippet volunteered by Thibault.' Jean gave a sad smile, 'Especially when he was chiding me for my ignorance of the matter and the rather naïve remark I once let drop, about this island really belonging to the English.'

Beaumont gave him a steady look.

'Is that what you think now?'

The question wasn't posed in the spirit of a challenge so Jean just shrugged and said that, yes, he supposed that he did. Thankfully Beaumont didn't react in the way that Jean remembered Thibault had. Rather he nodded a conditional agreement.

'I don't necessarily think you are right. In fact, in my position it would be intensely hypocritical of me to say that you are but I do know what you mean and I do have some sympathy with your point of view. However, we are in England. We did conquer them and William has assumed the throne. These are facts and I think it is only realistic to recognise them and proceed with our work here as sensitively as possible. Now then, to continue with the story.'

He then proceeded to inform Jean of the nature of the expedition, the landing and, importantly from Jean's point of view, some of the events that led up to the actual battle. He felt that he needed to get a feel for, not just the heroics of the day itself but the period immediately preceding it. Some of the personal touches that might have remained in Beaumont's memory and what he knew of the English preparations for defence. Suddenly Beaumont stopped, mid flow, and said to Jean.

'Lord Odo was involved in the battle. Since this is his idea, I am somewhat surprised that he didn't want to tell you all about it himself.'

Jean broke in. 'But he did, my Lord, that is, he does. He specifically mentioned that there were certain episodes in the fighting that he would describe to me personally.'

Beaumont looked hard at Jean.

'Did he indeed?'

A half smile appeared.

'Well, that might go some way to explaining this whole business.'

'My Lord?'

'This is something that I, or Josclin, would have mentioned anyway as part of your record but not, perhaps, in quite the same words that Lord Odo might have used. You see, LeBrun, there was a point in the battle where the English had the advantage of us. They occupied the high ground and our infantry, on our right, lost many men to the extent that we retreated, in some disorder, down the hill, pursued by the enemy. There was also a rumour, happily false, that Duke William had been killed. In short, the English were threatening to win the day.'

Jean leaned forward. 'But what happened, my Lord.'

'What happened, LeBrun, was that Lord Odo marshalled his cavalry, led them to the right wing of the conflict and reversed the situation. Within moments, his cavalry was inflicting carnage among the enemy infantry and chasing the few that survived back up the hill to their former position. You could say it turned the tide in our favour.'

Jean frowned. 'Then it was Lord Odo who was responsible for the successful conquest of this island?'

Beaumont gave a short laugh.

'Little more complicated than that, LeBrun, but I suspect that is exactly what your master would like the world to think. I'm afraid we are back into politics. King William has many enemies, in France as well as here and if it were thought that his occupation of the English throne were solely due to generalship other than his own, his authority here and in Normandy could well be compromised.'

Jean's frown deepened.

'So what should I do? How am I supposed to portray these events without giving offence to one party or the other?'

'I am here to give you information, Jean. How you incorporate it into your design is your affair. As I said, this battle was a complex business and could have been won or lost in several different ways. I have told you what happened. That should be enough to satisfy Lord Odo, although I expect he might have embellished the narrative somewhat. Do not forget, though, that their Majesties have now adopted your project.'

He raised an eyebrow. Jean was not at all comforted by the gesture.

Jean entered the chamber that had been allotted to him and found that thankfully, it was free from carpenters, master masons, military personnel or anything else that was likely to disturb his concentration. Some three hours later when the sun was well into its decline, much of what Jean had learned was sketched out and ready to transpose onto a fresh strip of unbleached cloth. He stood up straight and stretched, well pleased with an afternoon's uninterrupted work. Heavy treads and voices on the stair warned him that his period of quiet was coming to an end. These suspicions were confirmed when Guy entered in the company of a couple of masons, one of whom Jean recalled from his brief working visit to the cathedral close.

'Take no notice of us lad,' he boomed, 'These boys are going to let a bit more light into your life.' he winked. 'By the time they've finished, you'll be able to spot Wulfric before he gets anywhere near the tower. Right lads, just here I think. South facing. That way you should have more light for more of the day.'

He turned back to Jean.

'No sign of the Lady Beornwyn yet then? I tell you, it'll take more than the likes of Wulfric to keep her indoors, especially after what he's just done.'

'Any idea when she's likely to come to the castle?' Jean asked.

'None whatsoever my young friend' Guy replied. 'It'll come as a nice surprise won't it? Actually,' he went on, 'I'll have to stop Ranulph working on that thing he's just thought up because I need him up here to put a frame in this hole. Now! Why don't you let me help you move that table over there,' waving towards the far corner of the room, 'while these lads knock the stone out of the wall. That's it lads, there'll do nicely bout' five pieds by three should do it.'

He grinned at Jean.

'Just for you Jean, aren't you the lucky one?'

The apparently 'lucky' Jean shook his head at the sheer improbability of the situation and Guy's cheery attitude towards it but yes, he considered, he was the lucky one. At long last he could get on with his work again. He was going to be able to have light to see by and Lady Beornwyn's visit had been postponed for the moment. He leaned on the table, charcoal in hand and for the first time for ages, felt quite relaxed as he watched the masons chipping away at the stonework.

CHAPTER THIRTY THREE

Canterbury Castle

Beaumont stood for a moment looking at the door through which Jean had departed. He smiled to himself and tried to remember what he was like at that age. From what he had heard of Jean's youthful exploits from Odo he, Beaumont, had lagged way behind in matters of the opposite sex. In fact he had only ever known one women in that way in his life. He had married her and continued to love her devoutly. Then, to his everlasting grief, she had died soon after the Conquest. Unlike many of his contemporaries, Odo for example, his own life had been surprisingly chaste, not unlike young Thibault he supposed. His thoughts were interrupted by a knock on the door but before he could reach it, it had been flung open and he found himself face to face with his King.

For a split second Beaumont, a man renowned as one of the most articulate of his age, was speechless but not for long.

'Sire. I am so sorry that I was not at the gate to welcome you. I confess, we were not expecting Your Grace until somewhat later and I was not aware of your approach to the castle. I heard no fanfare or even the sound of your escort's mounts in the keep.'

He remained on the knee to which he had dropped at his first sight of William. The King laughed and bade him stand.

'That Robert, is because I am unaccompanied. Come my friend, let's sit down. No fuss, I insist.'

'You rode here alone Sire? No escort. Excuse me saying so but was that wise?'

'Damn it Robert. I'm not that well known in these parts and truth to tell, if I don't travel in state I don't have to spend so much of my valuable time gossiping to every self important dignitary that gets thrown in my path. That's why I've come to see you. You won't try and flatter me out of my wits and you will make a nice change from my errant step-brother. As soon as I landed, he was my first call. He wasn't expecting me either and I tell you it worries me when Odo looks guilty. Can't put my finger on it but he's up to something again.'

William walked away from the table and looked out of one of the arrow slits into the keep below. Beaumont had known and worked closely with his sovereign for a long time and knew that this was one of his habits when he had something on his mind.

He said nothing but waited for the King to continue. When he did speak again it was as though he was talking to himself rather than Beaumont.

'I wonder,' he murmured, 'Just how much that priest has on his conscience.'

He gave a short laugh and turned to Beaumont.

'In fact Robert, I wonder, does he have a conscience, what do you think?'

Beaumont thought carefully. He knew that the King's relationship with Odo was a mercurial one. Odo had done the King good service in the past but was it loyal service or was it merely motivated by that which brought great rewards in the form of power and land. The fact that they were related would not be an important factor in the King's mind. Half brother or not, William was only concerned with those things that cemented his own sovereignty here and in Normandy. He answered the question slowly and thoughtfully.

'I think my Lord Odo ambitious, your Grace...'

The King interrupted, 'Oh! Come on Robert. We are all ambitious. What sort of poor animal would man be if he were not driven by ambition? That wasn't my question and you know it!'

Beaumont stroked his chin and was still not prepared to be rushed into an answer.

'I presume your Grace that you have already come to your own conclusions. Your recent experience in Normandy with your son Robert has, I think, done little to encourage any confidence in my Lord Odo's absolute loyalty towards you. Did your Grace discover incontrovertible proof that Odo was implicated in the affair?'

Another dismissive snort of laughter from the King.

'Of course I didn't Robert. All I know is that my precious son didn't have the imagination or the courage to have acted on his own. He and Odo were always to be found muttering in corners and if they weren't plotting something or other they certainly weren't chatting over my next birthday gift. Mind you, Mathilde disappointed me with regard to that 'affair' as you diplomatically put it. Mother love is one thing, treason is another. Anyway, reading between the lines, as I always have to with you Robert, I take it you are of the opinion that brother Odo is not wholly to be trusted, am I right?'

'You have known that is my opinion for some time your Grace.' was Beaumont's reply. 'We have, after all, discussed this matter on many occasions.'

'So we have Robert, so we have. Just wondered if you've changed your mind or heard anything else I ought to know about. Oh! By the way, I understand that boy of Odo's is here with you in Canterbury.'

'You mean Jean LeBrun, your Grace?'

'That's the one Robert. Been planted here do you think? I've no doubt brother Odo would love to have a spy in your castle – especially as it's not really your castle but his. I expect he'd quite like to pick up the odd tit bit or two between you and Lanfranc.'

This time it was Beaumont's turn to laugh.

'LeBrun! I think not. Actually I'm not too sure that he loves his master as a good servant should. I certainly get the impression that he's much happier working here than at Dover.'

'No surprises there,' said William, 'I have heard that from other sources. Something to do with that nasty half-bred assassin of Odo's, what's his name, Wulfric?. Apparently he was given the job of looking after the boy and making sure that Odo's money for this ridiculous embroidery thing of his didn't get misused. I have to admit that, at this moment, I am having a problem understanding my Queenly wife. Apart from encouraging her son to commit treason against his father, she has, it seems, adopted this strange idea of my potentially treasonous half brother. All right, all right, I know...' he waved a hand to ward off Beaumont's half hearted defence of the embroidery, 'it's a women's thing this sewing and what have you but she's intent on seeing it through so I hope this young artist is getting on with it. I have been asked to report back you know.' He shook his head in mock despair. 'As if I haven't enough to do but you know the Queen...once she gets an idea into her head...'

Beaumont succeeded in not looking too amused and agreed with William.

'Yes your Grace, I do remember that her Majesty can be quite ...single minded.'

'Single minded!' exploded William. 'You have not the slightest...' he paused for a moment and gave Beaumont a keen look. 'Of course Robert, you're not married are you?'

'Not...No Sire'

'No children!'

'Well, no Sire, as I say I'm not m...'

'Oh! Come on Robert, that doesn't make any difference. Look at the saintly Odo. I shudder to think how many small Odos he's managed to replicate.'

He shook his head as if in amazement then suddenly thought, 'I say, Robert, you've never thought of marrying again?'

Beaumont shook his head.

'No Sire. I just haven't been fortunate enough to meet the right woman.'

'Humph' William growled. 'At least you're not like my second boy, you know, young William, he of the red hair. I fear his proclivities are not shall we say, strictly normal. Children! You don't know how lucky you are.'

Beaumont merely inclined his head and wondered if there was to be any more meat in this discussion other than excursions into the family closet. He was not to be kept waiting, for William immediately left his station at the window and rejoined Beaumont at the table.

'I'm told by Mathilde, that the work for this embroidery is to be undertaken by the School here in Canterbury.'

'This is true your Grace. LeBrun, through Lanfranc, has made contact with Lady Beornwyn and she has agreed to carry out the work – for the appropriate fee, of course.'

William nodded. 'I have heard that Lady Beornwyn's retainer has met with an accident. Is that right?'

'No accident my Lord, he was murdered and almost certainly by the Wulfric to whom your Grace referred earlier. If you cast your mind back your Grace, you may remember Warin, Beornwyn's man, at Hastings. He fought like fifty ordinary men and I can recall your Grace remarking at the time, that he was one of the bravest men in the field that day, on either side. He has never been a friend of ours but Beornwyn, on whom he doted, has always managed to keep him under some degree of control. From our point of view he has been useful because he has proved an admirable bodyguard for the lady who has placed great store on her ability to function without our protection. It has given her a particular status among her own race which she has, in her pragmatic way, used for the advantage of both our peoples.'

William again moved over to the window and appeared to be intently observing that part of the view that fell within his vision. Again he spoke with his back to Beaumont.

'Odo again. I might not always have been in sympathy with the way in which you and Lanfranc have striven to bring about an understanding between us and the natives. That is why Odo has been given such latitude. He believes in ruling by force, terror if need be and that is something I have always found easy to understand but as I get older and I listen to more people, like you and Lanfranc, the more I am beginning to respect your judgement in these matters. Do you think this might be a ruse of Odo's to undermine your work in this region?'

Beaumont shook his head.

'I do not think, your Grace that this murder was at Odo's instigation. It is my opinion that it was more personal than that. Warin, you may not be aware, killed Wulfric's father who was equally as evil as his son. It also appears that young LeBrun has not always treated Wulfric with the respect that he seems to think he deserves.'

'Just a minute Robert. Yes, I do remember now. Warin, Warin… Yes but, I thought we managed to kill him, not until after he'd dispatched many of our host admittedly, but I thought we'd cut him down.'

'No your Grace, he escaped. I think it was more important to him to remain alive so that he could protect his mistress.'

'He can't do much to protect her now can he?'

'Indeed not your Grace and I fear that Lady Beornwyn will not accept our protection although it was offered immediately.'

William let out a heartfelt 'Whew! For God's sake Robert, don't let anything happen to her now. Mathilde has a great respect for the woman and is depending upon her for this great embroidery thing. Do you know, I never thought the day would come when we would be talking about embroidery. By comparison, politics and government seem much safer. That said, I have a funny feeling that this project inspired as it was by my devious step-brother, is not too far removed from affairs of state or does that seem silly to you?'

Beaumont left the table and joined his liege lord at the window.

'Your Grace,' he said. 'I don't think it silly at all. If the English can be prevailed upon to embroider the history of our conquest of them, many of your troubles in this island may be over. Acceptance on their part of the event and pride that it is their skill that is being called upon to record it.'

'The design is ours though, isn't it Robert?'

'Inevitably your Grace. Would you like to meet the young artist responsible for it?'

'Of course I want to meet him. The Queen was quite taken with him and spent more time with him than her state duties should have allowed. I'm always interested to meet anyone who's not scared of Mathilde.'

Before leaving the room Beaumont inquired of the King whether or not he would prefer to change out of his rough travelling clothes into something more regal and fitting for appearing before his subjects. William looked down at his travel-stained riding wear.

'Change Robert! You must be joking. You're the one that needs to change. If we don't get an hours hunting in before the sun drops down you are likely to have a highly disgruntled liege lord on your hands. The subjects can wait. We'll see them later, by which time, my retinue should be here. I hope you can accommodate us all!'

#

The hall was packed with strangers. It had been impossible to miss the ceremony that had heralded in the King's retinue of knights, secretaries and priests who, by all accounts, had made their entrance considerably later than that of their master. It also included, much to Jean's consternation, the Earl of Kent. It was the first time that Jean had seen him since leaving Dover and his apprehension at the thought of the coming meeting, surely inevitable, was not improved by Odo's obvious displeasure at having to share his table in his castle with Robert Beaumont who was sitting on the right of the King. This was Jean's first good look at William. He had seen him before, at Dover, but then he was seated way below the dais and people like Kings were so remote that he'd hardly registered who it was.

It was different now though. Now he was seated among the lesser nobility, the squires and people of influence such as Josclin who, it has to be said, was civility itself. This brought him much closer to the men of real power and he had a good view of William who, unlike his half brother, seemed to be in an excellent humour. Both Beaumont and Lanfranc acknowledged Jean's presence with a nod and he found himself blushing in confusion as the other men at his board, to whom he was unknown, exchanged querying looks as they tried to place him in the hierarchy of the court. Odo ignored him.

As the repast drew to a conclusion and people started to vacate their tables, Jean's attempt to steal out unnoticed was foiled by a page who quietly came up to him and whispered in his ear that Lord Beaumont asked that he, Jean, should repair to his chamber and there await the arrival of certain persons of rank who wished to speak with him.

Jean's first thought was that this was what he had feared from the moment he first set eyes on Odo. His fiery patron would be angry at the way in which his great idea had been usurped by others but once back in the quiet of his room, Jean rightly reasoned that nothing that had happened had been of his making. As always he had merely been at the mercy of forces and people over which he had no control.

Not his fault if Lanfranc and Beaumont had taken him under their influence and as for the School of Needlework and Lady Beornwyn! Why there he was merely doing what he had been engaged to do in the first place. None of Odo's money had been misused so what was he getting so worried about. He stood and looked out of the hole in the wall, as it had been left by the masons and was further depressed to see that rain had started to fall and not a star was to be seen. It was going to be colder tonight with his room open to the elements. How long was it going to be before the frame was in place and it was glazed and who was supposed to be paying for it? He hoped that Odo wasn't going to have to foot the bill. That hadn't come within his budget.

The panic was starting to build again when the tread of boots was heard approaching along the corridor. The procession was led by the two customary men-at-arms who, having reached the doorway, stood guard over it. Then in walked the King, Robert Beaumont, Lanfranc and bringing up the rear, bigger and more opulent than all the others put together, his imagined nemesis with a brow like thunder.

It was however the King who commanded the attention of everyone present, including Odo and Jean. Not as burly as his half brother he was still an imposing figure, his height and carriage compensating for his comparatively simple dress. Even Lanfranc of Bec was fully and expensively robed, while Robert Beaumont's finery was the equal of Odo's who, as always, wore his status on his back. Without a word, King William walked over to the hole in the wall and looked out into the murky gloom. Beaumont idly wondered why it was that William seemed so drawn to windows, even when it was impossible to see much of what lay beyond.

He just stood there, silent, looking out for what seemed like ages to Jean who was desperately trying to subdue a sneeze. The rest of the party only looked down at their feet, none of them registering Jean who had retreated behind his table on which lay the strip of linen on which he had been working. Even Odo gave him not so much as a glance but kept his eyes on the floor. Eventually William turned slowly from the window and strolled over to where Jean was standing. Jean executed what he hoped was a passable bow then, as was his nature, looked William straight in the eye. William returned the look then nodded and walked behind the table where he bent over, the better to see the drawing. Jean moved to one side to give him space.

The scene was that of the Norman fleet disembarking at Pevensey. He turned to Jean who by this time was feeling irritable rather than awed. He was tired and in particular he was tired of people constantly interrupting him, even kings and earls and all the other representatives of a class that considered themselves better than he was. He was not in the mood either to tolerate much in the way of criticism so again he defiantly returned William's look who intensified the severity of his own piercing gaze. Jean, in fact, was more frightened of Odo than the King who, so far as he was concerned, was something of an unknown quantity. It was still with relief, however, that he heard William's approval of what he had just seen.

'You're an unusual young man. Oh! I don't mean any of this,' jabbing a finger on the picture 'I'm no judge of the quality of your work but I suppose it must be something special for all these important people to keep going on about it.' he sniffed. 'If you ask me it's taking up far too much of their valuable time but I dare say,' turning suddenly to Odo, 'What do you think brother, after all you're paying for it?'

Odo growled something under his breath and the King said, 'What was that, speak up, let's all hear what you have to say. This was all your idea, don't forget!'

Odo didn't move towards the table but growled, 'Yes, it was my idea and I must say I'm most disappointed. This was supposed to be an offering to the greater glory of our Lord and...'

'Which 'Lord' would that be then?' William interrupted. 'Anyway it looks all right to me but then, as I say, I'm no judge. Suppose you tell me what's wrong with it then.'

Odo fingered the heavy cross which he wore around his neck and turned on Jean.

'This is dead' he hissed venomously. 'No life, no colour. I didn't give you money for this' waving a dismissive be-jewelled glove at the drawing.

'My Lord!'

Beaumont's quiet yet authoritative voice cut through the chill evening air like a whip.

'As I understand it, LeBrun was provided by you with the necessary funds for having his work transposed into needlework. As for the colour or lack of it. I was present when the Lady Beornwyn requested that she work from charcoal drawings. That way, the dyes of her threads would not be colour contaminated by any colours in LeBrun's designs. She, I might add, is most impressed with Master LeBrun's work.'

There was silence for a while. The King went back to his inspection of the night sky and whistled softly to himself. Lanfranc was the next to break the silence.

'I can vouch for that Odo. It appears you have been nurturing a rare talent in your Normandy lands. It is much to your credit that you have been sufficiently observant to have recognised it and employed it. You will, of course, be the first to appreciate that such gifts as this young man possesses are too precious not to share with the rest of the world. I would not presume to speak for His Majesty,'

He dropped his head in a courteous bow in the direction of William's back.

'But I feel sure that he would consider it a wise and generous gesture, on your part, were you to release Master LeBrun from any feudal bonds that exist between you.'

Odo's hooded eyes engaged with those of the Archbishop but he could not detect any suspicion of irony in them. The King's back remained silhouetted against the night sky, rigid and unmoving as if he were lost in his own private thoughts and not connected with anything else that was going on the room. Jean wished that he could be swallowed totally by the gathering shadows of the corner into which he tried to become invisible.

Without turning, the Kings spoke and, unusually, his tone was almost conciliatory.

'As you well know, brother, nobody respects and upholds our feudal tradition more than I do.'

He turned and faced the small gathering.

'But you know I do, on this occasion, agree with the Archbishop. You will have lost nothing but one young man from your estate and in the long run, of what worth was he likely to prove? From what I understand, when the time came, he was not the ideal candidate to adopt his father's role and besides, I do believe that your niece would welcome this piece of extraordinary generosity on your part. Obviously, should you decide to adopt this sensible course of action, it would not reflect adversely on the boy's family in France. Would it?'

The question came out as a challenge. Odo swallowed and the normal resonance of his voice was somewhat muted. The bow was perfunctory.

'Of course not your Grace.' he cleared his throat. 'It shall be as your Grace wishes but my investment in this project has not been inconsiderable so perhaps...'

'Think of the glory brother, think of the glory.' was William's abrupt response. 'All right, you three. Enough of all this airy fairy sort of stuff. I have two countries to run and much as I regret the fact, I need your help. This young genius here also has work to do. I suggest we repair to ours and leave him to his. Agreed Odo?'

This time the bow was more respectful.

'Yes, your Grace.'

But before they left the chamber, William wheeled around in the doorway, causing the others to come to a sudden halt.

'There is one more thing Odo, that perhaps we should discuss here in front of LeBrun. Your nasty piece of work, what's his name...'

'Wulfric, your Majesty.' interjected Beaumont softly.

'Wulfric, Wulfric' mused the King making it clear from his expression that it was not a name which found favour in his mouth, 'That's the one. Hope you have him well reigned-in, brother. Not impressed with what I've been hearing here in Canterbury. As for Dover...the last incident at Dover did not impress the Queen, I can tell you and after the time I've been wasting on this young artist of yours, I would not like to think that he might be at risk from your pet assassin.'

Odo had the grace to look crestfallen but his reply, to the effect that he had not seen Wulfric or indeed had anything to do with him for some time or even knew of his whereabouts, was delivered with such obvious sincerity that all of those present had little alternative but to believe him. The King, however merely satisfied himself with a 'Humph' which signified neither disbelief nor acceptance of the statement.

When they had all gone and the sound of boots and armour had receded, Jean collapsed onto his pallet and just lay there, looking up at the rough timbers of the ceiling and wondered what the next surprise was likely to be.

At least it sounded as if he might be a free man, his own man, dependent on his own wits and skill to survive in the world. Two things were now obvious to him. He had better be good at what he did and he would do well to keep out of Odo's way, for the time being at least. God! But it was cold with that hole in the wall. He wrapped his cloak around him and snuggled down as deeply into the straw mattress as he could.

#

He woke early. It was still dark and he was stiff and chilled. That awful fog was wreathing in and around where the window was supposed to be and he was relieved to hear, on the other side of his door, the familiar cheery voice of Ranulph in lively conversation with what sounded like another workman. The knock came almost immediately and Jean bade them enter. It was a rather shivery and tousled Jean, his tunic covered in stray bits of straw, that greeted the two artisans as they entered.

'Morning Jean, here's your glazier, he's called Turvald and we've come to finish that off,' waving a mallet at the hole in the wall. 'We've orders to get a move on so we don't hold you up with your work.'

He gazed keenly at Jean who was trying to find the tear in the mattress where the straw had escaped. 'You get more important by the day, you do. Mind you, looking like that…look more like a scarecrow than a man of art.'

'Oh! Shut up Ranulph,' said Jean crossly. 'What happened about that invention of yours. I thought you were supposed to be working on that and had been taken off ordinary carpentry jobs?'

Ranulph dropped a pile of timber on the floor and walked to the window with his measuring twine and started to measure up for the frame. Meanwhile, his companion who seemed to be a man of few words, was busy mixing some mortar in a wooden pail.

'All in good time, my son,' replied Ranulph but with difficulty since both hands were occupied with the measuring while his stylus was clamped in his teeth.

'My orders were to get this done so you can be nice and cosy and your lovely artistic hands not get so cold for you to draw properly. Shan't be long. Just got to get these two frames right, pop the first one into place then Turvald here can do his bit.'

Jean stopped his valeting for a moment and for the first time that morning looked interested.

'Two frames, why two frames?'

Ranulph squared off a length of timber and replied without looking up from his work, stylus still clamped in his mouth.

'That's where this glass stuff goes, between the two frames, bit too fragile to mortar it straight onto the stone. Anyway,' he continued, 'That's what Master Guy has worked out. Me? I haven't a clue. First time I've ever had to fit one so we shall soon see if he's right. There we go.'

Jean turned his artist's eye on the glass, lying carefully wrapped in sackcloth on the floor and shook his head.

'That's too small to fit that window.'

The two craftsmen shook their heads in mock despair and for the first time Turvald opened his mouth. He spoke Norman like a Saxon, which he was but it was still easier for Jean to understand than a carpenter with his mouth full of stylus.

'That's what the frames are for. Not just stability but they're what has to fit the hole in the wall, not the glass.'

Jean nodded and wrapped his cloak round him. The morning was cold and he would be glad when the chill air had been kept out. He wasn't too sure about the light though. From what he could see of other glass and what he remembered from his visit to the tailor in Dover, this new glass stuff was all right but he would miss being able to see out of the window on a fine day. Often, when he was tired from bending over a board and concentrating on his drawing, he would take a break and just look out at whatever view was available to him. Sometimes it could even be inspirational.

Overlooking the bailey and the figures moving therein gave him ideas about dress or movement that he could then incorporate in his work. For now, during the chillier days of spring and most definitely during the winter, he would be glad of the added comfort afforded by the protection of this glass but when the sun shone... Still, for the time and money that was being expended on his behalf, he supposed he should be grateful so, brushing the last pieces of straw from his person, he watched as Ranulph and Turvald went about their work.

Soon he was invited over to inspect the results of their labours. It was neat, he had to give them that and he could feel no hint of a draught as he experimentally moved his hand around the perimeter of the framed glass.

'Careful Sir!' prompted Turvald. 'That mortar's still wet but when it's dry that there window will be firm as a rock and you'll be all snug and dry and be able to see better. Why don't Ranulph and me take your table over to the window for you and you'll be able to work directly under it.'

Ranulph nodded and together they each took an end of the board and carefully placed it under the new window. Turvald nodded appreciatively as he noted Jean's work.

'Why Sir, that is wonderful is that, if you don't mind me saying so. Perhaps I shouldn't, being one of the side that was beaten by your people but you have to give credit where it's due, especially where craft is concerned. Don't you think so Ranulph?'

Ranulph packed up his tools and laughed.

'Don't you worry my friend. Young Jean here is always being told how brilliant he is and not just by the likes of us. The great and the good think so as well don't they Jean?'

Turvald, however wasn't really listening. He was still intent on the panel Jean was currently engaged on which happened to be the opening of the battle scenes as told to him by Robert Beaumont.

'You know Sir,' he said at last when Jean was beginning to wonder if he would ever be rid of them, 'you ought to think about doing some designs for the coloured windows that everybody is getting so excited about.'

'Um?' said a preoccupied Jean.

'Oh yes!' Turvald continued, to Jean's growing exasperation, 'His Grace has already made a start with one of the clerestory windows. Eden it is and very nice too. Mind you the serpent is horrible. Good job it's a long way up otherwise it'd frighten the children silly. Mind you.' he continued reflectively, 'I suppose that's the main idea. Can't have the Garden of Eden looking too jolly otherwise Gawd knows where we'd all end up.'

He pointed to the drawing.

'That 'orse looks as it's had a nasty tumble. Whoops, there goes another one. They yours or ours?'

Jean let out a heavy sigh and Ranulph laughed.

'Come on Turvald, let the man get on. See you later Jean and if you see her Ladyship, don't forget to mention my idea.'

The unwilling Turvald was led out of the room protesting that he wanted to see what happened later but Jean was too immersed in his work to take any notice and the folds of linen looped over the end of the table coming to rest on the straw which, now having no draught to disturb it, lay placidly on the boards. His concentration was complete and now, not even the elements could disturb him.

CHAPTER THIRTY FOUR

The School of Embroidery

The wind was lashing the rain through the streets of Canterbury and the small group of men, doing their best to shelter from it, found little protection from the walls of the building on the corner. They were men-at-arms but un-mounted, a circumstance which did little to alleviate their spirits. They were still armed though, their heavy broadswords oiled against the wet and their shields forming a makeshift shelter over their heads. There were four of them and they were not in the least happy with their current assignment.

'If we have to do this, why in God's name can't we wait inside. Bloody rain,' one muttered, using his woollen mitt to wipe a dewdrop off the end of his nose.

'Stop moaning lad,' snapped the one in charge, 'We are here because we were told to be here and if we're told to wait outside, that is what we are going to do. I don't like this job any more than you do but orders are orders and take my word for it, Lord Beaumont doesn't tell us to do something unless he has a very good reason.'

Another one turned his head to one side and muttered out of the corner of his mouth.

'It's all right for him... Lord Beaumont's little lap dog.'

The other three tittered until Josclin swung the offending individual round by his cloak and slammed him against the wall.

'Look here lad,' Josclin hissed, 'I have been around a lot longer than you three and I have earned his Lordship's trust because he and I have been through a lot together. He is the best master you're likely to see this side of ... Prefer to serve under Lord Odo would you? I don't think so! Just keep quiet and do as you're told or you and me are going to fall out and believe me, you wouldn't want that.'

He thrust the soldier back into the arms of his two companions.

'Anyway, lads,' he continued in a more conciliatory tone, 'It's not me you need to lose any sleep about. You know full well why we're here so just do your job. Keep your eyes open and stay alert. Just watch each other's backs and mine too but most of all make sure nothing happens to the Lady Beornwyn.'

He cast a practised eye around the surrounding houses and the narrow alley.

'If anything happens to her Ladyship, we're all in deep shit.'

The men shifted their feet and looked uncomfortable. Grumble as they may, Josclin was perfectly confident about his small bodyguard. After all Robert Beaumont had ordered him to select them himself and he'd chosen those he knew would be the most reliable; but he understood soldiers and he was only too well aware that the better they were, the less they enjoyed duties they considered to be beneath their dignity such as this one.

Truth to tell, he wasn't too enthusiastic about it himself. It was one thing to hunt down an animal such as Wulfric, it was quite another to act as nursemaid to an extremely difficult Saxon noblewoman but so far as Lord Beaumont was concerned, Josclin just did as he was told. Pity about the weather though, the boys were right there, it didn't make life any easier. He sighed and checked that his sword was fully protected under his cloak. He didn't like hanging about but his orders were to be as unobtrusive as possible, so he couldn't very well knock on the door and ask how much longer her Ladyship was likely to be. There was no chance that she was going to walk from here to the castle without being aware of their presence but the less obvious it was, the more likely that she would tolerate it.

He didn't relish getting on the wrong side of Lady Beornwyn so, being the seasoned campaigner that he was, he leaned further into the wall to derive what protection he could from that quarter, wrapped his cloak more closely around him and settled down to wait for however long it took. His eyes however continually swept around the area and his sword arm was across his body, his hand resting on the hilt. He was reassured to see that his three men-at-arms, now that they'd had their statutory whinge, were also wide awake and stood back to back, alert and ready for any contingency.

Inside the building, the object of his reluctant attention stood looking down at her niece who was pursing her lips with displeasure and saying, 'Why not? We have been through all this before. It just doesn't make sense and you have a greater reputation for common sense than any other women in the city. So much so in fact,' she concluded with a pout and a futile stab at the lock of hair, 'most people are intimidated by it. So why not?' she repeated with greater emphasis.

Beornwyn sighed.

'I know what I said but after giving it much thought I have changed my mind. Your place should be here, supervising our ladies. Perhaps the time will come when you will be required to be directly concerned with the design but for the time being I would prefer to deal with that side of the matter myself. It is not only a question of the artistic work you understand but there are other considerations to be taken into account. Such as...'

'Such as what, Aunt?' Alysoun interrupted. 'What sort of considerations can there be from which I should be excluded? As for our women here...'

She quickly glanced around the room in which eight or nine women were concentrating on their embroidery frames. Their concentration was assumed in most cases as they were much more interested in the conversation taking place in front of them. Occasionally one of them would leave her work and step over to a brazier which stood in the middle of the room. This brought her closer to Beornwyn and Alysoun and she would spend rather longer than was necessary pretending to warm hands which had become stiffened by the needlework and the cold.

When she returned to her frame, her companions would give her an enquiring look which she would return with raised eyebrows and a perhaps a wink. These needlewomen were beginning to look forward to these clashes of will which, just lately, seemed to characterise the relationship between their two supervisors. It created a welcome diversion from the less interesting tasks which occasionally fell to their lot and since they spent most of their time here in some awe of the formidable Beornwyn, there was some entertainment to be found in the younger women's occasional moments of mutiny.

As if sensing a challenge to her authority, Beornwyn shifted her attention from her niece to her other charges and with a sharp bark of a cough the women quickly dropped their eyes to their work. Alysoun had not finished however and she pursued her argument by including the needlewomen. She waved her hand at them.

'Look Aunt, just look at them and look at what they are doing. Badges for Lanfranc's household servants. For goodness sake, they can do those with their eyes shut. I am not needed here at the moment but I do need to know what is going on with this huge project of ours and be honest, you need me to know as well. Please Aunt, you know I'm right. Why won't you take me to the castle?'

Beornwyn took herself to the centre of the room and kneaded her large hands over the brazier. Not because she was cold but she needed time to think. Alysoun was winning more and more of these arguments, she reflected resignedly. She was getting tired and Warin's murder had affected her deeply. She wondered, was it time to hand over more of the responsibility to her niece? Alysoun was more than capable, of course she was but that wasn't the point. At least, not in this instance it wasn't. The point was ... what was it exactly?

She looked at her young ward. She was lovely, even with that petulant exasperation she assumed during these minor skirmishes. That wisp of hair, why on earth didn't the girl cut it off? Forever getting in her eyes when she was working and despite herself, Beornwyn couldn't help smiling at her and the smile became wider as soon as she realised that Alysoun's scowl deepened as a result. She thought she was being laughed at. Impulsively, Beornwyn moved over to her and hugged her. The women, needles suspended, gave each other imperceptible signs of approval at this show of affection but Alysoun was not to be bought off by it and she stiffened in her Aunt's embrace.

She did not try to push away though, she really did not wish to upset Beornwyn but she did want her to know that she was not going to be placated by a hug, no matter how well meant. After a moment, Beornwyn released her and held her from her at arms length.

'I'm sorry' she began, 'You know that I value your opinion, especially on a project as important as this and of course I would not have contemplated accepting the commission had I not been sure of your support but…it's just that…your safety is paramount and I worry so much about…'

This time Alysoun did push her away, albeit very gently.

'No!' she said firmly. 'Not this time. Yes, all right, I know you worry about me and after what happened to … but you can't keep me a prisoner here all the time and it's not only my safety that is concerning you is it? It's something else. It's something to do with the designer? Is that what this is all about?'

This time it was she who held her aunt at arm's length while she studied the mixed emotions flitting across the face of the older woman.

'I am right aren't I? That's what is worrying you isn't it? Why? Am I not sensible enough not to be swept off my feet by the sheer brilliance of this man? Are his looks as awesome as his talent? Why don't you want me to meet him, what is it about him that concerns you so much?'

By this time any pretence of embroidering Lanfranc's badges had been totally abandoned and such needles as happened to be drawing thread through canvas, were not wielded with the sort of care expected of the alumni of the school. Beornwyn immediately reverted to the disciplinarian and snapped,

'Get on with your work and be certain that I will not accept anything that is less than perfect.' To Alysoun, she said.

'Not here. Not now. My personal chamber.'

Upon which she swept out of the room, Alysoun following, her head bowed. Before closing the door behind her, she could not resist a fleeting glance of triumph at the women, who were already murmuring excitedly to one another.

Once in Beornwyn's chamber, neither spoke for a minute. Evidently Beornwyn was trying to collect her thoughts while Alysoun, sensing victory, although not unkindly, was content for her to do so. Eventually Beornwyn, having taken up her favourite position leaning on her table, gave a rather sad smile and Alysoun, well though she knew her aunt, was constantly surprised how a simple smile transformed that formidable patrician face into something that was almost beautiful.

'Alysoun, my angel.'

Another pause during which Alysoun stood quietly, her eyes firmly fixed on the floor although, inwardly, she was impatient to hear what was coming next.

'Alysoun,' her Aunt repeated. 'You do me an injustice, although it has to be confessed, it is but a small one. I am most concerned for your safety, especially in the light of what has happened. You cannot, in all fairness doubt that, but you are also partly in the right. I know I have to take the blame for accepting the work but I did so for reasons that, at the time, seemed perfectly sound. Both the Archbishop and Robert Beaumont, possibly the two men in the world for whom, as you know, I hold the greatest respect, impressed on me the possible importance of this commission. They also thought that I would find the young artist responsible for its design, sympathetic to our requirements and someone with whom we could work creatively and productively. They also though, when pressed, gave me some indication of his background and character which, it has to be said, do not exactly come up to the standard of his artistic abilities.'

She took a deep breath.

'This young man …has…has… a history of familiarity with members of our own sex. There now. I've said it and I have no doubt that what I have just told you is precisely what you expected to hear. Furthermore…no, please let me finish. Furthermore, I fully expect you to make the point that all this has nothing whatsoever to do with you or any work in which we might happen to be engaged but you must admit my dear, that in many of the ways of the world you are inexperienced and … and……'

Alysoun was unable to restrain herself any longer and couldn't subdue a raucous snort of unladylike proportions. The glisten in her blue eyes that Beornwyn had mistaken for incipient tears of sympathy only revealed themselves to be tears of unresolved mirth. In the end she flopped down on the stool again and howled with laughter. Beornwyn, somewhat discomfited, could only shrug her shoulders and express the opinion that her ward was behaving in a manner not entirely fitting that of a young and carefully nurtured young woman. Still hiccupping slightly, Alysoun stammered out her apologies and leaning forward, placed her small hand over that of her aunt in a gesture of appeasement.

'I'm sorry Aunt,' she said, 'but I am not a child and you yourself have never, never…'

'Never what Alysoun, never known a man?'

Beornwyn completed the sentence for her. She continued, her customary musical voice more gruff than it usually was.

'There is much about me of which you are ignorant, my dear. I have lived through more turbulent times than you. I have seen and experienced things that, I would hope, are beyond your imaginings and I would do anything to keep you safe and shield you from such things. I do not mean to be over-protective but I cannot help myself. Of course, you are quite old enough and certainly intelligent enough to look after yourself but...'

'Oh Aunt!' Alysoun broke in. 'If only you knew. Most girls of my age are already married and with children. Many of my childhood friends are and they talk to me. I listen to our women when they talk amongst themselves. I know what men are like and what they want and I have to say... the thought of it does not altogether displease me. Oh dear! Does that make me wicked and immoral in your eyes?'

Beornwyn shook her head.

'Of course it does not. It simply means you are a normal, healthy child and I am glad of it. It still does not stop me from fearing for your welfare though, does it?'

Alysoun sprang to her feet.

'Come Aunt. Let us go and visit this licentious young Norman.'

She grinned mischievously.

'I can't wait to see him now that you have told me what he is like. Let us go now, this minute.'

'But it is raining,' protested her Aunt, 'Can we not, at least, wait for the rain to stop?'

'No, no, no Aunt. We must go now. I'll fetch our cloaks.'

She ran from the room leaving Beornwyn looking after her, shaking her head and frowning heavily. Within seconds she was back.

'Just one more minute Aunt, I have just to supervise a delivery of new wool, it will take but a moment.' and off she ran again.

This time it was five minutes before she returned and with another breathless apology she announced herself ready to be on her way to meet, as she put it with a grin, 'This wicked Norman artist.'

The rain had actually stopped but the waiting body guard were hardly any happier with their duty and Josclin had to work overtime to keep them alert by pointing out shadows from the surrounding buildings and pretending that he could hear footsteps approaching and it was with considerable relief that he heard the bar on the inside of the door being lifted. He urgently beckoned his men to him and repeated the orders he'd given them time and time again. Their presence must not be too obvious to their charges. They must keep a respectful distance from them, watch their language and, above all, stay alert and on guard.

The rain might have eased but the water had swept a lot of household waste down into the centre of the main thoroughfare and the two figures, one taller than most men and slightly stooped, the other youthful and upright walked on either side to keep as much of the filth off the hems of their garments as they could. This separation did little to assist their dialogue but it was easy to see that the elder kept turning her head as if to avoid answering the other's continuous pattern of questioning.

Suddenly Beornwyn held up an imperious hand, not only to quieten the enthusiasm of Alysoun but to motion to her to stop her progress. They turned and faced each other and then Beornwyn turned a further ninety degrees until she was looking back the way they had come. Their bodyguard who had done their best to stay as inconspicuous as possible, which wasn't all that difficult when taking into account the numbers of pedestrians, donkeys, sheep, shoppers and sellers that cluttered up the main street. They were, however, four men-at-arms who, to the rest of the good people of Canterbury meant little, as soldiers were always somewhere about the town but to Beornwyn they might as well have been sent by the Devil himself. She stood there in the murk, magisterial and foreboding enough for those close to her to shrink back as she raised an accusing finger and aimed it at the unfortunate group of men.

'How dare he!'

She exclaimed in tones as musical as ever but edged with contempt, 'How dare he countermand my wishes in so flagrant a fashion.'

Small groups were now gathering. So long as her anger was directed at somebody else, Lady Beornwyn in a temper was always good value. Here, against four burly representatives of Norman repression it was not to be missed.

Alysoun felt embarrassed and sorry for the men who were obviously only carrying out orders. Orders moreover, that had been given for the benefit of Beornwyn's protection and security. Not so the appreciative audience who held their local patroness in awed affection and relished any opportunity to see her exercise her aristocratic Saxon authority.

'All right, don't block up the way. That's enough, get back to your work or whatever it is you're supposed to be doing.'

Josclin knew well how difficult Beornwyn could be if she really put her mind to it so he wasn't prepared to let this little problem get too far out of hand. He decided the best way was to be assertive himself. He came right up to the imposing form of the lady and bowed, but not too deeply. Through Robert Beaumont, he had come to respect the Lady Beornwyn as much as the next man and he had long learned that she cared little for subservience, even if she did insist on getting her own way most of the time.

They looked squarely at one another. Beornwyn's voice was quieter when she spoke but she made no attempt to disguise her displeasure.

'Well Josclin! You were there when your master and I were discussing my safety. The fears for it, if I recall correctly, were his and not mine and again, if I recall correctly, I openly and clearly stated that I did not wish him to provide me with an escort,'

She leaned her head to see past Josclin's broad shoulder, the other three men-at-arms standing awkwardly together although still appearing vigilant.

'Let alone a small army such as you have there.'

Josclin lifted two gauntleted hands in supplication.

'My Lady, I know, I know. My Lord felt that you did not sufficiently appreciate your vulnerable position. Especially now that maniac is at large. You of all people, my Lady should have fears for not only your own welfare but that of your ward.'

He leaned forward slightly so that only she could hear him.

'It is my Lord's opinion that Warin was not only killed because of some feud between him and Wulfric. Me? I am no more than a soldier and a servant my Lady but please believe me when I tell you that my Lord Beaumont has good reason for ordering me to deliver you safely to the castle, where he waits upon you both.'

He bowed briefly to Alysoun who nodded in return.

Beornwyn was not to be mollified however.

'Humph! I hope what I am about to hear at the castle will fully justify this… this military expedition.' she softened slightly, 'You are an honest man Josclin but,'

Her chin lifted and she once more became the one in command.

'Heed me carefully. You and your men will do your duty. I know you better than to try and deflect you from it, but you will do it inconspicuously. So move back and let us continue on our way unencumbered by soldiery.'

Josclin bowed again and turned back to his men. Before he had reached them, Beornwyn, always cheered by a successful encounter with the other side, took Alysoun's arm and went on her way down the main street, nodding regally to all the bobs and curtsies that were aimed at her.

They crossed the river and carried on down the busy thoroughfare, their progress halted from time to time as various townspeople stopped to show off their new babies or some new wares just arrived from across the sea. Alysoun had always been aware of how the local population of Canterbury respected her aunt but she never failed to be surprised at the degree of affection in which she was held. Beornwyn was truly loved by many of these people who saw behind the haughty, distant, authoritarian figure to the warmer, accessible lady who had worked tirelessly for the good of the community.

Now that the rain had stopped, the cottages and hovels were emptying fast. They turned right into Stour Lane, narrow and unpaved. The mud here was thick in places and as ever, mixed with the sort of town waste that made walking difficult and unpleasant. Half way down, Beornwyn slipped. Not seriously. She didn't fall but her grip on Alysoun's arm tightened and her head went back. It went back just far enough to be missed by the arrow, that thudded into the adjacent door frame.

Within a split second they were bundled roughly into the doorway. The shaft of the arrow was still quivering until a gloved hand stopped it so that its trajectory could be more easily judged. Josclin sighted along it's length.

'Peter, Bryce', he ordered urgently, 'The building over there. Second story!'

The house that he indicated was one of the tallest structures in the vicinity. As with most of the buildings in the area it was constructed mainly of wood but unlike most of its neighbours, it had an upper floor which probably meant that it was the property of a tradesman. The ground floor would be his workshop or showroom and the upper, the living quarters for the family. It was unapproachable directly as it stood in the cluttered maze of alleys that constituted this part of the city so the two men-at-arms would have to reach it the best way they could. Consequently, Josclin correctly judged that whoever had fired the arrow would be well away from his firing position by the time the soldiers reached the building. Nevertheless, he impressed on Bryce and Peter the need for caution.

'If that's who we think it is, he'll have disappeared down some dark hole before you get to him but he's a devil. Keep an eye out for each other at all times and don't go poking around in dark corners or shuttered rooms. He'll see you first and if he does you're dead, two to one or not. Right go...'

Meanwhile, the two women found themselves the objects of some curiosity from the members of the household into which they had been bundled so unceremoniously, not least because they seemed to have been the target of some maniac bowman. Although known to each other, Beornwyn knew everybody in Canterbury whatever their station in life, it was not often the householder's wife and her assorted snotty brood had come into such close contact with the illustrious dame and her niece and they seemed to be at a loss how to cope with the situation. Awkward bobs from the mother and the elder daughters were mingled with unblinking stares and sniffs from the younger contingent.

Beornwyn nodded agreeably to them but deep down she was shocked and frightened and leaving Alysoun to handle the uncertain social obligations, she beckoned Josclin to join her, just inside the doorway but out of any firing line.

Josclin, whose profession was violence, recognised that his charge had been shaken by the incident and he found himself feeling a twinge of sympathy for a lady who, hitherto, he had regarded as more intimidating than any women had a right to be. He hastened to reassure her.

'Don't worry my lady. I doubt if those two that I've sent off will do any good and as soon as they return we'll continue to escort you to the castle.'

He immediately had cause to reassess his sympathetic opinion of Lady Beornwyn who snapped

'Worried! Who said I was worried. You look to your men Josclin and pray to God that they do return in one piece. You and I both know who was responsible for this knavery, but why?'

She turned to him with genuine inquiry in her voice.

'Why, all of a sudden now? His revenge was directed at poor Warin, not me.'

Josclin shook his head.

'I have no idea my Lady. You would be better to ask your questions of my Lord. All I do know is that we are going to get you and the young lady to the castle as soon as I think it safe.'

'YOU think it safe Josclin?' she gave a short laugh, 'You have almost failed once, what makes you think that he will not succeed the next time?'

'Next time my Lady, you will walk with us around you and he would need to come out into the open if he means to harm you. This one doesn't like coming out into the open and…'

'NO!'

Josclin looked up sharply, as did everyone else in the room.

'I will not be marched into Canterbury castle by a guard of Norman men-at-arms. I will walk freely in this town and you Josclin, although you might have my grudging regard, will not persuade me otherwise.' her voice softened, 'I do not however, speak for my niece. If you would concentrate your efforts on her security I would be grateful.'

Alysoun dropped the grubby hand of the child whose fingers she had used in an effort to teach it to count to five and distract it from some of the drama.

'Certainly not Aunt. I walk with you or not at all.'

Beornwyn bent to her. 'But child, you don't…'

Alysoun held her now somewhat less than immaculate finger to her aunt's lips.

'Not another word Aunt. I walk with you and that is that.'

Josclin shuddered inwardly at the thought of not one but two headstrong women to guard against assassination. Give him a platoon of men to command any time. He looked out of the doorway and saw Peter and Bryce picking their way through the mud towards him. Needless to say they were unencumbered by a prisoner but at least they appeared to be unharmed. When he turned back to marshal the other member of his force he noticed that Lady Beornwyn's niece was standing in the doorway, trying to extract the arrow from the door frame. He sighed as he went to her.

'You'll never pull that out my Lady. That arrow tip has been double fired. It's designed to go through armour if there's a weak spot. It would have gone clear through that frame if it hadn't been oak.'

She looked wonderingly at him as she ran a finger along the flight.

'It's quite beautiful, almost graceful.' she said, 'Would one of your men try to cut it out for me?'

Josclin looked at her for a moment and then, with a sigh of resignation, beckoned Peter over.

'The young lady would like that arrow. See if you can get it out for her.'

Peter frowned at him.

'What does she want...'

'Don't ask. Just do it lad. Try not to spoil the flight.'

'Try not to spoil... but'

Alysoun looked up at him.

'Please.'

She said simply and without another word Peter nodded, drew a wicked looking blade from a scabbard at his belt and went to work on a particularly unyielding chunk of seasoned oak.

Beornwyn was making for the doorway when Josclin stopped her with an apologetic cough.

'What now Josclin? We are late enough already and if we do not get to the castle soon, your Lord will start to get anxious and before we know it, he will send an entire regiment out to make sure we arrive safely.'

Josclin mustered enough authority to look her in the eye. They were about the same height.

'My Lady. I am sorry but I must insist that you wait until we are ready. Lady Alysoun, for some reason or other, wishes to have the arrow that so nearly succeeded in killing you and it will take a moment or two for my man to extract it from the door frame.'

'Arrow!' exclaimed Beornwyn, as if this was the first she had heard of it.

'Why, in the name of God, child, do you want an arrow?'

'Please Aunt, indulge me. I would just like to have it. It is not every day that my favourite Aunt narrowly escapes death and I would like to keep it as a talisman.'

Beornwyn looked hopefully at Josclin but this time he avoided her glance and went over to assist Peter who was making slow work of the task. She groaned.

'Oh, very well. Incidentally, I am not your favourite Aunt, I am, as you well know, your only Aunt and I am asking you to make haste. We do not have time to spare for these fooleries.'

Peter redoubled his efforts and handed the arrow, the head somewhat flattened but otherwise intact, to Alysoun who grinned her thanks at him. This caused him to blush and his comrades to smother their grins at his discomfiture.

Josclin eventually organised their interrupted progress and while he allowed Beornwyn her space, he insisted that two men-at-arms proceeded the women by some five paces while he and the other brought up the rear, a similar distance behind.

Beornwyn, her arm protectively about the shoulders of Alysoun, felt her shiver slightly. The child had been frightened, she realised. She hadn't shown it but the seriousness of the event had not escaped her and that was why she had insisted on retrieving and keeping the weapon that had come within, literally, a hairsbreadth of killing her aunt. When she spoke of keeping it as a talisman, that was exactly what she had meant. Just a small act of defiance perhaps but it showed spirit and Beornwyn loved and respected her the more for it.

They encountered nothing else untoward as they neared the castle. As soon as the guards manning the outer gate recognised and admitted them Josclin breathed a sigh of relief and dismissed his men. The unfortunate Peter was still being nudged and teased by his fellows, especially as Alysoun made sure of thanking him prettily for his efforts on her behalf. Beornwyn too, thanked Josclin graciously for his protection and not for the first time that day that grizzled old soldier was forced to revise his opinion of her.

The bailey, as ever, was busy with all the day to day activities necessary to the castle community and the two women constantly found themselves greeting various craftsmen, domestic staff, clerks and clerics. As a frequent visitor, Beornwyn was known to most of the inhabitants but Alysoun, who had far less to do with the civic affairs of the city, still found herself the object of considerable interest. This was especially so with regard to the pages and the younger knights who were taking advantage of the break in the weather to exercise their combat skills in the open, where swords and other weapons could be swung with much more freedom. Beornwyn, ever anxious for the well-being of her niece, was quick to notice the effect she was having on the men and for the first time since her narrow escape, tried to make some sense of this irrational foreboding about this particular visit to the castle. Fortunately Robert Beaumont forestalled any further anxieties by meeting them at the foot of the tower.

Gracious as ever, he greeted Lady Beornwyn with a warmth that was obviously genuine. With Alysoun, who he hardly knew, he was more reserved and bowed gravely to her. If he was surprised to see this demure young woman carrying an arrow he was gentleman enough not to remark on it but when she asked him if he would be kind enough to point out the smithy to her, so that she could have it re-headed, even he could not resist a slightly quizzical look at Lady Beornwyn.

She, Beornwyn, had been hoping that there would be time enough for the story of the arrow to be related by Josclin when he made his report to Beaumont but apparently it was not to be, so playing down the drama of the event, she quickly acquainted him with facts of how the arrow came to be in Alysoun's possession. As she had feared, Beaumont requested a fuller explanation than she thought strictly necessary and said that he would question Josclin more fully later. He went on to insist that she either stayed in the castle or be prepared to accept whatever measures he considered adequate for her protection. He turned from Beornwyn for a second and transferred his attention to Alysoun.

'If you would let me have that arrow Mistress Alysoun, I will have one of my people take it to the armoury and re-headed.'

He held out his hand for the arrow and she passed it to him.

'Thank you.'

He then turned again to Beornwyn.

'My Lady, I have always liked to think that we have worked well together for the good of the people of this region and it is for this reason, together with the respect in which I hold you that I consider it important to look to your safety as far as it is in my power to do so. Today, you could so easily have lost your life to Wulfric who might well be working alone. To be honest with you, I don't know for sure whether he is or not. All I do know is, that if he had succeeded in killing you as he did the lamented Warin and it became known to the citizens of the city that now their beloved Lady Beornwyn had died at the hands of one of Odo's people, the consequences for our reconciliatory work here could be disastrous. So please, allow yourself and your niece here to submit to my protection and care.'

Alysoun plucked at his sleeve to gain his attention.

'We will my Lord' she said, 'You have my word, my Aunt will be quite happy to be escorted through the town by a whole army, if you consider it necessary.'

'Now, just a minute…'

Beaumont found himself swung around by his other sleeve in the direction of Beornwyn who did not look at all happy.

'AUNT! Please Aunt. You know my Lord is speaking sense.' Alysoun's voice was respectful but firm.

'I know nothing of the… o h! Very well Beaumont but this is for the sake of my niece not me and I hope you understand that?'

Robert Beaumont bit his lip but managed to hold Beornwyn's outraged look.

'Of course my Lady. I understand completely. Now, if you forgive me, I think we ought to proceed with the purpose of this visit and see what progress is being made by Master LeBrun.'

Beornwyn eyes clouded over momentarily but she nodded and with a lady on each arm Beaumont led them up the steps of the tower.

CHAPTER THIRTY FIVE

Caen

Mathilde was sitting with her ladies, embroidering and exchanging gossip. She missed Mirabelle who had made her laugh and had an incisive intelligence that almost matched her own. With William away so much of the time, defending his rights to his territories here in France, she really had few people in the court to whom she could relate. She sighed and spent the next few moments concentrating on her needlework until the memory of Thibault struck her and her hand hovered over her stretched linen while she let her mind wander. Such a waste to have somebody of Thibault's integrity, vegetating his life away in some House of God. A less worldly version of Robert Beaumont, he would have made a good trusty administrator here or over in England.

That young artist LeBrun! Now his was another talent worthy of cultivation and amusing to boot. Still, he must be left where he was. This was important work on which he was engaged and although originally at the instigation of Uncle Odo who, she smiled to herself, was actually footing the bill for his work, the finished article was going to reflect considerable glory on the House of William of Caen.

LeBrun... Thibault... Her thoughts came round in a circle to Mirabelle again. Ah well, she thought, William was expected at any time and she would soon have other subjects to discuss. She reapplied herself to her needle and deftly, for she was a fine needlewomen, stitched in the form of a stag. William adored his hunting and this was to be a napkin for his birthday. Another year, bringing with it, perhaps, another set of problems. It shouldn't be long now and William would be with her and she could catch up on all the news and that was what she really liked. To know what was going on.

From below came the sound of the drawbridge windlass and the clatter of hooves. Her women had heard it too and without a word from their mistress, began to quietly pack up their silks and their frames. William always preferred to be welcomed alone so, one by one, they approached Mathilde, bowed and rustled out through the rushes to the door at the rear of the chamber, opposite to that which William would enter. Mathilde did not put aside her work but replaced it with one on which she had been creating a design for a cushion cover, because a birthday present is a birthday present and should be a surprise.

The noise of approaching boots became louder and within moments, the door was energetically flung open, causing the rushes closest to it to scatter as William entered. He was flushed and happy from his exertions and looked fit for a man of his years. He was getting on for fifty now. Mathilde looked up from her work and waited for him to approach her. He raised a hand in greeting and immediately strode over to the window. From there, he looked down on to the great doors guarding the inner keep through which he had just entered and which were now firmly barred. The drawbridge was raised and the castle was secure. Not that he had any immediate worries but he always liked to reassure himself that his guards had not relaxed their vigilance just because their Duke was not currently in conflict with any of his neighbours.

Having satisfied himself on that point he turned to his consort who, having continued her embroidery while he was otherwise engaged, set down her frame and said, 'Well?'

Still looking out of the window, William's voice was neutral when he turned to speak.

'de Courcy mentioned that he'd called in at St Steven's, making arrangements for his third daughter's admission to the order. Poor devil has more daughters than he knows what to do with and stays awake at night worrying about dowries and that sort of thing. Do you know, he...'

'St Stevens?'

The Queen's tone suggested that her interest in de Courcy's brood was not uppermost in her mind. He noticed her embroidery frame was lying untouched on her lap though, a sure sign that he had her attention. He turned back to his window and appeared to be concentrating on the view. Some pigs were defying the swineherd's attempts to round them up and the spectacle had attracted most of the inhabitants of the bailey, knights, artisans and a few other younger boys who took full advantage of the situation to rush around and impede the meagre progress made by the hapless swineherd. When he smiled, it was Mathilde's curiosity which caused his lips to twitch, rather than the pantomime being played out below him.

'William!'

He took his time to turn in response to her call and by the time he had done so, the smile had disappeared and he merely let out a disingenuous, 'Um!'

'William,' she went on, 'I don't suppose that de Courcy mentioned seeing Thibault did he?'

'Well yes, as a matter of fact he did. What made you ask?'

'Nothing in particular,' came her reply, 'but oddly enough I was thinking about him only a few moments before you came in. What did de Courcy have to say about him?'

'Well, he said he thought that Thibault looked a great deal better than when last he'd seen him.'

Her hand began to move to a thread on her cuff but she was aware that William was waiting for her to begin fussing with it so she withdrew it and made to pick up her embroidery frame. He frowned, she had disappointed him by depriving him of a teasing remark. Instead she smiled at his frown and said, 'That is nice to hear.'

This time she really had spoiled his fun. His frown deepened to one of genuine enquiry. He moved towards her.

'Is that all you have to say?'

She looked up at him as he stood over her and said.

'What else would you have me say, my love?'

He scratched his head.

'Well, I did think you would be rather interested in the news. I had always assumed that you had plans for young Thibault, providing of course that he did not intend to incarcerate himself in that place for the rest of his life.'

She returned her eyes to her stitching.

'Why ever would you assume that, William? Naturally, since that business with Mirabelle and the state of the poor boy when I brought him back over here, I have retained some interest in his welfare but that is all.'

The King turned abruptly and made for the sanctuary of his window again. Eventually he turned and said, 'Oh come on Mathilde. Whenever you take an interest in anybody, their welfare is one of the last things you consider. So what is it with Thibault? I would be very surprised if you and I were not of one mind here so stop being difficult and feminine and say what you have to say.'

She replied, quite sweetly, 'I was not aware, William, that 'being difficult' was exclusive to my sex, however, I too would not be surprised to find that we shared similar views on this matter. So far as I know, the only person for whom our wretched kinsman Odo has shown any real regard is Thibault.'

William nodded his agreement. She continued. 'Ah! I see we are of one mind. Strange is it not, that Odo, one of the most thoroughly corrupt people imaginable, should bestow whatever spark of humanity he possesses on one of the most honest and reliable men to be found in either of our two domains.'

William started to say something but she pre-empted him with a wave of her needle.

'Yes, yes, I know. Robert Beaumont and Lanfranc are both trustworthy but they are worldly men, political animals and they know that their interests are best served by serving you honestly. Odo is never happy unless he is plotting something. Perhaps Thibault could bring himself to re-enter Odo's service. He now knows Odo for what he is but if my uncle's affection for him remains undiminished, Thibault might just be privy to thoughts that would otherwise not be available to us.'

William nodded.

'I guessed that was the direction in which you were heading and you could be right. Certainly Odo is not going to bare his soul to Robert or Lanfranc. Firstly because he can't stand either of them and secondly he knows full well that they would report everything back to me. No, the idea is not unreasonable but then, coming from you, my love, I would not expect it to be. Of course, for it to come to anything at all, we have to presume that Thibault will be willing to do what we ask of him and that Odo will confide in him as he did previously.'

The Queen shrugged.

'What have we to lose? I suspect that Thibault is still an Achilles heel, so far as Odo is concerned. The man has to love something for God's sake whereas Thibault probably still imagines that Odo was responsible for Mirabelle's death. That being the case, would he not welcome the opportunity to do Odo harm? As I say, what have we to lose? If my predictions are correct, we will have a window into Odo's mind. If not, we are no worse off than we were before.'

William was silent for a moment then gave a short laugh, 'Well! Talk of the devil, guess who has just walked through the gate?'

CHAPTER THIRTY SIX

Canterbury Castle

Jean brushed a fly away from his work. Although the window provided him with more light it also seemed to intensify the warmth of the emerging sun which encouraged all sorts of insects to materialise. Not for the first time, Jean wished that they had left the open window as it was, so that he had more natural illumination and fewer unwelcome visitors. The fly continued to buzz and for the moment, Jean was distracted.

He straightened up and looked around this room that had been allotted to him and felt a sudden lurch of homesickness. His mother perpetually concerned for his welfare, his father, stern and unbending but well meaning and his brothers and sisters. How were they all? Did they think of him at all? Not that he deserved it if they did because since he had been over here he had scarcely given them a thought, which was hardly surprising with so much going on. Not very nice of him but perhaps one day...the fly re-settled on the battlefield and once again Jean brushed it away only this time he managed to sweep his drawing stick to the floor, where it broke.

He picked up the pieces of charcoal, smiling a little to himself as other memories, hidden over the last few months, began to rise to the surface. His friends from the village and the girls. The girls! He hadn't thought of that sort of thing for a while now. He had the odd disturbing dream but hadn't really thought about girls in that way since riding through the village on the way to Canterbury and the housewives had taunted him from their doorways. He felt himself stirring but then the memory of Mirabelle washed through his mind like a wave of cold water. That had been the last time and look how it had ended for her. Poor Mirabelle, he thought and come to think of it, poor Thibault.

He walked back to his trestle and stared gloomily at what he had accomplished. How much more would there be to go before he was free of it and could revert back to being a normal healthy male with desires other than working to please the likes of Lords Odo, Beaumont and Lanfranc, not to mention the King and Queen.

He ran his fingers through his tangled hair. If anyone, a year ago, had offered him the opportunity to be doing what he was at this present moment, he would have jumped at it. To be allowed, actually allowed, to spend his time doing what he loved best and be cosseted for his art was beyond any imagining but now…now he thought it might be quite pleasant to just be an ordinary young man enjoying the things that all ordinary young men were supposed to enjoy.

He looked again at his work and pursed his lips. Not bad but would it be good enough for the Lady Beornwyn? From what he'd seen of her, he quite liked her, even if she did look like a horse. He also imagined that she could be quite unforgiving if crossed. Nevertheless, fierce though she undoubtedly was, there seemed to be some sort of mutual respect existing between them. Funny that! Him a Norman country boy and her a high born Saxon noblewoman but there was something definitely there and if this was to be a successful collaboration then a creative alliance of some sort would have to be devised.

He pulled the table back from its position under the window, it was too hot. Perhaps someday somebody would come up with a way of opening the damn things when the weather was warmer. His last panel depicted some of the battle scenes, as described by Beaumont with Josclin filling in the occasional gap in the narrative.

A gust of air blew under the door, indicating that one of the doors leading to the bailey had been opened and Jean watched the dust motes float and fall from the light in the window. They settled momentarily on his table and he wondered if all this effort would prove just as ephemeral. He settled again to illustrating some of the earlier battle scenes. One of the significant events, according to Beaumont who advised Jean not to omit the record, was the death of Harold's brothers. Jean glanced at his notes; Gyneth and Leofwin. Funny names these Saxons had but apparently it was these two and the force they commanded who had been unwise enough to forsake the relative safety of the high ground they held and, mistakenly believing William's infantry to have been in retreat, followed them down the slope.

This decision, which Beaumont had described as "militarily unwise" and Josclin as "fucking stupid" had cost them their lives and possibly even an English victory. Jean didn't really bother about these tactical aspects of the conquest. He was no soldier and his only real interest was to create some pictorial record of events as simply as possible. By now he was quite adept at this technique which was just as well, considering how long this record was supposed to be.

Gyneth and Leofwin having been accordingly dispatched, Jean consulted his notes on what came next. Thankfully, not a great deal. He looked at the folds of linen concertinaed on the floor. If nothing else, there would be plenty for her Ladyship to look at. Whether or not she liked what she saw he would soon find out as he heard her unmistakable voice in conversation with Robert Beaumont as they approached his room. He glanced around quickly. Too late to do anything now but it didn't seem to be too untidy. His straw mattress lay neatly rolled in one corner and apart from some small piles of charcoal shavings, the floor was tolerably clean. He pretended to be concentrating on his work as they entered and to his surprise, the first sound he heard was a very audible intake of breath coming from the doorway. He looked up sharply and on precisely the same beat, he and Alysoun exclaimed, 'YOU!'

For a few seconds nobody said a word and then Beornwyn, frowning in bewilderment said, not unkindly, 'Alysoun, have you and this, this young man met on a previous occasion?'

Without waiting for a reply she turned to Jean with a touch more edge to her voice.

'Master LeBrun, you have told me nothing of this.'

Neither of the young couple answered the questions aimed at them but continued to look at each other in total disbelief and it was Robert Beaumont who eventually broke the ice by saying.

'Well that should save a lot of trouble, no need for introductions.'

He turned to Jean and coughed in order to deflect his attention away from Alysoun but it took two such clearings of the throat before he managed it.

'I must say LeBrun, you might have had the goodness to mention this before. I was under the impression that, apart from Guy and his inventive carpenter, what's his name, that you knew of nobody here in Canterbury.'

Jean merely shook his head so Beaumont continued.

'This young lady is the niece of Lady Beornwyn and an expert in the field of embroidery and design. One of the foremost in the country if her aunt is to be believed'

He gave a bow to Lady Beornwyn.

'Never mind that' snapped the lady, without even acknowledging Beaumont's courteous gesture. She turned to Alysoun.

'How did this happen, why wasn't I informed that you already knew this man?'

Alysoun's response was equally short.

'I haven't met him Aunt. I don't know him from Adam. It is just that when I was in the cathedral, inspecting the kneelers in the choir, he sort of well... sort of...'

'What' barked Beornwyn, 'Sort of what exactly?'

'I sort of fell over her my Lady.' Jean's voice was respectful but it was unmistakably tinged with amusement. He went on, 'You see, I thought she was somebody else but it was just a silly mistake and then we sort of got tangled up and...'

'Tangled up!'

Beornwyn's voice had temporarily lost its normally attractive timbre. Beaumont was biting his lip furiously while Alysoun could not stem a most unladylike snort of laughter which, if nothing else, seemed to relieve whatever tension existed in the room.

'As the boy said, it was nothing more than a silly mistake. We didn't even exchange a word, let alone introduce ourselves to each other.'

The word 'boy' stirred Jean out of his good humour and he retorted, in the best English that he could muster, 'I might not have said anything to you but you, Lady, if I remember rightly, had quite a lot to say to me and very unflattering it was too.'

Her head lifted, her eyes sparked and she made her reply in impeccable Norman, 'Master LeBrun, if that is who you are, with your pitiful grasp of our language I am surprised that you could understand anything of what I said.' she dismissed him and turned to her aunt.

'So this is him Aunt, how disappointing.'

Both Beornwyn and Beaumont frowned at this display of discourtesy and Jean blushed scarlet, something he had not experienced for a very long time. His eyes were fixed on his board while he tried, without any apparent success, to think of something equally cutting in return. The truth was that he really had made a complete idiot of himself in the choir of the cathedral and now couldn't possibly understand how he had managed to confuse this… this girl, with someone as reptilian as Wulfric. Nevertheless, as the silence in the room lengthened into an eternity, he felt he needed to assert himself somehow or other so, ignoring Alysoun, he looked directly at Beornwyn and said.

'If I have offended your Ladyship, I ask your pardon. I would also ask to be released from this undertaking and be allowed to return home where my talents, if such they be, might not be appreciated to any great extent but at least they are not life threatening. Nor do they continually necessitate my having to deal with those who are superior to me in social rank.'

He again delivered this speech in Saxon and added dryly.

'That is if your Ladyship can understand what I am saying.'

Robert Beaumont and Beornwyn looked at each other while Alysoun merely gave one of her dismissive snorts and moved over to the trestle to look at Jean's latest efforts. Jean moved out of her way, to the other side of the table and inspected his grimy hands. It was Beaumont, ever thoughtful and diplomatic, who spoke first. When he did so, it was quietly but the edge of authority could not be mistaken.

'I cannot speak for Lady Beornwyn of course, or for that matter, her niece.' he gave a small bow of the head in Alysoun's direction, 'But I don't think that the Queen would be happy for you to do that and if the Queen were not happy, then the King...'

He paused for a moment to allow the words to take their desired effect and then continued.

'And then, of course, there is the Earl of Kent. This was his idea originally and although their Majesties have registered their interest in the project, my Lord Odo would be loath to lose the veneration that this finished work is likely to bring him. My Lord Odo is not a man to take disappointment lightly. Of course, if you really wish to abort your work then there is nothing I can do to stop you but I would advise you to think most carefully. What do you say my Lady?' turning to Beornwyn.

Hitherto, Beornwyn's mouth had been set into a tight disapproving line but before she could say whatever it was on her mind, Alysoun spoke up. She was still at the table running her fingers over the outlines of Jean's drawing, just as she had with the first set that she had seen. She didn't acknowledge Jean's presence at all but spoke almost to herself or at least to the cloth under her fingers.

'There can be no question of not finishing this. Of course he must and we must waste no more time in setting about our work. This is much too important. I don't care about the King and Queen and even less about that odious Bishop...'

Beornwyn put her fingers to her lips and whispered, 'Hush.' but Alysoun was too far into her own thoughts to allow them to be interrupted.

'This,' she pointed to a figure, 'Must be in red. No, no not all of it. The front of the horse in red the rear in green. That way, with the other horses behind, as he has drawn them, we can add to the depth of his illustration.'

Her voice started to rise in volume as she warmed to her theme.

'Don't you see, it will be a new way of depicting a scene. It will give it new..., Oh, please Aunt, what is the word... a new dimension. No, another dimension.'

She pulled the linen across the table to see the preceding frame. She frowned and bit her lip. No one else in the room spoke although, once again, Beornwyn and Beaumont exchanged glances. Jean, still smarting from what he saw as Alysoun's arrogance, pretended to study the chair against which he was leaning but even he could not mistake the controlled excitement that seemed to emanate from this uppity young woman.

Pity, he thought to himself, as he made a fruitless job of trying to flatten his own thatch, that she couldn't bring her hair under better control. She obviously held her own with her redoubtable aunt and from the way he was hanging on her every word, Lord Beaumont seemed to find her quite fascinating. Typical of the aristocracy, whatever their race or culture. They always stick up for one another.

Alysoun's forehead furrowed even more deeply and she looked up at Beornwyn.

'Of course you are quite right Aunt. A border must be added. Two, in fact; top and bottom.'

Jean pushed the chair back with a violence that caused the others to look up. He started forward towards the table and Robert Beaumont stretched out a hand and gently restrained him by his elbow. Alysoun, a hint of a smile playing around her mouth, shook her head.

'Don't worry Master LeBrun. I have no intention of spoiling your design.' She pushed her hair back under her cap and beckoned to him with the other hand.

'Come here, let me explain.'

Her tone was not in the least patronising, rather that of an equal with a shared interest and Jean looked up at Beaumont who promptly released him. He moved to the table, opposite to Alysoun and looked at where she was pointing. She giggled quietly and shook her head.

'Not there Master LeBrun, here with me.'

Once more her tone was completely neutral without the slightest hint of flirtation or command.

'Of course I do not intend that your design be altered in any way. I love it but can't you see? If we added a border here and here,' she pointed to the top and the bottom of the frieze, 'we could flesh out the story that you have, so effectively, illustrated.'

He looked at her but her face gave no hint of irony. In fact she was not even looking at him but still concentrating her gaze on the drawing.

'Do you see what I mean?'

Still her eyes remained fixed on the table in front of her. Jean looked at her long and, he guessed, clever fingers.

'Well…' he began hesitantly, 'Well… not really. Surely this is only meant to represent what happened, why does it need anything adding to it? Unless I've missed anything out of course,' he added.

He was desperate not to be made look stupid by this self confident young women but he was not going to pretend to understand something that he had not.

'Come on,' she cajoled, 'Look at it through the eyes of someone who hasn't seen it before. I am not too worried about the story. That takes care of itself, what concerns me is the overall feel of the piece.'

She invested the word 'feel' with such passion that Jean looked at her again to see if she was being in any way sarcastic but she was still riveted to what was in front of her. Jean looked again. Still he failed to see what it was that she was looking for so he swallowed, shrugged his shoulders and said.

'You will have to tell me I'm afraid. I just don't know what you're talking about.'

Suddenly she was looking at him.

'Why do your people always do that?'

He frowned. This time there was a suggestion of humour in her voice.

'Do what?' he said.

She shrugged her shoulders, in imitation of him. 'That' she said.

'Whenever one of your people doesn't know something or is dismissive of something, they always do that.'

She did it again and he automatically repeated the movement when he replied.

'I don't know.'

Upon which she burst into a peal of laughter and the two onlookers could not even restrain their own mirth. The only one present who couldn't see anything to laugh at was Jean who stood there not knowing whether or not he had made himself out to be complete idiot. His discomfort was quickly diffused by Robert Beaumont coming over to him and saying.

'She is absolutely right you know, LeBrun. It seems to be a particularly odd habit of our people. But I think the Lady Alysoun wishes to explain something to you.'

He indicated the drawing.

'I know nothing about such things of course but I think she is of the opinion that your illustration of events...' he turned to Lady Beornwyn, '... while, in every way, masterful...'

Beornwyn gave a perceptible nod of agreement.

'...might even be improved upon by the additional elements in the form of borders which um...'

Beaumont was interrupted by Jean, who suddenly seemed to have found his tongue.

'Why?'

Beaumont shrugged his shoulders.

'Well, to be honest with you LeBrun...I think it is because.... because... I have no idea whatsoever,' he eventually conceded.

It was an obviously amused Alysoun who came to his rescue.

'Master LeBrun. As my Lord says, your designs are wonderful and I know of no one who could have executed them better. As my Aunt will tell you, I have skill with a needle and I can create pictures in my head but I have no skill in draughtsmanship. Your work is good. It is very good but it is a straightforward historical narrative. In my opinion, it requires another dimension. Something that would help the onlooker identify more closely with the various elements of the story. For instance, what you are portraying is a series of events leading up to and including your conquest of our peoples....'

She said this without any visible indication of rancour and Jean surmised that her creative interest in the project outweighed any feelings she had for the Conquest but he was wrong!

She went on, 'But if you don't mind me saying so, this is typical of your attitude towards art. Most of your architecture, brilliant and innovative as it may be, seems to be created for one purpose only – to show your supremacy over us. This...' sweeping a hand over the table of drawings, 'seems to be much in the same vein. No doubt your final panel will show the coronation of Mathilde as Queen of England.'

A servant knocked, entered and handed Alysoun her repaired arrow. She ran her fingers along the flights and gave Jean a look that dared him to challenge what she had just said. He couldn't. His look became more challenging though.

'I can only agree that yes that is my plan for the last panel but what of it? I am only following orders and anyway, what are you talking about? What is wrong with Norman architecture? From what I can see it is only about a hundred times better than anything you Anglo Saxons have managed to build and what is more,' he continued, trying to ignore her snort of derision, 'why shouldn't my countrymen impose their cultural superiority if they want to? We won didn't we and another thing...'

He was stopped in full flow by Beaumont's cough.

His Lordship was shaking his head at him. Jean frowned, first in frustration in failing to find an obvious ally and then in disbelief as the arrow twanged between his feet and stuck in the boards, its momentum gently moving the straw that lay around it.

Having recovered his wits, he was furious. He pulled the arrow out of the floor and waved it at Alysoun. Beaumont intervened.

'LeBrun these times are still not easy. We have to try and understand each other a little better.' He glanced over to Lady Beornwyn who said nothing but nodded warily. Alysoun's head was up however and she looked decidedly unrepentant. Beaumont crossed the floor, took the arrow from Jean and handed it back to Alysoun with a imperceptible shake of his head. She gave a deep sigh and lay the arrow back on the table.

'Right!' said Beaumont, 'where were we? You, Lady Alysoun, were, I think, trying to make a point to Master LeBrun here. Something to do with creating art for it's own sake and without any particular political agenda in mind. Do I understand your reasoning correctly?'

She looked at him gratefully.

'Indeed you do my Lord. All I am trying to say is, if you leave your work as it is, it becomes no more than a history lesson but if you decorate it, it can become a true work of art. Let me see now…'

She walked the length of the table and back, her eyes still engaged with the drawing.

'Look, when a scribe writes, all he is doing is putting words on parchment. Virtuous and worthy enough but, when he decorates it, illuminates it with highlights, colours and scrolls, it becomes a work of art. Do you not see?'

Jean's expression remained stubbornly blank.

'Oh dear.'

She sighed again but instantly became re-animated.

'Look, Master LeBrun, have you never seen any of our own art, our carvings our jewellery, metalwork, weaving designs, anything at all?'

'Alysoun!'

Beornwyn spoke wearily.

'I think that is enough for the moment. I am tired.'

She turned to Beaumont, 'I have to admit that the earlier incident has effected me more than I thought.'

She turned back to Jean.

'Master LeBrun, the continuation of your design has more than lived up to the standard of the first panel. I knew I was right to undertake the commission and although I sometimes find it difficult to understand the workings of my niece's mind, I am sure that what she has said will be worthy of your consideration. Please excuse her enthusiasm and directness. I would not have her any other way but those that do not know her can sometimes find her challenging.'

Jean, for the umpteenth time, wondered how it was that these aristocratic people, could suddenly turn on the charm. As for her niece, perhaps she was right about his designs. Perhaps they could benefit from some new ideas which might enliven his narrative. Perhaps he'd think about it and see if he couldn't come up with something of his own.

In the meantime he contented himself with a nod and a grunt of agreement.

'Well!'

Her Ladyship said, with obvious relief.

'That is that for the moment. We will continue our deliberations on the morrow, if that suits you?'

The question, Jean noted, was directed at Beaumont, not himself. Obviously he had been granted enough courtesy for one afternoon and the thought made him smile a little to himself. One thing he wasn't going to do was shrug his shoulders.

Alysoun did not seem too eager to go and lingered at the table, tracing over the pictures with one hand while the other clutched the arrow tapping the flight on her chin.

Actually, Jean thought, she's quite pretty. As she followed her aunt and Lord Beaumont out of the room she gave a last lingering glance over her shoulder at Jean's drawings then, as she passed him, shot him a brief thoughtful look but said nothing by way of a farewell.

Jean heard their footsteps down the stairs and returned to his work. He felt like setting fire to it.

CHAPTER THIRTY SEVEN

The School of Needlework

Beaumont made his farewell to the two women and stood on the steps, watched them cross the bailey, making certain that Josclin and his three men were in close attendance as they exited the postern. Once they had passed through and out of his sight, he remained, still looking after them until, after a glance up to Jean's window, he turned and made his way back to his apartments with just the ghost of a smile on his face.

#

In the town, a shadow detached itself from a doorway and moved in the direction of the School of Needlework.

#

Beornwyn and her niece made their way back the way they had come. They were hemmed in by their escort and it was not long before Lady Beornwyn turned to Josclin and snapped at him to allow them some degree of freedom. Alysoun, still clutching her arrow, turned and gave Josclin a sympathetic grin but this time there was no way that he was going to allow himself to be bullied out of what he perceived to be his duty and his tone, as he answered his charge, was only just respectful. In short, he made it clear that their protective formation would remain intact. A stony glare from Lady Beornwyn was duly ignored and the rest of their journey was silent, uneventful and uncomfortable, especially from the point of view of those lesser citizens of Canterbury who were shouldered aside by this square wall of bodies.

'Aunt?' Alysoun ventured at one point.

'Not now my dear.'

Having arrived safely at the School, Alysoun took herself off to her design table and stared anew at the length of linen that lay draped over it. It was, in fact, her aunt who eventually broke the silence once Josclin had departed, leaving two of his men guarding the front door.

'Well?'

'Um'

'What did you think?'

Alysoun raised her eyes reluctantly from the table.

'Think! About what Aunt?'

Beornwyn waved an impatient hand.

'Come child. You are perfectly aware what I mean. Just be honest with me, that is all I ask.'

Alysoun wrinkled her forehead in mock perplexity.

'Honest, Aunt?'

Beornwyn stamped an oversized foot.

'Stop playing games girl and tell me, plainly, what you thought of today's visit.'

Alysoun regarded her thoughtfully.

'I thought you were very lucky to escape this arrow. You were nearly killed you know.'

Beornwyn raised her eyes heavenward and gave an exasperated sigh.

'Not that, not that. I am only too well aware of that particular drama. You are being deliberately obtuse, child. You know full well that I am referring to the work that we are about to undertake. Has what you have seen today made you more enthusiastic for it or less? It is not too late you know. We can still give the boy back his money and advise him to look elsewhere for the needlework.'

Alysoun's head snapped up.

'Elsewhere Aunt! How can you even think of such a thing. Leaving everything else aside, you have already told Le…, whatever his name is, that we are interested in doing it. How will it look if we, proud English remnants of a rapidly declining nobility, can't keep to an agreement made with an ordinary, base born, Norman youth?'

Beornwyn studied her long fingers and said nothing for a moment. Then, with a quiet smile she said tentatively.

'Ordinary?'

'Yes Aunt, he is ORDINARY. As ordinary as you can get!'

A pause then, her head down and voice almost inaudible, 'It's his work that is extraordinary and that's why we have to continue with this commission and when we do we will set our own Saxon mark upon it. All right, all right,'

Her head came up and her eyes locked with those of Beornwyn, 'The narrative design will be his but we will have some say in the addition of borders and the accompanying text. That way we will have set our own mark on a work of art that will possibly intrigue the world long after we have gone.'

She was tapping the arrowhead on the table to emphasise her point and went on.

'Believe me Aunt, if we do not, this embroidery will be claimed by the Norman people as all their own work and our contribution will be forgotten. We are already, not yet eleven years after the invasion, saddled with a reputation of being little more than barbarians. In some ways this can be seen as our last significant gesture of defiance.'

'Yes, my dear but…'

'I know what you are going to say, Aunt, that they have paid for it and, thanks to Jean…thingummy…designed it but we will have had our say and we will be known as the people who actually made it. You do see don't you?'

'Yes dear, of course I see what you mean. In fact if you remember I had already mentioned something like this myself but…oh, for goodness sake! Stop playing with that infernal arrow. There are risks, Odo's no fool, he will see what we have done and more importantly, so will Mathilde and it is she who seems to have taken over this project.'

She shook her head doubtfully and walked over to Alysoun.

'I am not concerned for myself, you know that, but I am worried that you could become the object of their malice. That arrow you keep playing with should serve as a reminder of what they are capable. Although we are lucky, in that we do have good friends in Beaumont and Lanfranc but they can only protect us up to a point.'

She then said, although not so much to Alysoun as to herself.

'Mathilde, I think could also be an ally.'

'Well there you are then, Aunt. That settles it. We might not have that many Norman friends but those we do are, at least, powerful.'

Having delivered what she considered to be the last word on the subject, she then went on to talk of the practical matters that she had raised with her Aunt earlier. The quality of the wool and the linen backing, the number of ladies they were likely to need and the dyes that would have to be sourced. Beornwyn listened but walked about the room restlessly, as though still considering the implications of what they had just discussed.

'You are going to need The Bestiary are you not?'

Alysoun looked up.

'Of course I am and that copy of the Aesop. We might as well use them both to flesh out the borders. The only thing is…. well, the boy will have to have them. You and I do not have a good enough freehand to lay down the design directly.'

Her eyes twinkled.

'Can we trust them to him do you think? After all, I can only remember two or at the most three occasions when you have entrusted them to me and one of those was when I was about five and you didn't dare let me touch the pages. You turned them for me and explained what they were.'

Beornwyn's expression softened.

'That seems such a long, long time ago. Anyway, do you not think you might show our young protégé just a shade more respect. You should really not refer to him as a boy. I doubt you are as old as he is.'

Alysoun frowned.

'Protégé! Since when has he become OUR protégé? Surely, he is merely to be the agent of what is to be our triumph and anyway,' she continued, 'Age has nothing to do with it. What about rank, what about race?'

She affected an air of being shocked and walked slowly around the table to join her aunt, whom she regarded with a slightly crooked smile.

'I am surprised at you, I really am. Of all people, I expected you to keep this young, yes Aunt, whatever else he is, he is definitely young, Norman upstart at arms length. Heaven knows, you went to enough trouble to keep me away from him. Why! If I hadn't…'

'Yes, all right, ALL RIGHT Alysoun.'

Beornwyn looked down on her with a severity that never quite matched the smile lurking around the corners of her mouth.

'Since you are young, unworldly and, I shall forever regret having said it, pretty-ish, I thought that you might be a distraction to him. That is why I was anxious that you not meet with him.'

She turned away and Alysoun responded with one of her unladylike hoots of laughter.

'A distraction, Aunt, me? What about him being a distraction to me and my work? I mean to say, he's not bad looking and although not exactly oozing with charm he…'

'What do you mean 'not bad looking' child? I thought you'd hardly looked at anything beyond his work. If I thought for one instant that …'

Alysoun stood on tiptoe and held a delicate finger to her Aunt's mouth.

'My dear Aunt, I have met the boy – yes, boy – but twice. The first time he knocked me down and trod all over me and the second time he barely spoke to me save to question my motives for wanting to make his work more interesting. So there you have it. On the first occasion he annoyed me and on the second, I annoyed him. Hardly a recipe for a passionate liaison is it? Oh, by the way, you never did tell me what basis you had for suggesting he had a reputation. Something to do with some drawings of his, was it not?'

Beornwyn snatched her hand away, took a step back and wagged a large finger at Alysoun.

'Rumours, that is all. Rumours and suggestions made in passing and I dare say, in jest but so far as you are concerned my dear, I take no chances. I know you think that you are well versed in the ways of the world and I have ordered your education to that end but there are still things that...'

'That what Aunt?' put in Alysoun, who by this time was well into her mischievous role.

Beornwyn took a deep breath, then noisily exhaled in a defeated sort of way.

'Oh, child! Since you obviously know what I am talking about, why do you go on about it. Please, just take my advice and tread warily as far as that young man is concerned. And stop teasing me. It has been a long and difficult day. I am tired and am going to my bed.'

She went up to Alysoun, bent down tucking the stray strands of hair back into her headdress and kissed her lightly on her forehead. She was halfway to the door when Alysoun softly said, 'Before you retire, Aunt, could I please have The Bestiary and the Fables? I have some ideas in my mind which I would like to put in order before I go to sleep.'

Beornwyn inclined her head and indicated that Alysoun should follow her into the next room. There, she detached a key from the chord around her waist and unlocked a large press which stood in one corner. From it she extracted a sheaf of vellum, roughly but securely bound with leather thongs and then more vellum sheets, this time protected by thin wooden boards. She gently blew dust off them and turned to Alysoun, holding them out to her, almost reverentially, with outstretched arms.

Alysoun stood for a moment, looking at her Aunt rather than the treasures to which she was to be entrusted. Beornwyn nodded to her and pushed the volumes a little further towards her, nodding her permission for Alysoun to take them. Alysoun then took a step towards her Aunt and carefully transferred the offering to her own hands. Beornwyn gave her a gentle smile and without another word, turned and left the room. Alysoun watched her go through the door and close it behind her before carrying the manuscripts to the table. Then she hesitated and instead of putting them on the table, pulled out a stool which sat underneath and placed them on that, pushing the stool back under the table without even glancing at the valuable objects.

'Later' she murmured to herself. 'First I must have another look at the design of the first panel, just to see what and how will best fit in the borders.'

It was getting dark so she fetched and lit two candles as well as lighting the sconces on the wall. Then she gave her attention to the design lying in front of her, tracing around the pictures with a forefinger of one hand and the arrow tip of the other.

She was completely oblivious to all else, the voices from the street outside, the bell tolling the curfew, the rustling of an inquisitive mouse in the wainscot and especially to the figure that noiselessly crept up behind her and clapped a hand over her mouth and a vice like arm around her waist.

His voice was sibilant, excited, menacing and right in her ear.

'Aren't you the pretty one? My master has never seen you has he? He would love to…rectify that omission. But I found you first didn't I? Finders keepers I think.' The hand around her waist began to move slowly down towards her pelvis but still she was trapped between him and the table. She could feel his hardness pushing against her.

He giggled.

'Master Jean's other pp…pictures! Do you like them? I do, much better than those there. Oh dear! Perhaps he hasn't shown them to you yet.

He pushed harder and his hand moved between her legs, rubbing, his chin on her right shoulder, whispering obscenity after obscenity. His right hand still clamped over her mouth, quite a sweet smelling hand, she was surprised at herself for noting and all the time rubbing and grinding against her.

As quietly as she could, she moved her head a fraction. It was enough to bring the arrow up over her shoulder with all the force she could muster. She felt it strike flesh. He shrieked and released her. She turned, her small hands unclenched, determined to put up as much of a fight as she could with her fingernails but what she saw when she looked up made her gag momentarily. His hands were up to his face, the shaft of the arrow sticking out through his fingers, together with a thin stream of blood and mucus.

The point of the arrow was firmly implanted in his cheek and he continued to scream, afraid to pull out the barb and tear the wound further. Anger then replaced the fear she had felt and she struck at him with her fists and her feet, screaming at him.

He backed off, suddenly turning on his heel and staggering out of the door through which she supposed he had made his unseen entry. She started to follow him, then felt her knees go like jelly and she had to support herself on the table.

When next she looked up, the room appeared to be full of people. Beornwyn, looking white and shaken, was there, a blanket thrown around her bony shoulders. The men-at arms that Josclin had left on guard, swords drawn and looking behind the wall hangings and rather ridiculously, she noted, under the table.

Beornwyn immediately enclosed her in the blanket and held her close.

'Ssh now. First things first. Are you all right?'

She pushed her niece away from her briefly so that she could look at her properly, then immediately returned her to her arms.

Looking up, she turned her attention to the soldiers.

'There has been an intruder. No harm done by the look of things but the first thing I want you to do is find out how he got in without anyone hearing him. I came through this door,' she indicated where she had entered the room, 'So he must have come through that one. That is assuming he didn't get past you without you noticing?'

The soldiers looked at one another then rushed out to where she had indicated. She sat Alysoun in a chair and stood over her, holding her hand and gently stroking the back of it. Alysoun smiled faintly through her tear filled eyes.

'You used to do that to me when I was little and had hurt myself.'

She held the hand to her cheek and breathed in deeply until she felt she had control of herself and could trust herself to speak sensibly. Still shocked, she needed a few moments to unscramble the thoughts that were jumbled up in her mind. The attack could not have lasted more than a moment at most, but she knew that it was important she should remember as much detail as she could and relate the facts as accurately as possible. Consequently, she squeezed her Aunt's hand and remained silent. The only noise in the room now was that of her breathing and Beornwyn had the sense to continue in her role of protector, rather than that of inquisitor.

After another couple of deep breaths, Alysoun calmly recounted what had happened but without dwelling on the physical degradation that she had undergone. Still not composed enough and feeling unaccountably ashamed, she was not quite ready to relive that part of the assault.

'It's all right Aunt. I'm not hurt, only a little shaken and nothing, so far as I know, has been taken or damaged.'

She nodded towards the books on the stool.

'He couldn't have been after those could he? I mean, how would he have known, we only…'

'If it was who I think it was, no my angel, that wasn't what he wanted. He is the very devil, how ever did you frighten him off? He fears nothing and feels nothing. Why he…'

'Me! Frighten HIM off Aunt? And he does feel something, he feels pain. Devil he might be but his reaction to my wounding him was all too human. You must have heard him scream.'

Beornwyn put her hands up to her mouth.

'Oh my God, Alysoun. That was him screaming? I thought it was you, that is why I…You wounded him but how? He is renowned for his fighting skills. That is if I am right and it was him. What on earth did you do to him to make him scream like that?'

Alysoun shivered slightly and said.

'I stuck my arrow in his face. It was horrible, horrible. There was blood and…and…'

'It's all right my lovely,' crooned her Aunt. 'It's over and he's gone.'

A shadow of a smile crossed her worried face.

'But you must admit, the justice of it is unbelievable. What a way to return his property. He shoots at me and misses but you didn't, my dear. You scored a bulls eye.'

Alysoun pushed her away.

'No! Surely not. It couldn't have been Wulfric. If I'd known it was him I would have fainted with fear.'

She shivered and again Beornwyn held her. There was a further commotion and one of the guards came back into the room, looking grim.

'We have found where he got in My Lady.'

The two women looked at each other and then at him.

'How?' Beornwyn demanded. 'I have always taken great pains to ensure the security of this building. The front entrance, which you were supposed to be guarding, is the only vulnerable access.'

He shook his head.

'Sorry Ma'am but whoever has the job of securing your storeroom hadn't made a very good job of it.'

Beornwyn looked at him and shook her head in disbelief.

'But that is impossible fellow! To get in he would have had to force open the hatch in the road and then somehow get through the door at the top of the cellar stairs. The hatch is bolted on the inside and the cellar door on the outside. Always.'

The man shook his head again.

'Not today it wasn't Milady. None of the bolts were pushed home. That's how he got in, no doubt of it.'

She stamped her foot.

'I tell you, fellow, those bolts are always secure. If there is one thing that Warin is…was…'

She faltered and looked to Alysoun who, much to her surprise, stood up and put a hand to her forehead. Not as her Aunt supposed, because she was feeling faint but because she had just remembered something and she wished she hadn't.

'It was me Aunt. Do you remember, before we left for the castle, we had a delivery of wool and I was so anxious not to keep you waiting that once I had seen it safely into the cellar I rushed back and it must have been then that I… Oh God! I am so sorry.'

Beornwyn said nothing for a moment then, after an admonishing shake of the head, merely said, 'Well, my dear, I think we can fairly say that it is a mistake for which you have paid dearly although, had it not been for your courage, it could have been so much worse. I know that I can never replace Warin but we should seriously give some thought to introducing a male bodyguard into the household. This time you were lucky but ...'

She let the thought hang in the air and they both quietly pondered the implications of it until the guard coughed politely to re-engage their attention.

'Excuse me ladies but I think we should get word to the castle, to Master Josclin or his Lordship. I don't want to think of the trouble I'd get into if either of us went leaving you here alone with only...and there is no way I could allow ...'

'Allow!!'

Lady Beornwyn drew herself up to her full height and the guard took an involuntary step back. Alysoun took hold of her Aunt's arm, looked up at her and shook her head.

'He's only doing his job, Aunt and he is absolutely right. Of course neither of us can go and neither should they. We'll wait until morning and then Josclin will be here to relieve them.'

She nodded towards the two guards, who stood uncertainly in the doorway through which the intruder had left.

'That, I think, will be better than anybody making their way to the castle in darkness, don't you agree?'

The two men looked at each other and the one who seemed to have assumed responsibility for them both said.

'Yes M'am but...' he gestured towards the front entrance door they had been guarding originally.

'It's all right,' Alysoun said, 'we can all stay in here together until dawn which, heaven knows, cannot be too far away by now. What do you think Aunt?'

Beornwyn merely nodded agreement and hustled out to find more cushions and covers saying that if they all had to stay up all night they might as well do it as comfortably as possible.

Alysoun, feigning a calmness she did not possess, picked up The Bestiary and began looking through it. The two soldiers, relieved at being under cover, hunkered down on the floor, their backs to the wall doing their best to look alert.

CHAPTER THIRTY EIGHT

The Castle, Canterbury

The following morning, Jean woke early with an aching head and furred tongue. He'd had no wine the previous evening, despite being urged to take some by Robert Beaumont, who seemed to think that Jean was out of spirits. He sat on the corner of his cot and ran his hand through his hair. He wondered if he was ill. He frowned to himself as he made an effort to gauge what exactly his feelings were. Well, last night he had certainly not talked as much as normal. He had been sitting next to Josclin, who usually had to put up with all sorts of questions about the battle and who was where in the action but it was Josclin who had indicated to his master, with a nod in the direction of Jean, that the lad was not his usual annoying self, hence Beaumont's remark and offer of wine.

Hauling himself to his feet and trudging to the door, he fetched in the bowl of water that had been left outside. He carefully rolled up his drawings and placed them out of the range of possible splashes and commenced his rudimentary ablutions. He found himself doing everything more slowly than usual and began to wonder if, in fact, he was suffering from some mild and unspecified illness. His customary approach to washing was to all but dive into the basin and get it over with as quickly as possible but today he was deliberate and thorough in his movements. He felt no pain. No other outward sign of a malaise apart from this ...this annoying feeling of being withdrawn and ... It was this damn design, that's what it was. Alysoun's comments were sticking in his mind like a burr on a blanket and he couldn't shift them. The infuriating thing was that she was right. His instincts told him that she was right but he couldn't for the life of him see what it was that she was getting at. He flung his rag into the bowl and picked up his drawings again. He spread them out and tried to look at them through somebody else's eyes – her eyes, damn it! He tried to remember what colour they were but couldn't.

If she was so clever, why didn't she design something that was more in accordance with what she wanted? He almost wished he was back under the direct control of Lord Odo. At least Odo knew nothing about art.

He suddenly stopped and lifted his head and listened. There it was again.

No mistaking it. He whirled round, ran through the door and down the stairs to the great gates which guarded the tower. They were open. He took the steps two at a time, ignoring the shouts of the tradesmen and servants who were trying to make their way up the steps on their way to work. He took the last four steps in one, sprinted across the bailey, ducked under a low rail to the outer yard where the stabling was situated and skidded to a halt. He was right. Nero, saddled and about to be mounted by one of Odo's men-at-arms and non too gently either.

The horse scented Jean and gave another trumpeting neigh, followed by one of his welcoming snickers which was cut short by his rider roughly jerking on the reigns to pull his head up. Jean ran over and grasped the bridle, soothing the animal by gently running his hand down its nose.

'What the hell do you think you're doing with my horse? Who told you…?'

'Who do you think, boy?' gruff and surly, typical of one of Odo's ruffians thought Jean.

He wrenched Nero's head away from Jean, the horse wheeled around and Odo's man shouted over his shoulder.

'Anyway boy, it isn't your horse is it?'

'No, not exactly but…'

He stood for a moment and watched Nero exit through the gate and stayed listening until he could no longer hear his hoof beats. True the horse wasn't his so he had no right to feel aggrieved at the real owner wanting his property back but still he'd grown fond of the animal and had made a point of seeing him every day, even if he didn't have the time to ride him. Sadly he shook his head; something else to add to his accumulating list of problems. Not that being without a horse was that important. He had no time to spare for that sort of thing and if it was really necessary for him to be mounted, he had no doubt that Robert Beaumont would be happy to lend him something from his own stable.

In the meantime he had to re-address the question of work. He supposed that, before too long, Beornwyn and her niece would turn up at the castle and make further criticism of the drawings and he was still nagged by the thought that they had every right do so. If only he could determine what the problem was before they descended on him with their patronising ways.

Idly he kicked his foot through a pile of damp sand that had fallen from a passing cart and stopped, transfixed by the result of this random act of childish ill humour. Where the pointed toe of his boot had struck, the disturbed sand had parted in the shape of an arrowhead. Where had he last seen… Of course, it was that arrow in Alysoun's hand. Although why, in God's good name, she wanted to carry that gruesome object about with her he couldn't imagine. But no! That was it. She had been tapping with the arrow on his drawings while she had been talking and he hadn't been listening to her at all. He had been distracted by this young noblewoman using an arrow as a pointer and only had half an ear to what she was actually saying. True, he recognised it as criticism of a sort but the actual content had not penetrated what he now began to think of as his thick skull.

He continued to scuff about in the sand as if some picture might miraculously appear in it and it did. Not very graphically it's true but the content of his design was running clearly through his mind and then... then. He let out a gasp of complete exasperation. She was right. Of course, she was right – well, up to a point anyway. He ran his fingers through his hair, still damp from the morning wash.

Thoughtfully, he made his way back to the tower, so wrapped up in his own ideas that he failed to hear Ranulph call to him from the other side of the yard. A second shout stopped him in his tracks and he waited with barely concealed patience while Ranulph came to him, dodging porters, squires and labourers for whom the day's duties had just started.

'Glad I've caught you Jean,' said Ranulph, 'cause just I've finished the full scale version of this embroidery thing. It's a bit heavy but I think I can manage to lug it up to your room. Trouble is, all these other bastards working on the building here think that I've been given preferential treatment to get this job done and they've gone all huffy with me.' he sniffed, 'Mates! I tell you, when it comes down to it, you're on your own in this world.'

A perplexed Jean could do little more than offer token sympathy and just at this moment, the last thing he wanted was a complaining Saxon carpenter going on about his weird invention. Nevertheless, he had shown initial interest and more to the point, Lord Beaumont had given it his blessing, so he begged Ranulph to leave it for a day or two because, quite honestly, he had a lot on his mind. He could tell that Ranulph was thinking "Oh right then, you as well" but he didn't say anything, merely gave a philosophical nod and told Jean that he would see him when it was convenient. Jean started to apologise for his ill humour but settled for thanking Ranulph, giving him a conciliatory pat on the back and continued up the steps to the great tower.

Back in his room, he remembered that he hadn't yet had any breakfast. He was about to dash down to the kitchen to remedy the situation when there was a knock at his door and one of the servant girls came in to refill his pitcher and empty his wash bowl. Before she disappeared, he asked her if she would fetch him some bread, beer and anything else that might be available. She gave him a neat little bob and within half an hour she was back with some food, by which time Jean was immersed in his work and failed to notice its arrival. If she hadn't given a tentative little cough, he would probably have gone on working until it was time for his midday meal. As it was, he turned from the table, just in time to see her exit through the door.

'Just a moment,' he said and she half turned to face him.

'Yes Sir?'

A timid little voice which suited the tiny figure, standing in the doorway with her eyes firmly fixed on the floorboards.

'Thank you.'

He said, as much for the title she had bestowed on him as the food she had delivered. She lifted her head for the briefest second, gave another of her quaint little bobs and ran off down the passage. Jean had, however, seen enough of her to register that she had had beautiful brown eyes in a elfin face and, although a slight little thing, a promising body under her shapeless drabs. He also noticed that she didn't smell too fresh which was a pity because tidied up a bit she could have been quite attractive. He carefully placed his charcoal stick on the drawing table and moved over to the trestle, next to his mattress, on which he stored his personal bits and pieces and ate his food. He had just raised a mug of ale to his lips when his hand was stayed by the thump of heavy feet progressing along the corridor and before he had a chance to swallow anything, there was the formidable figure of Josclin framed in the doorway and just visible beyond him, two of his men.

'You still having breakfast young man? Dear oh dear, we've done a day's work by this time. Anyway, we're just off to the Lady Beornwyn's place to relieve the guard there. His Lordship wondered if you wanted us to take any of your work over there for you.'

Still chewing on his first mouthful of the day, Jean replied, 'No thank you Josclin. Since I'm not good enough to be allowed over there, they can come here and fetch it if they want it.'

Josclin looked quite relieved that he wasn't going to have carry rolls of decorated linen through the town but couldn't resist having a parting dig at what he considered to be an unsuitable occupation for a full-bloodied male.

'I suppose that's what they call artistic temperament is it? I would have thought they would have welcomed you at the School of Needlework with open arms. Ah well, better get on with some real men's work.'

Jean just gave him a grin and retorted that it was a pity that all these real men, and heaven knows there had been enough of them, had thus far failed to capture a miserable little specimen like Wulfric.

'I'll see you later, lad.' growled Josclin and started to take his men back down the corridor.

'Oh Josclin!' Jean called after him.

'What?' Josclin came to a reluctant halt.

'Good morning.' Jean cooed.

Josclin made a rude sign and continued on his way.

Jean grinned to himself and went back to his table. He thoughtfully picked his teeth with one of the small sharpened sticks that he kept for the purpose, then chewed on some parsley. He had always practised some form of oral hygiene and wondered if that little servant girl did the same. He rather doubted it, not if the rest of her was anything to go by. Still, that was not his concern, he had work to do. Those damned borders again.

He moved over to his work table and looked at the last panel. It looked fine to him but then again… Well, if the high and mighty Lady Alysoun wanted borders he supposed he would have to draw them but she was going to have to tell him what to draw. Everybody else had so why not her?

CHAPTER THIRTY NINE

Dover Castle

The two men stood looking at each other, neither speaking, nor moving. Eventually it was Odo who broke the stalemate. He lifted up his arms towards Thibault and said.

'My dear boy, I cannot tell you how pleased I am to have you back with me.'

Thibault made no move towards him and Odo dropped his arms. Thibault still said nothing. Odo took a step towards him and Thibault remained as impassive as he had on first entering the chamber. Odo's hand strayed towards the table at which he had been working prior to Thibault's entrance. It hovered over some parchment and then away again. His expression was a genuine mixture of sadness and puzzlement. Eventually he moved, putting the table between himself and his Squire. He sat heavily in his chair and sighed.

'You blame me don't you? That girl! You think that I had something to do with her death and you blame me for it.' Odo continued, 'Thibault, you must believe me when I tell you that I played no part in that sad young woman's death at all. We all have our suspicions who the culprit was but,'

Thibault broke in, his voice taut.

'Wulfric, my Lord?'

'Exactly, my boy, Wulfric.'

Odo spread his hands in a gesture of hopelessness. Thibault responded in a tone of chilling neutrality.

'But, my Lord, Wulfric is your man, is he not. He is your creature. Has nothing been done to apprehend him?'

Odo's brow furrowed.

'I am sorry to see that your absence from my household has distanced us somewhat and made you forgetful of your position. It is not, I think, for you to question me. I have already told you that I was in no way responsible for what happened. Do you presume to doubt my word?'

His brow cleared and he shook his head sadly. He rose and again he held out his arms.

'Come, my son. Let us not fall out over this business. Why, you scarcely knew the girl and yes, Wulfric has done business for me in the past but now he is gone. Some say to Canterbury but no one knows for sure.'

He moved around to Thibault and grasped him by the shoulders.

'I cannot begin to tell you how pleased I am to have you back in my service Thibault and I have to say, in the short time that you have been away you have matured greatly and, what's all this?'

He took a step back and indicated Thibault's sombre apparel.

'Not taken orders have you my boy? You always took a pride in your appearance but I must say this matches your present mood. Come, my son.' he clapped his hand on Thibault's shoulder, 'Say that we are to be as we were before your hasty departure from Dover.'

He put his hand under Thibault's chin and turned his head so that Thibault had no choice but to look directly at him. There they stood for a moment like a father and son attempting a difficult reconciliation.

'You have my word Thibault,' said Odo gravely, 'I am not responsible for what happened nor, I might add, can I quite understand why you should have taken it to heart in the way that you did. You and she were not exactly,' he gave a dismissive laugh, 'No, of course not. So why did you react in the way that you did or was it for some other reason?'

Thibault said nothing and only gave a brief shake of his head before saying.

'It is of no consequence whatever, my Lord. As you say, I am back in your service and as ever, yours to command.'

His tone was still neutral and although Odo sensed the restraint he was happy to have his favourite under his roof again and he said as much. Thibault nodded and asked if there was any service in particular that his Lordship had in mind for him. Now that he was back, he would much prefer to be given some responsibility, rather than revert to his former lifestyle of practising for the joust and other sporting activities. Odo thought for a moment, then walked back to his table and started to sort through the pile of scrolls and vellum that lay there. He looked up at Thibault, appraising him, then beckoned him over to him.

'Thibault, if there is one characteristic with which I would associate you, it is honour. It is something you shared with your father. You have always been trustworthy. Suppose I entrusted you with a task which is, shall we say, delicate. Would you be willing to perform it for me?'

Thibault answered, 'Of course, my Lord.'

Odo looked up at him but saw nothing in Thibault's blue eyes. He looked very tired but then, he had just made the journey from Normandy to Dover so he had every reason to look tired but Odo was looking for something else and try as he might, he could detect nothing but clear honesty in those eyes that looked steadily back at him. Still he hesitated a fraction longer, pretending to peruse some document. Eventually he invited Thibault to sit opposite him.

'The fact is, my boy, I am anxious about the way in which my authority appears to be usurped in Canterbury.'

Again he looked closely at Thibault but detected nothing more than polite interest, he continued.

'Robert Beaumont, another honourable man, as you were never tired of telling me, and that sanctimonious prelate, Lanfranc, seem to have been given far too much latitude in governing a wealthy region which was supposed to be in my gift.'

Again he paused but found no reaction other than a studied interest.

'Also, your former charge, LeBrun, appears to have been taken under the wing of my illustrious brother and his wife.' his voice became harsher, 'Regardless of the fact that it was my inspiration in the first place and my purse that funded it in the second. To cap it all, William and Mathilde have promised LeBrun his freedom on the completion of his work. Oh yes, Thibault, their Majesties have done.'

He cleared his throat and made a conscious effort to control his anger.

'Well, that is as may be. I dare say they have their reasons but this brings me to the point in question.'

A third check on Thibault's response again revealed nothing to Odo so he continued.

'I need somebody I can trust to have a look at what is going on in Canterbury,' he waved a hand, 'A quiet word with Beaumont perhaps. As we've just reminded ourselves, you and he always got on well together. I would just like to know how the land lies over there. What they are all up to and, so far as LeBrun is concerned, I'd be interested to know what progress he is making with my brainchild. If I remember correctly, you two never got on particularly well but then, considering the difference in your station, there was no reason why you should. Not exactly a task worthy of your talents is it Thibault? I need hardly tell you that discretion is of the utmost importance, so far as they are concerned, it need be no more than a social call.'

He looked at Thibault, 'What do you think?'

Thibault replied that, of course, if his Lordship thought he was the right man for the task, he would willingly undertake it. When did his Lordship want him to start?

Odo nodded. 'Well, you look as though you could do with good night's sleep. If you feel like it, why not ride over tomorrow. Your horse is back in the stable by the way.'

For the first time Thibault registered some slight emotion.

'Nero, back in the stable? Why, where has he been?'

Odo replies airily, 'Oh yes, well, LeBrun rode him over to Canterbury.'

'LeBrun!' echoed Thibault.

'Yes, LeBrun. He needed to get over to the School of Needlework in Canterbury. He needed a mount. You had taken yourself off so I lent him Nero.'

'I see, my Lord. I think I might just go over to the stable and check on him now, before I retire.'

Odo chuckled.

'That is typical of you Thibault. From what I hear LeBrun hasn't hurt the animal but go and put your mind at rest by all means and Thibault... I am truly delighted to have you back.'

'Yes, my Lord. Thank you, my Lord.'

Thibault nodded a bow and left the chamber. As he did so, his mentor was absently running a be-ringed finger down a column of figures, wondering if he had made the right decision to confide in Thibault as he had.

#

At roughly the same time that Odo of Bayeux was torn between checking his revenues and experiencing a vague unease with regard to Thibault's loyalty, Josclin and his two men were clattering up to the School of Needlework. He had hardly eased himself out of the saddle when the door was flung open and one of the men he had left on duty the previous night rushed out to tell him of the young Lady Alysoun's ordeal. Ordering the new guard to hand their mounts over to their relieved colleague and follow him he ran into the building, sword in hand, to be met by a cool and collected mistress of the establishment who instructed him to calm down and put up his sword. Josclin, after looking around as though he expected to see armed assassins lurking in every corner, did as he was told while Lady Beornwyn gave him a clear and concise account of what had happened, only omitting the more intimate details of her niece's experience.

He looked hard at Alysoun who was quietly sitting at the table toying with breakfast.

'There is nothing I can add, Josclin. My Aunt has told you everything that took place. Oh!' she suddenly thought, 'can I order you and your men some breakfast? The two guards that were here all night have already had theirs.'

'No thank you, Lady Alysoun,' replied Josclin, who was beginning to suspect that anybody engaged in any activity of a creative nature tended to take their breakfast a lot later than the rest of the working world.

'I do want to take a thorough look around the premises though.'

He deferred to Lady Beornwyn who replied that of course he must do whatever he felt necessary but a search had already been made. He nodded but said it wasn't him that had made it so if her Ladyship didn't mind...

'No, of course I don't mind. I quite appreciate that you have our interests at heart but we shall be very surprised if you find anything that we might have missed.'

Josclin grunted and calling one of the new guard to accompany him, started to clump his way around the building.

The two soldiers of the night watch had taken the remaining relief to one side and were excitedly telling them of the night's events. Lady Beornwyn stood behind Alysoun's chair, stroking her shoulder with one hand while she ran the other wearily over her brow.

It didn't take Josclin long to ascertain that the intruder was no longer in the building but he was anxious to hear, in some detail, the injury that Alysoun had inflicted on the man and just how she had managed it. He sat opposite her at the table while she went through it again, Beornwyn still standing at her back and massaging her shoulder. When she had finished, Josclin shook his head.

'You were very, very lucky Milady. I can't see that it could have been anyone but Wulfric and even if I were to best him in a struggle, I should think myself a fortunate man but you? The wound that you inflicted on him, would you say it was serious?'

She frowned and then shuddered at the memory.

'To be honest Josclin, I couldn't say. I was so frightened and all I know was that he screamed like an trapped animal and he couldn't...that is, he couldn't seem to remove the arrow. His face was...'

Beornwyn broke in.

'For God's sake man, what do you expect the girl to tell you, other than what happened?'

Josclin moved uneasily in his chair, then rose.

'I don't suppose any of you,' he included the two old guard in the question, 'have any idea how he might have got in because, mark my words, if I find that either of you two have been negligent in your duties, my Lord will see to it that you...'

'It's all right Master Josclin,' Alysoun got to her feet and taking her Aunt's hand in hers moved over to him.

'We do know how he got in. Your men found it. They were in no way to blame, they have been more than diligent. The fact is, the fact is,' the words came out in a rush, 'It was my fault' and she proceeded to tell him about the cellar doors and the wool delivery and concluded, 'so you see Master Josclin, if I had been more careful, this whole nightmare could have been avoided.'

Josclin stroked his chin with a gauntleted hand.

'We can only be thankful, Milady that your carelessness didn't end in tragedy and it goes without saying that I greatly admire your fortitude. Now!' he immediately became businesslike, 'I shall leave the new guard here while I return to the castle with the old and make my report to my Lord. I have little doubt that he will want to ride over here as soon as he has the facts. Please secure the doors after we have gone and allow no one, and I must insist on this, no one whatsoever an entry' Beornwyn started to protest but he held up an apologetic hand.

'Not even the ladies of the School, my Lady. When he arrives, my Lord might advise differently but until that time, please do as I ask.'

Beornwyn gave a wry little laugh and said, 'Very well, Josclin, if you insist. You, of all people, are aware of how much I dislike the restrictions that protection imposes on me but above all else, I must think of my niece's safety.'

'Indeed you should Ma'am. The more so now that she has bested Wulfric. He will not take kindly to that and we must all be on our guard. You did well, Lady Alysoun but I think that your resourcefulness can do nothing but add to his desire for vengeance. I must go. My Lord will be with you before the day is out, I am sure of it.'

So saying, Josclin gave some last minute orders to the new guard, made his salutations to the two ladies and left with his men, the new guard bolting the doors behind them.

CHAPTER FORTY

The Castle, Canterbury

When Jean was working, he was oblivious of most things but he couldn't help but be distracted by a commotion which seemed to originate at the main gate and intensified into the bailey. Mainly shouting. He thought he detected Josclin's voice, and hoof beats skidding to a halt. By the time he had got to his window there didn't appear to be much to see but the voices, loud and urgent, continued up the steps to the main tower door only to become more muffled as they continued through the building in the general direction of Robert Beaumont's suite. He listened for a little while longer to see if footsteps were heading in his direction but they were not so he went back to his work. Nothing to do with him, thank goodness, but then, why should it be?

He had enjoyed a good run of uninterrupted creativity, probably the best since he had started. Information on the great battle had been forthcoming from both Beaumont and Josclin and he reckoned he had enough notes to see him through to the end of the project. As the conquest unfolded under his stylus, he again reflected how strange it was that the reports of the events from his Lordship and Josclin were so different in tone. According to Josclin, it had all been a foregone conclusion from start to finish but Beaumont's recollections seemed much more balanced and less triumphant in tone. That was as maybe. The fact was that, whatever the truth, it was not, thankfully, his responsibility to analyse the battle, only to record it to the best of his ability.

Then, the footsteps he had half expected earlier, could now be heard making their way towards him. He sighed and dropped his charcoal on the table as Robert Beaumont appeared in the doorway, accompanied by a red faced and sweating Josclin and two armed soldiers. Beaumont wasted no time in coming to the point.

'The Lady Alysoun has been attacked. Last night at the School. Josclin has just come from there.'

He anticipated Jean's question and went on to tell him that the young lady was unharmed. Since Josclin knew the facts at first hand, Beaumont indicated that he should take up the narrative. The old soldier was still breathing heavily and it occurred to Jean that he was in fact, just that. A man still vigorous but no longer in his prime and probably aware of his declining strength. Josclin then relayed his story, presumably just as he had to Lord Beaumont and once more Jean marvelled that he was seen as important enough to be included in the matter.

As soon as Josclin had finished though, Jean inquired as to the identity of the assailant.

'Was it Wulfric, do you think?'

'Course it was,' growled Josclin but Beaumont was a little more circumspect and said.

'It was almost certainly him but we do not know for sure. The Lady Alysoun had never seen him before but from her description, yes, there is little doubt.'

'And this arrow that she stabbed him with,' said Jean 'was that the same one you told me about, the one that just missed Lady Beornwyn, the one that she kept fiddling with when she was here yesterday?'

'Apparently,' Josclin continued. 'I have to say that she showed great initiative, not to mention courage. I'm not sure that any of my lads could have done any better. What bothers me now is that Wulfric is wounded and likely to be even more dangerous than he was before. Unless the wound is fatal of course,' he continued thoughtfully.

Beaumont shook his head.

'A cheek wound is likely to be painful rather than mortal but Josclin is right, we must be even more on our guard which brings us to where we are now.'

He waved a hand around the room.

'From now on, a guard will be posted at your door.'

Jean could not subdue the look of annoyance that flashed across his face.

'Do not worry, Master LeBrun,' Beaumont went on, 'He will stay on the other side of the door and will have strict instructions not to disturb you. Now, I must accompany Josclin to the School of Embroidery. We have to ensure that they are adequately protected and it is better that I inform Lady Beornwyn myself. She will not be happy but now that her niece has been attacked, one hopes her attitude towards our concerns for her safety might have been tempered somewhat.' he smiled ruefully and continued, 'Although, of course, one can never be sure. I will see you on our return.'

He nodded his farewell as did Josclin and they left the room. The guard outside the door shut it behind them.

Jean wandered over to his window and watched them mount and make their way to the postern. Lord Beaumont, Josclin and four men-at -arms riding escort.

Lady Beornwyn heard them coming, long before they clattered up to her front door and raised her eyes heavenward. Alysoun said softly, 'It is for our protection, Aunt. After what happened to me last night do you honestly think that Robert Beaumont is going to leave us without increased security?'

'That is as may be, child,' her aunt retorted, 'But you can already hear the neighbours and their friends gathering outside to see what all the fuss is about.' she sighed, 'you are, as ever these days, right and since I would not have anything happen to you for the world, I suppose we must subject ourselves to Robert behaving like a wet nurse.'

Alysoun grinned.

'I have a good mind to tell him what you have just called him…'

Beaumont entered, Josclin at his heels, just in time to see Lady Beornwyn waving an admonitory finger at her niece. He stood, one hand on the hilt of his dagger and the other stroking his chin. He looked from one to the other of the ladies.

'At least no real harm done, I hope. Are you fully recovered from your experience Lady Alysoun? It must have been terrifying for you.'

She dropped him a token curtsey.

'Thank you my Lord. It was horrible but it could have been very much worse. When you consider that it was my negligence that allowed the brute to enter this house I suppose you could say that I escaped quite lightly.'

'Indeed you did,' Beaumont rejoined. 'As it is, I can only commend your courage and resourcefulness.'

He turned to Lady Beornwyn, 'I am going to leave you three guards, Beornwyn, one of whom, I suggest, you keep with you at all times. It cannot be long now before Wulfric is taken but, in view of the humiliation visited upon him by the actions of your niece, we must now be even more vigilant.'

Beornwyn went over to him, took his arm and steered him away from the others.

'Robert, I fully understand your concern but you must appreciate that we are about to be engaged on this mammoth task imposed upon us by your foul compatriot.'

'Not to mention their Majesties,' murmured Beaumont.

'Yes all right Robert, them too but I cannot operate a school of embroidery properly with soldiers hanging about the place. My ladies would feel most awkward and their concentration severely compromised. This very afternoon I have called them for an introduction to the project and I am not happy to think that our conference is going to be held with men present, especially men bristling with weapons.'

Bearing in mind his earlier injunction, she looked to see if Josclin had overheard but he was deep in conversation with Alysoun.

Beaumont smiled inwardly at her exaggeration but realised, as usual, that he would get nowhere by pressing his argument too strongly.

'Very well, my Lady. We will allow your workroom to be the exception together, of course, with your private chambers but I must insist that a guard be on duty outside the door of any room that you and Alysoun might be occupying. Will you agree to that?'

'Thank you Robert. By the way, there are one or two things I would like to discuss with you at more length and at a more appropriate time. Would you be free to dine with us here tomorrow evening?'

Beaumont had never before thought of Lady Beornwyn in the role of hostess, gallantly stifled his surprise at the invitation and accepted graciously. They then rejoined Alysoun and Josclin at the other side of the room. Josclin had been attempting to find out more about the extent of Wulfric's injury but there was little that Alysoun had not already told him.

Beaumont and his lieutenant, after some last minute instructions to their men, then took their leave, Beaumont again expressing his appreciation of the invitation he had just received.

'You have asked him to dinner, here?' said a somewhat incredulous Alysoun.

'You never invite anyone here for anything except to sew. What on earth for?'

'What is the matter, child? Don't you like Robert Beaumont?'

'Yes, of course I like him Aunt but ...dinner! What are we going to give him?'

'How should I know!' came the answer. 'Call cook and we'll see what we have in store and if we don't have it, we will ask her to get something in.'

'But...'

'Oh! For goodness sake Alysoun, please don't go on so. There are things I want to discuss with Beaumont and with Beaumont alone so please, child, let us leave it at that. Now call cook and when we have dealt with menus we must start thinking about this afternoon's meeting.'

Alysoun shook her head, successfully dislodging the errant locks of hair, and went to do as her Aunt had asked.

#

This time it was not the footsteps of soldiers that disturbed Jean but the pangs of hunger. There was no sun so it was not easy to be exact about the time but if his rumbling stomach was anything to go by it was definitely long past lunchtime. He went to the door, opened it and encountered his guard, whose presence he had completely forgotten. He nodded to him and started to walk along the passage, only to find the man-at-arms following him. He stopped and told him that it was more important that the contents of his workroom be protected than his own person. He waved towards the room.

'What's in there can't protect itself,' he said. Then touching his dagger, 'I can, so just get back there please and don't let anyone in. I won't be long and I promise you, you won't get into trouble.'

The guard looked unconvinced but did as he was told and Jean made his way in search of food. Usually there was a servant or two hanging about the place. Granted most of them were Saxon, surly and stupid but what about that little girl, the one that had brought him his breakfast. She was nowhere to be seen so he hurried on down the steps towards the kitchens and there she was, walking up towards him.

On seeing Jean, she stopped and pressed herself against the wall, eyes firmly fixed on the tread on which she was standing. He carried on down the couple of steps which brought him down to her level. She pressed even further into the wall and Jean said, very quietly.

'What's your name, girl?'

In a barely audible whisper she said, 'Aveline, Sir.'

'Well, Aveline, I think that is a very pretty name but would you be offended if I called you Avis, for short?'

She raised her head slightly but did not look at him directly.

'Offended, Sir? No Sir, of course not, Sir.'

Jean was surprised that she spoke to him in good Norman. He had assumed that, like most of the other servants, she was a local girl. For the moment though, his hunger was greater than his curiosity.

'Is there any chance that you could find me something to eat, Avis? I seem to have missed lunch in the hall.'

She raised her eyes briefly and again he was struck by how lovely they were in contrast to the rest of her drab appearance. 'Of course, Sir, I'll bring it to your room, shall I?'

He tried smiling at her but she wasn't looking. 'Thank you Avis, that would be fine.'

She turned and began running down the steps, then stopped, turned and this time, looked directly at him.

'Sir, I'm sorry, Sir but, why Avis?'

He started down towards her but she visibly flinched so he stopped where he was.

'It's Latin for bird. Do you mind? Because if you do, I am happy to call you by your real name.'

'No Sir. Thank you, Sir. I like Avis.' She turned and ran on down the stairs while Jean, musing over this strange, child-like creature, returned to his room and a relieved man-at-arms.

CHAPTER FORTY ONE

The School

Under the watchful eye of a man-at-arms on the main door, a dozen women of assorted ages entered the School of Embroidery. They were quite used to the sight of Warin standing there but the sight of a fully armed Norman soldier was the cause of much more excitement and when they found another one, guarding the door to the sewing room, the verbal buzz rose to new heights. So much so that when the Principal of the School, together with her niece, entered the room it was some time before order could be restored to the level at which the voice of Lady Beornwyn could make itself heard.

She apologised for the presence of soldiers but did not go into any detail as to why that presence was necessary. This session was going to be difficult enough without those sorts of distractions. She began by briefly describing the commission in general terms, the story to be illustrated and the proposed destination of the finished work. Her needlewomen nodded their understanding of the project and Beornwyn paused for a moment before telling them of the dimensions of the piece and for a while she was unable to continue, such was the cacophony of excited comment that greeted her announcement.

She paused to let it die down and then, thankfully, handed over the rest of the session to Alysoun who reported on the progress of supplies for the work. Wools of the highest quality had been sourced and passed to the dyers. The dyes were setting and the unbleached linen was already in store. She checked to see if there were any questions.

Twelve arms shot up and Beornwyn groaned. She had hoped that this preliminary meeting would prove to be a mere formality and the women would be content to absorb without discussion, the basic facts of the work to be done but obviously this was not going to happen.

Alysoun patiently dealt with most of the queries raised by the assembly.

No, it would not be possible to ensure that there would be sufficiently large batches of particular colours since the dyers could not guarantee exact continuity for the quantities of wools they were likely to need. What colours would they be using?

Alysoun told them that there would be at least eight, possibly more and that they, the individual needlewomen, would be able to choose what colours to use since, given the complexity of the narrative, to allocate a particular batch to one person would be impossible. An elderly, though sprightly small nun raised her hand.

'Lady Alysoun, given the remarkable length of completed work, how are we going to break it down into manageable pieces?' Out of courtesy to her hostess, she spoke in Saxon although her accent was Norman. Alysoun, conversely, replied in Norman, such was her affection for this woman who had known her since she was a small child.

'Sister Marie, we will complete the work in sections. The designs have already been broken down into narrative lengths and we will work them in turn. I think that you, Sister Marie, will be given the task of joining the lengths together since it will require work of the very finest quality.'

The old nun acknowledged the praise with a faint nod of her head and the next question concerned, almost inevitably, the identity of the designer or designers.

Lady Beornwyn brusquely remarked that the designer was not likely to be known to any of them but they had her assurance that the work was extremely well executed and she hoped that her school would do justice to it. She went on.

'We have brought you here today to give you some idea of the magnitude and importance of this commission. It was originally, and it pains me to admit the fact, the brainchild of Lord Odo. Since my abhorrence of that particular nobleman is well known, you may gauge how important I consider this embroidery to be and I might add that my opinion is shared by Duke William and his Consort. The design is nearing completion although it is our intention to embellish it with borders and a commentary. I will be responsible for the latter and my niece for the content of the former. If there are no more questions I suggest you all await a summons to the School when we have decided a starting date.'

A few hands had been raised but quickly dropped to the pretence of arranging headgear or adjusting cloaks. They began to shuffle out, talking eagerly amongst themselves and noting, again, the two guards they passed on their way to the street.

Lady Beornwyn and Alysoun saw them off the premises and settled down to discuss the detail of the embroidery. What stitch to be employed in what area and a general outline of colour choice for, as Beornwyn gently pointed out, it was all very well to give them carte blanche but they didn't want to end up with a two hundred and fifty pied-long rainbow.

Colours were the least of Jean's problems as he persevered with his black and white battle. A knock on his door indicated lunch and the diminutive Aveline, dwarfed by a huge platter of fruit, cheeses and bread was protectively ushered through the door by his guard. As she entered, she smiled a thank you to the guard who gave her a fatherly smile back. That was a smile more than he had ever got out of her, thought Jean. He motioned her to place the platter on the table by his cot.

'Do you know him?' Jean asked, nodding to where the guard had stood.

Once more she reverted to her usual shy self.

'Yes Sir.' she murmured.

Jean went to her and placing the tips of his fingers under her chin, very gently lifted her head. Her eyes though, remained firmly fixed on her feet. Jean released her head which promptly went down again. Then he had a thought, 'Avis, would you like to see what I've been doing?'

Almost imperceptibly she nodded and taking her elbow, Jean led her over to his panel depicting the latter battle scenes. Very slowly she raised her head and looked down onto the table. She gave an involuntary gasp and Jean released her arm and left her there while he returned to his lunch. All the time that he was eating, she just stood. She didn't move from one end of the table to the other nor, so far as Jean could tell, did she move anything other than her eyes across the scene in front of her. Very occasionally, she gave another little gasp and appeared to lift one hand to her mouth. Eventually, Jean wondered if she was quite right in the head and then she turned round and looked at him. She looked directly at him and her eyes were shining. She tried to speak and then shook her head as if the effort was too great for her. Jean put down a hunk of bread and cheese and went over to her and studied her face. 'Are you all right?'

Again she shook her head and then said simply.

'I was there!'

Jean looked closely at her. Her eyes, which he had always thought lovely, were now positively luminescent and for a second it was he that was speechless. He tore himself away from her and went over to the table, turned and grinned at her.

'Come on Avis, you couldn't have been there. For one thing you are a girl and another, you are far too young. Oh! Wait a minute. I see. You like my drawing so much that it made you feel that you were ...'

'No, Sir. No! I was there. Ask him, Sir.' She pointed to the closed door and it took Jean a second or two to realise she meant the guard on the other side of it.

'All right, Avis. Why don't you tell me about it. Don't let him in here, we'll never get rid of him.'

He grinned at her again and immediately thought he'd lost her. Her animation disappeared and she dropped her head.

'Please,' he pleaded. She continued to look downwards but slowly began to talk, 'I was four years old. My mother died and my father was…well he was horrible. I still get nightmares, all the time. Anyway, we lived at Saint Valery and I remember it like it was yesterday. The huge, huge, fleet that put in there after the winds had driven them from the Dives. The night before they sailed over, I ran off and hid in one of the boats under a load of banners.'

Jean looked disbelievingly at her. 'How old were you?

'I've just told you Sir. I was four, well, four and a half.' she pointed to the door again.

'Yes, all right Avis, I believe you. Go on. What happened then?'

'When we got to these shores they unloaded the boats and they found me. Some of the men wanted to leave me there on the beach but some of the others, he was one,' she indicated the invisible guard. 'thought I would bring good luck to the expedition and they took me with them.'

Jean gave her another friendly grin. 'Well, you did, didn't you. They won.'

She returned his grin with a shy smile of her own.

'Yes Sir.'

'Go on, what happened then?'

'One of the farriers took me to the top of a hill and put me on his shoulders so that I could see the battle and I did see it,' she continued with a hint of defiance. 'Just like you've done it over there, it is wonderful, what you have done. I'm sorry Sir. I didn't mean to…'

Jean shook his head. 'For goodness sake Avis, don't apologise. You have just paid me a great compliment and I'm proud of it but don't stop there. How come you are here in Canterbury? I would have thought they'd have kept you in Dover or Hastings.'

'It was on one of Lord Beaumont's ships that I hid and when Lady Beaumont came over here she looked after me for a little while…until…'

Jean stopped her. 'Lady Beaumont? I didn't know there was a Lady Beaumont.'

Avis bit her lip and looked as if she were about to cry. When she spoke it was almost a whisper.

'She died. She used to tell me stories and Lord Beaumont would laugh at them and…'

She stopped and looked away from Jean. He put a hand on her bony shoulder and much to his surprise, she didn't shrug it off as he half expected her to. After a pause, she continued, 'After she died, Lord Beaumont wouldn't have anything to do with me. He said I could stay in his household but he told all the other servants to keep me away from him.'

It all started to come out in a rush now.

'He and his Lady were so… he missed – misses her very much and they never had children of their own so…' The tears started to wet her long lashes and roll down her none-too-clean cheeks. Jean waited for her to compose herself. She sniffed away her tears and smeared the grime further around her face with her hand. Jean removed his hand from her shoulder and resisted the temptation to give her a cuddle. If only she had been a little more wholesome. Then he thought, he hadn't always been so fastidious.

'You all right now?' he asked.

She nodded wearily and moved to clear away the remains of Jean's lunch. He stopped her, his hand on her shoulder again.

'Lord Beaumont…' he started. 'Lord Beaumont hasn't actually been unkind to you has he. I mean …' This time she did shake off his hand.

'Never,' she said vehemently. 'He is the very best and kindest of men. It is just that I seem to make him sad and he doesn't have time to be sad. He has so many important things to do.'

Jean nodded sympathetically. 'I must admit I would have been more than shocked had you told me differently. Thank you for your story Avis. I know it can't have been easy for you. Oh! Just before you go, would you do something for me?'

She dropped her eyes again. 'Of course Sir, anything.'

'You are a very pretty girl, Avis. Why don't you …does it never occur to you to…'

His courage failed him. 'Oh! Never mind. Off you go.'

#

Beaumont and his small entourage made their way back to the castle, threading their way slowly and carefully through an assortment of stallholders, merchants, vagrants and goodwives. They were met with the customary variety of bows, attempted curtseys, deliberately turned backs and the occasional outright hostile glance or gesture. Beaumont sighed to himself and wondered how long it was going to take before their presence here was accepted by the local population and he was one of the less despised Normans. He adjusted his grip on the reigns as his horse swerved slightly to avoid a stallholder who had moved into the road to field a dropped ball of twine.

'Well, Josclin. What do you think?'

Josclin, who had been silent thus far, absently leaned forward and patted his horse's neck.

'Think, my Lord! You mean about Lady Beornwyn and her niece? I think the young lady is in great danger. Her aunt less so, perhaps, although this bastard is so unpredictable …'

'I agree.' Beaumont replied. 'It is not going to be easy but I think Lady Alysoun should be moved to the castle where we can keep an eye on her. Lady Beornwyn won't like it but it makes so much more sense. Alysoun and young LeBrun should be working together anyway. If only Beornwyn were not so inflexible but I suppose I can see her point. She, at any rate, has to remain at the School to supervise things and they really should be getting on with this damned embroidery. The Queen is not renowned for her patience. Ah well! I suppose I could broach the subject tomorrow at dinner.'

They arrived at the postern and Beaumont reached into his purse to throw a coin to a beggar, little more than a heap of rags, sheltering under the wall.

Jean was looking out of his window when Lord Beaumont, Josclin and the two guards from the School arrived back and handed their mounts over for stabling. He had not, however, noticed an earlier arrival whose horse had made its lone entry only some thirty minutes previously.

He moved away from the window and back to his table, critically regarding his day's work. He had not been totally happy with it lately and he couldn't think why. He glumly supposed that it had something to do with the high and mighty Alysoun and her comments.

Jean heard footsteps in the corridor; Lord Beaumont coming to report on his visit to the School no doubt and quite likely the bearer of further incomprehensible instructions from the two Saxon noblewomen. The footsteps certainly sounded like his Lordship's, by now they had become quite familiar to Jean and were accompanied by another pair, probably Josclin's. Jean steeled himself for the customary sarcastic comments.

A few murmured words with the guard outside the door and Lord Beaumont entered. Jean turned back to his drawing, pretending to put some finer touches to it so that Josclin would be deprived of the opportunity to deliver some scathing remark about the idleness of the creative spirit, when he felt a familiar touch upon his arm. He whirled round.

'Thibault! What the devil are you doing here?'

Thibault took a pace back and regarded his erstwhile companion.

'Master LeBrun, you have charcoal all over those nice new clothes. You look like an…like an artist.'

Jean frowned, 'Come to that Thibault, you look like a priest. You haven't changed then!'

Thibault suddenly let out a burst of unexpected laughter.

'Jean, I never thought I would hear myself saying this but it's good to see you.'

Jean's face cleared immediately and he too laughed.

'Yes, Thibault. Likewise. It's good to see you but why the...'

He gestured towards Thibault's sombre costume. Robert Beaumont broke in.

'Jean, Master Thibault has spent some time back home in Retreat. However, now that he is back with us, I have no doubt that he will revert to his old finery. If only to make you look less like a courtier' he added with uncharacteristic irony. 'Now, I must attend to business. I will leave you two to become re-acquainted.'

'My Lord.' Jean stopped him before he could leave.

'Yes, LeBrun.'

'The Lady Alysoun, is she all right?'

'Quite recovered, Jean. I am sure she will be happy to learn of your concern. Until later.'

Jean turned to find that Thibault was still looking at him.

'Lady Alysoun, eh? My word, Jean, you have come up in the world. She likes hair like yours does she?'

'Oh shut up, Thibault. I really am pleased to see you. Come on, sit down and talk to me. By the way, what are you doing over here in Canterbury? Shouldn't you be back at Dover toadying up to the great Lord Odo, your father figure and mentor in chief? Mind you...' he went on, ignoring Thibault's warning look. '...the last time I saw you two together, you were trying to kill him if I remember rightly. With this very dagger too.' He unsheathed the dagger from his belt.

Thibault nodded sadly.

'Yes Jean. I owe you for what you did that day. Had you not stopped me, I could well have killed him although I have a sneaking suspicion that people like Odo do not die easily.'

Jean looked at him seriously.

'Thibault, there is something I need to know. Mirabelle...'

Thibault pressed his fingers to his eyes with something more than an expression of mere fatigue, as if he was shutting something out. Eventually he said, 'No Jean. It wasn't me. It couldn't have been me. I would sooner my life had been forfeit than Mirabelle's.' He shuddered. 'In the few hours we had together, she taught me more about life than I had ever learned on the battlefield.'

Jean stared at him disbelievingly.

'You what, Thibault? You're telling me that you and Mirabelle...Oh my God, I never guessed. Thibault, I'm so sorry. What can I say. So what happened?'

Thibault told him everything, as much as he could, although it was obvious that the memory was still very raw. He told of how he had returned to Mirabelle and how he had found her lying on her bed, still not cold but soaked in her own blood. Her clothes had been torn off her and she had been sliced vertically from her throat down to her... he stopped. Jean said, 'So, what did you do?'

'You know what I did. We have just been talking about it. Obviously I didn't really believe that Odo had personally killed her. Of course I didn't, but I was pretty sure that he knew who did. I cannot believe that I looked up to him for all those years, Jean, I really can't. You must all think me such a stupid innocent and I am.' he reflected for a moment. 'Correction Jean, was.'

Jean nodded.

'It had to be Wulfric, didn't it? Do you know of anyone else who could have done that to her?'

Thibault got to his feet and walked to the table, his back to Jean.

'Of course it was Wulfric. He is one of the reasons that I am here in Canterbury although Odo doesn't know that. So, Jean, what is all this about a Lady Alysoun then, a Saxon Lady is she?'

Jean grinned.

'Saxon, yes. I'm not absolutely sure about the 'Lady' though,' he went on. 'Actually, Thibault, she was attacked last night by that bastard Wulfric. '

Thibault's head shot up. 'Was that why you were asking Robert Beaumont if she was recovered?' Jean nodded.

'What happened then?'

Jean related all that he had been told by Lord Beaumont and Josclin and when he had finished the telling of it Thibault gave a whistle of admiration.

'That took a lot of courage on the part of the young lady. She is young I take it? This arrow with which she wounded Wulfric, where did that come from then?'

Jean told him of the attempt on Lady Beornwyn's life, adding that Alysoun was her niece.

'Really,' countered Thibault. 'I was not aware that the famous Lady Beornwyn had a niece.'

'Indeed she has, Thibault, and if you would care to, you can meet her tonight.'

They both looked around to find Robert Beaumont lounging, nonchalantly, in the open doorway. He continued, 'We are invited to dinner, at least I am but I am sure that her Ladyship will not be averse to entertaining you, Thibault, as well. No Master LeBrun, I cannot guarantee you a welcome at her table. You know how these things work so you will have to eat alone, here in the safety of the castle.'

He gave Jean an apologetic smile.

'So, Thibault, if you would care to meet me at the stables in say, an hour, we can ride over together. There are one or two things we should perhaps discuss.'

Thibault signified his assent with a bow and turned to Jean after Beaumont had left.

'Sorry, my friend but they are aristocrats. As his Lordship said, you know how these things work.'

Jean looked rebellious for a second but then changed to a look of resignation.

'Don't worry about me Thibault but watch out for Alysoun. If she could do what she did to Wulfric you might find yourself on the menu as the main course.'

Thibault grinned and said that it made a change to find a young woman who was impervious to Jean's rather obvious charms. Jean contented himself with the remark that the nobility in general, and Lady Alysoun in particular, could all go to hell so far as he was concerned.

Thibault's grin faded. Not because of Jean's remark but because during this exchange he had wandered back to Jean's work table and studied the latest panel on which Jean had been working. He gave another low whistle of admiration.

'Seriously Jean, this is brilliant. Have you got the rest of the battle scenes here?'

Jean said he had and arranged them on the table. Thibault turned to him.

'These really are excellent. Look, I'd better go. I don't want to keep Lord Beaumont waiting. I'll look forward to seeing you on the morrow and telling what a wonderful evening I spent in the company of the redoubtable Lady Alysoun.'

Jean made a face at him.

'You'll probably get on brilliantly together. She's just like you were when I first met you; arrogant as they come and treating us ordinary peasants like rubbish. Go on, go and enjoy yourself.'

After Thibault had left, Jean went to put the panels back in order. He sighed to himself and decided to stretch his legs before getting back to work again. Perhaps, when it was time, he could get Avis to bring some supper to his room. He went out, telling his guard that he was just going down to the bailey for a few minutes, also to have a quick word with the man about Avis. At first the guard had looked a bit blank but when Jean reverted to her proper name, Aveline, the guard gave him full chapter and verse on the girl, corroborating everything she had told Jean, even down to the unhappy estrangement between her and Robert Beaumont.

The guard, who was called Amaury, shook his head sadly when telling Jean how Beaumont had been almost unhinged with grief at the sudden death of his young wife and instructions had been given that the child, Aveline, should not be permitted within his sight. Of course, in a community such as a castle it was an impossibility for them never to catch the occasional glimpse of each other but there was no longer any communication between the two. Amaury went on to say that his Lordship's edict went against everything that his Lordship was known for, he being one of the kindest and most thoughtful of masters, and those that had known the girl from the time of the Conquest tried to compensate for his behaviour by giving her whatever comfort and protection that was in their power to offer her. The strange thing was though that Aveline, herself, seemed to have shrunk from any form of contact which promised affection so it had got to the stage where, other than a friendly salutation from her erstwhile friends, she kept herself to herself. Pity really because she was nice little thing and life had not been kind to her. Jean nodded in agreement and decided to find Avis and ask her to fetch him some supper. He could then have another chat with her. Maybe even make her feel a little more wanted as a person.

Robert Beaumont and Thibault walked down to the bailey together in the company of the ever present Josclin and a small escort of three men. At the bottom of the steps, Beaumont instructed Josclin to take the men to the stables and see that their horses were ready. Beaumont took Thibault by the arm and said, 'Before we set off, Thibault, why don't we take a turn around the bailey and talk one or two things over.' He walked his companion to the centre of the area, where they were unlikely to be overheard, and turned to him.

'I take it that you were sent here by Odo to, shall we say, take a look around, see what is going on in what he fondly imagines to be his personal territory and report back with your findings.'

Thibault nodded. 'You are very direct my Lord but then, I would expect nothing less from you.'

Beaumont raised an eyebrow.

'Well?'

Thibault spoke slowly and deliberately.

'My Lord Odo is anxious that you and Archbishop Lanfranc are establishing a power base of your own here in what, as you rightly point out, he regards as his personal fiefdom. He is the Earl of Kent.' Thibault added dryly.

'Indeed he is,' retorted Beaumont, equally dryly. 'Well, let us put things in the right context shall we? I am here at the request of The King who considers, not unrealistically I think, that his esteemed step brother, has enough fingers in enough pies to keep him busy for the rest of his life. I would not presume to speak for Lanfranc but I will say that he and I have long been in broad agreement how this region might best be administered to the advantage of our Sovereign. You know me, Thibault, I am not a self seeking man neither I think, are you. Are you?' he repeated, turning the statement into a question. Thibault's response was swift.

'I am not my Lord. You asked me why I was here and I gave you a forthright answer. Lord Odo also wished me to report on the progress made by Master LeBrun. From what I have seen I don't think he will have any problems there although I cannot yet vouch for the making of the piece.'

'Don't worry Thibault, after tonight you will have all the information you need to make a full report to my noble colleague. Now that we have cleared the air somewhat, let us be on our way. I cannot, by the way, vouch for the quality of Lady Beornwyn's table so you may have to make allowances for the Saxon palate.'

He stopped and turned to Thibault again.

'There is something else on your mind I think. I imagine it is something personal so I will not press you but Thibault, you and I are statesmen at heart. We are not comfortable in matters of deceit and intrigue. We are happy to administrate laws and policies, not of our devising, so long as we consider them reasonably honest and just.' He put a hand on Thibault's arm. 'You make a poor spy, Thibault and if you find that your loyalties are torn, then I can only advise you to serve those whose views most closely mirror your own.'

Thibault gave a bitter laugh. 'Oh, I shall my Lord, I shall.' He stopped and grabbed Beaumont's wrist. 'What, in God's name, is going on there?'

The clouds, scudding across a watery moon, had cleared momentarily. Beaumont followed Thibault's pointing finger. There, bathed in an almost supernatural light, was a slight figure at a water trough, which stood against one of the workshops inside the bailey. The figure appeared to have little apparel, saving a shift and was pouring buckets of water over its head. Hidden by the darkness, it was revealed only by this brief splash of moonlight, only to disappear again as the moon vanished behind another cloud.

The two men stopped for an instant and then Beaumont gripped Thibault's elbow and almost dragged him through the gateway into the stable area. Once there, he tersely ordered Josclin and his men to mount, indicated that he and Thibault should also do so and once mounted, led the way out of the postern without explanation or looking at any of them.

#

Jean had moved his table, as he often did during the hours of darkness, under the wall, to which three sconces had been secured in a line. During the evening and quite often if the skies were dull and overcast, these lights provided him with the means to work for much longer stretches than would have been otherwise possible. He had returned from visiting the bailey and after a few words with Amaury, who was shortly to be relieved by a new guard, he was well into the rhythm of his drawing. He paused to rub his eyes which were beginning to feel tired and he couldn't face the thought of joining everybody else in the great hall for the communal dinner; especially so since Beaumont was absent and the place tended to get even hotter and rowdier without the sobering influence of authority.

He thought, not completely kindly, of Thibault and Lord Beaumont having a civilized dinner at Lady Beornwyn's from which he had been excluded but at least, he consoled himself, he didn't have to pretend to be nice to the hostess's niece. He decided that he would have to go and chase up Avis or one of her colleagues. He had barely risen to his feet, when there was a knock on the door and the new guard, whose name he never got to know, opened the door and ushered in Avis herself.

As usual, she gave a neat little bob and with downcast eyes said that she had noticed that Master LeBrun wasn't at dinner and could she bring him something to his room. He gave her another of his encouraging grins and said, 'Avis, you must have read my mind. I was just about to come looking for you and here you are, saving me the trouble. Yes Avis, indeed I would be grateful for something to eat and while I am eating it, as we did at lunchtime, you shall cast your expert eyes on my afternoon's work and tell me if it is a true picture of what you witnessed years ago from the vantage point of a farrier's broad shoulders.'

She looked up at him then and her pretty eyes sparkled.

'Oh! Can I Sir? I'll just nip down and bring your pie.' She looked down again. 'When I saw you weren't down in the hall, I made sure I saved you a piece.'

Jean said, 'Thank you Avis. That was very thoughtful of you.'

She looked up again and blurted out. 'It's quite a big piece Sir.'

'Is it now,' said Jean with mock solemnity. 'In that case, perhaps you might like to share it with me?'

'Oh! No Sir. I couldn't do that. That would be …'

Jean grinned again. 'Well, let's see how big it really is shall we? Then we'll see, I must confess, I am very hungry.'

Another quaint bob and she was out of the door, her small feet rapidly pattering down the passage. Jean, who's natural response to Avis's painful shyness was to smile, found himself frowning and telling himself he must be careful with her feelings. She was such a vulnerable little thing who had been badly hurt in the past and there was no way that he was going to add to her pain. Strange really, he felt almost protective towards the girl. While he awaited her return, he strolled back to his work and started tidying up the parts of it which, on a fresh viewing, didn't quite meet his standards.

Avis was back in no time at all, laden with fresh ale, a clean beaker and the promised pie which, as she had told him, was a sizeable portion. Jean hardly looked up from his work and asked her to put it all down on his other table, which she did.

'Do you want to come and have a look?' Jean asked, his mind still on his illustration.

'I don't want to disturb you, Sir.' came the hesitant reply and Jean could hear her making for the door again.

'Hey, don't go yet.' he glanced over his shoulder at the meal she had bought. 'Anyway, I thought you were going to help me eat that enormous helping you've just brought in.' He watched her struggle with her timidity and said again, 'Tell you what, Avis, why don't you come over here and see what I've done today, while I sit over there and get started on that pie?'

She nodded and made her way over to the drawings. Jean gestured for her to stand alongside him while he deftly, with a few lines, drew in a couple more lances for the Norman cavalry. He looked sideways at her and saw that her eyes were transfixed by his dexterity. He smiled to himself. Not the first time he'd seen that happen but now his hormones were much more under control, so he said gently, 'Why don't you stay, like I said and I'll get on with my dinner.'

She didn't answer just nodded her head and Jean suddenly saw that she was different. Her simple scarf was usually worn over her head but now it lay across her shoulders and her uncovered hair was less tangled and brighter. He only just managed to restrain his first impulse which was to sniff but he needn't have bothered. She had obviously taken the trouble to bathe but she couldn't have taken the hint from what he had failed to say to her earlier. Perplexed, he left her to examine his work while he quietly got on with his dinner. While he was eating she didn't say a word but, as with the previous occasion, seemed to be mesmerised by what she saw in front of her. Jean finished his meal and asked Avis if she would like something of what was left. She shook her head, still saying nothing until Jean was beginning to find her total absorption in his drawing slightly bizarre. He put aside his platter and joined her at the table. When he was standing beside her she pointed at one of the figures, turned and looked at him with big, serious eyes. At last she spoke.

'I'm sorry, Sir, but is that Lord Odo?'

Jean looked at the figure to which she was pointing and said.

'Yes, Avis, the one with the staff, cheering on Thibault and all the other squires.'

She shook her head.

'I'm sorry, Sir but it cannot be him. He carried a huge mace and he…'

She squeezed her eyes shut and put a hand up to her mouth.

'I didn't like him, he frightened me. Nobody liked him. He was cruel and wicked.'

She opened her eyes again and looked at Jean.

'And he's a Bishop too.' she whispered.

Jean patted her hand that was resting on the table. She snatched it away and gave him a reproachful look.

'It's all right Avis,' he soothed. 'I am not going to do anything. Now then! This business of Lord Odo at the battle. That was very clever of you to remember that after all this time. The thing is, you see…' he went on, 'You are absolutely correct. Odo did go into the battle with a mace and he did… well, what you said he did, but men of the church were not supposed to do that and I have to tell you that Lord Odo is the man who has ordered me to do all this,'

Jean indicated the drawing.

'And Lord Beaumont suggested it might be wiser for me to show Odo, not waving a lethal mace about but a fairly harmless piece of wood. You see this is supposed to hang in Lord Odo's new cathedral in Bayeux and I think, between you and me, he would prefer all the people who see it to think that he had conducted himself as a good priest should. There, now you know.'

She moved her hand back to where it had been and her little finger gently touched that of Jean's. He did nothing and she gave a little sigh. Jean moved away and said, 'What about that pie now, it was delicious.'

Avis just gave another little shake of the head and put her scarf back over it.

'I'll just clear the things, Sir. Thank you for letting me see it again.'

Jean made no move to stop her as she made for the door, nor did he say anything.

Just before she went out, she lifted her head and gave him the most fleeting of smiles.

Feeling slightly silly at this unaccustomed role he seemed to be playing, Jean shrugged his shoulders as though to dismiss the whole episode, picked up one of his toothpicks and thoughtfully started to clean his teeth.

CHAPTER FORTY TWO

The School

The five riders drew up to the School of Embroidery but in a far more sedate fashion than on Robert Beaumont's last visit. The horses were walked up to the building quietly, there were no shouted orders and no audible clink of weaponry. Josclin talked to the guard on the main door, ascertained that there had been no further hint of trouble, knocked just hard enough to announce their presence to the guard inside and the two guests were ushered through the door to meet their hostess. Beornwyn looked sharply at Robert Beaumont when she saw that he was accompanied by a tall young man dressed in dark robes. Her guest wasted no time in making the necessary introduction. Beaumont then introduced Thibault to Alysoun who also looked at him coldly and made no effort to respond to his introductory bow. Beaumont could plainly see that an explanation was expected for the appearance of this uninvited guest.

'Lady Beornwyn, I know you will forgive me for imposing on you in this fashion but I thought that, if you had invited me here to discuss matters of policy in the town, it might be more pleasant for Lady Alysoun to have some less tedious company than we might be able to provide.'

He drew her Ladyship to one side and said quietly.

'I can vouch wholeheartedly for this young man. He is far too honourable for his own good, comes from a noble family of which he is the only survivor. I cannot claim that he is landed because he is not but he can number among his friends, their Majesties and, for what it is worth, Jean LeBrun.'

She gave a snort of dismissive laughter.

'You really think that a recommendation, my Lord?'

Beaumont shook his head.

'More than that, he is the sort of person we need to look to for the future. We will not always be here, Beornwyn and the true unification of this island can only be assured if there is another generation to take over where we leave off.'

A begrudging, 'Humph' was all Beaumont's reward for his little homily but it was enough. He knew Beornwyn would accept Thibault's presence with the graciousness of which she was capable when the occasion demanded. What he didn't expect, when they joined Alysoun and Thibault, was that the couple appeared to get on so well. They were sitting at the table, quite close together, pouring over the pages of some old book or other. Alysoun looked up.

'Aunt, I have been showing Master Thibault some of the designs I think we should incorporate into the borders of the embroidery.'

She giggled and pushed back a lock of hair into her cap.

'Master Thibault thinks that what's-his-name will be most annoyed at my suggestions.'

'Master LeBrun or Jean, as I believe his given name to be,' prompted her aunt, 'I would suggest, my dear, that you treat Master LeBrun with the respect that his talent deserves. What say you Master Thibault, I understand that you are well acquainted with the young man?'

Thibault stood and bowed, 'Indeed I am Lady Beornwyn. He is, I believe, extremely talented although I have no knowledge or understanding of these things.'

Beornwyn looked at Beaumont and said, 'I see. Tell us a little about yourself and what it is of which you do have an understanding.'

'Very little, I fear, my Lady. I was a youthful participant at the battle in '66 since when I have been bound as Squire to Lord Odo, my father having been slain at Hastings.'

'Lord Odo!'

Beornwyn spat out the name as if it were a particularly distasteful morsel of food. She looked again at Beaumont and this time her look was far from friendly. Thibault could hardly help but notice and added hurriedly.

'I am no longer bound to him my Lady.'

Beornwyn sniffed, 'What did you do that displeased him?'

'Nothing, my Lady. It is I that have severed the ties between us.'

She sniffed again. 'You! I cannot imagine that he has taken very kindly to your decision. Do you not fear harsh retribution from his Grace's hand?'

Thibault gave a bitter smile, 'His Grace is not yet aware of my decision, my Lady.'

Beornwyn looked from him to Beaumont and back again and then nodded thoughtfully.

'I hope you intend to be very careful, young man,' she said, 'Lord Odo is not to be lightly crossed. When first you joined his service, I take it that you were unaware of...of his...'

'No, my Lady. I was not but now I see things very differently although,' he added heavily, 'It took others to convert me to my present understanding of his character. By the way, Mistress,'

He turned to Alysoun.

'I understand that you had a particularly lucky escape the other night. I must congratulate you on your courage.'

Alysoun barely acknowledged the praise, then beckoned him back to her side and the book they had been looking at earlier.

Thibault was far from comfortable. He found the room too warm and he was surprised that the pulse, beginning to throb in his temple, was not obvious to the young lady at his side. His hand instinctively went to it and a shudder ran through his body. Alysoun shot him a quick look.

'Are you unwell, Master Thibault? Oh, I know,' she went on teasingly, 'I expect you're starving. Why is it, Sir that all young men seem to be perpetually hungry? Is it all this pointless exercise they seem to think so necessary to their welfare?'

Beaumont laughed at her observation.

'It is a long time since I was a young man, Lady Alysoun, yet I would like to think that my appetite can match that of Thibault's.'

Alysoun wagged a warning finger at him, 'Then we shall see, my Lord, if we cannot satisfy your appetite with our Saxon fare.'

The meal concluded. Both men signified by looks to each other that it had, indeed, been very good and the conversations continued. Occasionally all four joined in but, while Beaumont and Beornwyn talked of charters, law enforcement and local dues, the younger pair continued to scan the pictures in Alysoun's Bestiary, from which she intended to decorate the panels in Jean's design. It was Beornwyn's next pronouncement which was totally unexpected and, to Alysoun at least, completely surprising.

'Robert!' said the lady, nothing in her voice giving any indication of the effort it took her to say what she did, 'I would be much obliged to you if you would take my niece under your protection and afford her sanctuary at the castle.'

For a moment nobody said anything at all but looked at their hostess as if defying her to repeat her statement. Then Alysoun rose from her chair and said, 'Aunt! I'm sorry but did you...'

'Yes I did. Come here my dear.'

Alysoun slowly moved to Beornwyn's side and her Aunt took her hand.

'Alysoun, I cannot bear the thought of anything happening to you again. I cannot risk it and it makes sense for you to move to the castle where his Lordship, Josclin and his men can shield you so much more effectively. We had this building guarded and still Wulfric was able to reach you and now he has even more reason to harm you.'

She gave the hand a squeeze.

'There is something else. You keep saying how necessary it is for you to work directly with LeBrun, to decorate these blessed borders that you keep on about. Well, why not stay there until the work is complete. I have this feeling that the sooner it is all over and done with, the easier our lives are going to become.'

She turned to Beaumont, 'Well Robert, you would be agreeable? It goes without saying that my niece's welfare, both moral and physical, would become your responsibility.'

Beaumont cleared his throat. 'You might not believe this, Beornwyn, but I was going to make the same suggestion. In fact, it was one of the reasons why I accepted your invitation this evening although, I must say,' he added quickly, 'the quality of your table has made the experience even more worthwhile.'

'Yes, all right Beaumont, there's no need for all that courtly rubbish. You'll do it though?'

'I will be honoured, my Lady.' was Beaumont's response.

Alysoun looked seriously at her Aunt.

'Are you going to be able to manage here? I mean there is going to be so much to do and...'

'Nonsense!' was Beornwyn's businesslike retort, 'You have made all the necessary arrangements for stock, our ladies have been organised. All I have to do is supervise and sew in the commentary but that can be done last of all.'

'But Aunt!'

'But nothing, child. How on earth do you think I managed before. You haven't always been here to order me about. Now, that is settled. As I say, I shall be happy when this whole exercise is behind us and we can return to some semblance of normality.'

She turned again to Beaumont. 'I am depending on you Robert.'

He nodded. 'Why do we not take her back with us tonight? We came with an escort and one of them will be happy for Lady Alysoun to take his mount while he walks at the horse's head. Once we reach the castle she will have a personal guard, day and night.'

He looked at Thibault.

'Why don't you stay here and see if Lady Alysoun requires assistance with her effects while I organise Josclin and the escort.'

'But my Lord,' began Thibault, shaking his head as if trying to rid it of a painful thought. Alysoun giggled at his discomfort.

'Don't worry about me Master Thibault. It will take me five minutes to collect every thing I need but you can carry these if you will.'

She thrust the Bestiary into his outstretched hands, together with another volume which Thibault recognised as Aesop's Fables.

Beaumont returned, announcing that everything had been organised and that one of his escort would be pleased to allow Lady Alysoun his horse for the short journey to the castle. He gave a smile and went on to say that, ever since Alysoun had appeared at the castle carrying her precious arrow, she had become something of a heroine to the garrison and even more so when it was learned of her vanquishing Wulfric with the very same weapon.

Within minutes Alysoun re-appeared, as she had promised, and her goodbye's with Beornwyn took the form of an intense hug which the older lady seemed reluctant to break. Alysoun was helped into the saddle by Josclin and the soldier, whose mount she had requisitioned, seemed more than happy to walk at his horse's head.

They made their way down the deserted street with Lady Beornwyn standing at her doorway in the company of the guard. She did not wave and Alysoun did not turn her head. Only Robert Beaumont turned in his saddle and gestured his farewell and thanks with a languid wave of his gauntleted hand.

Even at walking pace, it did not take them very long to reach the castle. They were just approaching the Gate House when Nero, who hitherto had been more than happy to be re-united with his old master, suddenly shied away from something in the shadow of one of the Gate House towers. Thibault's knee bumped against that of Alysoun, to whom he apologised and he immediately brought Nero under control as they entered the castle grounds. They dismounted and handed over the horses to be taken to their stables. Alysoun took the arm of Lord Beaumont while Thibault and Josclin brought up the rear.

Thibault turned to his companion, 'Not like Nero to get spooked like that. What do you think caused it?'

Josclin looked back to the Gate House and shook his head.

'It could have been a number of reasons. I can't say that I saw anything untoward but…Oh! I know. It was probably that beggar that sits there. His Lordship likes to toss him a coin every time he leaves or enters the place. Stupid if you ask me. Could even be leprous but my Lord is too soft hearted. I'll get one of my lads to shift him tomorrow but don't say anything to his Lordship.'

Lady Alysoun was escorted by Beaumont to the living quarters where she was assigned the best available room which turned out to be a small suite only slightly less comfortable than that of his Lordship. Josclin chose one of his best men to guard her door, there being no other entrance for them to worry about and soon the guards were the only inhabitants of the community who were not asleep.

For most of them, their slumbers were undisturbed but for a few, of whom Jean was one, the piercing screams of a vixen roused them momentarily. Not for long though, after all it was the mating season for the local foxes.

CHAPTER FORTY THREE

The Castle, Canterbury

Nero's young groom was another whose rest was briefly disturbed and he, unlike Jean, did not find it quite so easy to get back to sleep. The horses seemed more restless than usual and since he had a genuine regard for his charges, he stayed awake for as long as it took them to quieten down again. Even so, he was the first of the stable lads to rise and it was still dark when he tiptoed out of the stall and made his way to the trough in the Bailey to splash water on his face and to rinse out his sleep-dried mouth. He dipped his hands into the cold water and immediately withdrew them with a gasp.

Gingerly, he put them in again and, yes, he hadn't been mistaken. There was something in there and it felt horrible. Not having a light to investigate further and not sure that he wanted to anyway, he ran to the Barbican and called to the guards. One of them came down and roughly told him to keep his voice down but reacted swiftly on being told of why he had been roused. He took a sconce from the wall, lit it and together with the boy, hurried over to the trough, held up the torch and swore quietly to himself.

He told the lad to run back to the Barbican and bring another of the guards. Having done so, the two men conferred in low, urgent voices and it was decided that one of them should wake Josclin. The one that remained at the scene told the shivering lad to get himself back to the stable and get some more clothes on. Captain Josclin would certainly wish to hear from his own lips what he had found. The lad did as he was told and was back at the trough just before Josclin came running up, still pulling on his woollen overshirt.

Josclin had brought another light with him and he instructed the two guards to remove the corpse from the trough. He brought the torch up to it and all four of them gave a sharp intake of breath and instinctively crossed themselves. Josclin's voice was harsh and bitter.

'You two stay here. You, boy, what happened?'

The lad told him what he could but since he hadn't actually seen anything it was unlikely to prove useful. Once Josclin had heard what little he had to say, he told him to get himself back to the stable. As he turned to go Josclin called him back.

'What happened here was closer to you than the rest of us. Are you sure you didn't hear anything strange? The boy shook his head and mentioned that he thought the horses were unusually restless and it was that which had disturbed him but apart from that…Oh yes, he did hear that the foxes were up to their fun and games again but since that had happened quite a lot recently, he hadn't given it a second thought. Josclin nodded thoughtfully.

'Neither had I, lad, neither had I. It could have been a vixen of course. I heard it too but just like you …go on then, get about your duties.'

The boy immediately did as he was told and Josclin turned to his men.

'Right, I'd better wake up his Lordship. Don't suppose he'll thank me for it but it has to be done. Stay here and keep your eyes and ears open and watch your backs. We all think we know who did this so I expect he'll have disappeared by now but we might as well not take any chances.'

With which he turned on his heel and made his way to the Keep. He didn't hurry because for one thing it would do nothing to bring the victim back to life and for another, he wasn't quite sure what he was going to say to his master.

#

Apart from the occasional lowly scullion engaged on night duties, there was still no one abroad yet in the living quarters. Nevertheless, Josclin kept his eyes open and was alert to every movement or sound which, inevitably, turned out to be a hound scratching or a cat stirring somewhere. He arrived at the door to Robert Beaumont's apartments and he stood at it for a moment, his hand raised to knock. He dropped the hand, then raised it again. When his fist did make contact with the board there was nothing hesitant about it and the sound reverberated along the gallery.

He did not have to wait very long. A slightly tousled but wide-awake Beaumont opened the door, took one look at Josclin's grim face and ushered him inside. Josclin did not wait to be invited to give an explanation. Without ceremony he said.

'There has been an incident, my Lord.'

Beaumont's hand flew to his mouth.

'Oh my God Josclin, not Lady Alysoun?'

'No, my Lord. Aveline, she's dead. Murdered. One of the stable lads found her in a water trough.'

Beaumont paled visibly and almost staggered.

'Aveline!' He whispered the name. 'How was she… did she drown, was she…?'

'No, my Lord,' Josclin broke in savagely, 'She had been slit from throat to crotch.'

Beaumont reached for a flask on a table and poured liquid into a goblet. His hands were shaking. He offered the flask to Josclin who shook his head and said nothing. Beaumont took a sip from his goblet and made a visible effort to pull himself together. Josclin looked steadily at him, his expression a mixture of anger and compassion. Beaumont drew a deep breath, 'Josclin, I … I only saw her last night. I…'

'Yes, my Lord,' Josclin broke in, 'I was there my Lord, if you remember. You dragged Master Thibault away from the spot, the same place where she was discovered this morning.

Beaumont sank into a chair.

'Oh! May God forgive me Josclin, what have I done?'

Josclin let out a weary sigh and this time there was no anger, only sadness in his voice.

'You have done nothing my Lord. We, all of us here at the garrison are to blame. She didn't want for affection, my Lord. All of my men who had known her since she was a toddler had a soft spot for her but after…after her Ladyship was taken from us, the child withdrew into her own grief and would have little to do with any of us. Some found it difficult to understand why your Lordship saw fit to sever all ties of affection between yourself and Aveline but I understood, if that is any comfort to you, my Lord.'

Beaumont rose to his feet and attempted a smile.

'I appreciate your words, Josclin but no, it isn't any comfort. Where is the child now?'

'I gave orders that her body was to be left where we found it my Lord.'

'Very well Josclin. I'll get dressed and come down with you. I would like to carry her to the chapel myself, if you think that the men won't regard the action as too hypocritical on my part.'

'I'll see that they don't my Lord.'

Beaumont came over and put his hand on Josclin's shoulder.

'That wasn't what I meant Josclin and you know it. Give me but a moment and I will be with you. While you are waiting, think if there is any way by which we might hunt down that evil creature. I take it that Wulfric is your favoured suspect?'

Josclin nodded vehemently. 'No doubt in my mind.'

Moments later, Robert Beaumont emerged from his bed chamber, lacing up his tunic. Josclin helped him with his cloak and noticing that Beaument's hands were trembling, fastened it with a plain pin. All his attire was plain. Robert Beaumont always wore quality clothing but Josclin had not seen him attired so sombrely since Lady Beaumont had passed away.

As they made their way down the spiral staircase, Beaumont led the way and over his shoulder, said.

'Well?'

'Well my Lord. The first thing we should consider is the security of Lady Alysoun and Master LeBrun.'

Beaumont nodded his assent and Josclin continued, 'Next we have to discover how Wulfric got into the Bailey without any of the guards seeing him. This must mean that he has found some way of getting in other than through any of the gates, all of which are guarded, so I suggest that I take some men and scout around the outside of the castle walls then…'

Beaumont held up a hand to stop him and turned and looked up at him.

'Even better, why don't you and Thibault both search separately? Take three men each, and patrol half the perimeter. Talk to people, ask if they've seen anything, anybody unusual. Yes, yes , Josclin, I know what you are going to say, Wulfric operates in the dark and no one will have seen anything but do it. It's worth a try.'

Josclin added quietly.

'I've seen something my Lord, so have you! That beggar outside the Barbican or whatever it was that Thibault's horse shied away from last night.'

Beaumont slapped a palm to his forehead.

'Oh my God, Josclin and to think that I gave him charity every time that I passed him. It still doesn't explain how he got in, but… Make a start just as soon as it gets light. Wake Thibault, pick your men with care and pray God we will scotch that reptile before he kills somebody else.'

That said, they both hurried to the bailey and joined the guards that stood by the water trough. Beaumont, avoiding the eyes of his men, knelt and tenderly lifted the tiny wet and bloody corpse into his arms. He just stood there for a moment then turned to Josclin, saying in a low voice, cracking with emotion.

'Give me some time, my friend. Carry on as we proposed and report to me as soon as you find anything but for now, I need some time to reflect upon my failings.'

Bearing his light burden, he slowly made his way to the chapel as if the load were leaden.

Josclin immediately became all action. He turned to the guards and told them to get back to their posts and that they would have to stay on duty since the rest of the garrison would be engaged on a search. He then looked up at the barely lightening sky and hurried into the keep, to check on the guards allotted to Alysoun and Jean and to wake up Thibault.

Jean had managed to sleep through all this excitement as, indeed, did most of the occupants of the castle. He was, however, woken earlier than he was wont to be by the sound of heavy objects being dragged along the corridor and voices outside his door. He groaned, turned over, stretched and yawned his unwilling way into a morning that didn't sound as though it was going to start too well. Wrapping a blanket around him, he opened the door and was not very happy to find Ranulph standing there, apparently trying to explain to the guard the purpose of the selection of timber propped up against the wall. Jean groaned again but this time in frustration, as he jerked his thumb towards the room to indicate to Ranulph that he should bring himself in, together with his invention, assuming that is what it was. The guard gave Jean a pitying look as he closed the door on them.

'All right, Ranulph. You've carted it up here so you might as well put it together and show me how it's supposed to work.' He peered gloomily at the collection of wood.

'It doesn't look anything like that model you made.'

Ranulph replied cheerfully, 'I dunno, I really don't. For someone who's supposed to be taking the artistic world by storm, you 'aven't much imagination 'av you?'

Jean yawned.

'Oh! Just get on with it, Ranulph. I haven't woken up yet, let alone washed or had breakfast. By the way, you haven't seen Avis on your travels have you?'

Ranulph looked up from banging two pieces of timber together. 'Avis! Who the 'ell's Avis?'

'She's one of the servants. Little thing with lovely eyes, except she seldom lets you see them.'

'Oh yea! Like that is it?'

'Oh, shut up Ranulph and just get on with it. That banging is beginning to give me a headache.'

After about thirty minutes during which, if anything, the banging got worse, Ranulph walked over to Jean who was looking out of his window at something going on below him. Ranulph tapped him on the shoulder and Jean turned around and said, 'There seems to be a lot going on out there this morning. What's that all about?

Ranulph tipped his cap back, scratched his head and looked out of the window.

'I dunno but you're right. Josclin's up to something or other and...' elbowing Jean to one side, 'Isn't that your old mate, Thibault, all geared up for action. Doesn't look very soldierly though, does he? Looks more like a priest playing soldiers.'

Now it was Jean's turn to scratch his head.

'No, that's Thibault all right. Anyway, it's nothing to do with us. Show me how this contraption of yours is supposed to work then.'

'Well,' began the proud inventor, 'It's like this. These two end bits, the ones that look like saw horses with one half of the top 'V' missing, we just drop these as far apart as you want to allow for the length of canvas to be worked. If you look 'ere you'll see two holes have been reamed in them, one at the top and one at the bottom. Now, these 'ere lengths of timber have got a peg cut out at each end and these pegs fit in those 'oles, see?'

Jean intimated that, no he didn't see. Ranulph started to look a touch exasperated.

'Look, what's the single most important thing about an embroidery frame? It keeps the material tight, right? Now look. These lengths of timber with the pegs can be used to keep the two ends rigidly apart because they've holes drilled in them at intervals. So you just fit the pegs into the holes in the end pieces and then adjust the length to the length of fabric you're working on. All you 'ave to do is pop a dowel through two corresponding holes in these horizontal timbers, right?'

'Yes, I can see that, Ranulph, but so far all you have is two saw horses with two of the top bits missing and some lengths of wood to keep them apart. How do you fit the linen into that contraption?'

Ranulph said, 'Ah!' and disappeared into the corridor, returning with two rollers of the type used to move heavy weights, such as blocks of stone, over short distances. They were, however, much thinner than those and smoothed to a fine finish. They also had pegs, this time stuck into each end and Ranuph proceeded to drop the pegged rollers vertically into holes that had been drilled out of the angle of the two saw horses.

At long last Jean was beginning to see what this contraption was about and Ranulph soon confirmed that he was right.

'There you go, Jean. Fix one end of the panel to one roller, stretch it over to the other one, roll it up as tight as you want and jam in a couple of wedges to stop the rollers from moving.' He looked at Jean expectantly but before Jean could express what he thought he was interrupted by voices from the corridor, one of which caused him to groan audibly. Ranulph looked at him expectantly.

'What in the name of God, is she doing here?' Jean expostulated. Again the voice, this time raised in anger, brought another groan from Jean who sank into his chair, his head in his hands.

'That Avis, is it?' Ranulph asked. 'I thought you wanted to see her. Don't look much like it now, does it. Bit of a firebrand is she? Mind you,' he added reflectively, 'there's some who quite like that sort of thing but I wouldn't 'ave thought that you were…'

He threw a protective arm over his invention as Alysoun swept furiously into the room followed by a distraught looking guard whose fighting abilities were somewhat limited by the two very heavy looking books that he was carrying in his arms.

She stood, arms akimbo and glared at Jean who glared warily back.

'I understood,' she began waspishly, 'that I was brought here for my protection, not as a prisoner or is that how you Normans always treat a guest? I completely failed to realise that my every movement was to be shadowed by this…this. Oh for goodness sake, fellow, put those down somewhere and get out.'

She pointed first to Jean's worktable and then to the door. The guard sheepishly put the books where she had indicated and clanked out of the door where he could be heard complaining to his fellow, Jean's guard. She then turned an even more hostile eye on Jean, 'Well, Master LeBrun, I suggest we waste no further time and make a start on these borders. I realise that you have yet to complete the whole narrative but the sooner I can get some of the panels over to my Aunt, the sooner we can make a start on the embroidery itself.'

Jean rose unwillingly to his feet, determined not to be intimidated.

'Lady Alysoun!' he began as forcefully as he could. 'I have yet to prepare myself for the day. I have not yet had any…'

Her attention switched to Ranulph and his collection of wood.

'What in God's name is that contraption supposed to be and who are you?'

Ranulph whipped off his headgear and made a surprisingly passable bow to the young lady.

'Ranulph, my Lady. Carpenter and…' His voice failed for a moment and he gestured towards his frame.

Ignoring Jean, she crossed the room to get a closer look at Ranulph's pride and joy. She looked at Ranulph for an explanation. Jean sat down again and prepared himself for the verbal demolition of Ranulph's invention. He was to be disappointed.

'Explain it to me, Master Ranulph.'

Her tone had changed, had become almost gracious and Ranulph hastened to tell her what it was all about. They conversed in their own language and although Jean managed to pick up quite a lot of the conversation, he was left with the unhappy feeling that perhaps some of it, the bits he couldn't quite understand, were directed against him. Anyway, Alysoun appeared to be genuinely interested in what Ranulph was telling her and walked around the frame, nodding approvingly as Ranulph explained it to her. Eventually she turned to a hungry Jean and said sweetly, 'You see, Master LeBrun, it takes one of our own race to apply his obvious intelligence to our problems.'

She turned to a beaming Ranulph.

'Now Master Ranulph, what you have designed is quite ingenious but not, I fear, suitable for our work, '

Ranulph's beam faded and Jean perked up a bit.

'But,' she went on, 'That is not to say we cannot put it to some valuable use. You see, there is no way that this,' she pointed to the frame, 'can provide the degree of tension required for embroidery.'

Ranulph's face fell and Jean shook his head in sympathy. She looked pointedly at Jean before continuing.

'But I am sure that it will be invaluable as a support for our ladies to work on the lengths of cloth that Master LeBrun has deemed necessary for his design. The embroiderers will still be able to use their own frames but if that can be set at, say, knee height, several embroiderers can work on the same length at the same time. Do you understand what I am saying?'

He nodded vigorously and said that, of course he could reduce the height of the end pieces to whatever her Ladyship desired. No trouble at all. He looked triumphantly at Jean who shrugged, then remembered Alysoun's reaction to the mannerism and wished he hadn't. She gave a little smile to herself and took herself back to the work table where she started to inspect his latest panel.

Jean and Ranulph looked at one another. Ranulph nodded towards Alysoun's back and Jean shook his head vigorously. Ranulph then cleared his throat and announced that he ought really to be going since his overseer had given him orders to start his normal duties as soon as he had finished with the presentation of his frame.

Alysoun turned from the table, thanked him politely for his efforts on behalf of the School of Embroidery. She promised him that she would ask Lord Beaumont to arrange for it to be transported thither and that she would deem it a great favour if the inventor himself could install it and instruct the staff in its use. Ranulph blushed, managed another bow of sorts, winked at Jean and left the room. Alysoun assumed her normal brisk nature and announced to Jean that it might be better if they wasted no more time and made a start on designing and drawing in the borders. By this time, Jean was rapidly running out of patience with Alysoun's overbearing attitude and while he was prepared to accept it from the aunt, he drew the line at being bossed about by the niece. Accordingly, he mustered as much dignity as his unwashed and famished condition would allow and informed Lady Alysoun that, until he had remedied those two conditions, he was not going to do anything.

She regarded him solemnly for a moment, brushing her top lip with her forefinger and then said.

'Master LeBrun, I apologise. I thought you would already have breakfasted and prepared yourself for the day. A servant saw to my personal needs some time ago and I'd assumed you had enjoyed the same service.'

Jean broke in. 'The servant that came to your quarters, was she small and slim with big…?

Alysoun stood up a little straighter.

'Big what, Master LeBrun?'

'Eyes, Lady Alysoun. Big, dark eyes. Quite beautiful eyes actually.'

Alysoun put her head on one side and looked at him as if she were seeing him properly for the first time.

'Not exactly, Master LeBrun. He was fat and really rather ugly – actually.'

Jean frowned, not so much at her remark than at the commotion, the third that morning, which appeared to be going on outside. In seconds the door had burst open and Josclin, Thibault at his heels, came in looking flushed, with exertion or anger, Jean had no way of knowing. As it turned out it was a mixture of both.

The two men made a token salutation to Alysoun, then Josclin came straight to the point. 'Master LeBrun, Amaury, one of your guards, tells me that you and one of the servant girls, Aveline, seemed to have some sort of understanding, his word not mine. Well?'

Jean looked from one face to another, including that of Alysoun, who was listening intently.

'No Josclin, we didn't have any sort of 'understanding' as you call it. She looked after my needs here, my food and drink but that was all. If you must know, I felt sorry for her. She told me her story, her journey over here when she was little more than a baby, the tragedy that affected both her and Lord Beaumont but that was all. If you're asking me did I like her, the answer is yes I did. If you're suggesting it went further than that then you've got it wrong, because it didn't. Why? What's all this about? Has something happened to her?'

Thibault, who had hitherto been silent, came over to Jean and put a hand on his shoulder.

'She's dead, Jean. She was found early this morning, she had been brutally murdered and we are almost certain that Wulfric is responsible.'

Jean sank down in his chair, obviously shocked and upset. Josclin turned to Alysoun.

'I'm sorry my Lady but despite her lowly station, Aveline was very popular among the garrison here. Master LeBrun was one of the few people who, it seems, had her confidence and it is important to find out if he could tell us anything that might help us in our searches.'

Jean just sat and shook his head while Thibault's hand rested on his shoulder. For a moment nobody said anything but Josclin broke the silence by announcing that they must get on with the search. He impressed on both Jean and Alysoun that they must not move about without their escort. Thibault nodded his agreement.

'Jean,' he said, 'I am going now with Josclin to expand our investigation outside the castle walls. However, I must return later to Dover. My Lord Odo will be anxious for my return.' he smiled ironically and continued 'and my report. I'm sorry Jean but we will track him down. It seems we both now have good reason to see him brought to book.' Jean looked up at him and, for a fleeting moment, imagined he had seen that look on Thibault's face on another occasion. What was it exactly? Then Thibault gave him one last sympathetic pat on the shoulder. Both men made their bows to Alysoun, turned and left the room.

Alysoun started towards Jean, then stopped.

'Master LeBrun, I will instruct the guard to have food and water brought here. Once you have refreshed yourself, we will commence our work. I am sorry about your friend.'

Jean slowly rose from his chair and shook his head.

'She wasn't really a friend, I just felt sorry for her. Don't worry about the guard. I presume both our bodyguards are outside this door. I'll get one of them to accompany me to the laver. If it's all the same to you, I'd rather wash in private and as for breakfast, that can wait. All of a sudden I seem to have lost my appetite.'

She watched him leave the chamber and heard him in conversation with one of the guards. Alone in the room for the first time, she took a look around. Nothing extraordinary but quite orderly. Funny, but she'd expected the place to be a mess. Why was that, she wondered. She absently picked up one of the sharpened sticks with which he cleaned his teeth. At least he looked after himself properly and again, she wondered to herself, why she should have thought otherwise and what about the servant girl. The poor thing had probably taken a greater liking to LeBrun than he had realised.

Not just a womaniser then, he was altogether more complex than she had bargained for. Then the memory of Wulfric's assault upon her came over her like a wave and she had to sit down in Jean's vacated chair until the nausea left her. It could so easily have been her fate. She rallied, forced herself to her feet, took a deep breath, walked over to her books and opened one, the Fables. She searched among the rolls of completed panels and sorted out the first ones, the ones that she intended they start on. By the time that Jean came back, she had sorted out which of the Fables would best suit her purpose.

CHAPTER FORTY FOUR

The Castle, Canterbury

They had been working for over two hours; Alysoun picking out the illustrations and directing Jean, who copied them into the empty borders of his design. It was proceeding much better than either of them had anticipated. From Jean's point of view, the work was much less boring than he thought it would be. He had never had much experience of reproducing existing art work before but he found that he was able to do so in such a way that he could impose his own style on the weird birds and animals that appeared in Alysoun's book.

She, for her part, took a vicarious pleasure in selecting those themes which might just blur the message that the work was intended to convey. Jean, who seemed to be remarkably familiar with the Fables of Aesop, not only impressed her with this knowledge but also confirmed for her, his skill as a draughtsman. He worried her slightly at one point when he questioned her choice of subject, wanting to know why the theme of deceit had appeared so much at the beginning but happily, this was precisely the sort of ambiguity at which she was aiming.

'Deceit?' she said, 'Surely, Master LeBrun, your informants made you aware of what these scenes were all about.'

He looked at her, doubtfully.

'Yes, of course they did. All these early scenes illustrate, or partly illustrate, the dishonest way in which your Harold succeeded King Edward who had promised the throne to our Duke William or King William, as he rightfully is now.'

'Exactly,' she smiled almost sweetly at him. 'Deceit, terrible wasn't it?'

All he said was, 'Umph, what's the next one then.'

What did surprise her was the speed at which he reproduced these pictures. In fact she was having quite a problem keeping up with her selections. Eventually though, Jean's hunger was starting to re-assert itself and he flung down his stylus and stretched.

'I'm hungry. I'm going to get something to eat. Do you want to come or shall I have something sent up here?'

She shook her head. 'No thank you, I'm not hungry. I'll stay here and sort out what to include in the next panel.'

He shrugged and left her to it. On the way out, he picked up one of the guards and asked that he accompany him to the kitchens. While they made their way Jean asked if he had any news about the hunt for Wulfric. The fellow said that he'd heard nothing since Josclin and Thibault had left to continue their search, but there was not a man in the garrison, low or high born, that was not anxious to see Aveline's killer brought to justice.

#

It being less costly to throw up three walls than four, a number of the poorer inhabitants of Canterbury, living on the Southern side of the town, had taken advantage of the solidity of the old Roman wall, itself part of the castle's fortifications, to erect their lean-to hovels. As the prosperity of the town increased, many of them had been abandoned for something more substantial and nearer to the centre of activity. It was in one of these deserted and dilapidated hovels that Josclin now stood in the company of six of his men. It was Thibault who'd found the place in his searches earlier that morning but, for the reasons he had explained to Jean, he had made his excuses and goodbyes to Lord Beaumont and was on his way back to Dover.

Josclin had added Thibault's three men to his own three and the seven of them, crammed into this small and foul smelling ruin, were giving each other uncomfortable looks. The building or what was left of it, for half the thatch was lying on the floor and one wall had all but collapsed and was hanging on by a few worm eaten timbers, was rank and gloomy. Thibault had also discovered the bloodied rag in one debris strewn corner which might have come from nothing more than an isolated domestic accident but on the other hand...

What was more significant though, was the hole in the back wall which was not so much a hole as a mouth of a narrow tunnel, the end of which could not be seen. This, Thibault had discovered by ordering his men to tear down a pile of old boards and bales which had kept the opening hidden from casual view. All this, he had reported to Josclin before making the short journey to Dover and it was this hole or tunnel that now occupied the attention of Josclin and his men. Josclin felt the hilt of his sword.

'Right! This obviously leads somewhere into the castle and it shouldn't be too difficult to find out where. Any of you heard of any secret passages, escape tunnels, that sort of thing?' They all shook their heads and mumbled to one another but from the looks they were giving each other and the way in which they backed away from the hole, it was obvious that none of them were especially keen to investigate it further.

'All right, all right, I'm not suggesting one of you is going to be made to crawl up there. What we'll do is this. You,' he pointed at one of them, 'go and find a rabbit and you,' he pointed to another, 'requisition a ratting hound from somebody. Shouldn't be too difficult, we've all seen them about the place. Off you go and be sharp about it.'

The two men he'd selected left the hut looking happy to be out of the place. Josclin turned to the others.

'Right! Let's think about this. Where do we reckon that tunnel is likely to lead to, bearing in mind that it's not running in a straight line? You can see it isn't because it curves almost immediately. Any ideas?'

His men all looked at one another, then at him. One of them went outside, the better to orientate himself. He came back.

'Not sure, Sir but so long as it doesn't deviate too much, I reckon it should come out somewhere near the garderobe.'

Josclin permitted himself a rare smile.

'My thoughts exactly. Just the way a sewer rat would get in. Henri, you and Georges go and take a look but be careful. On your way and keep your eyes out for the other two and tell them to get a move on with those animals. Off you go now. Look for anything to indicate that those latrines haven't been used for anything other than that which God intended.'

The two men left and Josclin pursed his lips. He should, by rights, have reported this find to Lord Beaumont and for all he knew Thibault had done so before he left, but he just wanted a little more firm evidence before disturbing his Lordship. Also he was loathe to leave the other two soldiers there on their own. He did not have the luxury of too many men, the garrison was not large since most of Odo's squires and others in his entourage had been recalled to Dover. He had the two guests to protect and their guards needed changing frequently. Even the most diligent of soldiers could only be relied upon to keep awake for relatively short periods of time when all they had to look at was a wall with a door in it. He made a few rapid calculations. It was going to be a question of juggling his resources without compromising the men's efficiency. Also, he was not too happy with a single guard looking after Lady Alysoun and young LeBrun, there should have been at least two but now there could be no question of that.

Then there was Lady Beornwyn and her establishment and all the guards had to be relieved at some time. As soon as he'd found out exactly how significant this tunnel was, he'd take himself off to the grieving Lord Beaumont and go through it all with him. The hurried scuffle of boots interrupted his thoughts and the men he'd despatched to the garderobe re-entered the hovel. Henri and Georges came in, removing their protective headgear and wiping their perspiring brows. Josclin looked hard at them.

'Well? You haven't spent much time looking. Easy to find was it?'

Georges shook his head. 'No sign of anything anywhere close to where we thought it might be. The garderobe's definitely not where he's getting in. The holes go straight down and out over the fosse,' he sniffed, 'you can smell them from here.'

'What about the bars over the jakes?' asked Josclin. 'They all secure and not been interfered with recently?'

Georges shook his head again. 'No Sir, we checked the lot, all secure and mortared in place.'

Josclin sighed. 'Right, we'll just have to start from this end then won't we? Where the hell have those other two got to? They...Ah, about time!'

The two men ducked under the filthy blanket that served as a door and stood in front of Josclin, one clutching a large docile rabbit and the other a bad tempered terrier which looked as though he'd sooner have a go at the men-at-arms than he would the rabbit. The guard had taken the precaution of muzzling the animal with a length of rag and it didn't look at all grateful for the attention.

'Sir!' Henri spoke up.

He was older than the rest and he had probably served longer under Josclin and therefore Beaumont, than any other man in the garrison.

'Yes Henri, what is it?'

Henri puckered his already wrinkled brow.

'I don't quite understand, Sir. There's a tunnel, or at least we think that's what it is. Why don't we just set a fire at the bottom of it and let the smoke do the rest. Why do we have to bother with this... this menagerie?'

He waved dismissively at the drowsy rabbit and the growling dog.

'First thing I thought of, old friend, but then I thought again. I don't like the combination of fire and castles. There is still a hell of a lot old wood in this castle and although it's being rebuilt and re-designed, I don't think that his Lordship would thank us for burning it down. Neither, I imagine, would Lord Odo. Just think about it lads. Any of you fancy the responsibility for burning down Odo's Canterbury fortress?'

They all shook their heads and Josclin contented himself with a nod before he went on.

'No, let's try these firs.'

Jerking a thumb at the rabbit and dog which, by this time, was becoming more and more irritable. The soldier put down the rabbit at the entrance to the tunnel and it sat there cleaning it's whiskers with its paws. Josclin nodded to the dog handler who set it gingerly on the floor before whipping off the makeshift muzzle. Before making for the rabbit, the dog found time to administer a lightening nip on the ankle of the man who'd been looking after him. None of them were wearing full armour and the soft boot offered him little protection, if the oath that he let out was anything to go by. The rabbit, sensing that he was next on the terrier's menu had already disappeared around the bend in the tunnel when the dog tore in after him, barking madly and scrabbling wildly with his claws on the sandy incline. For almost a minute there was silence in the hovel and the tunnel, then a blood-curdling screech rent the air. They all looked at one another until Henri observed that it sounded as though the dog had caught up with the rabbit. Josclin nodded his agreement.

'You're right Henri. That was a rabbit squealing not our man, though I'd have thought that,' he broke off as another scream rent the confines of the tunnel. Josclin's head shot up.

'Now, was that the rabbit! What do you think Henri?'

The older man rubbed his chin.

'Well', he began slowly. 'I wouldn't be too surprised if that wasn't the rabbit again.'

Josclin looked at him and then reluctantly agreed.

'Right then, we'd better get digging hadn't we? You,' he indicated the soldier that had found the rabbit, 'try and find Master Guy of Falaise and ask him to let us have some tools. The rest of you stay here. I'm going to report to my Lord and check that our two guests are still in one piece. If anything has happened to them we might as well all go up there and join the dog and the rabbit.'

He left the lean-to shack and made his way back into the Bailey and walked over to the tower. This time there was no hesitation when he reached Beaumont's quarters and he hammered on the door as soon as he reached it. It was opened immediately by Beaumont himself.

Josclin reported what had been found and Beaumont said, yes, Thibault had already told him of the suspected tunnel but had been forced to return to Dover as there were more important political issues at stake. Josclin sniffed. Political issues did not concern him but what did was the immediate welfare of the garrison, Lord Beaumont and the two young guests under Beaumont's and therefore Josclin's, protection.

'It was suggested that we try and smoke him out, my Lord. That is if he is stuck somewhere in the tunnel.'

'I would rather we didn't resort to that, if you don't mind, Josclin. We have enough problems without all going up in flames. This…this rabbit hunt that you have organised. No results from that?'

'No my Lord, not as yet. I suspect that the dog has killed the rabbit and is quite happy to stay up there, living off it until it's all gone although,' he thought for a moment, 'that second scream that came from there. That could have meant that whoever is in the tunnel, and we must assume that it's our quarry, has either killed the dog or been attacked by it or, then again, it could have been the rabbit having a second yell.'

He thoughtfully tapped his fingers on the hilt of his dagger.

'I'll tell you what we do for the moment, Josclin,'

Josclin looked up, 'Sir?'

'We do absolutely nothing. Obviously you'll leave a couple of men there but bring the rest of them up here and station them around those parts of the castle in which that tunnel is likely to emerge. Get them to sit quietly for a time. See if they can detect any noises of trapdoors, murder holes or mining activity. We might not be under siege but by God Josclin, there are times when it feels like it. Before you leave, I wish to apologise for my behaviour earlier. I should not have allowed my emotions to interfere with my duties. Thank you for taking them on your shoulders.'

Josclin took a step back and bowed. 'Not at all, my Lord . Those of us that have served you since the great battle fully understood your feelings. If that poor girl's death has done nothing else, it has served to demonise her murderer and replace fear with anger in the hearts of the men. I'll just go and check on Lady Alysoun and young LeBrun and then I'll carry on with your orders.'

Beaumont stopped him as he was marching out. 'I'll see to them Josclin, you get on with re-organising your men. Oh, and one more thing. I have sent a message to Lord Lanfranc, asking him to spare us four of his personal guard. I'm sure he will happily agree, on the understanding that if his God can't protect his person then nobody can.'

'Thank you, my Lord. That will be most useful. I'll be on my way then.'

Beaumont nodded and Josclin walked out. Before his boots could be heard on the stairs, Beaumont, himself had exited his rooms and was making his way to Jean's studio. He strolled along the gallery, pausing to try the latch to Lady Alysoun's apartments and was pleased to see that the room was locked. He proceeded onto Jean's room and the two guards, on catching sight of him, stopped their murmured conversation and stood looking alert, one either side of the door. Beaumont nodded to them and knocked. There was no answer. He knocked again, this time more loudly and the guards looked at each other and he at them. He knocked a third time and without waiting for any answer, pressed down the latch and entered the room.

He was highly relieved to see that there wasn't anything going on that he hadn't expected. The two of them stood hunched over the worktable, Alysoun referring to two large open volumes while Jean was concentrating on copying an illustration from one of the books onto the border of his original design. He was glancing quickly from the page to the linen and his charcoal was fairly flying over the surface.

Beaumont coughed. Nothing. He took a step closer and coughed again. This time Alysoun whirled around. Her cap had moved right to the back of her head and blond hair was cascading quite freely down the sides of her face. She looked, Beaumont thought, quite flushed and almost exhilarated. He felt a frisson of anxiety then she grinned at him and held a finger to her lip, indicating Jean with her other hand. Beaumont returned her grin and gave a nod of understanding.

While he was certain that nothing untoward had taken place between these two young people he resolved that in fairness to Lady Beornwyn, if not to his own stewardship, he would somehow have to arrange a discreet chaperone of some description. Still, that was possibly the least of his current concerns.

Jean finished sketching in his fantastic animal, copied from the Bestiary and Beaumont noticed that he was already engaged on the scene depicting Guy delivering Harold into the care of William. He was not aware of how long they had been working together but like Alysoun, he could not help but be impressed by the speed by which Jean worked. When she considered that their host had waited quite long enough, Alysoun tapped Jean on the arm to indicate they had a visitor. Jean unwillingly disengaged himself from the panel but when he saw who had interrupted him, his brow cleared and he greeted his Lordship with one of his open grins and a perfunctory bow.

'Please don't stop. I am sorry to have interrupted you but I was anxious to see that you and Lady Alysoun have everything you need. Unfortunately, Thibault has had to return to Dover but I have no doubt that, as soon as his duties there allow, he will return to spend some time with you. There is one other thing, Master LeBrun, that I would mention...'

Jean looked, first at Alysoun then enquiringly at him. Beaumont studied the panel in front of him, whether with interest or to give himself time to collect his thoughts, Jean wasn't sure. Eventually he looked up and said simply, 'Jean, I understand that you showed some small kindness to, and interest in, one of my servants, the child that was brutally murdered.' he cleared his throat, 'You may be aware that she, when an infant, was a favourite of my wife. What I mean to say is that I am grateful for your kindness. I am sure that Aveline ... '

Jean closed the conversation by saying that he had done nothing except listen to the girl's remarkable story and allow her to watch him while he worked. It was very sad that her short life had been so horribly terminated. He then changed the subject, aware that Beaumont was finding it difficult.

'What of Wulfric? Has there been any news, my Lord?'

Beaumont nodded. 'Yes indeed, Jean. There has been some development but at this stage, we are not sure just how helpful it is likely to be. Your friend Thibault discovered a possible secret passageway into the castle, through the old Roman wall on the South side. Josclin and his men are investigating it as we speak.'

Jean ran a heavily charcoal stained hand through his hair.

'That seems odd, my Lord.'

'What's that Jean, what seems odd?'

Jean, seemingly perplexed, continued to transfer charcoal from hand to hair and Beaumont was quietly amused to see that Alysoun was looking as though she would dearly have dearly liked him to have stopped doing it but didn't quite have the courage.

Beaumont repeated his question.

'What is it that seems odd to you?'

Jean's reply was considered and thoughtful.

'I would have thought that if Thibault had found this...this tunnel, or whatever it is, he would have wanted to have stayed to investigate it himself. I mean, that's what he's like. He's so conscientious it's not natural.'

Beaumont shook his head.

'I am perhaps privy to certain things that you are not Master LeBrun. The situation at Dover is complicated. Your friend is in a difficult position and knowing my Lord Odo, as you do, I am sure you understand what I mean.'

Jean shrugged.

'Of course my Lord.'

He looked at Alysoun.

'If Lady Alysoun and you, my Lord will excuse me, I would quite like to finish another couple of panels before the natural light goes completely.'

He picked up a newly sharpened stylus and prepared to return to the table when he was stopped by Beaumont's gentle touch on his arm.

'Before you do, there is one more thing I feel I should mention but I'm not quite sure how to put it.'

Alysoun and Jean frowned at one another and then focussed their attention on Beaumont, who stood there for a moment stroking his chin. He cleared his throat again.

'The thing is...the thing is, Lady Alysoun, your being here, working alongside Master LeBrun, was subject to the understanding that you be... you be...'

He groped for the correct word. Alysoun's hoot of laughter resolved his problem.

'Chaperoned, my Lord?'

She didn't even look at Jean.

'Chaperoned! You think I need protecting from him?'

Her tone and the way that she indicated Jean was not, Jean thought, very complementary so he made sure that his scorn matched hers.

'Huh! Quite right my Lord. She is probably safer in this room with me that she would be in her precious School of Embroidery.'

He reinforced this remark with another, 'Huh' and returned to studying the point of his stylus.

Alysoun first of all looked outraged then puzzled and finally turned her back on both men and quietly pushed her hair back into her cap. When she turned back she was quite composed although Beaumont imagined that if she could think of the right words, she might have had a lot more to say. As it was, he held up two placatory hands and said soothingly, 'Well, I think if we say that you have not one, but two God fearing men to look after you, there is unlikely to be anything for anybody to worry about. I imagine that no mention need be made that they are actually on the other side of the door. Yes, I think that will suffice. Is there anything else?'

Alysoun said, 'Yes, my Lord. If it could be arranged for the finished panels to be taken to the School of Embroidery, I would be grateful. I know my Aunt is most anxious to make a start on the needlework. Oh, and yes. Would it be possible for that craftsman, what is his...'

'Ranulph,'

Broke in Jean, still concentrating on the point of his charcoal.

'Yes, that's it, Ranulph. If he could be helped to transport his frame there as well,' she pointed to the back of the room, 'And given the time to demonstrate it to my Aunt, that would be most helpful.'

Beaumont walked over and looked at it.

'So this is the finished article,' then said, 'I am sure that we can see to that. When we change your Aunt's guard, it can be done at the same time. One final thing, so far as we are aware, Wulfric is still at large so I must insist that you do not go anywhere without an escort.'

Alysoun's eyes twinkled.

'Anywhere, my Lord, absolutely anywhere?'

Beaumont sighed audibly.

'Within reason, Alysoun, within reason, you know full well what I mean. Until later then.'

He bowed, Alysoun gave a smooth curtsey and Jean just nodded. If he was the hired help, he was damned if he was going to play the courtier. He started to draw, freehand and out of his own head, the last of the battle scenes. The point of his charcoal broke at the first angry stroke.

The Lady Beornwyn was missing her niece quite dreadfully. Despite her anticipation of this and her stoical nature, it was far worse than she had ever thought it might be. She had, however, made the decision that Alysoun was likely to be safer within the walls of the castle and she would not alter it. Had she been made aware of recent events, she might well have thought differently but as it was, the news of the servant girl's murder had yet to reach her. She now was impatient to start on the embroidery. That, at least, would help to keep her mind occupied and stop her fretting so much about Alysoun. She had not long to wait. Before the end of the afternoon, the now familiar sound of the guard could be heard approaching the School. She noted, with relief that they appeared to have brought something with them from the castle, other than their customary weapons and rations.

Amaury, for he was about to stand his first guard at the establishment, courteously introduced himself to the Dame and conveyed the greetings of Lord Beaumont together with those of her niece. She enquired, as casually as she was able, as to the well-being of the young lady and Amaury was happy to inform her that she was busy working with Master LeBrun and had settled comfortably into her quarters. He went on to say that he had brought three panels, completed to the satisfaction of Lady Alysoun and there should be more arriving with tomorrow's guard. He duly handed Beornwyn the lengths of illustrated linen, carefully folded and wrapped in calfskins to protect them from the steady drizzle that had started to fall. He and the other replacement guard carried them into the building and, under Beornwyn's careful direction, deposited them in the sewing room.

At first, Beornwyn hadn't noticed the presence of the stocky Saxon artisan who lingered at the entrance with a handcart full of what, at first glance, appeared to be a random selection of wooden bits and pieces. When she returned from the workroom, Ranulph had brought himself in out of the wet and was lovingly guarding his pile of wood. He made one of his bows to the lady and Amaury made the necessary introductions, leaving all other explanations to Ranulph.

Beornwyn had already made the arrangements for her ladies to start work on the following morning and the presence of an inventive workman had not been factored into the equation. Eager as she was to inspect the designs, she was gracious enough to give some of her valuable time to Ranulph, who assembled his frame in the workroom and took care to inform her Ladyship that, without the encouragement given to him by Lady Alysoun, he would not have presumed to take up her valuable time. Just as her niece had, Beornwyn could see that for the lengths of panel on which the stitching was to be worked, some form of support could indeed be a useful aid. Therefore after some discussion on a likely suitable height of the frame, it was agreed that Ranulph should return the following day to make the requisite adjustments. Before he left her and in the cause of demonstration, he and Lady Beornwyn had hung the first of Jean's panels on the frame.

Left to herself again, Beornwyn returned to the workroom to make a closer inspection of the design. She smiled to herself at the choice of border design and concluded that, with her commentary stitched in Anglo Latin, it was very unlikely that the origin of the work would ever be questioned. The designer might be Norman but her School produced the finest needlework of any institution anywhere and this extraordinary record of the subjugation of her people would, if nothing else, confirm the supremacy of Saxon craftsmanship.

She ran a large index finger over the drawing on the panel, tracing King Edward's court, Harold's ride to Bosham, his subsequent cross channel voyage to Pontheiou and the events that followed. Traces of charcoal adhered to the finger and she thought that, before starting work, the scenes should brushed over lightly with a fine brush to remove the excess residue of charcoal while keeping the lines of the drawing intact.

For the first time since she had left, Alysoun had not entered her thoughts and for the first time in many years, she felt the first stirrings of excitement at the challenge which lay ahead.

CHAPTER FORTY FIVE

The Castle, Canterbury

A pile of labourers' tools stood neatly stacked in one corner and the men seemed to be a little more relaxed, otherwise the dilapidated hovel appeared much as when Josclin had left it. He reported his conversation with Lord Beaumont to the guard, ordered two of them to stay there and keep alert and told the others to get back to the castle and wait for him at the garderobe. As they went out, Josclin went over to the stack of tools, spades, spikes, mallets and so forth and calculated what would be the most constructive use for them.

Then he thought about what Beaumont had said and it made sense. If Wulfric was still holed up, so long as they could locate the entry point in the castle and guard it, he wasn't going to go very far. That was supposing that Wulfric was inside the tunnel. If he wasn't, there was not much they could do about it anyway so they might as well wait until Lanfranc's men appeared and Josclin's men could be sent off for a period of well earned rest; Something that he also would have welcomed at that point in time. He might have the reputation of someone who never needed sleep and was always on duty, and to some extent it was a well deserved reputation but, he reflected wryly, he was just as human as the rest of them and he wasn't getting any younger. He nodded to the men he was leaving to guard the tunnel and told them that they would be relieved at the first possible opportunity. He then made his way wearily back to the castle to see if there had been any developments there.

It appeared that the men selected had made another good search of the area where it was thought the tunnel might have emerged. They'd banged on walls and partitions but by the time Josclin arrived on the scene there was nothing at all to indicate anything hollow behind any of them, so he was reduced to leaving men to watch over any spots which might prove to be remotely vulnerable. Having informed this group, as he had the two outside, that he would relieve them as soon as he could, he left them to it and made his way to the kitchens to find something to keep him going for a little while longer.

He need not have worried because nothing emerged from the supposed tunnel, not even a bad tempered terrier and there was nothing found inside the castle through which an intruder might have secret access. Guy had also surveyed the fortification from the outside but even he, who could probably have constructed a Norman castle in his sleep, could not locate a covert exit from a tunnel which might have run in any direction. His suggestion was that his men dig their way carefully into the tunnel from the side to see if that would help determine the way it ran. Since the old Roman wall, into which the tunnel had been dug, formed not only the Southern boundary of the castle but was also part of the foundations, he was understandably wary of attacking it with too much enthusiasm. Therefore, like Robert Beaumont and Josclin, why not just wait for a few days to see what happened.

#

Throughout this period of drama and the ensuing period of waiting for something to happen, Jean and Alysoun were making steady progress with their work. Not only was Jean sketching in the borders at a prodigious rate but he had already made a start on the last battle panels. All that would then be left of the actual narrative would be the scenes depicting, literally, the crowning moment of the whole historic event, the coronation of King William. Other than the fact that Jean had been told that the ceremony took place at Westminster on the Christmas Day following the great battle, he had but scant knowledge of the proceedings. He therefore decided he could give rather more reign to his imagination than hitherto he had allowed himself.

Alysoun, who had visited Westminster, although not of course as a witness to the Coronation, was able to give him some details about the interior of the Abbey which he duly intended to work into his design. However, since all coronations consisted mainly of thrones, crowns, orbs, sceptres and archbishops, he had plenty of his own material on which to draw.

He also thought it only fair that Queen Mathilde's coronation should have representation, even though it was an entirely separate event, held two years later at Winchester. Alysoun thought it vulgarly excessive to portray, not just one but two triumphant symbols of Norman oppression and said as much to Jean. His immediate response was that she confine her input to the borders and leave him to finish the work for which he had been made responsible. It was, he reminded her, Mathilde who had taken his part against Odo and it was probably she who had prompted William to insist that he, Jean, be released from any feudal restraints on completion of his work. That being the case, there was no way that Queen Mathilde would be omitted from the design.

In Jean's mind, Alysoun's contribution was virtually at an end. Once she had run out of interesting beasts and Aesop offered no more sly innuendos, Jean assumed that there would be little for her to contribute after the early scenes. Not that this fact worried him at all, he merely gave an exaggerated sigh and carried on at seemingly breakneck speed, sketching in hunting and battle scenes. Alysoun began to wander around the room and after a while, Jean said, 'For goodness sake keep still, just because you have nothing to do now. Look, I tell you what, why don't you start to tidy up the finished panels and get them ready to be taken over to the School? That's if you don't mind and it's not too menial a job for you!'

She started to say something in defence of her dignity but decided against it. He had spoken without looking at her or stopping his drawing. She could not believe that anyone could concentrate as he did and still know what was going on around him but she started to do as he suggested and fold up the completed work. This was exactly what she had been hoping to do. There was one more statement she needed to make and it was one that she hadn't had the courage to do or persuade Jean to illustrate for her.

While engaged in doing the borders, she had kept one of the earlier panels back from delivery to the School. It had not been difficult. Once Jean finished a panel, he lost interest in it and she had found it quite easy to hold this panel back by the simple expedient of repeatedly moving it to the bottom of the pile waiting to be taken away. She always suspected that Jean worked at such a rate he had not bothered to take any notice of continuity. Although chronologically later lengths had already been taken over to the School, it didn't matter that much at this stage. When it did become important was when all the lengths were being joined up and that would be the very last thing of all to be done and probably months and months away.

With her back to Jean's worktable, she very carefully, so as not to smudge the design, folded up the linen and told Jean that she was going back to her room for a while, leaving him to work on his own border vignettes of husbandry, war and hunting. This suited Jean, who was not especially happy to have to surrender his control over the design, even of the borders but also because, for the first time, he was working as much from his imagination as from written or mental notes which, for him, was an infinitely more interesting proposition. Just as she suspected, he didn't even turn around. He just grunted something unintelligible and probably unflattering and carried on drawing another dead soldier or whatever it was he was doing.

She slipped out of the room with the panel under her books, was joined by her bodyguard and made her way back to her own quarters. Once inside she carefully unfolded the canvas and stared at it thoughtfully. This was not going to be easy. First she had to experiment. Tentatively and with the tip of a fingernail she rubbed at the mythical figure that Jean had sketched into the border. This beast had been her suggestion and it was not until he'd nearly completed the border on this piece that she had thought about doing what she was now about to attempt. Very, very gently she scratched away at the figure and very, very slowly, it started to disappear. With enormous patience, she succeeded in deleting it. True, a little smudging was left but now she was confronted with the part of her plan that she was not certain of being able to accomplish.

She sat back on her heels and thought. Not having a table to work on, she was forced to use the wooden floor as a work surface and she only hoped that it would prove suitable for what she had in mind.

She rose to her feet, instinctively brushing the fragments of rush that had adhered to her gown and looked down on the small blank space. Then she picked up her book of Fables and leafed through until she found what she was looking for. Tucked away in one of the pages, a tiny scrap of parchment on which she had made a rough copy of one of the many examples of graffiti that graced many of the buildings, public and private, in the town. She had been told by Beornwyn that some of these amateur artworks were extremely old and had been there for perhaps many hundreds of years. Indeed, there were even some of the later ones to be found on the School of Embroidery walls, the perpetrators being fully aware that the building sheltered mainly ladies of a gentle and retiring disposition.

Alysoun reflected sadly that poor Warin had often spent wasted hours removing the more offensive offerings, only to find that they had been re-drawn a few days later. Alysoun was only too well aware of her limitations as a draughtswoman, but in this case, this tiny isolated case, she told herself that it was unlikely to be noticed. Thus fortified by her decision, she sharpened a fine stick of charcoal of which, since Jean's original order, could be found all over the place and once more sank to her knees in front of the panel.

Moments later, she sat back on her heels again and regarded her efforts with something akin to satisfaction. She giggled to herself. It was pretty rough but all in all, not too bad an effort. Was that what men were really like, she wondered. How unpleasant to be burdened with something like that all the time, but no, all her knowledgeable friends had assured her that these rude drawings were far too exaggerated. It was just how men liked to think of themselves endowed.

She giggled again but soon stopped. How would Lady Beornwyn view this particularly lewd illustration. Once the reasoning behind it was explained to her, assuming that she needed an explanation, Alysoun felt sure that she would understand and not be too worried by it. The Normans who viewed it would be unlikely to think that it was anything other than an attempt at crude humour on the part of the designer. The designer, Jean, what would he think? He would hate it although he had already been happy enough to include the Adam and Eve illustration which Alysoun had suggested but then, that had biblical associations. Anyway, if what had been said about Jean's early drawings was true, the ones that had first caught the attention of Lord Odo and, she shivered at the thought, Wulfric, then he would not have much cause for complaint. Or would he?

Rather to her surprise, Alysoun reflected that she had quite enjoyed the short time she had spent in Jean's company. They had worked together well and she thought that a degree of mutual respect had begun to grow between them. He was much more complicated than she had first thought. That business with the servant girl, the way in which he and Robert Beaumont almost treated each other as equals and then there was his talent. She loved watching him work, his self belief in his creativity which excelled her own but more than anything, his sheer down-to-earth normality and his refusal to be cowed by anything or anybody.

She gave another shiver and wondered why. It was not cold and she could only think that her act of defiance had, perhaps, been taken a little too far and she was suffering a pang of apprehension. Too late. Her task now was to get it back in its place and have it taken to her Aunt by the next change of guard. Accordingly, she carefully folded the panel again, put it under her books and carried it back to Jean's studio in the company of her ever-vigilant guard.

Her arms were full and the burden quite heavy so the guard opened the door for her, standing aside to allow her to enter. Before he managed to shut the door behind her, she had caught her toe in a particularly tangled pile of rushes and fell headlong, her precious cargo scattering over the floor with The Bestiary, much the heavier of the two volumes, hitting the back of Jean's ankle. He shot up from his stool, hopping on one leg and giving a reasonable imitation of Alysoun's language in the cathedral on the occasion of their first meeting, only this time it was in low Norman not bog Saxon.

'What, in God's name, is the matter with you woman? Why can't you move about like everybody else instead of… that hurts, that does.'

He rubbed the back of his ankle while the two guards, his and Alysoun's, looked at him reproachfully and helped her to her feet. Flustered and furious with herself, she waved them away and bent down to retrieve what she had dropped but Jean had already and protectively, claimed his canvas and was gently refolding it when he stopped, stared and stared again. Alysoun, who was unhurt, took one look at his face and started to laugh. It was the last thing she wanted to do or should have done but she couldn't help herself. The more she tried to stop it bubbling up, the more it became impossible to stop and in the end, her stifled snorts had become a fully fledged howl and she was forced to flop down on Jean's vacated seat, hands up to her face and blonde hair all over the place.

When Jean spoke, his tone was of the sort generally used to calm a frightened horse or an agitated village idiot. Quiet and restrained but firm.

'It's all right, Lady Alysoun,' placing undue emphasis on the title. 'Just tell me what this is supposed to be about.'

He tapped the offending border.

'You drew this didn't you. Why?'

She wiped her eyes and looked up at him and again, his expression caused another smothered hoot of mirth. She shook her head helplessly and he shook his in mock sorrow.

'Oh dear! Oh dear! What are we to tell Lady Beornwyn. That her oh-so-perfect niece has suddenly lost her mind. She might dress like a nun but draws like a...'

She regained a vestige of control.

'All right, Master LeBrun, that's quite enough. I have not been allowed to see them but I understand that your talents also embrace, if that is the right word, pictures of an ... an erotic nature. This was not intended for your eyes. If you find it offensive, I apologise. I...'

Jean held up a charcoal begrimed hand.

'Did I say I found it offensive? No, I didn't but if you must know I think the execution of the subject is dreadful. A child could have done better. What in the name of Heaven is it supposed to represent?'

Her chin came up.

'I am surprised you feel the need to ask that question, Master LeBrun. I would have thought it quite unambiguous and as for a child doing better. I obviously have not had your experience in drawing genitalia of the opposite sex.'

Jean stood open mouthed, 'But...but that's different, you're a girl and anyway, who told you about my... you know?'

'That is not important Master LeBrun and for your information, I am not a girl. I am a young lady of noble descent. Your commonplace morality means nothing to me'

Jean took a step back.

'Here we go. Same old thing. Them and us. Well, whatever airs and graces you want to give yourself, that,' he tapped the drawing. 'is rubbish. Now, why don't you tell me why you felt the need to spoil my work.'

Alysoun took a deep breath and shook her head. Jean, for the life of him, could not understand why she kept that wonderful hair imprisoned in that drab black cap thing she always wore.

'Do you know who that woman is, that you drew there with the priest?'

She pointed to the illustration just above her crude drawing.

'Yes,' Jean replied, looking puzzled.

'Of course I know who she is. She's Aelfgyva, however you're supposed to pronounce it. Anyway, I think it was Lord Beaumont who told me. No, just a minute, it might have been Thibault, come to think of it. Anyway this Aelf... whatever. She was promised by your Harold to one of our noblemen. I can't remember which one. Does it matter?'

Alysoun shook her head again. 'Not to you I dare say but to us, yes. Aelfgyva was Earl Harold's sister. Your people put about that, as part of his so called oath to William, she was, as you say, supposed to be betrothed to one of your nobles and before you ask, I don't know which one either. She was actually though, betrothed to Hakon, her cousin who, as you have recorded, was a hostage of your William and...'

Jean interrupted, 'Yes, yes, I know all this. For God's sake, it's all on here, just as I was told it.'

He pointed out the figures on the canvas.

She bit her lip.

'Why don't you look a little closer. Not just at that scene with Aelfgyva and the priest in the chapel but to your illustration immediately before it; the part where Earl Harold is actually pointing out the nobleman to whom Aelfgyva is being given.'

She pointed at the scene in question and Jean shook his head in irritation.

'God damn it, Lady Alysoun, I drew it. I don't have to look at it. I'm sorry I can't give you the name of your precious nobleman but I thought we'd agreed that it wasn't important.'

'Please, Master LeBrun, then I will explain.'

Jean gave heavy sigh, smoothed out the panel and bent over to look more closely. He then groaned.

'What have you done now? First of all you have the nerve to replace my perfectly good border picture with some disgusting, badly drawn portrayal of a man in rut and then you have the effrontery to deface one of our nobles, the one that is about to take Aelg..., whatever her damn name is, with a moustache, a crooked one at that. If I might remind you, once again, Lady Alysoun, your job is getting the needlework done and mine is the design from which you work. I only hope that you can sew a hell of a lot better than you can draw. And another thing...'

She laid a placatory hand on his, which he promptly snatched away, giving her a look she found difficult to interpret.

'It's wrong, all this.'

She waved a slender hand at the panel.

'First of all, Earl Harold was not sent to Normandy to confirm the promise that William would accede to the English throne on King Edward's death. He was sent, by Edward, to negotiate the release of two hostages, relatives of Harold, Hakon and Wolfroth. Actually, they were not even hostages, kept in Normandy as a surety for William's succession, as your people would have it but rather his wards who Harold was to bring back to England with him. Aelfgyva is in Rouen, not for betrothal to one of your knights but one of ours, Hakon and as you have shown in your design, Harold is indicating the man with his hand; the man is now wearing a moustache because that is the facial adornment of our menfolk, not yours. So all I have done is changed one of your knights to one of ours, just to keep the record straight, you might say. As for the moustache being crooked, I'm sorry about that but if you think about it, it's a sort of insurance for you. If questioned about it, you could just say it was a slip of the charcoal, so to speak.'

Jean drew breath to say something but she forestalled him and went on, 'You have said nothing about the man with the axe, also naked I might add, who appears next to the figure which I have just added. You put him in, at my instigation, without any problem...' Jean interrupted, exasperated.

'Of course I did, I thought it was just another character out of your book of fables or something. Anyway, you have had me drawing all sorts of artisans and peasants with their implements, ploughing, sowing and the rest, why not one with an axe, hacking away at some tree or other?'

'That figure represents Hakon, Master LeBrun. That is why I wanted him under your Aelfgyva. He is symbolically naked because of his forthcoming nuptials with that lady.'

Jean sank down onto his stool and put his head in his hands. When he looked up, he thought he hardly dared ask the next question.

'If that is Hakon, who then is that ... that monstrosity that you have added next to him? No don't tell me it's... it is isn't it?

She bit her lip again.

'Indeed it is, Master LeBrun. That priest is not blessing Aelfgyva, he is caressing her. Now, which cleric of your acquaintance would be most likely to caress the face of a virgin Saxon lady, about to be betrothed to another man?'

Jean groaned again, this time with real feeling. 'Oh no! Do you realise the trouble I am likely to be in when all this gets out. All I have ever done, ever wanted to do,' he emphasised, 'was to record, as faithfully as I could, events which have been related to me by other people. Anything other than a purely artistic interpretation was never part of my commission and now you have changed all that by... by insisting on turning the whole thing into an exercise in Saxon propaganda.'

He banged his fist on the table and raised his voice. A guard opened the door and then closed it, winking to his companion.

'Lover's tiff?'

Jean glanced at the closed door and lowered his voice.

'Lady Alysoun! They are going to crucify me for this. I've been promised my freedom and Lord knows what but when they see what you've done. What I've done or supposed to have done, Odo will feed me to his dogs. Thank you very much your Ladyship, thank you very much.' he repeated bitterly.

Alysoun went to lay a restraining hand on his arm but stopped herself. She moved to the other side of the table, leaning on it, facing him.

'Listen to me, Master LeBrun. Nobody will notice anything. I will wager whatever is in my power, nothing will be noticed. It is far too subtle and your design is so incredible that everything in it will be taken at face value.'

She leaned slightly closer and said very quietly.

'If you do not believe me, just ask Lord Beaumont, when next he visits, what he thinks of this particular panel.'

She moved back again.

'And, by the by, Master LeBrun, I would deem it a great favour if you would cease to use my title when addressing me. You have the habit of making it sound like an insult.'

Jean looked up at her, then back to the panel.

'Um! All right, we'll ask his Lordship, just casually, what he thinks of this but if he notices anything untoward, I dread to think what will happen to me.'

She stood up straight.

'Don't worry Master LeBrun. If anything is said, I will take the blame. Tell him that I have done it without your knowledge.'

Jean gave a negative shake of the head but relaxed slightly and roughed up his hair. He then turned to her.

'By the way, I would deem it a great favour if you would cease to use my title when addressing me. You always seem to make it sound like an insult.'

Their eyes locked for an instant, then she giggled.

'Very well. You can just call me Alysoun and I will just call you LeBrun.'

If Jean intended a riposte he never got around to it because the familiar sound of guards standing up and the inevitable heavy footsteps in the corridor prevented any further conversation on the topic.

It was, as Jean anticipated, Josclin, who announced that the new guard for the School was about to leave and were there any further designs ready for delivery. The two young people looked at one another. Alysoun said 'Yes' and Jean, on the same beat, said 'No!'

Josclin sighed and asked if they could please make up their minds and Jean, very firmly said.

'No Josclin, there is nothing ready at the moment. Thank you all the same.'

Josclin left the room, shaking his head. Jean turned to Alysoun and told her that there was no way that panel was going to leave his studio until Robert Beaumont had cast an approving, if innocent, eye over it.

Alysoun made an over-elaborate curtsey and said, 'Of course, it would be just as MASTER LeBrun wished!'

CHAPTER FORTY SIX

The Castle, Canterbury

Josclin hauled himself from his cot and sat for a moment, planning the day ahead and brooding over the fact that the last few had been unaccountably quiet. A veteran campaigner, he was never totally happy if things became too peaceful. He pulled on his over-shirt and boots, tested the edges of his sword and dagger and made his way to the lavabo. A quick duck of his shaven head and he was ready for yet another day in the service of his master.

Breakfast could wait. There was just enough light and time to make his first visit of the day to the various posts around the castle. Since it was the furthest, he decided to start with the two who were guarding the tunnel. This was turning out to be something of a waste of time. They never had anything to report and there was obviously nothing very much alive in the hole, except, in all probability, the dog and he was probably quite happy to stay where he was with a whole buck rabbit to himself.

Josclin frowned. Funny though, you would have thought it would have wanted water by now. They had tried calling it to come out but it was such a surly animal, it probably preferred the company of a dead rabbit to that of a bored soldier who was just as likely to take what was left of the rabbit and give the dog a good kicking. Josclin rounded the corner to the South of the castle and saw one of his two guards standing outside the tumbledown hovel holding an extremely dirty child, a boy, by his ragged jerkin.

The boy was struggling and the soldier was having quite a problem retaining his grip on the urchin who, for something so diminutive, was putting up quite a lot of resistance. Josclin strode up to the pair and demanded to know what all the fuss was about. By now, the guard had managed to grab a handful of filthy hair and by this means was able to keep the urchin at arms length, thus avoiding all the waving arms and feet aimed at that area of the soldier's anatomy most precious to him. Josclin stood, arms akimbo, in front of them.

'Yes, all right. That's enough now. Calm down boy or I'll take my belt to you.'

To the guard, 'What's all this about then?'

The guard tweaked the child's hair tighter, causing it to yell.

'Dunno Sir. Caught 'im tryin' to sneak into the place.'

He jerked a thumb towards the door of the hovel.

'Can't understand a word 'e says Sir. He's local. I've never been able to get 'old of their heathen jabber.'

Josclin looked sternly at the boy who defiantly stared back at him although for a moment he stopped struggling. Josclin spoke to him in Saxon.

'Why were you trying to get in there lad, what do you know about this place?'

The boy sniffed and attempted another ineffectual swipe at the guard.

'Don't know 'nuffin about it. I want my dog back. You stole my dog and I want 'im back.'

Josclin nodded, 'It was your dog was it, the one we...er... borrowed? Small black and white terrier thing, very bad tempered. Is that the one?'

'Bloody well is!' the boy struggled, 'and I want 'im back.'

Josclin stroked his chin and regarded the filthy object with a mixture of amusement and distaste. He crouched down in front of the lad, taking care to keep out of range. 'What's his name then, this dog of yours?'

The child looked up at his captor as much as to say, thank goodness someone with some intelligence has arrived on the scene.

Josclin nodded to the guard to release the child and repeated the question. 'Go on then, what's his name?'

'Wuff', said the boy, then added proudly, 'I thought of it all by myself.'

'Did you now,' said Josclin admiringly, 'Well, I think that's a brilliant name for a dog, don't you?' he added, turning to the guard who nodded, not having the faintest idea what the discussion was all about.

'Tell you what,' continued Josclin, 'Why don't we go in there and see if we can find Wuff. I expect he comes when you call him doesn't he?'

'Course he does,' the lad replied scornfully, 'I've trained 'im 'an all.'

Josclin stood up, careful not to take the boy's germ ridden hand and led the way into the hovel. The other guard stood up and reported, as usual, that nothing had been heard or seen. Josclin stood between the tunnel and the boy.

'How old are you, son?'

The lad tried to look tall but he didn't come much higher than Josclin's knee. He said he was five, the same age as the dog. In fact, he went on, they were born in the same bed at the same time. At this, the second guard, who did have some understanding of the local language, could be heard muttering.

'Same mother too I shouldn't wonder.'

Josclin brought himself down to the boy's level again.

'Now son, I want you to call your dog. The thing is, he chased a rabbit up there a couple of days ago and we haven't seen him since but if you call him…'

The boy didn't wait to be asked twice, he ran around Josclin and stuck his head into the hole and screeched, 'WUFF! WUFF come here, come on out. Come on. NOW!'

There was an audible scuffling sound coming from the tunnel and the three soldiers looked at one another. A second or two later, the scuffling turned into an extremely dirty but happy looking mongrel terrier that was standing in front of his equally scruffy owner, furiously wagging a stumpy tail.

Josclin was the first to speak, 'What's that in his mouth?'

He moved to the dog who promptly stopped wagging and started growling. Josclin turned to its owner, 'Can you tell him to drop it?'

'Course I can,'

But he seemed so intrigued by Wuff's trophy that all he did was kneel down so that he could get a better look at it.

'Tell him to drop it now, son,' said Josclin quietly, 'Now, please.'

The boy got up and gave the required command and much to Josclin's surprise, the dog did just as it was told and dropped the human hand it had been carrying, at his young master's feet. The boy leaned forward to pick it up but Josclin said sharply.

'Leave it.'

He looked at his men, then back to the boy.

'All right, son. You've got your dog back, now take him off home.'

The lad pointed at the hand, torn and filthy with strands of sinew sticking out of the end but easily recognisable for what it was.

'Can I 'av that, Mister? Wuff found it. It's mine by rights.'

Josclin felt in his pouch and tossed the lad a small coin.

'Have that instead. Off you go now and be quick about it before I change my mind and take my money back.'

The lad stood thinking for a moment then turned around and whipped out of the door followed by the filthy dog, that seemed torn between relinquishing his gruesome treasure and being re-united with his master.

When they had disappeared, Josclin picked up an old lathe and tentatively prodded the limb, then gingerly turned it over.

'Is it him, Sir?' One of the men asked, 'Is it Wulfric's hand?'

'How do I know lad,' was Josclin's terse reply, 'I've never met the man. I wasn't here when he came to the castle to see my Lord Beaumont and even if I had seen him, do you honestly think I'd recognise him from that?'

He prodded the flesh again.

'So far as I know,' he continued, 'there's only one person here that spent any time with Wulfric and that's Master LeBrun. Hope he's not too squeamish because I have little doubt that his Lordship will want him to take a look at it, just in case. Stay here and don't let that urchin and his dog anywhere near the place. I'm going to report to my master.'

He noticed the two men looking warily at the dismembered limb.

'Don't worry, it won't hurt you and even if the rest of the body comes down looking for it, the two of you shouldn't have too much trouble beating off a one handed, half starved piece of shit like Wulfric.'

He shook his head in mock exasperation, left the hut, looked at the rising sun and judged that even if his Lordship had not yet broken his fast, this was important enough to disturb him.

Robert Beaumont agreed with Josclin. Although it was probably unlikely that a person could be identified by a severed or torn off hand, it was worth asking Jean to take a look at it. If he could identify it with any certainty, then the rest of Wulfric's remains were likely to be stuck in the tunnel, he could be forgotten and without the threat of his presence, things could get back to normal. The two men made their way to Jean's quarters and found him there staring at the panel lying on his work table, pursing his lips and shaking his head. Robert Beaumont spoke first.

'Good morning, Jean. We are sorry to disturb you at this hour of the day but I think it best to speak with you before Lady Alysoun makes her appearance.'

Jean looked first at Beaumont and then to the offending panel.

'Why my Lord, has she spoken to you about…?'

Josclin cut in brusquely, 'Master LeBrun, we need you to come with us. Now, if you'll be so good.'

Jean looked from one to the other but there was nothing in either of their faces to indicate that he was about to be taken to task so he gave one of his shrugs and said that, of course, he was free to do whatever they wished.

He covered the offending panel, found his cloak and the three of them left the fortification and made their way to the Southern boundary. Before they entered the ruin, Beaumont stopped Josclin from leading the way and turned to Jean.

'Jean, I won't beat about the bush. A body part has been found in there. A hand, to be precise. That is all. At present anyway. Since you spent more time in Wulfric's company than anyone else we know, Lord Odo excluded of course, we would like you to have a look at it and tell us if you think it might possibly be his.'

Jean made a face.

'A hand! Not much to go on is it? I take it this is something to do with that secret passageway you mentioned. Is that where it was found?'

Beaumont nodded.

'I'm afraid it's a bit chewed up but just have a look. It won't take more than a minute of your time and it could be important.'

The guards duly stood up as they entered and Jean's eyes were immediately drawn to the hand lying on the dirty floor. Rather to Josclin's surprise, he didn't hesitate but crouched down and held out his hand for an implement to turn it over as Josclin had done. He bent forward and inspected it minutely. Beaumont looked at Josclin who gave a grudging 'Umph' of approval. They looked at Jean expectantly when he rose from his haunches.

'Wulfric's,' he stated confidently, 'definitely his.'

'How can you be so sure?'

Josclin's question loaded with disbelief. Jean turned to the four men in the room, 'All of you, stand in front of me and hold your hands out like that.'

He demonstrated by holding out his hands, flat with palms down. They copied him and he inspected their fingernails.

'Thought so,' he said, 'The fingernails on that hand are perfect. All right, they might be a bit longer than when I last saw them but their shape is unmistakable. Even you, Lord Beaumont, who does not work with your hands as do the rest of us, even your fingernails are uneven and broken. There is only one man I have ever seen who had perfect nails and that was Wulfric. The hand too. He had small hands and that is one of them. I'd stake my life on it.'

Beaumont looked thoughtful. He turned to Josclin.

'So far, so good then, but I think we are going to have to excavate, even if only a fragment of wall. If the rest of the body is up there, I suppose we can assume that Wulfric hid himself there and ultimately perished from the wound given him by Lady Alysoun. I would like to make sure though, then we can consider the whole affair to be at an end.'

He turned to Jean, 'Thank you Jean. That has been most helpful. When you return to the castle, would you locate Master Guy and have him bring a couple of his men here. You had better return to your work. This time, I hope in the knowledge that your safety is well and truly secured. You might tell Lady Alysoun what has happened and that she is likely to be able to return to her Aunt as soon as she wishes.'

Jean acknowledged Beaumont's thanks and went in search of Guy, who was fascinated by what Jean had to tell him. He, in turn, collected two of his local masons, most of the Norman artisans were occupied by the rather more ornate requirements of the cathedral, and hurried to the South wall where he started to confer with Lord Beaumont and Josclin. Jean strolled back to the kitchens and sorted himself out some breakfast before returning to his studio with a ewer of fresh water from which to clean his teeth and wash. He then cast a jaundiced eye over the panel which had been the cause of all his tribulations the previous day.

#

Having been shown the evidence in the ruin, Guy shuddered, remembering the occasion on which that very hand had nearly dislocated his shoulder. He went back outside with Beaumont and Josclin and stood back, casting an expert eye over the massive stonework looming above them. It was decided that the first thing to be done was to complete the demolition of the lean-to and clear it all out of the way, leaving the wall and the entrance to the tunnel completely open. With the assistance of the two guards, this was accomplished in no time at all. Again Guy stood back from the wall and tried to judge where the tunnel might have led. Supported by the others, he came to a rapid conclusion that it was best to excavate, carefully and horizontally into the bend itself. Then they might at least have some indication of the direction in which it led.

The stones in the wall were huge and he had to make certain that enough were left in place to support the enormous weight bearing down from above. Accordingly, he gave orders that a number of stout props be brought onto the site so that they could be inserted as soon as the first stones were removed. It was well into the evening by the time that these were in place but then, everything seemed to happen at once. It became obvious that it was not a tunnel at all.

What had been thought to be a bend turned out to be little more than a small cave where the hole terminated and there, curled up like an obscene foetus, were the unpleasantly rotting remains of Wulfric, the skin and bones of a rather fresher rabbit draped over one shoulder like a cheap mantle. That it was Wulfric was undeniable. Both Beaumont and Guy recognised him immediately and there was that wound in his cheek which had plainly turned septic and was still suppurating, even in death. The corpse was also lacking the hand which, they supposed, had been torn off by the dog, it having run out of edible rabbit.

Once the body had been brought down to ground and laid there, the small group of men present stood regarding it with repugnance. Josclin was the first to voice what all the rest were thinking.

'Not much of a specimen was he. You wouldn't think something like that could be the cause of so much trouble.'

Robert Beaumont agreed and mused that the creature had died much as he had lived, in a hole and in the dark. He had probably crept in there when it had become obvious to him that his wound was killing him. Only Guy noticed that there were no weapons on or near him. Josclin agreed that it was strange but then considered it likely that Wulfric had hidden them somewhere in the vicinity since, once he was holed up in his cave, they would not have been much use to him. To make absolutely certain, he would organise a search sometime the following day, once it became light enough. His words suddenly made them conscious of how quickly the evening was dropping in and they started to disperse.

Josclin asked Beaumont if he should stand down the guard and it was agreed that now there was very little point in keeping them on duty. It had been a hard period for all of them and Josclin asked if Lanfranc's men might be retained for a further couple of days, in order to continue to share the duties searching for Wulfric's weapons. As for the personal bodyguards allocated to Alysoun and Jean, Beaumont recommended they be retained for the time being. Josclin was surprised by this, considering that the danger had passed but Beaumont explained his reasons.

'It is like this, Josclin. It is not so much the threat of assassination that now worries me, it is the problem of er…well, the problem of propriety.'

Josclin looked puzzled, as Beaumont had feared he might, so he went on.

'Lady Alysoun and Jean. They are both young and working as they are, in close proximity with each other, I feel it incumbent on me… that is I promised Lady Beornwyn.'

Josclin's brow cleared.

'I see my Lord. I never gave a thought to that sort of thing, occupied as I was with the threat of Wulfric. Yes, I suppose they should be … although a guard outside their door is hardly likely to prevent them getting up to anything they shouldn't. I must say that I would be very surprised if a young lady of her station were to allow Master LeBrun any liberties of that nature.'

'Perhaps not, Josclin, perhaps not, but at least I can say to Lady Beornwyn that I had some measures in place. Oh, yes and by the way, the aforementioned noblewoman was apparently quite taken by your man Amaury. She thought he was quite courteous, for a military man that is. Perhaps you would see to it that he is Lady Alysoun's bodyguard or however you want to describe his duties. I think Beornwyn might like the idea that her niece is under his protection, for whatever reason.'

Josclin nodded cheerfully, 'Very well, my Lord. I'll see to it, I take it tomorrow will be soon enough since, unless we've got things badly wrong, the young people will at least be sleeping in their own rooms.'

Beaumont grimaced.

'Don't even think of that, Josclin. Goodnight.'

'Goodnight, my Lord.'

#

The two young people in question had spent their day very differently to those occupied in recovering Wulfric's remains. Jean couldn't help being preoccupied with his part in the affair and Alysoun too found the news of the find almost disturbing, rather than comforting. There was also the matter of the disputed panel about which Jean was increasingly worried and Alysoun a shade more conscience stricken. She didn't really want to get Jean into trouble and she was beginning to think that her rebellious input had been slightly over ambitious. In short their combined minds were not really on their work. Jean hated it when it was like this. If he couldn't devote his entire being to this design, then he became frustrated and irritable with himself. She, guessing that this was how he felt, was tentative and distant with him.

By the middle of the afternoon they had recovered somewhat and Jean had started to sketch out his coronation ideas on a piece of board, supplied to him by Ranulph. These would then be transferred to the actual linen to be embroidered. Alysoun was again fascinated by the way that he worked and if she thought he was quick at laying down the finished design, he was even faster when sketching in his roughs. He explained, on being asked why, that it was important to illustrate his ideas before they left his head or were replaced by another set of thoughts.

They sat together at the table and this was the first time that he had actually let her into his space while he was working like this and not concentrating on his lines to the exclusion of everything else. Occasionally, Alysoun would move a finger to a particular point and ask him, 'what' and, 'why.' Sometimes their fingers would touch lightly as they moved them about the board. The first few times, they both withdrew them as if scalded but later on they lingered for a second or two.

Throughout the entire day, they had never addressed each other by anything but their given names and at the end of it, when they went their separate ways, their 'goodnights' were just on the warm side of social politeness.

Neither slept well that night and neither could have explained why.

CHAPTER FORTY SEVEN

The Castle, Canterbury

As if taking its cue from the good news of the previous day, the new one dawned bright and clear, and it was a buoyant Robert Beaumont who strode confidently into Jean's studio. Its occupant, just risen from his disturbed night, was still in the process of trying to quell the riot of thoughts that had kept him from his sleep. He groaned at the exuberant interruption, as Beaumont heartily wished him a good morning and all but slapped him on the back by way of a greeting.

Beaumont then explained that he had decided to take himself over to the School of Needlework and personally deliver the good news to Lady Beornwyn. Was there any message Jean wished him to deliver, or completed panels, or was there any service at all that he, Lord Beaumont, could render Jean, with regard to the redoubtable lady. Despite his semi-conscious condition, Jean couldn't help smiling to himself at the thought of a Norman nobleman running errands for him but quickly composed himself and apologised for not yet being fully awake, explaining that he had not passed a very restful night. Beaumont looked concerned and said, 'I'm sorry to hear that Jean. Something to do with all the excitement of yesterday was it?'

'Something like that my Lord,'

Jean's response was guarded and he walked over to join Beaumont, who was standing at his drawing table looking at the results of Jean's work of the day before.

'Ah! I see you have started on the coronation scene. Excellent! I look forward to seeing it finished and,' he went on, 'I cannot wait to view the completed embroidery although I expect it will be many months before Lady Beornwyn considers it ready for display.'

Jean nodded in agreement.

'Yes, my Lord. Obviously I have no knowledge of the technique but like you, I don't expect we shall see it for a very long time to come. It is one thing to do what I have done, that takes no time at all. But to stitch in the design with wools, all in different colours, I dread to think how long it will take.'

Beaumont nodded cheerfully, 'Indeed, indeed Master LeBrun, but just consider this. None of it would have been at all possible without your masterful designs.'

Jean gave a self deprecating smile then suddenly remembered the damned panel that Alysoun had worked on. Perhaps this was the best time to submit it to his Lordship's inspection. As he hesitated, the day seemed to lose some of its early morning promise.

'My Lord,' he began awkwardly, so much so that Beaumont raised an elegant eyebrow and wondered what was coming next. He really hoped it wouldn't be anything to do with Lady Alysoun, which in a way of course it was.

Jean sorted out the offending panel from the others. With care and not a little trepidation, he laid out on the table and said casually.

'My Lord, I cannot remember who it was that gave me the details for this particular scene. Was it yourself or could it have been...?'

Beaumont swiftly scanned the piece.

'No Jean, you are quite right, it was me. If you remember, you had considerable difficulty pronouncing the name Aelfgyva when I told you about her. Think yourself lucky you only have to draw it and not spell it.'

He laughed and Jean just about managed to join in. Then the laugh seemed to be stuck in Beaumont's throat. He coughed.

'Obviously I haven't seen the borders before. That is, after all, why we have Lady Alysoun as our guest but has she...did she...' he pointed to Alysoun's contribution.

'Oh yes, my Lord. That is...she didn't but I...I did.'

'I see.' Beaumont rubbed his chin, 'And she ...'

Oh yes my Lord.' Jean thought frantically, 'I did it but it was her idea. Something to do with the forthcoming nuptials of Aelg...Ael... what's-her-name and the business of um... procreation...that sort of thing,' he concluded lamely.

'Ah! I see,' mused Beaumont again, 'Well, I'm not sure what her Aunt is likely to say about it but I have no doubt that it will be acceptable if Lady Alysoun has agreed to it.'

'You see Jean,' he went on enthusiastically, 'this is exactly what this is all about. Our two cultures working together, in harmony, to produce a finished product that will be admired for years, perhaps even centuries to come as an example of peaceful co-operation between the conquerors and the conquered. No, Jean I think this is excellent although, if you will forgive me for saying so, that particular character there is not quite up the standard of your best work.'

Jean was quick to admit that, no, his Lordship was absolutely right, it wasn't something of which he was particularly proud but that apart, he hoped that the rest of the piece met with his Lordship's approval.

Beaumont said that indeed it did and now he must be off.

'I'm taking Josclin with me. He deserves a couple of hours break from this place. He is supposed to be searching for Wulfric's personal armoury but his men can do that. Oh, there is one more thing. I requested that Amaury take over the duty as your personal guard until Lady Alysoun returns to her Aunt. I think he has stood at your door before and is pleased to hear that he is to do so again.'

'Thank you, my Lord. I like the man. It was he that told me of Av...'

'Of what Jean?'

'Nothing, my Lord. I was just about to say I, too, shall be pleased to see him again.'

Beaumont nodded, waved farewell and promptly walked into Alysoun as she entered.

'Ah! Alysoun. We are just off to see your Aunt. Would you care to come with us? Now that there is no danger lurking there in the form of your old enemy, I suppose there is no reason why you should not return and take up your needle.'

Alysoun flushed and said, slightly too quickly for Beaumont's peace of mind.

'Thank you, my Lord, but I have not quite finished here with Master LeBrun.'

Beaumont regarded her quizzically.

'Oh! I was under the impression that your contribution to the borders had come to an end.'

He looked over to Jean and continued.

'Am I not right in saying that all that remains to be done are the Coronation scenes? Can they not be designed out of your fertile imagination Jean?'

Jean was about to say that, yes, of course they could, borders and all when Alysoun broke in.

'He has not yet seen the Abbey, my Lord. I have and he needs me to describe the interior. Don't you Jean?'

Beaumont winced at hearing her referring to Jean informally. Especially as he had only ever been in their company when they hardly seemed to be able to address each other with little more than veiled civility, but he could hardly force the girl to accompany him so he left them to whatever it was that fate had in store for them. On his way to meet Josclin at the stable, he encountered Amaury who was about to relieve Jean's guard. He stopped him and, as diplomatically as he could, requested that Amaury look into the room from time to time, just to enquire if Lady Alysoun or Master LeBrun were in need of any refreshment or anything. Happy to have passed on his responsibilities for Alysoun's moral welfare, he met up with Josclin and as

Jean looked out of his window, he could see them riding out of the bailey towards the town.

Having seen the two men on their way, Jean turned from the window to Alysoun.

'Whew. That was close, I thought his Lordship was going to see through all that Saxon nonsense you'd introduced into that Aelf...what's-her-name scene.'

Alysoun shrugged off her cloak, 'I told you he wouldn't and that you had nothing to worry about. I don't suppose he said anything at all, did he?'

Jean grinned, 'As a matter of fact he did. He pointed out that dirty picture of yours and said he didn't think it was up to my usual standard.'

She grinned back, 'I told you. Shall we start then?'

'No!' retorted Jean, I'll start and you only say something if you think I'm going wrong.'

They, or rather Jean, worked until lunchtime when he was overcome by hunger. Thanks to Lord Beaumont, he had gone without his breakfast. He opened the door and asked Amaury if he would arrange for someone to bring up some food. When Jean had shut the door again Alysoun turned to him and said, 'Have you noticed anything about the new guard of ours?'

Jean replied, not really but he'd known the man before and had always found him obliging and polite. Alysoun pursed her lips.

'No, it isn't that, although I'm sure he's an admirable man. It's just that he keeps looking in on us. Didn't you notice?' Then she thought for a moment, 'No, I don't suppose you did, you never notice anything do you?'

He shook his head, 'Not when I'm working, no, but I wish someone would hurry up with some food, I'm starving.'

It was not long before there came a knock at the door and they both moved over to his living space to eat. At least Jean wolfed his down while Alysoun ate sparingly and looked as if she was mildly troubled by something other than hunger.

Once Jean had finished, he carefully sharpened one of his toothpicks and while Alysoun was at the window, he cleaned his teeth and announced himself ready to resume work. The last panel was going well. They sat together at the table, their heads sometimes closer than either of them realised. She watched him quickly copy his scenes of celebration and rejoicing and, as ever, was mesmerised by the self assurance of his skill. Suddenly it hit her. A feeling which was so new to her, she gave a little involuntary gasp. This was coming to an end. This thing, the nature of which was unlikely ever again to be attempted, was drawing to its close. Not her involvement, obviously. The needlework had yet to be done and she would be kept busy with her needle for many months to come but as for seeing the concept unfold in front of her, it was nearly over. The sheer originality and breadth of its creation was about to finish. She wondered how she was going to compensate for the loss.

She moved a little to one side, the better to bring Jean into a clearer perspective. Such was the intensity of his concentration, there was never any fear of him catching her looking at him. His tongue protruding ever so slightly, his hair too long and apparently not subject to any of the usual laws of tonsorial gravity, his clever, slender fingers deftly outlining and shading and his long, supple body bent over easily and, she drew a sharp breath.

Although he was intent on his drawing to the absolute exclusion of anything else, she KNEW, at that precise moment, that he wanted her. She knew it as plainly as if he had cast his charcoals to the far corner of the room, thrown her on to the table and taken her on top of his triumphant coronation scene. Yet he had done or said nothing which might have given the slightest indication that anything of the sort was passing through his mind. Rather, it was quite the opposite. While his initial hostility had disappeared, she still had the feeling that he quite disliked her. She was mature enough to know that this dislike had little to do with any physical desire a man might feel for a woman but there was something there and she knew it with a certainty that surprised and even shocked her.

What about her then? She automatically dropped her inspection of him and sightlessly studied the scene on the table. She knew that she was blushing because she felt the heat rise from her covered throat to her unprotected cheeks but it didn't matter because he wasn't aware of her presence let alone her emotions. A tiny shudder went through her. She was being silly, that was all, imagining things. Her Aunt's unwillingness for them to meet and other thinly disguised hints from Thibault, among others, confirmed her suspicion that Jean had plenty of experience in the arts of love whereas she had none. Of course she knew what it was all about and had secretly and without shame enjoyed private and personal moments of physical satisfaction, but a man! The memory of Wulfric forced itself horribly into her mind and this time her shudder was more pronounced. She quickly turned away but it was too late. Jean said, testily, 'What do you think you're doing Alysoun? I'm trying to work and you start shaking the board. Now look what you've made me do!'

'I am so sorry, Jean. I don't know what came over me. I suddenly remembered…remembered…Oh, forget it! It's nothing. I'm sorry.'

Jean gave her the sort of look that might have been bestowed on a clumsy toddler, which had the immediate effect of making her bridle, chasing all her fanciful ideas out of her head.

'I have said that I am sorry, Master LeBrun. If you were expecting a more abject apology, you can just forget it.'

Jean's temporary irritation with her interruption evaporated just as quickly and he grinned at her.

'You see, Lady Alysoun, that's the trouble with you high-born noblewomen; always in the right, never in the wrong, whereas us poor peasants were put on this earth to take the blame for all your mistakes. Now, if I may be allowed to get on with what I'm supposed to be doing. The sooner I am finished, the sooner you can be back at your precious School of Needlework in the company of ladies of your own class. Although I hate to think what happens if one of them makes a mistake. No, don't tell me, you haul in some inferior yokel and punish him instead. Now, if you don't mind; I must finish this.' Another grin at her reddening features and he bent to his work.

Alysoun was left wondering why on earth her thoughts had travelled in the direction that they had. If he was attracted to her, he had a very funny way of showing it. What was wrong with her then? If her suspicions were correct and this infuriating young man was as experienced as he was reputed to be, why hadn't he...well, whatever it was that men did when they were that way inclined. Thibault hadn't signified any interest either, other than a brother might towards a younger sister so what was it that she was lacking?

#

Amaury was an easy going sort of fellow but conscientious and that was one of the reasons that Josclin singled him out for duties that required not only diligence but sometimes a touch of diplomacy. This duty he had now, for example, suited him down to the ground and he remembered with some pleasure how Master LeBrun, seemingly becoming more important a personage by the day, had showed real interest in poor little Aveline. So Amaury had done as Lord Beaumont had intimated he should, just opened the door very occasionally and very discreetly and checked that the young couple were immersed in nothing other than the work they were there to perform. Certainly nothing to report thus far and judging from the mild altercation in which they were involved at the moment, it looked as though there was unlikely to be anything much to report in the near future.

He supposed it was all right for him to listen at the door as he was because, truth to tell, he didn't feel very comfortable opening it too often. The last time, Lady Alysoun had given him a very strange look. Had he not been eavesdropping quite so intently though, he might have noticed something. As it was, he saw nothing and heard nothing. In fact his throat was cut so swiftly and efficiently, it was doubtful if he even felt anything. If he did, it was too late and with little more than a faint gurgle, his body was gently lowered to the floor, his lifeblood pumping out of him at a mortal rate.

The door was then opened, much more quietly than ever poor Amaury had managed it. Alysoun, still in a state fluctuating between confusion and anger looked up expecting to see their over-zealous guard peering round the door and ready to give him a piece of her mind.

Instead she smiled broadly and said, 'Thibua...'

The smile faded and she delivered the last syllable in a whisper. She nudged Jean who reacted as he had before.

'For God's sake, Alysoun, will you...' he looked up, saw her face and followed her terrified gaze. He slowly rose to his feet.

'Thibault?'

He flashed a glance at Alysoun, then back to Thibault.

'Oh my God! Thibault! Not again. Not like the last time.' He motioned Alysoun to keep behind him and took a step towards the man with the knife. He noticed the blood flicking from the point as Thibault raised it warningly. When Thibault spoke, his voice was perfectly controlled and normal. Nothing different about it at all. Just as if he was embarking on an ordinary social conversation.

'Hello Jean.'

He laughed, as if Jean's reaction was in some way ridiculous .

'Don't look so worried Jean. We are friends, aren't we? I wouldn't hurt a friend. What sort of person do you think I am? No. It's her. I know she's nothing to you, Jean so it won't mean anything to you at all, will it? You see, she has to go Jean. Just like all the others.'

Still making certain that he kept himself between Alysoun and Thibault, Jean too tried to keep his voice normal and calm.

'Others, Thibault? What others would they be?'

Alysoun was still behind him and with their backs to the wall they edged round the room towards Jean's living area.

'Oh, you know as well as I do, Jean. Mind you,' he continued, still in a conversational manner, 'There might be some of which you were not aware but there were some things I didn't think it right to share with you. Not once we had become friends.'

Jean effected a mirthless smile, 'Quite right, Thibault. You did the right thing there. That knife.'

He nodded towards the blade, still with an obstinate drop of congealing blood hanging from it.

'Looks like a good one Thibault, really sharp.'

This time Thibault laughed genuinely.

'So it should be.' he didn't look at it as he spoke. 'Wulfric's knife, this was.

He always had the best of weapons. Mind you Jean, you still have my dagger, if my memory serves me right.'

Jean nodded, 'I do Thibault, I do. Would you like to have it back?'

Thibault shook his head.

'No, of course not. You keep it and I'll keep this one. It only seems right somehow, me and Wulfric shared lots of things. We liked working together.'

'Did you now, Thibault, but he's dead now, isn't he? Did you ...Wulfric... you know?'

Thibault shook his head again. 'Kill him? Of course I didn't. She did. Didn't you, Lady Alysoun?'

He looked at her, over Jean's shoulder. He pointed the knife at her.

'She killed Wulfric and I buried him, well, sort of buried him but that's not why she has to die, Jean. She has to die, like all the rest of them had to.'

He lowered his voice to a confidential whisper.

'They want to destroy us, Jean, they all do.'

He looked directly at Alysoun again.

'Just like the rest, she is the embodiment of Eve and they lead us to sin, just as Eve did Adam. They use us in their filthy ways to have mastery over us. Come on, Jean, you must know that, you know what they are like. Remember Mirabelle.?'

Jean's voice was still calm but he was thinking furiously.

'Of course I do, Thibault. I was there wasn't I? Just after...'

Thibault gave one of his rare smiles. 'I was good wasn't I Jean? I even had Lord Odo fooled and believe me, that isn't easy.'

While Thibault was talking, Jean, keeping a terrified Alysoun behind him, had reached his living space and they were backed up against his small table. Thibault took a step nearer.

'Time now, Alysoun. Stand aside Jean. You are the last person I want to hurt. Stand aside. Now please. PLEASE.'

He came nearer and they could see his jerkin was covered in blood, as was his crucifix with which, for once, Thibault was not obsessively fiddling. The blood they supposed to be Amaury's. Thibault was looking perplexed that Jean still stood his ground. Jean, arms outstretched behind him to cover Alysoun as best he could, felt her slip something small and sharp into his left hand. Thibault came closer, now almost pleading.

'Please Jean, move aside so that we can finish this. There is so much to do, we must get on.'

He was almost on top of them now, shaking his head sadly at Jean when Alysoun suddenly moved. 'NO!' shouted Jean and moved to cover her again but Thibault had already struck and as the knife sank into Jean's stomach, he brought up his own hand jabbing the toothpick into Thibault's right eye. Jean collapsed to the floor.

Thibault roared with pain and raised his knife on the now unprotected Alysoun. Suddenly he stopped like a statue, Josclin's thrown dagger still quivering in his back and Jean's toothpick embedded in his eyeball.

Alysoun leaped out of the way as his body fell across that of the recumbent Jean.

'Quickly,' she shrieked at Josclin. Stop the bleeding, he might be still alive.

Josclin stepped forward, hurling Thibault's corpse out of the way and kneeling over Jean who was bleeding massively from his stomach wound. Alysoun looked around the room frantically, ran to the work table and snatched up the coronation panel. Together, she and Josclin used it, binding it again and again, to try and plug the wound.

CHAPTER FORTY EIGHT

The School of Needlework

A subdued Robert Beaumont found himself ill contrasted with a bright autumn day when he was admitted to the School of Needlework by one of Lady Beornwyn's servants who, after taking his Lordships cloak, announced him to the three people assembled at Beornwyn's table. Beaumont gravely greeted them, after which Lanfranc was the first to speak.

'Well Robert?'

'Thanks to your dispensation, my Lord Archbishop, the coffin was disinterred and is now on its way to Dover, escorted by Odo and his men.'

Lanfranc nodded reflectively and for a moment there was a heavy silence. The Lady Beornwyn cleared her throat.

'The other matter, Robert, what of that?'

Beaumont sank into his chair and passed a weary hand over his brow.

'That, Beornwyn, was not quite so straightforward. After much negotiation, Odo was persuaded that, if he were to call here and insist on inspecting the work you have thus far carried out, you would refuse to have anything more to do with it. The entire project, together with the noble Lord himself, could go to the devil as far as you were concerned.'

Beornwyn nodded gratefully. 'Thank you Robert. As we all know, I could not bear to have that monstrous cleric set foot on these premises. I only hope that you will not be made to suffer for communicating my detestation of the man in such an honest fashion.'

Beaumont took a mouthful of wine.

'Have no fears Beornwyn. So long as we have the support of their Majesties, Odo will do nothing. As ever, he will be far too busy plotting something else at this moment and he knows that we know that he is, if not the substance of it. It can only be a matter of time before he is alienated from his King.'

He took another sip of wine, relaxed more into his chair and continued.

'To be honest with you, my real concern was how to explain to their Majesties that there was to be no final panel, the one depicting their glorious coronations. The panel that Lady Alysoun and Josclin used to...' his voice tailed off.

Alysoun spoke up, her voice controlled, but only just.

'Really my Lord? The Bishop of Bayeux, William and Mathilde must surely be aware that to have those scenes illustrated by a different hand would diminish the importance of the whole work. We could not possibly agree to work on anything that was not part of Jean…of the original design.'

For some reason, Beaumont found it difficult to respond directly to Alysoun and he addressed his reply to Beornwyn.

'I believe the mitigating fact in respect of that particular matter has been that their Majesties accept a degree of responsibility for returning Thibault to these shores. Of course, once the embroidery is in France, it will be theirs to do with as they wish.'

Alysoun glanced at her Aunt who gave her an almost imperceptible shake of the head; a warning that it was best to leave matters where they were. Alysoun, however, had not finished.

'My Lord, did Odo request the return of Wulfric's remains as well?'

For the first time Robert Beaumont turned to her and found himself lost for words. She had changed, literally. That is, she was no longer wearing her black shapeless costume with the old fashioned cap and scarf but had been transformed into a totally different being and an extremely lovely one at that.

Beornwyn could not but help notice his obvious distraction.

'They were her mother's, Robert. I decided that it was time for her to come out of her chrysalis. You know as well as I do that recent events have affected her spirits and I thought it might be good for her to dress up a little.'

It seemed to Beaumont that it was rather more than 'a little'. Her underskirt, so far as he could see in the dim light, was of a sage green, fitted at the top but long and flowing from her waist which was encircled by a cross-over belt, hanging nearly to the floor. Her gown, a lighter green with very wide sleeves decorated with lace, as was the neck and a bliaud or over-mantle which was also, to his unpractised eye, yet another shade of verdant green. Her blonde hair was hanging in broad plaits and her head was covered by a white silk guimpe which had been tucked into the neck of her gown. He sighed to himself and Alysoun gave one of her giggles which brought the whole company down to earth again.

'I am sorry Lady Alysoun.' Beaumont stood up and bowed, 'You asked me a question and I was so taken by your…your transformation that I failed to hear what it was.'

Alysoun waved away the apology.

'I only asked if Wulfric's remains were taken by Lord Odo at the same time as those of Thibault.'

Beaumont shook his head, 'No, Odo was only really interested in Thibault. Nobody could understand that particular relationship. Almost that of father and son. If my Lord Odo had any finer feelings, then it was Thibault who was the sole beneficiary of them but then, it seems it was only recently that Thibault had been made aware of his benefactor's true nature. As for Wulfric, he was little more than an assassin who seemed to have enjoyed killing for it's own sake, whereas Thibault! I think Thibault was genuinely out of his mind. You know that his father was beheaded at Hastings? Thibault was at his side and it is possible that the incident completely unhinged him. He was so young and had been gently reared. What puzzles us all so much is that his insanity and his activities escaped everybody's attention, even that of Odo although of course, one could never be absolutely sure of that. He and Wulfric were always careful to limit their dreadful crimes to unfortunate girls of the servant class so it is only now that some of these incidents have come to light.'

Lanfranc broke in.

'I quite agree, Robert. I had never heard anything but good of the young man from every quarter, including their Majesties, but I think we should try and put all that behind us now and look more to the future than the unhappy past. Now, tell us, Lady Beornwyn, how goes your great endeavour? Are you happy with it?'

Beornwyn contented herself with a look at her niece before saying, 'Yes, my Lord. There is much still to do but I think I can say that we are not displeased with it.'

As she said it, she gave an involuntary glance in the direction of the workroom next door where the fabulous serpent of embroidery was resting on Ranulph's frame awaiting the continuing attentions of the embroiderers the following morning. Alysoun followed her glance.

'Working to that design has been an absolute pleasure for us all,' she said, a slight choke in her voice. She suddenly stood up.

' Aunt, my Lords, please excuse me.'

She left the table and, somewhat hampered by her unaccustomed finery, left the room. The three remaining occupants looked at each other.

'How is he, Beornwyn?' Beaumont asked softly.

She smiled, leant over and patted him on the hand.

'He will do, Robert, he will do. His wound is deep but is healing. His hand though, his drawing hand is of greater concern to us. As you know, tendons were severed as he attempted to ward off the dagger thrust. None of this is helping Alysoun's work though. She is in and out of that room fifty times a day. He is still weak mind you, but with Alysoun's help, he will mend and before you ask me Robert,' she turned to include Lanfranc, 'And you, my Lord, yes, I am content with matters. They will make their way, I am sure of it. He is, of course, not one of our people and his rank is not what I would once have wished it to be. That said, things are changing and he risked his life to protect my niece. That is quite enough for me.'

Beaumont vigorously signified his agreement.

'Quite right, Beornwyn, although their ultimate deliverance has to be attributed to your request that Josclin, on his return to the castle, collect your niece and escort her to you here. If he had not…'

Lanfranc nodded and then turned to Beornwyn, 'I think too, that you need not concern yourself with their future, assuming of course that they are intent on creating one together. Knowing LeBrun as I do, I am confident that he will, in time, adapt his considerable skills to his other hand. The number of commissions for the new coloured glass, new building decorations and I don't know what, will keep him in demand for years to come.'

The three of them continued in similar vein until Lanfranc touched Beornwyn's arm and pointed to the doorway

'Ah! Here comes your niece.'

Alysoun, looking slightly flushed, took her place at the table.

'He's gone back to sleep.'

She gave a little laugh of embarrassment as they all looked at her. She thought for a second, then turned to Robert Beaumont, leaning confidentially towards him and speaking as quietly as decorum would permit.

'My Lord, who was Mirabelle?'

About the author

John Hallam Lott has a degree in History and studies philosophy. He has written a number of short stories for radio and is a prize-winning poet.

He lives with his wife in a particularly beautiful region of Northern France and does much of his thinking and planning while walking the surrounding countryside and, from time to time, some of the sunnier parts of Europe.

NON-FICTION

Make Do & Cook

Learn the secrets of 10 important foods and how to cook healthy, delicious meals on the smallest budget

by Patricia Mansfield-Devine

Make Do & Cook teaches you how you can eat well on a budget. Whether you're a student, a pensioner or a parent with a family to feed, this is your guide to making tasty, cheap and nutritious meals without spending hours in the kitchen. It includes chapters on savvy shopping, menu planning and budgeting, essential ingredients and 100 simple and delicious recipes.

NON-FICTION / COOKING / FOOD

For more information, go to: www.webvivantpress.com

www.ingramcontent.com/pod-product-compliance
Lightning Source LLC
Chambersburg PA
CBHW031057260626
47172CB00001B/107